# GIRL EIGHT

*A Mercy Harbor Thriller: Book Two*

## Melinda Woodhall

Melinda Woodhall
Visit my website at www.melindawoodhall.com

Printed in the United States of America

First Printing: March 2019
Creative Magnolia

ISBN-9781090897305

*For Melissa Jean and Melanie Dee*

**Other books by Melinda Woodhall**

*The River Girls*
*Catch the Girl*
*Girls Who Lie*
*Her Last Summer*
*Her Final Fall*
*Her Winter of Darkness*
*Her Silent Spring*
*Her Day to Die*

Sign up for the Melinda Woodhall Thrillers Newsletter
to receive bonus scenes and insider details at
www.melindawoodhall.com/newsletter

# CHAPTER ONE

Ace stepped into the bright blue September morning and smiled; it was a perfect day to take the girl out to the farm. He strode across the brown lawn, the grass still dry and brittle after one of the hottest summers in Florida's history, and unbolted the garage door.

Stale, silent air greeted him. He paused, listening for any sound from above. Although he knew the room was securely locked and completely soundproof, he always took time to assess the situation before climbing the steep wooden stairs and unbolting the steel door. He liked to think his past reconnaissance training still came in handy after all these years.

Fiona Walsh was huddled on the bed in the corner, as usual, her once-glossy red hair hanging in limp, dull strands around her shoulders. She didn't look up as Ace walked in and turned on the light. The girl's pale blue eyes were numb, lifeless. She kept them trained on the ground as he considered her thin form.

*Yes, definitely time to give up on this one. She's lasted longer than most, but the thrill is gone.*

His eyes moved to a collection of photos taped to the far wall. The photos were labeled one through six. Each had been taken in the same shabby room, and each contained an image of a different terrified girl.

"Today's the day you make it onto the wall of fame."

Ace pulled out the photo he'd taken when Fiona had woken up in the room for the first time. She had been sitting on the same bed, the raw fear in her eyes matching that of the girls in the other photos.

Ace had already labeled her photo with a large number seven written in black marker. He taped the picture next to the others.

"I'm thinking seven must be your lucky number."

He produced a coarse laugh, and the raspy sound finally prompted a reaction. Fiona looked up with a start, as if awakening from a bad dream, and sprang from the bed without warning, her fingers clawing at his eyes.

"Whoa, there now, girl!" Ace shouted, losing his balance as a ragged fingernail scratched a bloody line along his cheek.

He easily captured her thin wrists and pushed her back onto the bare mattress. As she scrambled to get up, preparing to renew her attack, Ace stepped back toward the middle of the room.

He crossed his arms over his chest and waited, knowing the shackle around Fiona's ankle would save him from further injury. A drop of blood dripped from the scratch on his cheek and a red splotch appeared on his tan work boot.

He wiped the blood off his face with the back of his hand, angry at himself for letting his guard down.

The steel chain rattled against the rough wooden floor, then abruptly fell silent. She'd given up quickly this time. Her energy was running low, along with her will to resist.

Ace figured that was for the best. He enjoyed the challenge of breaking a new girl's spirit, but this girl's time was up; she'd been in the room for months now, and the novelty had worn off.

Besides, he needed the room free for the next girl.

Ace felt his pulse quicken at the memory of Doc's phone call the previous evening. Doc said he'd found a new girl that matched their strict criteria perfectly. If all went to plan, girl eight would be delivered within the next few weeks.

*Don't get ahead of yourself, Ace. You've got work to do here first.*

He sighed, knowing he had to dispose of the girl in front of him before he could move on to the next one. And the trip out to the old farm was always dangerous. There was always the chance he'd be seen; the chance he'd finally get caught red-handed after flying under the radar for so long.

*One careless mistake and I'll end up in a cell over in Raiford in no time.*

He needed to neutralize the girl before he attempted to take her outside. If given the chance she would alert the whole neighborhood that he'd been keeping her in the room above the garage.

No one had ever suspected the detached building held anything other than his old truck, the usual tools and lawn equipment, and a few cobwebs. No need to start raising questions now.

The citizens of Willow Bay were still reeling from a recent series of murders that had stunned the usually quiet town. Although the killer had been caught, many of the people in town were still on alert, expecting the boogey man to jump out at any minute.

Luckily for Ace, Doc had provided the perfect solution. It was a solution the girl would never be able to resist.

Ace reached into his pocket and pulled out a plastic bag. He dangled it in front of her, taunting her with the handful of white pills that rested at the bottom of the bag.

"I brought you some more candy, girl. Although I really shouldn't let you have it, seeing that you attacked me."

"My name's not girl. My name's Fiona. And I don't want your pills. I just want to go home. Please, just let me go home. I promise I won't tell anyone what you've done. I'll disappear and you'll never hear from me again."

She'd gotten the last part right, but the first part, well that wasn't possible. He'd made the mistake of letting girls go before, and it never ended well. Eventually, he'd learned his lesson.

*Always bury the evidence. That way it'll never come back to haunt you.*

Ace walked forward, bracing himself against another sudden attack. The floor creaked under his thick-soled boots as he approached and shoved the plastic bag at the girl, who now lay limp and weak on the bed.

"Don't act like you don't want 'em."

He waited for her to take the bag, impatient to get on the road. The day would only get hotter, and there was work to do.

Just as he had started to think he'd have to do it the hard way, she lifted a small shaking hand and took the bag.

* * *

The truck rattled along a narrow dirt road that led up to what remained of the old dairy farm. A faded *Willow Bay Dairy* sign leaned against the only structure still standing on the parcel of land that had been in Ace's family since the 1950s. The tin-roofed stable had functioned as a milking parlor with eight roomy stalls. The thin wooden walls and rusty roof had somehow withstood decades of blistering heat, frequent thunderstorms, and the occasional hurricane.

Ace circled the stable and then parked in the back, before scouting the surrounding area thoroughly. All was quiet. No signs of trespassing in the overgrown pastures or dense clusters of palmetto bushes.

He flung open the stable doors, allowing sunlight to flood in and light up the empty interior. At least it would appear to be empty to anyone who happened by and looked around. Just a hard dirt floor and eight empty milking stalls. Nothing out of place to draw further attention.

Satisfied that nothing was out of order, Ace walked over and removed a shovel from its hook on the wall. Liking the solid feel of the heavy tool in his hand, he turned toward the stalls. A number had been carved into a wooden beam on the back wall of each stall. Ace moved to stall seven and leaned the shovel against the wall before returning to the truck.

He took another furtive look around before rolling back the truck bed cover and surveying the girl's limp body. The fentanyl had worked quickly. Only the gentle rise and fall of her chest revealed that she was still alive. He had wondered if she'd make it all the way to the farm.

*Guess she's tougher than she looks.*

The thought prompted a raspy, satisfied laugh. He liked to put the girls in the ground still breathing. That way he never had to see them change. Never had to see them become stiff and blue and bloated.

He didn't want the image of the girl's dead and bloated body to stay with him. He preferred to remember his girls as they had looked when he'd first see them and taken their first photo. The memories and pictures were important; they helped him relive the good times after the girls had gone.

Ace opened the tailgate and tugged at the water-proof black tarp that covered the bottom of the truck bed. He pulled the girl toward him and wrapped the ends of the tarp around her thin body before hefting her over his shoulder and carrying her to stall seven.

He drew a large rectangle in the dirt with the shovel's cutting edge then lifted a heavy boot and stepped down hard on the shoulder, slicing into the ground. He tried to ignore the splotch of blood on his boot as he rocked the shovel back and forth, loosening the hardpacked soil.

Sweat beaded on his forehead and his back spasmed in protest as he bent again and again over the rapidly growing hole. It was hard work, and he wasn't as young as he used to be. Digging holes wasn't a job for an older man. But what choice did he have?

He paused to catch his breath and looked over at stall eight, his jaw clenching in a mixture of exhaustion and anticipation. The eighth stall was still empty, and Doc had already found the girl who would eventually fill it. A surge of energy flooded through him at the thought. He returned to his dirty work, this time whistling even as his arms trembled with the exertion.

A song was stuck in his head. Its words echoed through his mind over and over as he dragged the tarp to the hole and lowered it in.

*We live in fame, or go down in flame...*

The ends of the tarp slipped back, revealing the girl's slight figure nestled in its folds. Ace considered her fine pale skin and her fiery hair. His very own sleeping beauty. Only this fairytale princess would never be kissed and would never wake up.

He used his cell phone to take one last photo, then reached down and positioned the tarp back over the still, white face. He stood with some difficulty, his back and legs already weak and cramped. There was more work to do.

He flexed his hands, painfully stiff from grasping the shovel's handle, and tried to think of anything but the ache in his back, tried to focus instead on the next line of the song.

*Hands of men blasted the world asunder...*

He picked up the shovel and began to refill the hole. The work was tedious, but he knew he had to be patient. He had to make sure the stable looked as empty and abandoned as it had when he'd first arrived.

No one else came by the old place anymore, but you could never be too careful. It had been an active enterprise back in the day, and some of the people in town might drive by and get curious.

After he had restored the dirt floor to its original condition, he decided to drive into town. He needed to check in with Doc. As he steered the old truck toward the highway, the thought of Doc started him whistling again.

*Off we go into the wild blue yonder...*

The familiar tune and the blue sky ahead raised his spirits. He pushed his foot down harder on the accelerator, glancing back to see the stable disappear from view in the rearview mirror.

Girl seven had finally been laid to rest, and he couldn't wait for Doc to tell him all about girl eight.

# CHAPTER TWO

E den Winthrop watched the young women file into the sunny meeting room, her concern for them mingling with pride. They had all been through so much, and yet they had survived and were now here, at Hope House, fighting to rebuild their lives.

She noticed that several of the women were chatting and smiling, apparently starting to feel comfortable in the addiction treatment facility the Mercy Harbor Foundation had opened only the month before.

"I think this place is really starting to come together, Duke."

She looked down and raised her eyebrows as if expecting the golden retriever to agree. He looked at her and cocked his head, clearly needing time to think it over.

"Ms. Winthrop, have you seen Kara this morning?"

Eden turned to see one of the residents standing in the doorway of the meeting room.

"Sorry, Izzy, but I haven't. I'll go see if she's in her room. You guys go ahead and get started with your session."

Izzy withdrew into the room and Eden turned to walk down a wide, airy corridor, Duke following her at a quick trot. The golden retriever had acted as Eden's emotional support animal for years, and even though she felt like she'd finally gotten control of her acute anxiety, and hadn't had a panic attack in months, the loyal dog remained her constant companion.

Eden approached the room Kara Stanislaus had been assigned when she'd arrived at Hope House the previous week. She knocked on the closed door before trying the handle. The door wasn't locked, but Eden paused before entering.

"Kara? It's Eden Winthrop. You're late for your afternoon session with Dr. Bellows."

Hearing no response from within, Eden opened the door wide enough to stick her head inside. She saw Kara laying on the bed, her long, dark hair falling in a tangle over the side. The girl didn't move as Eden yanked open the door and hurried across the room.

"Kara? Kara, can you hear me?"

Eden gripped the girl's shoulders and gave her a gentle shake. Panic set in at the limp weight of Kara's body. Eden lowered her head and listened for breathing. Relieved to feel faint puffs of air on her cheek, she placed her fingers on Kara's wrist and detected an even fainter pulse. Eden turned and ran back down the corridor.

The group of women were seated in a circle in the brightly lit meeting room. Dr. Bellows sat with them, holding a clipboard and taking notes. He looked up as Eden burst in, immediately rising to his feet as he saw the fear on her face.

"Kara is unconscious, Dr. Bellows. You need to check on her."

Eden waited for the therapist to hurry past her and then followed him back down the corridor, dread settling in her stomach at the thought they might be too late.

"I went to check on her when she didn't show up for the session and I found her unresponsive. She's breathing and has a pulse, but she won't wake up."

Eden's voice caught in her throat and she forced herself to take a deep breath, knowing she needed to stay calm if she hoped to help the young woman.

Duke stood by the bed when they entered the room as if on guard, and he looked at Eden with worried eyes.

"It's alright, boy," Eden soothed. "The doctor's here now."

She turned to see Dr. Bellows lean over Kara and pull up one eyelid and then the other.

"Her pupils are severely constricted."

The therapist placed two fingers on her limp wrist.

"Weak pulse, shallow breathing."

Dr. Bellows looked down as Duke began sniffing under the bed, the dog's body tense and his bushy tail down.

"Have you found something, boy?'

Dr. Bellows reached under the bed and pulled out a prescription pill bottle. The cap was off and the bottle was empty.

"Methadone."

Dr. Bellows' voice was grave.

"She must have taken all the pills that were in this."

"Oh my god, how could she have...?"

But Eden's words were drowned out by Dr. Bellows' deep, urgent voice as he called 911.

"We need an ambulance right away. We've got a suspected methadone overdose. Young female, approximately twenty years old. Pinpoint pupils, weak respiration and pulse."

Eden listened numbly to the phone call, willing Kara to wake up and tell them it had all been a mistake.

*Did Kara do this on purpose? Or was this just a terrible accident?*

Dr. Bellows disconnected the call and pulled a package from the pocket of his lightweight blazer. He removed the wrapping to reveal a small white device with a short nozzle on top.

"This is naloxone."

Dr. Bellows tilted Kara's head back and inserted the nozzle into her left nostril. He pushed the white plunger on the bottom of the device before moving the nozzle to her right nostril and repeating the action.

He finally raised his eyes to look up at Eden, noting her confused expression.

"It's an antidote for opioid overdose. If you're going to run a rehab center you better have access to this."

Eden felt the sting of his words as she met his disapproving gaze.

"Right, so how do we know if it worked?" she managed to say, refusing to waste time defending herself when Kara may be dying right in front of her.

Eden wasn't the usual resource providing care to the residents, and she certainly didn't have medical training, but once this emergency was over, she promised herself she would verify with Reggie that all staff had access to the antidote.

Sirens sounded in the distance and Eden's heart jumped with hope. Maybe Kara would be all right after all. Maybe it wasn't too late.

Eden rushed toward the front of the building, waving to the ambulance. She ushered a paramedic carrying an enormous orange bag down the hall and into the small room where Kara lay on the bed, still unconscious.

Eden stepped back into the hall just as a second paramedic approached pushing a wheeled stretcher. She forced herself to stay quiet and not ask the questions that bubbled to the surface.

*Will Kara be okay? Will she survive?*

She knew the best thing she could do was stay out of the way and allow the medical professionals to take care of Kara. Her questions and concerns would only cause unnecessary delays.

Feeling useless, Eden decided to let Reggie Horn know what was going on. The director of the Mercy Harbor Foundation would want to know that a resident in their new addiction treatment facility had overdosed. And maybe Reggie would be able to find out what had happened, and how Kara had gotten access to a whole bottle of methadone.

The phone rang twice before Eden heard her friend's tense voice.

"I've heard an ambulance was called out to Hope House and I'm on my way. Do you know what happened?"

"It's Kara Stanislaus. Apparently, she overdosed on methadone. We found an empty prescription bottle."

"Is she going to make it?"

The fear in Reggie's voice matched her own, and Eden wished she could offer reassurance.

"Well, Dr. Bellows gave her an antidote. Nalo-something."

"Naloxone? That's good. Did he get it from our pharmacy?" Reggie asked, sounding relieved.

"He had it with him. Just pulled it out of his pocket." Eden remembered the doctor's critical comments. "He says everyone here should have it on hand."

"He's right, and we do have a supply of the kits in the pharmacy. Gloria is there today. She can provide an emergency dose to any of the staff. But perhaps Dr. Bellows didn't know that. He just started volunteering a few weeks back and is still getting used to things. We all are I guess."

Eden heard the doubt in Reggie's voice and felt a wave of sympathy wash through her. It hadn't been easy opening up the new facility in only three months, and they'd all worked night and day to get the place ready.

Their rush to open up Hope House had been prompted by the desire to create something positive in the aftermath of the recent tragic events in Willow Bay; the events had resulted in the death of three young women and the kidnapping of Eden's niece, Hope. Once Hope had been rescued and things had returned to normal, Eden and Reggie had decided to expand the Mercy Harbor services to help other young women fight addiction and avoid the terrible consequences that often followed.

"Well, Dr. Bellows must carry around his own supply," Eden reassured Reggie. "So, it worked out. I just hope it was enough to save Kara."

Just then the paramedics pushed Kara past Eden on the stretcher, a blanket pulled up to her neck and an oxygen mask over her mouth.

Eden rushed after the stretcher, trying to catch a glimpse of the girl's face, wanting to know if she had regained consciousness.

As she emerged from the building she saw the ambulance doors were open and waiting for the stretcher. She looked around and was relieved to see Reggie running toward her from the parking lot.

"Reggie, can you watch Duke? I'd like to ride with Kara in the ambulance."

"Sure, I'll keep him here with me. And he can always come home with me if needed."

Reggie's big brown eyes looked worried, but she smiled, her lips bright red against even white teeth. She bent over and ruffled Duke's fur.

"I'll be glad to have some company, and we'll be fine. Now go. And let me know what happens."

Eden waited for the paramedics to secure the stretcher into the back of the ambulance then climbed in and perched on a narrow bench. She watched the blanket rise and fall, letting the gentle rhythm calm her nerves and coax her own breathing into a deep, even pattern.

"You're going to be all right," Eden whispered and raised a hand to smooth back a strand of long, dark hair from Kara's forehead.

The trill of Eden's cell phone sounded in her pocket, and she hurriedly took out the phone and rejected the call, wanting to stop the noise. Looking down at the display she saw a phone number that had become increasingly familiar.

Leo Steele's handsome face flashed through her mind as she remembered the plans they'd made for that evening. The past few months had been busy for both of them, and tonight was supposed to be their first official date. She'd even bought a new outfit for the occasion.

Eden looked again at Kara's motionless form on the stretcher and sighed as she composed a text message.

*Sorry, must cancel dinner. Headed to ER. Will call and explain later.*

After switching the ringer off, she dropped the phone back into her pocket and listened to the wail of the sirens as the ambulance raced down the highway toward Willow Bay General Hospital.

# CHAPTER THREE

L eo read the incoming text message from Eden with a worried frown, then dropped the cell phone back on his desk, not knowing if he should be worried about her unexpected trip to the emergency room or annoyed that their big Friday night date had been canceled.

He'd been counting on a romantic candlelight dinner to take his mind off his increasingly obsessive search for his mother's killer. And he'd hoped the evening may be the start of a more intimate relationship with the woman who was constantly present in his thoughts but rarely with him in real life.

Before he could decide how he should respond to Eden's text, he heard the faint tinkling sound that indicated someone had opened the front door to the law office.

Loud male voices, followed by the quieter, amused voice of his paralegal, Pat, alerted Leo that Pete Barker and Frankie Dawson had finally arrived, thirty minutes late for their two o'clock meeting.

Leo stood up and walked down the hall to the lobby.

"Glad to see you guys are taking this investigation seriously," he said, looking at his watch and offering the two men a tight smile.

"Yeah, it's as serious as a heart attack, right Barker?" Frankie's voice cracked into a high-pitched laugh as he clutched his chest.

"Real nice, Frankie."

Barker rolled his eyes and looked over at Pat, who sat at the reception desk with a cup of tea in her hands and her little pug, Tinkerbell, curled up by her feet.

Pat Monahan shook her head and crossed her arms across her chest in a way that let Leo know she was becoming impatient.

"I've got work to do and you boys are keeping me from it," the older woman stated, turning to her computer and pushing her glasses on. "And you're interrupting Tinkerbell's nap."

Leo motioned for Frankie and Barker to follow him into his office and waved them over to a long table against the far wall. Piles of files, paper, and notebooks were stacked on the table, along with dozens of yellow sticky notes.

"Welcome to my war room, gentlemen."

"Well, it certainly looks like a bomb's gone off in here," Barker groaned, eyeing the piles of information that needed to be reviewed.

Leo regarded the retired detective. He looked healthy enough, but maybe the case would prove too much for the older man after his recent heart attack and unexpectedly early retirement.

"You know me, Leo."

Frankie dug a long, skinny hand into his pocket and pulled out a loose cigarette.

"I'm not good at all this paperwork bullshit. I'm better used out on the street, tracking down clues and creeps."

"Right, I agree," Leo replied, glad to see Frankie looking alert and sober. "Now put that cancer stick back in your pocket. This is a non-smoking office."

Leo searched through a tall stack of files, looking for the information he'd pulled together on the Natalie Lorenzo case. He grabbed a thick manila folder and opened it on the table in front of them.

Next, he picked up an even thicker folder that held all the information he'd collected on his mother's case over the years and arranged it next to the Lorenzo file.

"Our first task is to compare these two cases and see if we can find a link. Both homicides took place in Willow Bay back in 2006."

Leo put his left hand on the Lorenzo file.

"Natalie Lorenzo was strangled at the Old Canal Motel in May 2006."

He placed his right hand on his mother's file.

"My mother, Helena Steele, was killed two weeks later in her own bed. Her throat had been cut."

Leo stared at the men in front of him, willing himself to keep his tone neutral, his face impassive. He couldn't let them see how much it hurt him to speak of his mother's murder and the wrongful conviction of his father.

His family had been destroyed by the senseless act of an unknown killer. A killer that may still be out there, free to kill other women, free to destroy other families. Leo cleared his throat and continued.

"At this point, the only link between the two murders is the fact that two women were violently murdered in the town of Willow Bay within two weeks of each other. Other than that, they seem unrelated."

Barker pulled over a chair and sat down in front of the open files. He looked at the photo paper-clipped to the inside cover of the Natalie Lorenzo folder.

A thin woman with limp brown hair and red-rimmed eyes stared out at him. The look in her eyes told him everything he needed to know about the life she'd led before some sick bastard decided to end it.

"I never did see her alive," Barker finally said, wishing he'd never seen her dead either.

The image of her dead, bloated body had implanted itself in his mind, reappearing in dreams every so often, as if to make sure he didn't forget her.

"You and Ingram were on the case."

Leo reached out and snagged a newspaper clipping. An article on the homicide included a black and white photo of a younger, heavier version of Barker. He stood outside the Willow Bay Police department fending off a group of reporters.

Frankie leaned over Barker's shoulder and read the caption in a loud, cheerful voice.

*"Detective Peter Barker admits no new leads in motel murder."*

Barker glared over at Frankie, his fists clenching on the table in front of him.

"Very good, Frankie, I didn't know you could read."

Frankie's smile faded at the insult, making Leo wonder if they would all be able to work together effectively. He wasn't sure.

Pete Barker had been an old-school police detective before a heart attack gave him an excuse to retire early. He normally didn't hang out with wise-cracking ex-cons that boasted a two-pack-a-day habit like Frankie. At first glance, the men couldn't be more different.

And Leo was a workaholic defense lawyer convinced that the police had wrongly convicted his father. So, on the surface, the three men appeared to have nothing in common, nothing to bring them together and allow them to solve two cold cases that no one else cared about.

But Leo had known the men for years, and he had come to believe they all held the same view of the world. They were all jaded in their own ways, all willing to work outside the system, but deep down all three of the men wanted to see justice done.

"Can you both just cut the crap and give each other a break?"

Leo's voice was hard. The investigation meant too much to him to entrust it to anyone who couldn't focus on what was important.

"I asked you guys to help me because I need fresh eyes on these files, and fresh information from potential witnesses and leads. If you're going to spend all your time pissing each other off, then I don't need you."

"Sorry, Leo," Frankie muttered, fidgeting with the unlit cigarette. "I'll stop messin' around."

Barker relaxed his shoulders and gave Leo an affirmative nod.

"Yeah, you got it, Steele. All business from now on."

Barker began turning pages in the Helena Steele file. He stopped and stared at a photo of an attractive woman with dark, shoulder-length hair and a wide, friendly smile.

"I can see the resemblance," Barker murmured, not meeting Leo's eyes. "She looks like a nice lady."

"She was." Leo swallowed the lump that had risen in his throat. "She didn't deserve to die the way she did. Her killer is still out there walking around free, and my dad paid for what he did."

"It's a fucking shame," Frankie agreed, shaking his head.

Leo felt a rush of gratitude at the emotion he heard behind the words. Frankie knew what it felt like to be convicted of a crime he hadn't committed; he understood the grief and rage that had pushed Leo's father to commit suicide.

"Your mother worked at the old community health center?" Barker asked, staring down at a page of hand-written notes.

"Sometimes," Leo said. "She was a social worker for the county. She had an office at the center to meet with patients that had been tagged by the medical staff as potential victims of abuse or violence."

"You know Natalie Lorenzo had been attending a court-mandated substance abuse class there in the weeks before she died?"

"No, I didn't know."

Leo's mind churned with possibilities. Had they finally found a link between Natalie Lorenzo and his mother? Had the two women known each other? Had their killer been somehow connected with the health center?

"I don't remember all the details," Barker said. "It's been a long time. But I remember her police file included the court order about the community health center. Ingram and I went by there and talked to some of the staff."

Leo's heart pounded at the thought that Barker may have talked to his mother. Perhaps even taken a statement.

"We need to see the police files on the Lorenzo case," Leo said, staring down at Barker. "And you need to get them."

"Hold on, Steele. I highly doubt they'll just hand me the files."

Barker raised thick eyebrows and grimaced up at Leo.

"From what I've heard the chief put the whole department on notice. He was pissed that the story on Reinhardt went public before he could do any damage control. Said he'd fire anyone caught leaking to the press or sharing information outside the department."

"So, ask Nessa to do you a favor," Leo insisted, undeterred by the WBPD's new policies. "No one else has to know."

Leo knew that Barker's ex-partner, Detective Nessa Ainsley, would be the most likely source to help them out. She hadn't been on the force back when his mother had been murdered, but she was one of the few detectives that Leo trusted to do the right thing, no matter how hard it might be.

"I guess I can ask her," Barker muttered, not sounding very happy about it.

Leo patted Barker on the back and considered his next step.

"I'll check the legal files and business records for the health center. See if I can access a list of employees or patients somehow."

"And I'll scope out the neighborhood around the old health center. See if anyone remembers Natalie," Frankie offered.

Adrenaline pounded through Leo's veins at the thought that Natalie Lorenzo and the community health center might lead him to his mother's killer.

He studied Barker and Frankie with shining eyes.

"What are we waiting for? Let's get to work."

# CHAPTER FOUR

Nessa was starting to think she might be able to make it home in time to take the kids out for pizza, and that Jerry may even agree to treat Cole and Cooper to a Friday night movie when the phone on her desk began to ring.

"Detective Nessa Ainsley, how can I help?"

She held the receiver between her shoulder and her ear, automatically reaching for a notepad and pen.

"I thought you'd have snuck out by now, Nessa. Five o'clock Friday afternoon and you're still picking up calls?"

The sound of Pete Barker's gruff voice brought sudden tears to Nessa's eyes. They hadn't spoken in months; she hadn't realized how much she'd missed him.

"I was just leaving, actually," Nessa shot back, blinking hard. "Seems Jerry got used to me being around while I was recuperating and now he gets jumpy if I'm gone too long."

"Can't blame the guy, can you? His wife did get shot in the line of duty. Be glad you've got someone at home that cares."

Nessa winced at Barker's words. She knew he was right. She was lucky to have Jerry and the boys. After everything that had happened in the last few months, she should be thanking her lucky stars she was still alive to take her sons out to a movie and kiss her husband good night.

Poor Barker wasn't so lucky. He was alone now, and she knew he regretted spending so many nights away from the wife and daughter who were no longer a part of his life.

"So, what's the special occasion, Barker? You been missing me?"

"Every day, Nessa," Barker said, his voice soft, almost sad. "But that's not why I'm calling. I actually need a favor."

Nessa put down the pen and sat back in her chair, relieved that the last-minute call did not involve a complaint or an urgent request that would derail her plans for the evening.

"Oh, now I see." Nessa let her southern drawl creep into her words as she teased Barker, wanting to lighten the mood. "You've just been buttering me up with all that sweet talk so you can ask for a favor."

"I need to look through a couple of case files from 2006. Two cold case homicides I'm investigating."

Barker's words surprised Nessa into momentary silence.

"What do you mean *investigating*? Are you taking on private work now?"

"Something like that, Nessa. I'm helping Leo Steele investigate his mother's murder. He's convinced the real killer is still out there. He wants to find out who killed her, and he wants to clear his father's name."

Nessa digested the information, not sure how she felt about Leo Steele and Pete Barker investigating a case that the department had solved and closed long ago. The WBPD had gotten enough bad press lately. Chief Kramer would go ballistic if he found out Barker was digging around in old cases stirring up more doubt about the department.

"You said a couple of cases. What other case are you and Leo Steele working on?"

"The Natalie Lorenzo homicide. You know I was the lead on that case. I was partnered up with Ingram back then. I think I told you how that case shook me up."

Nessa didn't respond, but her mind flashed back to a conversation she'd had with Barker in the weeks after she'd been shot. They had discussed the Natalie Lorenzo homicide, and he'd told her that he had been the one to tell Natalie's twelve-year-old son, Vinny, that his mother had been killed. The encounter had left Barker with the conviction that he wasn't cut out to be a detective.

"And what does the Lorenzo case have to do with Leo Steele or his mother's homicide?"

"He thinks the cases may be related. That the same perp may have killed both Natalie Lorenzo and Helena Steele."

Nessa's mouth went dry at the idea. Had the same man killed the two women and gotten away with it? She coughed, reaching for her water bottle and taking a long sip.

"And what do you think, Barker? You investigated the Lorenzo case. You think that case matches up with the Steele case?"

"I don't know, that's why I need to see the files. In the Lorenzo case we interviewed loads of people, tracked down all the sexual predators in the area, but in the end, we never did solve it. I always assumed some sick john had ended up taking things too far then left town."

Barker hesitated, as if considering his next words, and then continued, his voice sounding cautious.

"But Reinhardt and Vanzinger worked the Helena Steele case. I only had peripheral involvement."

Nessa's throat constricted, and a dull ache started up in her stomach at Pete's words. Detective Kirk Reinhardt had turned out to be a dirty cop. And when Nessa had gotten too close to the truth, he'd shot her. She still had flashbacks of the rainy night and the explosion from Reinhardt's gun that had blasted her off her feet and sent her crashing to the pavement.

While her bullet-proof vest had stopped the bullet, her head had hit the pavement with force, and she'd been knocked unconscious. Luckily she'd come to in time to take down Reinhardt before he could hurt anyone else. Nessa squeezed her eyes shut against the memories, but she could still feel the rain on her face as she'd pulled the trigger and watched Reinhardt fall into the bloody puddles on the pavement beside her.

Leo Steele had been there that night. He'd helped save Nessa's life. His was the first face she'd seen after Reinhardt had fallen. As much as she wanted to turn Barker away and put Reinhardt and Leo Steele and everything to do with that terrible night behind her, she knew she couldn't do it.

She owed Leo Steele more than that. And she respected Pete Barker too much to refuse to help him out. He was a true friend, and she didn't have many of those hanging around these days.

"I can't give you the files, Barker, not without clearing it with Chief Kramer first."

"So, ask him. Tell him I just want to close out a case I left open. He may even appreciate the help."

"Yeah, and maybe pigs will start flying, too."

Nessa snorted, then lowered her voice.

"You don't understand the kind of pressure we've been under since the Reinhardt story blew up in the press. Investigators from the state and the feds came down here poking around. I bet Kramer was sweating bullets that they'd blame him. Things are just starting to settle down. He's not about to let Leo Steele reopen old cases that'll make the department look bad."

"I don't care who looks bad, Nessa, and neither should Kramer. If there's a killer in Willow Bay that's gotten away with two homicides, I think Kramer will want to know."

25

Nessa bit her lip and tried to think.

"He won't want to hear about it on Friday night. Let me think about it this weekend. In any case, I won't be asking him anything until Monday."

Barker sighed, and Nessa could imagine the deep frown mark that was probably appearing between his puppy-dog eyes.

"Nessa, I don't want to wait. We've finally got a lead. Something that could link the two cases. I can't just sit on it all weekend."

Nessa looked at her watch. It was now five fifteen. Traffic would be building, and Jerry and the boys were waiting.

"What kind of lead?"

"Both the woman frequented the old community health center around the time they were killed. Helena Steele was a social worker and Natalie Lorenzo attended mandated substance abuse classes."

Nessa wanted to scoff at the suggested link, but her past experience told her that it was just this type of seemingly random connection that could break a case open. Waving it off as a mere coincidence could prove to be a fatal mistake.

"So, what are you hoping to find in the files that can't wait until Monday?"

"I want to see if the reports list any common witnesses or suspects. Maybe someone at the health center that they both knew. I need to find out if anyone gets mentioned in both files."

Nessa looked at her watch again. Almost five twenty now. If she left it any later they'd never have time to eat pizza and make it to the movie.

"Listen, Barker. I can't give you the files without running it by Kramer first, but I'll find them and take them home with me tonight. That way I can look through them tomorrow morning for anyone connected to both cases or to the health center. If I find anything I'll call you tomorrow and let you know."

Nessa heard footsteps and then keys jangling in the hall behind her. She looked back to see Simon Jankowski stroll over to his desk and start unloading his backpack.

"I appreciate that, Nessa. I really do. I'll be waiting for your call."

Nessa hung up and shoved her laptop and a few files into her briefcase. She'd need to hurry if she hoped to make it down to the file room, check out the two files, and pick up Jerry and the boys in time to find an empty table at Pizza Express. Friday nights were always busy, and the boys would get grumpy if they had to wait too long to eat. She decided they'd have to wait on the movie, perhaps see a Saturday matinee.

"You leaving already?" Jankowski asked, booting up his laptop and arranging his coffee mug and files on the desk.

"It's after five and I've got a family to think about," Nessa snapped, instantly regretting her words.

Jankowski was going through a rough divorce. Friday nights on his own probably weren't his favorite thing.

"Sorry to ask. Just like to keep tabs on my partner."

"No, I'm sorry, Jankowski. Just rushing to get out. Jerry and the kids are waiting."

"No problem," Jankowski said, regarding Nessa with curious eyes. "Is everything okay? You look upset."

"Everything's peachy. Just in a hurry."

As Nessa hurried down the hall and made her way to the file room, she wondered if she should have told Jankowski about Barker's request. He was her partner now, after all. And he did have a right to know what she was working on. Especially if she was going to ask Chief Kramer for approval to help Barker.

But Jankowski's silence about Reinhardt's suspected involvement with a drug and sex trafficking ring had almost cost Nessa her life. She wasn't sure she could afford to trust him again.

# CHAPTER FIVE

Eden paused outside Room 324 and took a deep breath, suddenly scared to go inside. She'd been relieved to hear that Kara had regained consciousness and had been moved to a patient room for overnight observation, and she'd hurried up in the elevator without taking time to consider what she should say.

What was the appropriate thing to say to a young woman who had overdosed, and who might have been attempting to take her own life? Would Kara even want to see her, a woman she barely knew?

The setting sun was still visible through the west-facing window as Eden walked in and softly closed the door behind her. Kara lay in the hospital bed, her dark hair spilling over several white pillows propped behind her. Her eyes watered as Eden approached the bed.

"Oh, Kara, I'm so glad to see you're okay." Eden clasped the girl's small, cold hand. "You had us all so worried."

"I'm sorry about...everything. The nurse told me I'd overdosed, and they had to bring me here in an ambulance, but I don't remember anything." Kara stared at Eden with big, scared eyes, looking far younger than her twenty-one years.

"You don't remember taking the methadone?"

Eden wasn't sure she should be the one asking Kara questions. If the girl had tried to kill herself, she should be talking to a therapist. Someone like Reggie Horn or Dr. Bellows. Someone who would know the right things to say, the right questions to ask.

"Well, Dr. Bellows has me on methadone as part of my treatment, but I only remember taking the usual pills this morning. Gloria always comes around first thing."

"And you don't remember getting a prescription bottle and taking more pills?"

Kara shook her head firmly, her forehead furrowing into a frown.

"No, I never had a bottle or any pills. I'm clean now. I didn't even want the meth but the doctors keep telling me it'll help me readjust to being straight. Keep me from relapsing."

Eden knew drug addicts were often experienced liars by necessity, having to convince family, friends, and authorities that they weren't taking drugs, weren't hustling for drug money, but Eden thought Kara looked sincere.

*I just can't believe she's lying. She looks so upset, so scared.*

Eden watched Kara raise a trembling hand to her throat and begin twisting a gold cross that hung on a delicate chain around her neck.

"The people here keep asking me if I meant to hurt myself. They think I overdosed on purpose, but I *didn't*." Her voice cracked with emotion as she continued to twist the chain. "I would never do that to my sister. She's been through too much already."

Eden's heart ached at the girl's obvious distress, having experienced the pain of failing her own sister in the worst possible way. She forced thoughts of Mercy's death from her mind.

"Your sister? Should I contact her for you?"

"No, I don't want Anna to know what happened," Kara cried out, her hands grasping Eden's in panic. "She'll worry, and maybe even drag my little nephew over here to see me. They live over in Orlando and it's a long drive. I've caused enough trouble already."

"Okay, we won't call Anna," Eden soothed, trying to think of something to say to calm Kara down.

The girl needed time to think. She could call her sister and tell her what had happened once she was ready.

"How old is your nephew?" Eden asked, keeping her voice light. "What's his name?"

"His name is Nikolai, but we call him Niko. He's only two years old. But very smart. He already talks up a storm, or at least tries to."

A sparkle came into Kara's eyes and she sat up in the bed.

"I talked to him on the phone yesterday and he called me Auntie for the first time. I can't believe how fast he's growing up."

Eden grinned at the enthusiasm in Kara's voice, wanting to encourage her to talk more. Perhaps if she felt comfortable talking about herself and her family, she would open up about what had happened with the methadone.

"That's a lovely cross," Eden said, her eyes drawn again to Kara's hand nervously tugging at the chain.

"My father gave it to me," Kara said, looking down as if to reassure herself it was still there. "Before he died he gave one to me and one to Anna. It's all we have left of him."

"I'm sorry about your father."

Eden patted Kara's arm, regretting the way the girl's hazel eyes now appeared sad, the sparkle gone as she turned to gaze out the window, the sun's last rays glinting against the glass.

"I can't believe he's been gone over two years, but it feels like yesterday, you know?"

"I do know," Eden said, her own grief at losing Mercy still painfully fresh. "I lost my sister five years ago but it still...hurts."

Kara turned toward Eden, her forehead furrowing again in a sympathetic grimace.

"That's...terrible. I don't know what I'd do if anything happened to Anna. She and Niko are the only family I have left."

Eden forced herself not to react to the words that mirrored her own feelings for Mercy before she'd been killed. She hadn't thought she would survive losing her younger sister but giving up hadn't been an option. She'd had to be strong for Mercy's children. Hope and Devon had lost both their mother and their father on that horrible day, and they'd needed her.

"I think you'd surprise yourself. I didn't think I'd get through it, but I did. I had my nephew and niece to look after, and that helped. I feel very lucky to have them."

Kara bit her lip and blinked back tears.

"I've gotta get out of here. I need to see Anna and Niko. I need to tell them I'm sorry for leaving."

She squeezed her eyes shut and fell back against the pillows.

"I should never have left Orlando. Never have been so stupid."

"The only way you can help your sister is to get better. You need to get clean and strong. Then you'll be ready to be the best sister and aunt you can be."

"That's what I was trying to do," Kara insisted. "I was doing so well at Hope House. I just don't know how this happened. I don't know how I got...here."

Eden heard the frustration and confusion in Kara's words and wondered again if perhaps the girl really didn't remember taking the methadone. Could it really have been some sort of mistake?

"Yes, you were doing really well, and you'll continue doing well once you get out of here and come back to Hope House. You can't let this...accident...stop you from getting your life together."

"You mean you'd let me come back?"

The timid question made Eden smile even as her heart ached for the girl. Kara was still so young, and so alone.

"Of course, you can," Eden assured her. "We'll hold your spot until you're ready to come back. In fact, I'll check on you tomorrow and see if I can bring you back to the house myself."

Eden was glad to see a shy smile appear.

"Okay, I'll come back and finish the program," Kara said, sounding sure of her decision. "And then I'm going back to Orlando to help Anna and Niko. I'm going to be the best sister and aunt ever."

"I'm glad to hear it. Now you get some rest, and I'll come by tomorrow to see how you're doing."

As Eden took the elevator back down to the lobby, she checked her watch and saw that it was only eight o'clock. Would Leo have eaten yet? Perhaps it wasn't too late to go on their date after all.

Eden pulled her phone out of her pocket, suddenly remembering she'd turned off the ringer. Seven missed calls. Five of the calls had been from Reggie or other staff at Hope House, likely wanting an update on Kara. The other two calls were from Leo, but he hadn't left a message.

She quickly pressed the call back option, eager to hear his deep voice, wanting to tell him about her traumatic day. But the call went to voicemail and Eden decided not to leave a message. He had probably made other plans. Was likely out with friends enjoying his Friday night.

*Did I really expect him to just sit around waiting for me?*

The question lingered in her mind as she stood alone in the lobby waiting for her uber to arrive.

# CHAPTER SIX

Kara jabbed at the remote, bored with the selection of Saturday morning cartoons, infomercials, and local news available on the small television mounted above her hospital bed. She paused to watch the weather report on Channel Ten. Weather girl Veronica Lee pointed to a satellite image of a tropical storm brewing in the Caribbean. The curvy forecaster seemed excited to report the storm was heading toward the Gulf.

"Why is she always so cheerful about severe weather?"

Kara jumped at the unexpected voice beside her. She turned to see that Dr. Bellows had slipped into the room unannounced.

"Uh, I don't know. Maybe job security?" Kara offered, trying not to let him know that he'd startled her.

Dr. Bellows laughed and put his hand on Kara's arm.

"How are you today, Kara? Better than yesterday I hope."

Kara felt the urge to shrug his hand off her arm but didn't want to seem rude. After all, he'd come all the way to the hospital just to check on her.

"I'm feeling better, Dr. Bellows. Pretty much back to normal."

"That's wonderful. I wasn't sure I'd be able to pull you through when I found you yesterday."

Kara stared at him, her expression perplexed.

"You found me? You were the one who saved me?"

"Well, I asked Izzy to go find you and she alerted Ms. Winthrop, who found you unconscious in your room. She called me out of the session, and I managed to give you an antidote to counteract the methadone you took."

Kara blinked, not wanting to contradict the doctor but convinced that she hadn't taken methadone, at least not knowingly.

"Dr. Bellows, I took the pill Gloria gave me yesterday morning, but that was it. I didn't take any other pills, and I didn't have a bottle of anything in my room either."

"Calm down, Kara. I'm just telling you what I saw in your room. There was an empty prescription bottle and you were unconscious."

"But Dr. Bellows, I don't remember–"

"Call me Doc, okay? I think when someone saves your life it's appropriate to be less formal."

"Well...all right," Kara agreed.

Her frustration was growing at his refusal to listen to what she was trying to tell him.

"But I didn't take any pills. And I didn't want to hurt myself. I'm trying to get clean. I didn't even want the methadone anyway. That was your idea, remember?"

Dr. Bellows' face hardened at her words, and Kara cringed back against the bed at the contempt in his eyes.

"We talked in your last session about taking responsibility for your actions. That's one of the most important steps to recovery. It's disappointing to stand here and watch you blame *me* for your actions."

Kara wanted to protest, but something in the therapist's cold stare made her swallow her words.

*I'll just wait and talk to Ms. Winthrop. She'll believe me.*

Apparently satisfied that the matter had been settled, Dr. Bellows picked up the pitcher of ice water by her bed and pulled what looked like a small envelope out of his pocket. He opened the envelope and shook out two white pills.

"This is the follow-up dose to the antidote."

Kara stared at the pills in dismay. Pills had gotten her into her current mess; she felt sure more pills would only make things worse.

"I feel fine, Dr. Bellows. I don't need any more pills."

"So, you're a doctor now, Kara?"

His sarcastic words brought a flush to her cheeks, but she shook her head and didn't reach for the pills.

"Okay, I can't force you, but if you won't follow my orders then I can't be responsible for your well-being. We can't let you back in Hope House if you won't follow the rules."

Dr. Bellows gave a resigned shrug of his shoulders and set the cup of water on the table. Kara watched in dismay as he turned to leave.

"Fine, I'll take the antidote," Kara called out, "but I'm not taking any more methadone."

Dr. Bellows stopped and turned around, his expression impassive as he picked up the cup of water and held it out to her along with the pills.

"We'll discuss your treatment plan when we get to Hope House."

Kara swallowed the pills as Dr. Bellows retrieved a shopping bag that he'd left by the door.

"I've brought you clean clothes and a toothbrush. Get dressed and we'll get you out of here."

"You mean, like, now?"

"Yes, now. We need to get you back into treatment before they have you committed."

"Committed? What do you mean?"

"I mean the staff here have a legal obligation to report you as being a risk to yourself if they determine you tried to commit suicide. If that happens you'll end up in a locked psychiatric ward."

Cold fear flooded through Kara's body at the words.

*Will I end up in an asylum like my mother? Is that my fate, too?*

"They can't do that," Kara protested, but she grabbed the bag and stood. Her legs felt weak and shaky as she walked to the small bathroom. "I didn't do anything wrong."

Closing the door behind her, she untied the hospital gown and let it fall to the floor. Opening the plastic bag, she saw a white cotton sundress and sandals, along with underclothes, a comb, toothbrush, and toothpaste. She pulled out the dress and held it up, noting the frilly ruffles around the neckline.

*My size, but definitely not my style.*

The dress would have to do for now. She'd get back into her usual jeans and t-shirts when she was back at Hope House.

She got dressed, brushed her teeth, and ran the comb through her long, dark hair with a trembling hand. Looking into the small mirror, she noticed faint circles under her eyes and saw that her pupils looked tiny.

*Am I really well enough to be discharged?*

A wave of dizziness forced her to lean her head against the closed door. After a few minutes, she felt able to open the door and walk out.

"Okay, let's go," Dr. Bellows said, taking her bare arm and guiding her to the door.

"I'd like to say goodbye to the nurses. They've been so nice."

"Sorry, they've asked that we vacate the room immediately. A new patient is already on the way."

"Oh, well, okay then."

Kara let Dr. Bellows lead her down the corridor toward the elevators. He moved quickly and kept a firm hand around her shoulders to keep her from stumbling.

"I thought they took patients downstairs in a wheelchair," she said, worried that her legs may buckle underneath her at any minute.

"I told them I'd assist you. No need to be dramatic in any case. We'll leave the wheelchairs for people who actually need them."

Kara was surprised at the anger in his voice and the harshness of his words. Had she said something to offend him?

The elevator opened onto a busy lobby and Dr. Bellows hustled her quickly out the big glass doors. She was surprised when he approached a dark blue van with a disabled parking tag hanging on the rearview mirror. He took a key fob from his pocket and unlocked the door before helping her into the front passenger seat.

She stared out the window at the people rushing in and out of the hospital as Dr. Bellows hurried around the van and climbed into the driver's seat. He didn't wait for her to fasten her seatbelt. He started the car and reversed out of the parking spot, before heading the big van toward the exit.

Kara watched as the hospital receded in the side mirror, suddenly catching sight of a woman with blond hair that had stepped out of a car and was walking toward the hospital.

*Is that Eden Winthrop?*

Kara turned in her seat to look around, but the van swerved onto the highway and out of view of the hospital.

* * *

They drove in silence for several miles before Kara began to wonder where they were going. She wasn't familiar with the layout of the city yet, having come to Willow Bay only a few weeks before being picked up by the police on a drug charge and ending up in the Hope House facility, but she knew that they were traveling west, toward the coast, instead of east toward downtown Willow Bay.

"Where are we going, Dr. Bellows?"

Kara's throat felt thick and her words sounded slurred. She lifted a weak hand and motioned behind her.

"Hope House is back that way."

"I told you to call me Doc, and we aren't going to Hope House."

Kara's head began to spin, and her stomach churned as she tried to focus on the road ahead.

"Then where are we going?"

A sudden thought took hold.

*Is he taking me to a mental hospital? Will he let them lock me up?*

Her hand instinctively clutched at the door handle, and she managed a feeble pull before realizing the door was locked. Turning to look at Dr. Bellows, she saw a satisfied smile spread across his face.

"Here we are, then, safe and sound. No need to get upset."

Kara looked through the windshield, surprised to see they were no longer on the highway but had turned off onto a winding driveway. The van continued around a bend before parking in front of an impressive two-story house.

"Where are we? What is this place?"

"Let's just say this is a place we bring certain patients that need *special treatment*. It's more secluded here."

Kara's head began to spin again as she recognized the look of triumph in his eyes. She shrank back against the car seat and closed her eyes, trying to stop the spinning.

*He's gotten me just where he wants me. But why?*

She heard the driver's door open, and then a deep male voice spoke from somewhere outside the van.

"I see you made it, Doc. Everything go to plan?"

"Yep, mission accomplished, as usual. See for yourself."

Kara forced her eyes to open as the men walked over to the passenger window and looked in.

She saw Dr. Bellows standing next to a big man with thick hair and dark sunglasses. He opened the door and put a hand under her chin, turning her face up.

"She's a beauty."

"Yeah, I thought you'd be happy. And she shouldn't give you any trouble, at least not today. I gave her a little something this morning just to make sure."

"On top of the stuff you gave her yesterday? You trying to kill her before I even get her inside?"

The big man's voice sounded angry, and Kara recoiled, trying to pull away, but her body felt heavy and it was hard to move.

"And you can carry her inside, seeing you got her in this state."

"She'll be fine, Ace. Just wanted to make sure she didn't try to get away or cause any problems. She's stubborn. You might have a hard time breaking her in."

Kara felt rough hands seize her arms and hoist her toward the van's door. She raised one hand high enough to grab a clump of Doc's hair, pulling with all her might. He grabbed her wrist and gave a vicious twist, forcing her to release her grip. She felt her delicate gold chain break as he wrenched her out of the van and let her fall onto the hard concrete of the driveway. She clutched at her neck in panic.

*Oh no, my necklace. Where's my necklace?*

Her mind reeled as she fought against the effects of the drugs and an overwhelming fear.

*Will I ever see Anna and Niko again? Will they ever know what happened to me?*

She struggled to keep her eyes open as the world began to fade around her. A pair of thick-soled work boots appeared in front of her and she tried to focus on a red splotch that marked one of the shoes, but it was no use. She was so tired, and her eyes were too heavy.

Finally, Kara closed her eyes and allowed herself to escape into oblivion.

# CHAPTER SEVEN

Eden stared at the unmade, empty bed in confusion. She looked at the numbers on the door again. Yes, it was Room 324, the room Kara had been in the evening before. She walked to the open door of the little bathroom and looked in, knowing even as she did that Kara wouldn't be inside.

Eden studied the nightgown laying on the bathroom floor and frowned, pushing away a sudden sense of unease. She stepped back into the room and noted the half-filled cup of water on the table. The television was on and turned to the local news. It didn't appear as if Kara had been discharged.

*They must have taken Kara to another floor for some sort of test.*

Eden pressed the call button on the bed and then sat in a wooden rocker to wait. Within minutes a harried-looking nurse opened the door and looked around the room, her eyes finally settling on Eden.

The nurse's name badge identified her simply as Morgan. Eden wondered if it was the woman's first name or last.

"Sorry to bother you, but I've come to visit Kara Stanislaus and she's not here, as you can see. I'm wondering if she's been taken for some sort of test? I can always come back if needed."

Nurse Morgan looked at the empty bed, then walked to the bathroom and peeked in. She moved to the foot of the bed and picked up the chart.

"No, she hasn't been scheduled for any tests, so maybe she went for a walkabout. Sometimes people get bored and want to explore. Especially the younger ones."

"Could she have been discharged?"

The nurse wrinkled her nose and shook her head, making her blonde ponytail swing back and forth.

"Her chart wouldn't be here if she'd been discharged but let me go double-check at the nursing station."

Eden watched the woman hurry out of the room. She stepped to the doorway and looked up and down the hall, hoping to see Kara's dark hair and slender figure approaching, but the halls were empty.

Nurse Morgan reappeared, her brow furrowed.

"She's not been discharged, and no one has noticed a patient roaming around the halls."

The nurse pulled open a narrow cabinet and took out a see-through plastic bag. Eden could see jeans and a pink t-shirt inside.

"These were the clothes she came in," the nurse said, biting her lip. "And it looks like her hospital gown is on the floor in there."

Eden's pulse started to race as she turned to the nurse, her voice urgent. "How could she have left the hospital without any clothes, and without anyone seeing her?"

"I'll call security. Maybe they'll be able to track her down."

After Nurse Morgan had rushed off, Eden walked to the window and looked down at the streets below. She saw a line of cars waiting in the loading zone and noticed a woman in a wheelchair being loaded into a van. It made her think of Dr. Bellows and his wife.

When she'd entered the hospital earlier she thought she'd recognized Dr. Bellows getting into his dark blue van outside the hospital. She hadn't seen his wife, but she knew that the woman used a wheelchair, and had assumed he'd been taking her in for some sort of treatment or therapy.

Eden felt a twinge of guilt that she hadn't gotten to know Dr. Bellows and his wife yet, and still was unsure why his wife needed the wheelchair. She should have made more of an effort.

Of course, the therapist had only been volunteering his services at Hope House for a few weeks, and during that time Eden had been busy getting the facility up and running. But she suspected her busy schedule wasn't the only thing that had kept her from getting to know the doctor.

*Something about the guy just rubs me the wrong way.*

Eden looked further west, wishing she could follow the blue sky all the way out to the coast, finding it hard to believe a tropical storm was swirling beyond the clear, cloud-free sky. She supposed that weather, like some people, could be very deceptive; it was dangerous to accept either at face value.

* * *

Eden turned into the Hope House parking lot, navigating her big, white SUV into one of the spaces reserved for staff before turning off the engine and jumping out of the driver's seat. She saw Reggie Horn waiting inside the glass doors as she strode toward the entrance.

"Has Kara shown up yet...is she here?"

The words were out of Eden's mouth before Reggie could offer a greeting.

"No...no one here has seen her or heard from her yet. I asked all the staff and residents. Nothing."

Eden's heart sank at the words. After the hospital security guard had performed a search of the hospital and declared that Kara was no longer on the premises, Eden had hoped the girl would have somehow made her own way back to Hope House.

She'd told herself that Kara must have called her sister after all. Maybe Anna had driven over from Orlando, or maybe Kara knew someone in the area who had stopped by for a visit. The thought brought new worries as Eden imagined Kara driving off with someone that may lead her back to the life of drugs and addiction she'd been fighting to escape.

Reggie put a small hand on Eden's arm and squeezed.

"She'll show up soon I'm sure."

But Eden saw doubt in Reggie's deep, brown eyes, and her own doubt that she'd ever see Kara again began to grow. She looked toward the parking lot as a dark blue van pulled in and drove toward the staff parking area. An image of the same van outside the hospital that morning clicked into Eden's mind.

"Maybe Dr. Bellows saw her. Maybe he knows where Kara is."

Reggie turned to Eden, eyebrows raised.

"Why would Dr. Bellows know where Kara is?"

"Because he was at the hospital this morning. At least I think it was him. I saw him from a distance, but I'm pretty sure it was him."

Eden started out to the parking lot before Reggie could ask any more questions. She saw the therapist walk around to the passenger side and open the door. She approached just as Dr. Bellows was adjusting a backpack over one shoulder.

"Dr. Bellows? Can I have a minute?"

The therapist jumped at her words and turned toward her with wide eyes, obviously flustered.

"Uh, I guess so. What seems to be the problem?"

"I'm wondering if you saw Kara Stanislaus when you were at the hospital earlier. Perhaps you saw her or spoke to her?"

"The hospital?" Dr. Bellows looked confused as if he didn't know the meaning of the word.

"Yes, I saw you getting into your van outside Willow Bay General earlier this morning. You were in the disabled zone so I assumed you were with, uh...your wife."

Eden felt a warm flush creep up her cheeks. She couldn't remember his wife's name even though they had been introduced only a few weeks ago.

"Oh, yes. I had to take Terri in for her therapy session. We go to the attached rehabilitation center, so I don't really think of it as the hospital."

"Right, well, did you and Terri happen to see Kara while you were there? She's left the hospital without being discharged and we aren't sure where she's gone."

"No, I didn't see her, but I'm sure she'll turn up sooner or later."

He moved his backpack to the other shoulder and turned back to pick up a stack of files as if the conversation was over.

"Yes, I hope so, but it just seems so odd. Why would she leave like that without telling anyone?"

"Why do drug addicts do anything? Because they are slaves of their addictions."

He shrugged his shoulders, giving her a condescending smile.

"In my experience, this type of behavior is quite common, so I wouldn't get too worked up about it."

Eden bit her lip, refraining from telling the smug doctor what she thought about his callous advice, and instead moved aside to give him room to step back and close the car door. She dropped her eyes from his face, not wanting him to see her anger, and saw something shiny on the floor before Dr. Bellows slammed the door shut.

As he turned to face her she noted that his hands shook slightly around the strap of his backpack. Her eyes flicked up to his face and she saw his skin was flushed and his pupils had dilated, his eyes wide and dark. Her indignation turned to concern.

"Are you feeling okay, Dr. Bellows? You look ill."

"I'm fine. I just need to get into the session," he said in a clipped voice, pushing past her in annoyance. "I don't like being late. It sets a poor example for those residents who truly do want help."

Eden gaped at his retreating back, outrage seething through her.

Was the man implying Kara didn't want to be helped? How could he make such an assumption after only a few sessions with the girl?

Even Eden knew that a true evaluation of Kara's state of mind and a plan for recovery would take longer than a few hour-long sessions.

She wondered if he was the right choice of therapist for the vulnerable women at Hope House.

*And why was he sweaty and shaking? He almost looked scared.*

She wondered again about his visit to the hospital. Something didn't feel right.

Her eyes returned to the van, and she remembered the flash of gold she'd seen on the floor. She looked over her shoulder. No sign of Dr. Bellows. He was likely preparing for the afternoon session.

Eden stepped up to the passenger's side door and peered in, letting her forehead almost touch the glass as she strained to see in. Her pulse quickened at the sight of the delicate gold chain shining up from the dark carpet.

*Could it be? Could that really be Kara's chain in Dr. Bellows' van?*

Eden forced herself to step back and take a deep breath. She was being ridiculous and paranoid.

Why would Kara's necklace end up in Dr. Bellows' car? It didn't make sense. The chain likely belonged to his wife, Terri.

*Yes, it's got to be Terri's chain. And I'm sure Kara will show up at any minute still wearing the chain her father gave her.*

But doubt followed Eden as she made her way back inside the recovery center determined to call Kara's sister. If Kara was okay, she would have called Anna. And if she hadn't called, Eden would know for sure that Kara was missing.

# CHAPTER EIGHT

D oc opened the door to his house with an exaggerated sigh, relieved that he'd managed to oversee the group session without incident and leave the recovery center without seeing Eden Winthrop again, and without having to answer any more questions that he wasn't prepared to answer.

"Terri, honey? I'm home!"

He dropped his backpack on the floor and walked into the room off the hall that acted as Theresa Bellows' study. Sunlight flooded in through a big picture window, surrounding the woman sitting at the desk in a warm glow.

"Sorry, dear, almost done with this article. Give me five minutes and I'll make you a sandwich."

Terri looked around with a cheerful smile, her hands still flying across her computer keyboard, as Doc crossed over and kissed the top of her head, enjoying the silkiness of her dark curls against his cheek.

"Sure, no rush. I'll put on a pot of coffee."

The last drops of coffee dripped into the pot just as Terri pushed through the doorway and crossed to a kitchen counter that had been lowered to accommodate her wheelchair.

She stopped in front of an oversized bread box that dominated the countertop. The wood was worn, and the words *Fresh Bread* had faded into pale blue smudges on the front long ago, but Terri had inherited the box from her grandmother, and she refused to give it up.

"I made a fresh loaf this morning," she said as she cut off two thick slices. "Whole wheat just like the doctor ordered."

Doc watched her prepare the sandwich with a mixture of pride and sadness. She was a resourceful woman, refusing to let her medical condition, or her wheelchair, get in the way of the things she loved to do, but he knew it was hard on her to be confined at home so much of the time.

"Well, I'm glad you did. It smells delicious in here."

He poured them each a cup of coffee and set one cup in front of Terri before taking his sandwich and coffee over to the little table by the window.

"So, how're things at Hope House? Everyone getting settled in?"

Doc knew his wife wished she could help out at the new recovery center, too. Before her accident, she'd volunteered at several community centers and charitable organizations, always willing to give her time and talents to help those less fortunate.

It was hard for her to see him out making a difference while she was sitting at home writing the odd article for medical journals and healthcare websites.

"Things are still pretty unorganized over there, but I'm helping them out the best I can."

"Really? Is it that bad?"

Doc took a big bite of his sandwich, enjoying the fresh taste of the whole wheat bread, and tried to decide how much he could risk telling Terri. He finished chewing and assumed a look of worry.

"Well, just yesterday one of the residents got hold of a bottle of methadone and took an overdose. Luckily I thought to ask why she hadn't shown up for the session and they found her in time for me to give her naloxone before it was too late."

He shook his head and grimaced, liking the way her eyes widened at the story.

"Oh my god, is she okay?"

"Yes, the naloxone did the trick and she pulled through. But if I hadn't been there I doubt anyone would have noticed. The poor girl would probably be rotting at the morgue right now."

Terri put her hand over her mouth, visibly horrified at the image he'd conjured, then reached over to pat his hand.

"They sure were lucky to have you there, and it's a good thing they had the naloxone on hand. I'm glad it all worked out."

A prickle of irritation edged up Doc's back at Terri's words. It sounded as if she was giving nosy Eden Winthrop and her amateurish team at the recovery center half the credit for saving Kara.

"Actually, they didn't...have the naloxone I mean. I had the antidote with me."

"What...you carry around an injection kit with you all the time?" Terri's eyebrows rose in surprise. "I didn't know that."

Doc felt the irritation bloom into anger at the skepticism he heard in her voice. He'd heard that tone before, usually when she thought he was lying.

"No, not all the time, just when I'm volunteering at an addiction treatment facility run by incompetent people. But you wouldn't understand what's needed at a place like that anymore, would you?"

He regretted the harsh words as soon as he'd spoken. After everything they'd been through together, he knew he shouldn't take his anger out on Terri. She didn't deserve it.

*It's all Eden Winthrop's fault. That bitch has got me worked up.*

Terri lowered her eyes to her cup of coffee.

"No, I guess I don't know what it's like. It's been a long time since I worked at the community health center with you. I'm sure everything's different now."

Doc stared at his wife's lowered head with a familiar sense of helplessness and anger.

*Why did this happen to Terri? Why is she the one stuck in a wheelchair?*

He reached for her hand and held it, shame washing through him at the thought of his careless words causing her more pain.

"You know you mean everything to me, don't you? Without you I'm nothing. Absolutely worthless."

His softly-spoken words made her tighten her hand around his.

"That's sweet of you, Doc, but you shouldn't think that way. If something happens to me you'd still have your work. And you help so many people. Just think about how you're helping the women at Hope House. That's worth a lot."

Doc looked into Terri's trusting brown eyes and knew he could never tell her how he really felt. She wouldn't understand.

*Those women don't deserve my help; they don't even deserve to live.*

\* \* \*

After finishing his sandwich and draining his coffee cup, Doc headed out to his real job. The one that paid the bills and ensured that Terri had access to the best medical care and latest therapeutic treatments available.

The Behavioral Health Group of Willow Bay was a private counseling clinic for those who had the money or insurance to pay for premium care. Doc had founded the clinic after medical school. He'd decided to open his practice in sunny Willow Bay rather than his gloomier hometown of Ft. Wayne, Indiana.

There were too many bad memories back home, and besides, he had connections in Willow Bay that made the little town seem like a safe place to start fresh.

Doc had designed the modern, clean lines of the clinic himself, wanting the practice to appeal to a certain type of patient, hoping the exclusive clinic would attract people who had money and were looking for new ways to spend it.

A few well-chosen words could persuade such a person that weekly therapy sessions would change their lives, for a substantial fee.

Of course, the patients of his private practice had to be coddled and pampered, and they couldn't go missing without instigating a high-profile search. He'd known from the start that there would be no hunting among his private clients.

Better not to mix business with pleasure in any case. Any hunting would be done away from his home and away from his business.

Doc had found that community health centers, homeless shelters, and government-funded rehab facilities offered up the easiest selection.

A few weeks volunteering at a new place would often allow him to pick a target that met the strict criteria he and Ace had agreed on years ago. And sticking to their guidelines had prevented even a hint of suspicion or interest in their activities.

No one had ever suspected Doc was anything other than a selfless volunteer. No one had ever come to him inquiring about the young women he'd taken. No one until Eden Winthrop.

He gritted his teeth at the thought of Eden's interrogation that morning. Who did she think she was? Where he went and what he did was none of her business.

The memory of his impulsive response to her questions nagged at him. He'd told Eden that he had been with Terri at the hospital. What if she asked Terri about it? How could he explain why he'd been there? How could he explain why he'd lied?

Their mission was now in jeopardy and Doc needed to tell Ace. Ace would be mad, but he'd know what to do to fix it. Ace had always been able to fix their mistakes in the past.

But Doc didn't have time to call Ace just yet. The clinic's eating disorder support group met every Saturday afternoon, and Doc was scheduled to lead this week's session.

He could see some of the group members already arriving as he pulled the van into his reserved parking space and jumped out.

He hurried around to the passenger seat to retrieve his backpack then froze in confusion when he saw the gold chain on the floor. It must have fallen off in the brief tussle he'd had with Kara.

But how had he missed seeing it? A frightening question popped into his mind.

*Did Eden Winthrop see the chain this morning?*

He tried to remember their conversation, tried to picture where'd they'd both stood. But he'd been rattled by her sudden appearance and intrusive questions, and his mind now refused to cooperate.

He knew she'd stood next to him on the passenger's side of the van, but he couldn't be sure if she had been in a position to see the floor.

*Even if Eden Winthrop did see the necklace, she couldn't know it's Kara's, could she?*

"Dr. Bellows? Do you need us to help carry anything?"

Doc spun around to see two of the girls that attended the session staring up at him, their eyes hopeful. He produced the warm smile he always wore at his private practice and pocketed the chain. He'd give it to Ace later to dispose of properly.

"No, thank you, ladies, I've got this."

Doc swung his backpack over one shoulder and ushered the girls inside the sleek building. He kept a pleasant smile affixed to his face while watching the young women and girls file in and take seats in a circle of comfortable chairs, but the spark of panic he'd felt upon seeing the gold chain was growing.

He wasn't worried about the police. They wouldn't waste time looking for a runaway drug addict with a record. They never had before.

*But what if Eden Winthrop talks to Terri? Will she expose my lie?*

The phony smile fell away at the thought of his wife discovering another one of his lies. He needed to talk to Ace before things got out of hand.

"Okay everyone, take a seat."

Doc clapped his hands and stood at the front of the room waiting for the group to settle. He had to get away for ten minutes so he could call Ace.

"I'd like everyone to spend a few minutes writing down what you hope to achieve by being a member of this support group," he called out, picking up a notepad and ripping off pages to pass around. "Come up with at least three specific goals that you can share with the rest of the group."

All eyes looked at him in confusion. This wasn't the normal routine. Doc ignored their surprise and handed out pens with the *Behavioral Health of Willow Bay* logo before checking his watch.

"Okay, I'll give you ten minutes."

He backed out of the room, waiting until the door closed behind him to take out his phone and tap in Ace's number.

"Yeah?"

Ace's voice was impatient, but at least he'd answered. Doc had been afraid Ace would be too busy with the new girl to pick up.

"Someone came looking for Kara Stanislaus."

Doc glanced back over his shoulder, even though he was sure no one else was in the hall. He'd learned the hard way that you could never be sure who might be listening in.

"Who was it?"

"Some nosy bitch from the rehab center came around asking questions, saying the girl is missing."

The silence on the other end of the line scared Doc more than an angry outburst would have. What was Ace thinking? What would he do?

"I know exactly who she is. She's caused trouble before."

"It gets worse."

"Stop fucking around and tell me."

Doc took a deep breath and stared through the glass door, watching the women in the meeting room. A few were looking around as if they'd finished writing.

"She saw me leaving the hospital this morning. But before you get too upset, she didn't see who I was with."

"So, she knows you were there, and she knows the girl is missing."

"Right."

"Anything else I need to know?"

Doc thought about the gold chain in his pocket. He needed to get rid of it. He needed to give it to Ace.

But what would Ace say if he knew Doc had been careless enough to let Eden Winthrop see it?

"Well, I found something in the van that I need you to take care of. I'll give it to you and explain everything when we see each other."

"We can't meet here. Not until I make sure this isn't going to turn into a problem."

"Is it going to be a problem, Ace? Are we going to be okay?"

Doc cringed at the fear he heard in his own voice.

"Pull yourself together, Doc. As long as you let me know what's going on, I can take care of it, like I always do."

After Ace had ended the call, Doc sucked in a deep breath of air, then exhaled slowly. He had to finish the session as if all was well.

*Everything will be okay if I just keep calm and follow orders.*

Ace had never let him down, and he wouldn't start now.

All heads turned to him as Doc walked back into the room. Instantly he plastered on the obligatory smile and surveyed the group.

"Okay, everybody ready to share?"

But as the women started to talk, a feeling of impending doom took hold and Doc recalled the look of determination he'd seen in Eden Winthrop's inquisitive green eyes.

# CHAPTER NINE

Pete Barker shifted the weight of the box he was carrying and used his elbow to ring Nessa's doorbell. When he didn't hear sounds of life from inside, he sat the box at his feet and knocked on the door with a big fist. Within seconds he was rewarded with the sound of footsteps approaching. The door opened a few inches and a small boy looked out at Barker with suspicious eyes.

"Hey there, buddy, how you doing?"

The eyes blinked at Barker's cheerful greeting and the door closed. The chain rattled and then the door swung open all the way. Cole Ainsley stood in the doorway holding an Xbox controller in one small hand. He held out the other hand to Barker for a fist bump.

"Hey Mr. Barker, whatcha' doing here?"

"I'm here to see your mother. But I thought I'd bring over this stuff for you and your brother since I was already making the trip."

Barker turned to pick up the cardboard box that he'd finally found in his garage that morning after an extended search. It had been hidden by stacks of old *Newsweek* and *Time* magazines that he'd never gotten around to reading. The box had collected dust for years and held nothing of real value, yet Barker had to swallow a lump in his throat as he carried it into the foyer. It held the remnants of Taylor's childhood: games, toys, and sports gear that she'd left behind long ago.

"What's in there?" Cole asked with big eyes.

"Some toys and gear that my daughter doesn't need anymore. Thought you and Cooper might want some of it."

"Why doesn't your daughter need it anymore? Did she get new toys?" The boy's curly red hair and questioning gaze reminded Barker of Nessa.

*This little apple hasn't fallen far from the tree.*

"Well, she's grown up now and...gone. But I'm sure she'd be happy to see you guys enjoying this stuff."

"I'm in here, Barker!"

Nessa's voice called out from the kitchen and Barker moved down the hall, giving the cardboard box a sideways look as he passed. There was still time to carry it back out to the car if he wanted. But he shook his head and kept walking.

*Just let it go, Pete. No more holding on to the past, and no more moping around and feeling sorry for yourself.*

An acrid smell greeted Barker as he entered the kitchen.

"Something burning in here?"

Nessa looked around from the stove with an exasperated expression, picking up a towel and waving it around.

"Yeah, it's called lunch. I tried to make grilled cheese sandwiches and I guess I left the darn things in the pan too long."

Barker crossed the room and opened the window before pushing the fan button above the stove. He picked up a file folder on the counter and began fanning the smoke toward the window. The radio on the windowsill was tuned to a local country station and Barker recognized the song. It was a sad ballad that Caroline had liked. He switched off the radio.

"I was listening to that, Barker," Nessa complained, dropping the smoking pan into the sink and turning to face him. "There's a storm coming if you hadn't heard and I want to be prepared."

"Yeah, I know. I watch the news. But it sounds like it's still days away and it'll probably make landfall north of here."

"Thanks for the in-depth weather report. Maybe you've found your new career."

Barker rolled his eyes and sat down at the kitchen table. Piles of folders were arranged in stacks next to the remains of someone's half-eaten sandwich. He pushed the sandwich to the side and opened a folder.

"So, you find anything?"

"Well, I haven't had much time to look, but, yeah, I think I might have."

Nessa washed her hands and dried them on the dishtowel before sitting next to Barker at the table.

"I skimmed through the witness statements in both files and so far only one name stands out."

She opened a file to a page that had been bookmarked with a yellow sticky note and pointed to a name at the top.

"Penelope Yates was the social worker assigned to Natalie Lorenzo's case. Apparently, Natalie was in the process of trying to regain custody of her son and Penelope was helping her."

Barker nodded and scanned the report. He saw Marc Ingram's name at the bottom of the statement.

"Yeah, she was the one who found Natalie's body," Barker murmured, his stomach churning at the memory of the gruesome scene. "Ingram took her initial statement. She was pretty upset from what I remember. Couldn't tell us much."

"Yeah, I think you'll see that, according to Ingram, the witness was hysterical when he arrived and had to be transported to the hospital before she could give the statement."

"I don't blame her," Barker said. "I bet she still has nightmares about it. I know I do."

"Well, Penelope Yates was also questioned during the Helena Steele investigation. A detective named Tucker Vanzinger took her statement."

Barker's pulse quickened as he looked at the document Nessa had placed next to him.

"Vanzinger was Reinhardt's partner for a while," he said, trying to picture the young detective he hadn't seen in over a decade. "They worked the Helena Steele case together at first, but he left the force before it went to trial. He hadn't been a detective long when he was called out to the scene. I always suspected the case was too much for him to handle."

Barker flipped through the pages in the file until he came to a selection of crime scene photos. He tried not to react to the carnage depicted in the pictures. Blood spatter covered the wall behind the bed where Helena Steele lay, her head thrown back to expose a deep, bloody slash in her throat. The knife that had been used to kill her lay on the carpet next to the bed.

"Vanzinger stuck around long enough to talk to Penelope Yates."

Nessa handed Barker a bundle of papers held together with a thick rubber band.

"These are all the notes and related paperwork I could find related to the interviews Reinhardt and Vanzinger conducted as part of the Helena Steele investigation."

Barker saw Penelope Yates' name on the top sheet and read the synopsis statement before dropping his eyes to the signature of the investigating officer.

"Looks like Vanzinger asked Penelope Yates what she knew about Helena Steele and came up empty. He even states that Ms. Yates had been calm and cooperative during the interview but had no relevant information to add. He concluded that further follow-up wasn't recommended."

"Yeah, I can read, Barker. It's just that I find that statement a little strange when you compare it to the statement Ingram took from her after the Natalie Lorenzo homicide."

Barker stared at her with a blank expression and shrugged.

"Come on, Barker, don't you think it's unlikely Penelope Yates would act *calm and cooperative* while being questioned about a co-worker that's been violently killed only weeks after she found Natalie Lorenzo's dead body? Don't you think she might have mentioned that she'd found another woman's body only weeks before?"

Barker let Nessa's words sink in. She had made a good point, but he wished he had thought of it. He was the one who was supposed to be looking for some type of connection between the two cases and here was Nessa having to connect the dots for him. He must be losing his touch.

"Yeah, I see what you mean," Barker admitted, turning back to the Natalie Lorenzo statement. "If she was so upset after finding Natalie's body that she had to be hospitalized, I doubt she would forget to mention it a few weeks later. So why didn't she say anything?"

"And why didn't Vanzinger include this information in his report?" Nessa asked. "Is it possible he actually didn't know she had been a witness to the only other homicide in Willow Bay that year?"

Barker found himself staring at her again, not sure what he thought. He tried to remember Vanzinger. Had he been too inexperienced and green to ask the right questions? Or had he been ignorant enough to discount the connection?

"He was partnered up with Reinhardt," Nessa said, not trying to hide her disdain for the late detective that had tried to kill her only months before. "In my mind that automatically makes Vanzinger's actions suspect."

Barker knew that Nessa had every right to be biased about Kirk Reinhardt. The detective had been dirty, and he'd succeeded in fooling a lot of people for a long time. Had he already been dirty way back then?

"All I know for sure is that Tucker Vanzinger quit the force before the case went to trial. I haven't seen or heard from him since. But I think it's about time I look him up."

Nessa nodded and patted Barker on the back.

"Just be careful, Barker. You never know what you'll find if you go around stirring up old cases and pissing off ex-detectives."

Barker smiled at her words, but he was already trying to figure out how he could find Vanzinger. He had a vague recollection of Vanzinger and Jankowski riding patrol together before they'd been promoted to the detective squad.

*Maybe Jankowski has kept in touch with his old buddy.*

He glanced over at Nessa and decided not to mention the idea to her just yet. Jankowski was her partner now, and she may be offended if Barker decided to question him.

The kitchen door opened just as Barker started to stand up.

"Well, if it isn't Pete Barker! Long time, no see!"

Jerry Ainsley stood in the doorway carrying two bulging bags of groceries. Nessa hurried over and took one of the bags out of Jerry's arms and set it on the counter.

"Hi, Jerry, how've you been?"

"Pretty good, I guess. But I'd be doing a lot better if my wife worked less and took better care of herself. I worry about her."

Jerry looked at Nessa with raised eyebrows and shook his head playfully, but Barker could see the genuine concern that filled Jerry's eyes. Nessa had already been shot and had miraculously survived. It was only natural for Jerry to be scared.

An unfamiliar flash of envy jolted through Barker as he watched Nessa reach for Jerry's hand and squeeze it. He turned and walked toward the front door, wanting to get away from the domestic scene.

*I remember when Caroline worried about me. Back then it pissed me off. But what I wouldn't give now to hear her nagging.*

He stopped by the front door and looked down at the box of toys and games Taylor had left behind when she'd moved away. An ache started in his chest at the thought of driving away without them. Just knowing they were in the garage had made the possibility that she might come back someday seem real.

"What's that?" Nessa asked as she walked up behind him and followed his gaze.

"Just something I didn't want to leave in the car."

He picked up the box and turned back to Nessa.

"Take care of Jerry and the kids, Nessa. Believe me when I say that family is the most important thing in the world. Some of us just don't figure that out until it's too late."

Nessa stared at Barker in surprised silence.

"It's not too late for you, Barker," Nessa finally said, putting a warm hand on his arm. "I have hope for you yet."

But Barker wasn't feeling very hopeful as he drove back toward Leo Steel's office. He turned to assure himself that the box was safely in the backseat, relieved that he'd decided to keep it after all.

*I haven't given up on you, Taylor, and I never will.*

# CHAPTER TEN

**N**essa watched Barker's metallic blue Prius disappear around the corner before she stepped back inside. The pungent smell of burned food still hung in the air, reminding her that she needed to clean up the mess she'd made in the kitchen.

*And there's a heap of dirty laundry to do as well, Nessa. Don't forget about that.*

She made her way down the hall wondering why her weekends were often more stressful than a normal workday. The faint buzzing of her cell phone prompted a frantic search under stacks of papers and files until she found the phone wedged between her laptop bag and Cooper's baseball mitt on the kitchen table.

The number on the display was familiar, and for a split-second, Nessa was tempted to let the call roll to voicemail. Eden Winthrop wouldn't call her cell phone on a Saturday if the matter wasn't urgent, and Nessa wasn't sure she was ready to deal with another crisis right now. She was still recuperating from the last one.

"Hello, Eden, how are you?"

Nessa tried to keep her tone light. Maybe Eden was just trying to raise money for her charitable foundation. Maybe Nessa could simply agree to write a check to the Mercy Harbor Foundation and continue on with her chores.

"I'm sorry to bother you on the weekend, Nessa, but I don't want to wait until Monday to file a report, and I thought you might be able to help."

The strain in Eden's voice confirmed Nessa's worries; it wasn't going to be a quick call. Nessa listened to Eden's account of the last twenty-four hours with growing concern.

"So, this young woman at Hope House was found unconscious and taken to the hospital, and now she's disappeared without letting anyone know where she's gone?"

"Yes, that's right."

"And you think she might have hurt herself, or that something bad might have happened to her?"

"That's what I'm afraid of, but I'm not sure."

Nessa hesitated, knowing Eden wasn't going to like what she was about to say.

"From what you've told me Kara Stanislaus is an adult, and you have no evidence of foul play. That being the case, there's not a whole lot I can do at this point. Now, once she's been gone over twenty-four hours –"

"You can't be serious! Kara is missing and we're supposed to just wait until it's too late to help her...too late to do anything? What if she's hurt somewhere, or what if she's been abducted?"

Nessa frowned at the obvious distress in Eden's voice. Her emotional reaction likely stemmed from her niece's recent abduction. Even though Hope was safely back at home, the situation had been traumatic and would almost surely cause Eden to be overly vigilant with the women who turned to her foundation for help.

"What makes you think someone might have abducted Kara?"

Eden's next words were drowned out by the stomping of feet as Cole and Cooper led a trio of neighborhood kids into the kitchen and swung open the refrigerator. Nessa glared at the boys as she stepped out onto the back porch. She closed the door behind her, muffling the loud voices and laughter, but saw Jerry starting up the lawnmower.

"Eden, how about we meet over at the station in about an hour? You can file a statement and we can try to figure out if there's reason to think Kara Stanislaus may be in any kind of danger."

"Okay, I'll see you there. And Nessa? Thanks for taking my call."

After Nessa disconnected the call she leaned against the porch rail and watched Jerry push the lawnmower around their little backyard. When he looked over she smiled and waved, but her spirits sank at the thought of what his reaction would be when she told him she had to go into the station, and that the Saturday matinee would have to wait.

* * *

Jankowski was at his desk talking on the phone when Nessa walked in. He looked over his shoulder and raised his eyebrows, surprised to see her at the station on a Saturday. She hadn't worked a weekend since she'd returned to duty full time.

Nessa stuck her tongue out at Jankowski's broad back as she set down her laptop bag and water bottle. She could still see the look on Jerry's face when she'd left the house. Of course, Jerry always worried that she was working too hard or doing too much, but today he'd looked downright angry as she'd rushed out the door, leaving the sink full of dishes and loads of laundry behind. His parting words played through her mind.

*So, you're rushing off to save the day and leaving this mess behind for me to clean up? And let me guess, Jankowski will be there, too, right?*

Nessa could understand Jerry's irritation at her sudden departure, but his comments about Jankowski worried her.

*He can't possibly think something's going on between me and Jankowski, can he? He's gotta know there's not a chance in hell I'd do that.*

She looked up to see Jankowski grinning at her.

"Miss me too much to stay away?"

Nessa felt an irrational pang of guilt at his playful words.

"I'm here to take a statement from Eden Winthrop. She thinks a young woman may be missing."

Jankowski cocked his head, crossing thick arms over his chest.

"Eden's coming here? Who's missing?"

"A resident at that new rehab center," Nessa responded, already knowing where his questions would lead. "I think she said the girl's name was Kara."

"Is she a minor?"

"No, she's twenty-one."

"How long has she been gone?"

"Since this morning."

Jankowski snorted and rolled his eyes.

"An adult female with a history of drug use isn't seen for eight hours and we're supposed to open an investigation? Nessa, I know you feel like you owe something to Eden Winthrop, and I'm sure she's still traumatized by everything that happened...but encouraging her irrational fears won't help."

"This whole department owes something to Eden. She played a big part in bringing down Reinhardt and the traffickers from Miami. Not to mention saving *me*."

Nessa's phone buzzed on the desk and she looked down to see a text from Eden. She pocketed the phone and stood up, aiming a disapproving stare at Jankowski.

"The last time Eden reported a girl missing it turned out to be legit. I think we owe it to her to listen to what she has to say."

She hurried out of the room, not waiting for Jankowski to respond. When she reached the lobby, Eden was pacing back and forth, hands shoved into the front pockets of her slim, black trousers.

"Where's Duke?"

Nessa scanned the room for the golden retriever as Eden whirled around, offering her a wan smile.

"I left him at home with Barb and the kids when I went to check on Kara this morning. He doesn't like hospitals. I think it's the smell."

"I don't blame him," Nessa agreed, thinking of her own recent hospital stay. "He's a very smart dog."

Nessa led Eden to an interview room and motioned for her to sit.

"You want a cup of coffee or some water?"

"No thanks, Nessa. I don't want to waste any more time. I have a bad feeling, and the more I think about it the more convinced I am that something terrible has happened to Kara."

A deep voice behind them made both women jump.

"Hello, Eden. It's good to see you again."

Jankowski's face softened as he looked at Eden, and Nessa had to refrain from rolling her eyes. She'd almost forgotten her suspicions that Jankowski had a crush on the tall, curvy blonde.

"Hi, Detective Jankowski, I didn't know you'd be here." Eden's tone was apologetic. "Sorry to interrupt your day off."

"I was already on shift today and I'm glad to help. So, what makes you think something terrible has happened to...Carrie?"

"Her name is Kara Stanislaus and she's a resident at Hope House. When I talked to her yesterday at the hospital she was determined to complete the program and get her life together. Now she's just gone."

Jankowski sat at the table across from Eden and held up his hand.

"Hold on, let's take this step by step. Why exactly was Kara in the hospital?"

"When she didn't show up to her session we checked in her room. Found her unconscious with an empty bottle of methadone under her bed. Dr. Bellows thought she must have taken an overdose."

Eden looked at Jankowski and Nessa with worried eyes.

"But it's not that simple. Kara has been staying at Hope House because she's recovering from an addiction to opioids. Methadone is prescribed as part of her treatment, and the doctor assumed that she'd somehow ingested too much. He gave her an antidote, something called naloxone, and called the ambulance."

"What do you mean by she *somehow* ingested too much methadone?" Jankowski prompted. "Was it an accident or did she intentionally take too much?"

"According to Kara, it was neither. She insisted she hadn't taken the methadone, and she doesn't know how the empty bottle got in her room."

Jankowski raised his eyebrows, not bothering to hide his skepticism at the idea Kara hadn't knowingly ingested the pills.

"I wasn't sure I believed Kara either until Reggie got a call this afternoon from the hospital with the results of Kara's blood tests. The hospital said they found no trace of methadone in Kara's bloodwork."

Jankowski ran a hand through his thick hair and looked over at Nessa as if unsure what the next question should be.

"Do they know why she passed out?" Nessa asked, her concern growing.

"They said they would need to run more tests on Kara to find out if she has a medical condition or if perhaps she'd taken something other than methadone."

"Taken something else? Did the hospital say what it might be?"

"No, they just said that it's possible there were other drugs in her system, but more tests would be needed to be sure."

"So, it's likely she did overdose, but we aren't sure on what?"

Nessa couldn't tell if Jankowski was asking a question or making a statement, but she could see the remark had offended Eden by the flush of color that now painted her cheeks.

"The easy answer for everyone is that Kara is just a runaway drug addict that doesn't want to be found," Eden said, rising to her feet so that she towered over Jankowski. "But that doesn't feel right. None of this feels right."

"Please, sit down, Eden." Nessa put a hand on Eden's arm and squeezed. "We're listening, and we'll do what we can to find Kara if she is missing. But we need you to tell us everything you know."

Eden sank into the chair, her back stiff but her voice resigned.

"I'm not sure what happened, or why it happened, but I can tell you what I suspect."

When Jankowski opened his mouth to respond Nessa kicked him under the table, motioning for him to be quiet.

"Okay, that's good. Just tell us what you suspect," Nessa coaxed.

Eden swallowed hard and cleared her throat.

"I don't think Kara overdosed. I don't think she meant to harm herself. And I don't think she left the hospital on her own."

Nessa remained silent, nodding at Eden to continue.

"I think Dr. Bellows, the therapist who volunteers at Hope House, may have misdiagnosed the issue when he found Kara. And I think he may know where she is now."

Nessa blinked in surprise.

"You think this Dr. Bellows is involved with Kara's disappearance?"

"Well, Dr. Bellows was at the hospital around the same time Kara went missing, and I think I saw Kara's necklace in his van."

"Whoa, hold on you two," Jankowski said, sitting up straight in his chair. "We haven't even established that this girl is actually missing, and you already have a suspect in her disappearance?"

"Well, Kara Stanislaus did pass out for unknown reasons yesterday and had to be hospitalized," Nessa said, frustrated by Jankowski's outburst. "And today she can't be located at the hospital or at Hope House, which is her last known address. I think that would make most people wonder if something happened to her."

Nessa then turned to face Eden, offering a sympathetic smile.

"But you have to understand that we can't just assume Kara's missing. She's an adult, and unless we have evidence of foul play, we don't know that she even wants to be found. She may have her own reasons for leaving."

Nessa picked up a metal clipboard and handed it to Eden.

"Why don't you go ahead and fill out this missing person's report. Provide all the details you have, including contact information for Kara's family and friends. Add any insight you have into Dr. Bellows or anyone else who might know where Kara is or what happened to her. Once we have that Jankowski and I can review and make some initial inquiries."

Jankowski narrowed his eyes but kept his mouth shut as Eden began writing. After a few minutes, he stood and walked to the door.

"We'll give you some time to fill that out, Eden," he said. "Nessa, can we talk outside?"

Nessa stepped out of the room and closed the door behind her, bracing herself against whatever argument Jankowski was going to throw at her.

"The whole situation does seem suspect," he said before she could speak, "but the last thing this department needs is to be accused of police misconduct or incompetence."

"I know that, Jankowski. Calm down."

"Then you realize we can't start a manhunt for a woman that may not want to be found just because Eden Winthrop feels that something isn't right."

"No, but we can try to find Kara and ask her if she wants to be found. If she says that she doesn't want anyone to know where she is, we can just drop the whole thing."

Jankowski shook his head and threw up his hands.

"We start accusing some doctor of abducting his own patients and we're going to be looking at one hell of a lawsuit."

"No one is going to accuse anyone without evidence," Nessa said, her mind already calculating the plan of attack. "But we will need to speak to Kara's doctor. He may have information and, if he has nothing to hide, there's no reason he would refuse to cooperate."

"Right, and we're all going to win the lottery," Jankowski muttered. "You're delusional if you think some doctor is going to discuss a patient just because we ask nicely."

"Well, we can try."

"Not without the okay from upstairs. I've spent the last three months answering questions from the feds and getting my ass chewed out by Mayor Hadley, the entire town council, and anyone else who wanted to add their two cents about the kind of job we're doing. You think I'm sticking my neck out because Eden Winthrop has a bad feeling?"

"I thought you had a soft spot for her," Nessa teased, wanting to talk Jankowski back from the ledge.

"Maybe, but not soft enough to throw my career away," Jankowski snapped, his cheeks suddenly pink at the admission.

"Let's ask Chief Kramer then," Nessa suggested. "We'll let him decide if we should pursue the investigation and talk to the good doctor."

"Okay, let's ask the chief. After all, he gets paid big bucks to make these kinds of tough calls."

Nessa grinned up at Jankowski.

"So, you want to be the one to call him at home on a Saturday?"

"Dream on, Nessa. Your idea..."

Nessa grimaced as she took out her phone and dialed Kramer's cell number. The phone rang four times before she heard the chief answer. After a brief conversation, she hung up and shrugged at Jankowski who had been listening at her shoulder.

"You heard the big guy. We're to follow protocol and make sure Kara Stanislaus is missing at least twenty-four hours before we open an official investigation."

Jankowski nodded, not meeting Nessa's eyes.

"Right, and no interrogating anyone unless we have evidence some sort of foul play is involved."

Nessa thought about the chief's brusque assessment.

*That young woman has the right to leave town without us harassing her or her doctor. Let's play this one by the book.*

How was she going to tell Eden that they would have to wait until the following day to begin looking for Kara Stanislaus? And would Eden understand why they couldn't bring Dr. Bellows in for questioning? Nessa wasn't sure she completely understood the chief's reasoning either, but what could she do?

She stood outside the interview room, knowing she still had a decision to make. If she went against the chief's orders she'd put her job at risk, but if she agreed to *play by the book* as Kramer wanted, she might be risking a young woman's life.

# CHAPTER ELEVEN

Leo tried to focus on Barker's words, but his mind kept returning to Eden and the distress he'd heard in her voice when she'd called him from the police station. He was glad to be the one she'd turned to for help and advice, but her call had come just as Pete Barker and Frankie Dawson arrived with an update.

After twelve years of frustration and dead-ends, Leo felt sure that the connection between his mother's murder and that of Natalie Lorenzo was the key to finding out who had killed the women, and why. Now Barker had uncovered a common link between the cases. A known acquaintance of both women had been identified.

Leo pushed thoughts of Eden's call aside, reassuring himself he would call her as soon as Barker explained what he'd found, and once they had formulated a follow-up plan.

*Sorry, Eden, your missing girl will have to wait just a little longer.*

Barker snapped his fingers in front of Leo's faraway eyes.

"You in there, Leo?" Barker asked, his voice amused. "Or are you on planet Eden again?"

"Sorry, Barker, I'm all ears."

Barker dropped his notepad on Leo's desk and tapped on the name he'd written in capital letters across the top of the page.

"Penelope Yates. She worked with your mother at the community health center, and she was interviewed as part of the investigation."

"Okay, so how does she fit into the Natalie Lorenzo case?"

Frankie Dawson jumped up from the armchair he'd been sprawled in and slapped Barker on the back.

"Let me tell him, man. He's not gonna believe it."

Barker shrugged and sat back in his chair.

"Just tell me, Frankie."

Leo tried to rein in his impatience. He hadn't had a real lead in his mother's case for over a decade; now that he had one he needed to keep his cool.

"Penelope Yates was the chick that found Natalie's body," Frankie announced. "She was at the scene of the damn crime, man!"

Leo stared at Frankie as if he had spoken a different language. Was it possible that one of his mother's co-workers had found Natalie Lorenzo's body? Did the woman have information that could help identify the killer? Could she even be involved in the murders?

"Were you the one that interviewed her, Barker?"

Leo's eyes were hard.

"Was Penelope Yates considered a witness or a suspect?"

"Take it easy, Leo. She was never a suspect. She was Natalie's social worker. They'd been scheduled to meet at the community center but Natalie never showed. Ms. Yates went to the motel to check on her and found Natalie's strangled body. The poor woman had to be hospitalized she was so upset."

Leo nodded, letting out a tense breath as he tried to piece together possible scenarios. Penelope Yates had been assigned Natalie's case at the health center, and she had worked with Helena Steele at the same facility. Was Penelope somehow the link between the women and their killer?

"We have to find Penelope Yates as soon as possible. Do we know if she still lives in Willow Bay?"

Barker nodded.

"Yeah, Penelope Yates lives in a condo downtown. Like everybody else, her name, address, age, and most of her personal details are available online. No expectation of privacy anymore."

"Okay, so let's see if she'll talk to us." Leo reached for his phone.

"I was thinking a less direct approach may be best," Barker said, rubbing the stubble that was starting to sprout on his chin. "Get her talking casually and find out what she knows.

"So, you're thinking she might know something, or could even be involved?" Leo asked, his hand falling back to the desk.

"We can't be too careful," Frankie said, pacing around the room. "We gotta assume the worst and hope for the best."

"You're a real philosopher, Frankie," Barker snorted. "But in this case, I have to agree. We need to do a little surveillance, find out what she's like. Try to have a casual chat, see what she'll tell us."

"Great, I'll go talk to her now," Leo said, his mouth set in a firm line. "I'm pretty good at getting witnesses to talk."

"You could do that," Barker said slowly, "but then she may recognize you and clam up. And she may remember me from the investigation as well."

Leo and Barker watched Frankie stretch his long, skinny arms over his head and yawn. He frowned when he realized they were both staring at him.

"What? You guys want me to talk to the chick?"

"You're the only one she won't recognize," Leo agreed.

"Unless she hangs out at the racetrack," Barker added.

"Screw you, Barker." Frankie turned to Leo and nodded. "I'll do it, man. I'll be smoother than James fucking Bond. She won't know what hit her."

* * *

After Frankie had set out on his mission to track down Penelope Yates, Leo allowed himself to turn his thoughts back to Eden.

"Why the frown?" Barker asked. "I thought you'd be happy to finally get a hot lead."

"I am," Leo agreed, but he couldn't hide the strain in his voice. "It's just that Eden called earlier and said she thinks one of the girls at Hope House has gone missing. She's pretty upset."

Barker rubbed the stubble on his chin again as he considered Leo.

"You think maybe she's just a bit...well, paranoid? I mean after everything that happened, maybe she's a little too nervous."

Irritation mixed with guilt at Barker's words. Of course, it was tempting for him to blame Eden's anxiety and traumatic past for her suspicion that another girl had gone missing.

She'd been through so much, how could it not affect her judgment? Her sister had been murdered years ago, leaving her to raise her sister's children on her own, and then only a few months ago her niece had been kidnapped by a serial killer. Eden had a right to be scared; she knew first hand that the world was a very scary place.

"I doubted Eden before when she reported Stacy Moore missing, and I learned my lesson then."

Leo wasn't sure if he was trying to convince Barker or himself.

"She may have reason to be anxious, but she isn't making this stuff up. If Eden thinks a girl is missing, I believe her. And I want to help her if I can."

Leo stood and walked to the window. Clouds were starting to gather in the west. He wondered if they were the first signs of the storm that was heading for the coast.

"The police are telling Eden they can't open an official search for the girl until she's been missing at least twenty-four hours. By then the hurricane could be closing in, and I doubt a missing drug addict will take priority over a natural disaster."

"No, I don't imagine it would," Barker agreed. "If the mayor declares an emergency everyone's focus will be on evacuating low-lying areas and securing the town."

"I'm going over to Eden's and see if I can help."

Leo didn't mention that he was suddenly desperate to see Eden again. The possibility that he might actually find out who killed his mother had stirred up a tumult of feelings only Eden could understand. She knew what it felt like to lose a loved one to murder. She understood him as no one else could.

"If you want some help I'm available," Barker said, moving to stand next to Leo by the window.

"You and Eden saved Nessa's life, and she's one of the only friends I've got left, so I figure I owe you both."

Leo looked over at Barker, wondering about the older man's personal life for the first time. Did Barker have a family? Or was he all alone in the world? Leo knew how lonely an empty house could be. The thought made him even more anxious to get to Eden.

As he straightened the case files and paperwork on his desk, he picked up a photo of his mother and stared down at it.

She had been a good woman; she'd worked at the community health center in an attempt to make a difference in people's lives.

Her good intentions may have gotten her killed.

*Maybe it's true after all that no good deed goes unpunished.*

Leo thought of Eden's efforts to help those less fortunate. She had opened Mercy Harbor to help abused women after her sister had been killed by an abusive husband.

Then, when her niece was kidnapped by traffickers that preyed upon young drug addicts, Eden had opened up Hope House to offer treatment and refuge for young women at risk.

*Eden tries to help people that others have hurt. Just like my mother.*

The thought scared him. As he and Barker left the office, he wondered if Eden's good deeds would end in tragedy as well.

# CHAPTER TWELVE

Kara squinted up at the sunlight streaming in through the small window above her. Her mouth was cottony-dry, and for an instant she couldn't remember where she was, or how she'd gotten there. A persistent pain in her leg had pulled her from a deep and dreamless sleep.

Looking down she saw the source of the pain: a wide, metal cuff tightly encircled her ankle. A thick, steel chain connected the cuff to the concrete wall.

Memories clicked into place and Kara screamed in terror.

"Help me! Please, someone help!"

Her voice was weak and ragged, and the raspy screams tore at her dry throat before ending in a painful coughing fit.

She looked toward the door with frantic eyes, sure that the big man that had been with Dr. Bellows would appear at any minute.

*I have to find a way to escape. There has to be a way out.*

Forcing herself to take a deep breath, Kara surveyed the room, taking in the steel door, small barred window, and thick concrete walls. It had been designed to be the perfect prison.

The bed she sat on was bolted to the floor and held only a bare mattress. No sheets or pillows; no comfort had been provided.

She inched her feet toward the edge of the bed, wincing as tender skin throbbed under the close-fitting ankle cuff. The chain was long enough to allow her to put both feet on the floor; she tried to stand.

Her empty stomach heaved, and she retched over and over, but she had nothing to expel. Finally, her stomach stopped its dreadful spasms and she stood on wobbly legs, head spinning.

Fighting back tears, she stared at the chain, following it with her eyes to where it was anchored to the wall with a heavy metal plate and thick bolts.

She squeezed her eyes shut, not wanting to see how hopeless it would be to try to break the chain, or how unlikely it was she could somehow escape.

*I'll never get out. I'll be stuck in here forever.*

But then a cold realization settled in her stomach.

*Or at least until he, whoever he is, kills me.*

Kara shivered as she pictured the big man's rough face, and his cold, greedy eyes. He could come back any minute. What would he do with her when he did return? She looked up at the small window set into the slanting ceiling. It had thin, metal bars across it, but allowed natural light into the room. She could tell the sun would be setting soon. That meant she'd been in the room all day.

Whatever they'd given her had knocked her out for at least eight hours. Her eyes dropped down from the window and settled on a row of photographs that had been taped to the wall. She tried to focus her eyes, unsure of what she was seeing.

"Oh, no. Oh my god, no!"

She tried to scream again as she stared at the faces of the girls that had been in the room before her, but no sound would come. Fear had paralyzed her vocal cords, stolen her ability to scream.

There was no need to count the girls in the pictures. Whoever had taped the photos to the wall had already marked each with a big number. The last photo had been marked with the number seven.

The red-haired girl in the picture looked dazed. She sat on the bed that Kara now sat on, and she wore a white dress, very much like the dress Kara now wore.

In fact, each picture showed a different girl in a frilly white dress sitting on the same bed with the same look of fear in their eyes.

Kara shuffled forward, trying to get a better look at the photos, but the chain stopped her halfway across the room.

One of the girls had long dark hair and eyes that appeared almost black in the photo. Something about the girl reminded Kara of her sister. The thought of Anna made Kara's heart drop.

*What will Anna think when I never come home? Will she think I've abandoned her, or will she know something terrible must have happened to keep me away?*

Kara wasn't sure which would be worse. But either way poor Anna would be left on her own to care for baby Niko, and Kara would never see her sister or nephew again. Her hand instinctively rose to her throat, seeking the comfort the little cross provided, and it was only then that she remembered the gold chain was gone.

Fresh tears spilled from her eyes as she thought of her father's words as he'd fastened the delicate necklace around her neck with trembling fingers.

*If you wear this cross, then you won't be lonely, since part of me will always be with you.*

Kara had removed it only rarely since then, scared that she would lose the last, fragile link she had to the man that had been both mother and father to her and Anna since they were small girls in Prague. He'd brought them to the U.S., hoping for a new life, not knowing that a malignant force was already growing inside him.

For once Kara was glad that her father was gone. At least he wouldn't have to experience the pain of not knowing what had happened to her. He would be spared that much.

Lost in thoughts of her father, she didn't hear the steel door open until the big man was standing in the room, staring at her with a satisfied expression.

"So, you're already up and about," he said, shutting the door behind him. "I'm surprised. Doc gave you enough fentanyl to kill most people. He can get a little carried away sometimes."

Kara blinked at the casual words, trying to understand what he was saying. She hadn't overdosed on methadone after all. Dr. Bellows had somehow given her fentanyl. Had he set up everything to get her away from Hope House?

"Dr. Bellows drugged me? He planned...this?"

"That's what I just said, and you're lucky to be alive."

"But why? Why would he do that?"

"He did it for me. Because I asked him to do it."

He stepped closer, and she could see a faint scar on his cheek.

"And he did a good job finding you. I usually wait longer between girls, but he said you were special."

Kara recoiled at his words and sat back hard on the mattress, her eyes flicking to the pictures on the wall.

"So, you've noticed them already, then?"

Kara stared up at him in horrified silence. He seemed so matter-of-fact. Like having a collection of abducted girls on your wall is something anyone could have.

"You can call me Ace, by the way." He ran a hand through his thick thatch of hair. "And you should know that I didn't kill any of those girls."

He waited, as if expecting a reaction, then gestured to the wall.

"Those girls all left this room in the same condition they entered. And you can, too, if you play nice."

Kara felt herself wanting to believe the man's callous words. He was trying to give her hope that if she did what he wanted, he'd let her live.

But could he really have abducted and assaulted seven women and then just let them go without getting caught? Would he and Dr. Bellows have taken such a risk? She looked into his dark eyes, searching for any hint of compassion or warmth. She saw only the cold, hard eyes of a killer.

*He'll never let me leave here alive. Not willingly.*

But a small kernel of hope was growing inside her. Maybe if she pretended to believe him he would let down his guard. Maybe he would slip up and she could find a way to escape.

"So, you'll let me go? If I do what you want, you won't hurt me?"

"That's what I said."

Ace stepped closer, within touching distance.

"Of course, it also depends on other people keeping their noses out of my business. You see, some people are looking for you. If they get too close I might have to change my plans. And that wouldn't be good for you."

Kara felt her heart race at the idea that someone was looking for her. Trying to find her.

"Who is it? Is it my sister? Will you let me call her?"

Ace let out a raspy laugh.

"No, your sister isn't looking for you. And no, you don't get phone privileges. At least not yet, not before you earn them."

The look in Ace's eyes made Kara's stomach clench. She thought she might retch again but somehow managed to stay still. He reached out a rough hand just as the phone in his pocket buzzed. He kept his eyes on Kara's face as he took out the phone, then glanced down at the display.

"I've got to take this, but don't you worry, I'll be back soon."

Kara kept her eyes on the door after it closed behind him, sure he would walk back in at any moment. When he didn't appear, she let her eyes flick once again to the girls on the wall. They all looked as scared as she was now, and she somehow knew that the collection was the deranged man's memorial to the girls; they were all dead.

*And if Ace gets his way I'll be the next one on the wall. I'll be girl eight.*

# CHAPTER THIRTEEN

Eden couldn't stop thinking of Kara Stanislaus as she left the police station and steered her SUV toward home. After driving several minutes in silence, she turned on the radio, needing to drown out the anxiety that swirled through her mind. A weather report was in progress on WBRO, the reporter's voice shrill in the hush of the car's interior.

"...the hurricane is predicted to make landfall late Monday along Florida's gulf coast. We'll be tracking the storm's path throughout the next forty-eight hours and.."

Eden switched the channel to a cool jazz station that Hope and Devon refused to let her listen to when they were in the car. She felt her shoulder muscles relax as the smooth sound of a saxophone surrounded her. By the time she pulled onto the driveway and parked the car inside the garage, she'd managed to calm her nerves and push the disturbing events of the day to the back of her mind.

Duke was waiting for her as she entered the house, the energetic wagging of his tail giving away his excitement at her return.

"How was your day, sweet boy?"

She knelt next to Duke and pulled him in for a hug, grateful to feel his warm body next to her after the long, stressful day spent without him.

A delicious aroma led her into the kitchen, and she stopped in the doorway, watching Barbara Sweeney pick up a long-handled ladle to stir something simmering in a saucepan. The little window in the toaster oven revealed cheese melting onto generous slices of garlic bread.

"Barb, you're a life-saver," Eden said, dropping her purse on the counter and walking toward the stove to peek at the creamy alfredo sauce.

"It's not a problem, dear. I'm happy to have an excuse to dust off some of my old recipes." Barb moved to the sink and began to fill a large stainless-steel pot with water. "Now that you're home I'll put the pasta on."

Barbara Sweeney was a slightly older, slightly plumper version of her sister, Pat Monahan. She'd been helping out with the kids over the summer after Leo Steele had suggested the widowed woman might be just what Eden needed.

Leo knew Barb was dependable, kind, and trustworthy. She possessed all the qualities Eden had been looking for. The last woman Eden had trusted to take care of Hope and Devon had betrayed her, and Eden was still wary. But Barb had settled in quickly, and now Eden wasn't sure how they'd ever managed without her.

"What can I do to help?" Eden asked, her stomach growling as she remembered she hadn't eaten anything since breakfast.

"Dinner's almost ready," Barb said, checking on the bread, "and I'll call Devon and Hope down to set the table, but I imagine Duke and Lucky would enjoy getting out for a bit. They've been cooped up most of the afternoon."

Eden nodded and called to the dogs. Excited feet and tails filled the kitchen as Eden snapped on the dogs' leashes and opened the back door. Duke let Lucky scurry past him before looking over his shoulder at Eden, anxious for her to follow.

"Okay, I'm coming, Duke, let's go."

The early evening air was uncomfortably hot and muggy, and Eden's silky blouse clung damply to her shoulders by the time they'd walked around the block a few times and returned to the house. Eden was pleased to see Reggie's red Mini Cooper in the driveway.

Reggie was perched on a stool at the kitchen counter nibbling on a piece of garlic bread when Eden entered, followed by Duke and Lucky. The dogs were still frisky after their trip around the neighborhood, and they responded happily to Reggie's greeting.

"Hi there, Duke, how've you been, boy?"

Reggie scratched Duke's soft head and smiled down at Lucky, who was wagging his tiny tail in a frantic greeting.

"You must be Duke's friend, Lucky. I've heard all about you."

The little Yorkie stared up at Reggie with inquisitive eyes before scurrying around to stand by Barb's legs.

"Lucky can be a bit shy at first," Barb said, "but he and Duke are getting along nicely. They're good friends now."

Eden smiled at the words, wishing she could forget everything that had happened that day and let herself enjoy the houseful of family, friends, and delicious food. Everything seemed just about perfect for once. But the worry about Kara nagged at her, dampening her mood.

Footsteps sounded on the stairs and Devon bounded in, his big blue eyes searching for food. He grabbed a slice of cheesy garlic bread and stuffed half of it in his mouth before turning to Reggie and offering a gooey smile. Hope wandered in behind him, her eyes on her cell phone as she tapped in a message.

"Aunt Eden, is it okay for Luke to come over later?" Hope asked, not looking up.

"I guess so, as long as it's not too late."

Eden resisted an urge to snatch the phone from her niece's hand. Lately, Hope spent much of her time staring at the phone, waiting for messages from Luke Adams, and Eden worried that her young niece was getting too serious about the boy. They were both only fifteen, and Hope had already been through so much. She'd endured more tragedy and violence than most girls her age could even imagine.

But Hope now had a chance to live a normal life, and Eden knew that would inevitably involve boys and angst and all the other things that went along with being a teenage girl. So, for the time being, Eden tried to grit her teeth and allow Hope to navigate her first romance without too much interference.

Eden's thoughts turned to food as Barb carried heaping plates of pasta into the dining room. After some coaxing Reggie agreed to stay for dinner, and everyone gathered around the big table while Duke and Lucky lounged at Devon's feet, somehow sensing he would be the one most likely to sneak them a bite.

Eden attempted to keep up a cheerful stream of conversation throughout the meal, but she was growing more and more anxious to get Reggie alone. She wanted to talk about Kara, and she hoped that Reggie would have more information to share about Dr. Bellows.

Once the pasta had been consumed and the table had been cleared, Hope and Devon retreated upstairs, and Barb collected her purse and called to Lucky.

"Is everything all right, Eden?" Barb asked as she stood by the door, ready to leave for the night. "You seem...distracted. Is there any way I can help?"

"You've already helped more than you know," Eden assured the older woman, impulsively leaning over for a hug. "The alfredo was wonderful. You and Lucky go home and get some rest."

"Well, let me know if you need me to watch Hope and Devon tomorrow. I'd be happy to take them to church with me if you need time alone."

Eden watched Barb's big white Buick pull out of the driveway before closing the door and hurrying back into the kitchen where Reggie sat waiting, a glass of red wine on the counter in front of her.

"Where can she be, Reggie? What's happened to Kara?"

"I wish I knew, my dear. The poor girl hasn't returned to Hope House, and nobody there has heard from her."

"Was her sister's phone number in Kara's file?"

"Well, we found the emergency contact number Kara listed for Anna Stanislaus, but no one answered when I called. Just got one of those automated voicemails. I did leave a message with both my cell phone number and yours. I hope that's okay with you."

"Yes, of course, it is."

Eden checked her phone, making sure the ringer was on.

"She could already be back in Orlando by now," Reggie said, drumming her long, perfectly manicured fingernails on the table.

"I wish I could believe that, Reggie, but I just can't. Kara may have had an addiction, but she was in recovery, and she was determined to complete the program and return to Orlando to help her sister."

"Maybe she didn't want to wait. Maybe she wanted to go home and decided to just go."

Eden bit her lip., wanting to believe that Kara was safe, but the facts didn't add up.

"Kara was picked up on drug charges and the judge offered her the chance to go to Hope House instead of receiving a custodial sentence. Why would she risk dropping out of the program? She must know if she just leaves the judge could send her to jail."

Reggie's brow furrowed over her dark, worried eyes.

"I don't know, Eden. How can we ever know why some people make the decisions they make?"

"Okay, then tell me what you know about Dr. Bellows. He diagnosed a methadone overdose and that proved to be wrong as you know. And I saw him at the hospital this morning around the time Kara disappeared. But what I didn't tell you was that I think I saw Kara's necklace in his van."

"When?" Reggie stared at Eden with wide eyes. "Where?"

"This afternoon, outside Hope House. I saw a gold chain on the floor of his van. It looked like the chain Kara showed me yesterday. So, tell me. What do you know about Dr. Bellows?"

"I can't believe Dr. Bellows would do anything to hurt one of his patients." Reggie shook her head slowly back and forth. "He seems so dedicated. He's volunteered so much of his time for so many years. It just doesn't make sense."

"When did you meet him?"

"Well, I only met him about a month ago, when he came to Hope House offering to volunteer his counseling services. But I verified all his references, and he's been volunteering in the community for more than a decade. He also runs the Behavioral Health Group of Willow Bay, which is a private practice."

Eden considered Reggie's words, trying to match the arrogant and rude Dr. Bellows she'd met with the selfless, generous doctor Reggie was describing.

"And he's obviously a doting husband to his wife, who's in a wheelchair," Reggie added. "I find it hard to believe such a doting husband could be involved in Kara's disappearance. Unless..."

Reggie paused as if trying to put the pieces of a puzzle together.

"Unless what, Reggie?"

"Well, unless he assisted her in leaving the hospital at her request. Perhaps she wanted to go home without anyone at Hope House trying to stop her, and he agreed to help her."

"And why would he do that? Wouldn't that be a violation of ethics? Helping an addicted woman leave undetected from a court-mandated rehab program?"

Reggie shrugged her shoulders, and Eden saw that her friend didn't want to believe anything bad about Dr. Bellows. She wanted to retain the untarnished image she held of a dashing, selfless doctor.

"What do you know about his wife, Terri?"

"I have met her a few times. She's a lovely woman. Very sweet and intelligent. If I remember correctly, they met while they were volunteering at the community health center here in Willow Bay, back before it was shut down due to lack of funds."

Eden stood up and paced the length of the room, her nerves on edge, her head starting to ache.

"From what I can tell, Dr. Bellows is still head-over-heels for his wife," Reggie insisted. "They seem very happy together, in spite of her medical situation."

Doubts swirled in Eden's mind as she tried to make sense of what Reggie was telling her.

*Could a man that seems so caring and loving have done something terrible to Kara Stanislaus? Or am I imagining it? Has the past damaged me so badly that I've started imagining abductions and crimes?*

Eden wasn't sure what to believe, but she knew that she could never simply accept Kara's disappearance until she found out the truth, no matter where it might lead.

# CHAPTER FOURTEEN

Leo flipped on the headlights of his BMW as dusk cast deep purple shadows over the skyline. Clouds the color of fresh bruises hung over the city, hinting at the storm to come. He checked his watch again and pushed his foot down harder on the gas pedal.

"So, you and Eden are seeing each other now? You two an item?"

Leo kept his eyes on the road, wishing he knew how to answer Barker's question. When they came to a stop at a red light, he turned to Barker and nodded.

"If you ask me, yes. But I guess you'd have to ask Eden as well to find out if she agrees."

Barker looked out the window, his eyes scanning the sidewalks as if searching for something or someone. Leo had noticed him doing that a lot. Perhaps it was a habit he carried over from his years on the force; always on the lookout for suspicious activity.

"I just might do that," Barker murmured, his voice suddenly distracted as he caught sight of a tall woman standing on the corner.

The woman's back was turned to them, her long dark hair and slim-fitting jeans the only features Leo could see. Barker's attention stayed on the woman, and he looked away only after she turned around, revealing wide-set eyes over a turned-up nose.

They continued on in silence until the BMW turned into Eden's driveway and Leo parked behind a red Mini Cooper.

"Cool little ride."

Barker circled the tiny car before following Leo to the front step. The door opened before Leo could knock, and Eden stood silhouetted in the doorway, her hair a golden gleam in the brightly lit foyer.

Leo let his eyes linger on her face for a long beat, taking in the strained smile and the unmistakable worry in her green eyes. He recalled her often wearing the same expression in the days and weeks after she'd rescued Hope from Vinny Lorenzo. But he hadn't seen that look of anxiety in recent weeks, and he'd allowed himself to believe she was recovering.

Eden stepped forward and Leo instinctively pulled her into an embrace. He held her against him, feeling the stiff muscles in her back relax as he whispered in her ear.

"It's going to be fine. We'll figure out what's going on."

Eden nodded against his chest, then raised her head. He saw the shine of tears in her eyes as he lifted a hand to push a strand of silky hair back from her cheek.

"It just feels like it's starting all over again. A girl is missing, and no one seems to believe me."

"I believe you, Eden," Leo said, his voice firm. "And I've brought someone who can help."

Leo turned to Barker, who stood on the front step wearing an awkward smile. He waved at Eden and nodded a greeting.

"Hello, Ms. Winthrop. Good to see you again. It's been a long time."

Eden stared at Barker as if she'd seen a ghost, her skin turning pale as the blood drained from her face.

"What is he doing here?" she asked, her voice hoarse. "What does he want?"

Leo stared at Barker, his brow furrowed in confusion.

"Do you two know each other?"

"Well, yes...sort of," Barker stuttered. "I was one of the detectives assigned to investigate Mercy Lancaster's homicide. I met Ms. Winthrop as part of the investigation."

Eden lifted her hand to her mouth as if to stop herself from saying something she would regret. She took a deep breath and then lowered her hand.

"I'm sorry, Detective Barker. I didn't expect to see you and it just...well, shocked me. The last time we talked I believe I was giving a statement about what happened the night my sister was killed. I'm sure you can understand it was a very upsetting time."

"God, Eden, I'm sorry. I didn't realize..."

"Didn't realize what, Mr. Steele?"

Reggie Horn's voice sounded over Eden's shoulder, and Eden moved aside to reveal the diminutive woman. Reggie's mouth was set in a hard line, and she had both hands on her thin hips as she glared at Leo.

"It's not important, Reggie, let's all just get inside."

Eden motioned for the two men to follow her and Reggie back to the kitchen, but Leo saw that Reggie continued to watch him suspiciously. She'd already warned him off Eden once, and he had a sinking feeling she would do it again if given half a chance.

Duke blinked up at Leo when he entered the kitchen, and Leo walked over and ruffled the fur on the dog's head, but didn't speak, still worried about Eden's reaction to Barker.

"Can someone tell me what's going on?" Reggie asked.

"Detective Barker worked on Mercy's homicide," Eden said in a flat voice. "I was surprised to see him here. It's been a stressful day...but it's okay."

"So, what exactly are you playing at, Mr. Steele?" Reggie demanded. "Are you trying to stir up trouble, or does that just come naturally to you?"

Melinda Woodhall

"It's my fault," Barker offered, stepping into the room and facing Reggie. At six feet tall and two hundred pounds, he seemed huge beside Reggie's five-foot frame.

Reggie stared up at Barker, seemingly unperturbed by his heft, and raised her eyebrows as he explained.

"I should have told Leo about the investigation. I wasn't thinking that an unexpected reminder of such a painful past event would be upsetting for Ms. Winthrop."

"It isn't in the past for Eden, Detective," Reggie said, her tone softening at the look of remorse Barker wore. "She lives with her sister's death every day. She tucks her sister's children into bed every night because Mercy isn't here to do it."

Leo's heart clenched as Reggie's words hit home. The dead were never really in the past for those they left behind. He knew, because he lived with his mother and father's death every day, too, and they had led him to the quest that now dominated his life.

"Very wise words," Barker murmured, his eyes lingering on Reggie's solemn face. "I'm sure everyone here can understand."

Reggie nodded and stuck out a small hand.

"Since Mr. Steele didn't see fit to introduce us, I guess I'll have to do the honors. I'm Eden's friend, Reggie Horn. And I'm also the director of Mercy Harbor and Hope House."

"It's a pleasure to meet you, Ms. Horn. I'm Pete Barker, but most people just call me Barker."

"Well, I think I prefer Pete. And please, call me Reggie."

If Leo didn't know better he would think Reggie and Barker were flirting. Tucking the idea away, he turned to Eden.

"I'm sure you're anxious to talk about Kara. Tell us what you know. Barker is here to help."

\* \* \*

Leo listened to Eden's recap of the events leading up to Kara's disappearance. She'd gotten to the part about seeing a gold chain in Dr. Bellows' van when Barker interrupted.

"So, what do you know about this Dr. Bellows? You have any background information on the guy?"

Reggie stood and stretched her back, then paced over to stand by the window. The last vestiges of daylight lent a warm glow to her ebony skin, and Leo noted that Barker watched her with fascinated eyes as she spoke.

"I checked him out when he offered to volunteer at Hope House. We always run a background check, and I performed a reference check myself."

Reggie kept her voice calm and measured as if giving testimony in a court case.

"He's a well-regarded doctor in the community, a volunteer for many local charities, and a devoted husband to a woman that is paraplegic and uses a wheelchair. Everyone I spoke with gave him glowing references."

"And no reported incidents at anywhere he volunteered?"

"Not that I know of," Reggie said, then conceded, "but the old community health center was closed down years ago, so I wasn't able to talk to anyone there for a reference."

Leo's pulse began to beat faster at her words.

"You mean Dr. Bellows volunteered at the community health center downtown?" Leo's voice was hard. "When did he work there?"

Reggie shrugged and bit her lip as she tried to think.

"I believe he said he volunteered there several times. Both before his medical residency and then after he moved back to Willow Bay to open his practice. I think the last time was in 2006 or thereabout."

Leo met Barker's eyes, knowing the retired detective was thinking the same thing that he was.

*Dr. Bellows may have worked with my mother. He may have met Natalie Lorenzo, a drug-addicted woman like Kara. A woman that had gone missing before turning up dead.*

But could he share his suspicions with Eden and Reggie before knowing for sure there was a link? He didn't want Eden to worry about something that may prove to be unfounded. He needed to do some digging first.

Leo looked at Eden's anxious face, saw the nervous way she fidgeted with a napkin on the table, and knew he couldn't wait to talk to Dr. Bellows. If there was even a remote chance that the man was involved with the murder of Natalie Lorenzo or his mother, he couldn't sit by and let another young woman fall victim to the same fate.

"I think Barker and I should have a chat with the good doctor."

He stood and turned to Reggie.

"Do you know where we can find him? Do you have his home address?"

"He might still be at Hope House," Reggie said, her voice betraying her reluctance in sharing the information. "We agreed to start hosting NA meetings on Saturday nights for the community. Dr. Bellows should be there until eight."

Leo looked at his watch, his heart pumping at the thought that Penelope Yates was no longer the only lead on their radar. But they only had fifteen minutes to get to Hope House if they wanted to catch the doctor before he went home.

"I'm going to go now," Leo said, crossing to Eden and taking her hands in his. "But I'd like to come back after I talk to Dr. Bellows. I want us to spend some time together."

Eden nodded up at him, managing a smile as she walked with him to the door.

"That would be great. Leo. I'd rather not be alone tonight."

"Okay, then it's settled. Once I speak to Dr. Bellows I'll be back. Maybe I'll even pick up a bottle of wine. I think we both need to relax after the day we've had."

Leo waited until he and Barker were in the car, speeding toward Hope House before speaking again. As the lights of downtown Willow Bay approached, Leo spoke into the car's silent interior.

"I hope I'm wrong, Barker. But I have a bad feeling about the saintly Dr. Bellows."

# CHAPTER FIFTEEN

Doc stood at the back of the meeting room, listening to a young man share the story of his addiction and recovery with the other addicts in the room. The man, sporting long sideburns and a New York Yankees sweatshirt, had identified himself only as Tom, and he had been rambling on for almost five minutes.

As the wall clock behind Tom ticked toward eight o'clock, Doc lifted his hand to cover a wide yawn, trying to hide his boredom and disgust at the weak, whining people that attended the NA meetings.

"Thank you, Tom, for sharing your journey with the rest of the group," Doc called out as Tom finally took a seat. "It's now time to close out the meeting. Would anyone like to volunteer to lead tonight's closing prayer?"

A slim woman in stretch pants and a faded tank top raised her hand. She looked at Doc with puffy, wet eyes, and he saw that she was clutching a tissue in her hand, shredding it into little pieces that she let fall to the floor.

Doc nodded at the woman, barely able to hide his contempt. While most of the people at the NA meetings he hosted were numb, exhibiting little emotion, sometimes he'd get someone, usually a woman, that would be overcome with self-pity and subject everyone to a crying jag.

"What's your name?" Doc asked as the woman stood.

"I'm Laura, and I'm an addict."

Doc wanted to roll his eyes at the silly woman. Of course, she was an addict. Every loser in the room was an addict.

That's what made these meetings such perfect hunting grounds.

"Thank you for sharing, Laura," Doc said, offering up a warm smile. "Please lead us in the closing prayer."

Laura closed her eyes and clasped her hands in front of her chest. Her voice trembled as she recited the one prayer everyone in the room knew by heart.

"Dear God, please grant me the serenity to accept the things I cannot change, the courage to change the things I can, and the wisdom to know the difference. Amen."

Doc ushered everyone out of the meeting room before locking the doors behind him. He stopped in the administration office to collect his backpack, then headed out to the parking lot.

As he neared his van, Doc saw two men standing by the driver's door. His gut told him immediately that the heavier man was a cop. He knew the type too well, could tell by the way he carried himself. But the younger man was too well-dressed to be law enforcement. He looked at Doc with hungry eyes.

Whoever he was, he would be dangerous.

"Dr. Adrian Bellows?"

The man who looked like a cop squared his shoulders and positioned himself in front of the door to the van.

"Hello, gentlemen, how can I help you?"

Doc decided he'd play the helpful volunteer role with these two men. They didn't seem the types to be intimidated by the arrogant doctor routine he'd used with Kara Stanislaus and Eden Winthrop. Better to try to ingratiate himself, at least until he could find out who they were and what they wanted.

"We'd like to ask you a few questions."

"Sure, but since you obviously already know who I am, can I ask who you are?"

"I'm Leo Steele. I'm a lawyer and I represent Eden Winthrop, the founder of this facility."

Doc didn't allow himself to react to the words, but his pulse quickened at the man's last name. He tried to keep his expression neutral, wondering what they wanted, and what he was going to say.

*Just stay calm and play along. Find out why they're here.*

"Nice to meet you, Mr. Steele." Doc flashed a warm smile. "Eden Winthrop's an inspiring woman. I've been honored to volunteer here. The community needs more people like Ms. Winthrop and more facilities like Hope House."

Doc looked over at the older man and raised his eyebrows.

"And you are?"

"You can call me Barker, and let's just say I'm an interested citizen," the big man said, his voice flat. "Interested in finding out what you know about a young woman who's gone missing."

"Oh dear, someone is missing? How awful."

Leo Steele stepped closer, staring into Doc's eyes.

"Do you know where Kara Stanislaus is, doctor? From what I understand, you may be the last person to have seen her this morning at the hospital.

"No, actually, Mr. Steele, I didn't see Kara this morning. The last time I saw her was yesterday afternoon *when I saved her life.*"

"So, you weren't at the hospital earlier today?"

Doc felt panic rising in his chest, constricting his throat.

*They already know I was there. That bitch, Eden Winthrop, surely told them she'd seen me. The old cop is trying to trick me.*

"Yes, I was there, but I didn't see Kara."

Doc managed to keep his voice even.

"I was much too busy looking after my wife to notice anyone else. But now that I hear she's missing, I wish I'd thought to check in on her. Perhaps I could've prevented her from running off."

"So, you have no idea where Kara Stanislaus may be?" Leo Steele asked, still staring directly into Doc's eyes. "You didn't see her at all this morning, and she was never in your van?"

"In my van? Why would she be in my van?"

Doc clenched his teeth as he felt a wet trickle slide down his back. *Never let them see you sweat, Doc.*

Leo glanced over at Barker and gave a slight shake of his head, as if a silent question had been asked, and answered.

*What do they know? What are they holding back?"*

"Let me ask you something else."

Leo cocked his head, leaning in even closer.

"Do you remember a woman named Natalie Lorenzo? She attended an addiction treatment program at the community health center. You volunteered there as well, didn't you?"

"What? That...that old place closed down years ago," Doc stammered, stalling for time. "I couldn't possibly recollect every drug addict I've treated."

"I'm not asking you to remember every addict, Dr. Bellows, only Natalie Lorenzo. Do you remember treating her back in 2006?"

"No, I'm sorry, but I do not." Doc couldn't resist wiping his forehead with the back of his hand.

"Do you remember Helena Steele, a social worker who worked at the health center around the same time?"

Doc saw Leo's jaw tighten around the words, and he instinctively took a step back.

"No, I don't remember her, either. Is she related to you, Mr. Steele? I'm confused...what is this all about?"

Barker cleared his throat and put a big hand on Leo's arm as if holding him back.

"It's about two homicides, Dr. Bellows," Barker said. "It seems you are one of the only people we can identify that worked with both Natalie Lorenzo and Helena Steele."

Doc stared at Barker with narrowed eyes; his good doctor routine wasn't going to work.

If he kept talking he may end up making a mistake, and he couldn't afford to give the men any more information. They already seemed to know too much.

"I told you, I don't remember them. Now if you'll excuse me, I have to get home to my wife."

Doc stepped forward but Barker didn't budge.

"Was your wife with you at the hospital this morning, Dr. Bellows? Perhaps she saw Kara while she was there? Could we speak with her?"

"No, you may not." Doc's face contorted with rage. "My wife is a paraplegic who needs around-the-clock care. She doesn't need to be bothered by the likes of you."

"Okay, I can understand that. That must be difficult." Barker's face was impassive. "But I do have a few more questions."

"Get out of my way, Mr. Barker. I'm leaving."

Barker didn't move for a long second, then stepped aside. Doc pushed past him and opened the car door, but Barker put a hand out, grasping Doc's arm before he could get in.

"You know a woman named Penelope Yates, Dr. Bellows? She worked at the community health center, too, and we'd like to speak with her. Do you know where we can find her?"

"I haven't seen Penelope Yates in over ten years." Doc wrenched his arm out of Barker's grasp. "Now, leave me alone."

Doc climbed into the car and slammed the door shut. He looked over his shoulder as he pulled out of the lot and saw that the men were still standing in the same place, watching him drive away.

Their questions had stirred ugly memories, and as Doc steered the van toward home he couldn't stop thinking of that fateful night twelve years ago. The night that had turned a doctor, a man who had sworn to save lives, into a killer.

# GIRL EIGHT

*A muggy darkness surrounded the Old Canal Motel as Doc approached. Buzzing lights overhead lit up the corridor of Building D, lighting the way to Natalie's room. She'd told him she would be waiting in Room 407. She said she wanted to talk to him about her son. The boy she'd called Vinny. The boy she claimed was also his son.*

*Doc knocked on the door with a trembling fist, hating the fear that consumed him and made him weak. But more than that, he hated the woman on the other side of the door. The woman that was threatening to ruin his life and destroy his marriage.*

*His pulse quickened as the door opened to reveal a thin woman with limp brown hair and scared eyes. Doc knew she wasn't yet thirty years old, but time had taken its pitiless toll.*

*Long gone was the fresh-faced sixteen-year-old he'd last seen twelve years before. Natalie Lorenzo's face now told a tale of drug addiction and rough living, and the spark that had once warmed her light brown eyes had been replaced by a grim determination.*

*"Hi, Adrian. Come on in."*

*Natalie stepped back and motioned for him to enter, but Doc paused, turning back to search the dark night behind him, wanting to make sure he hadn't been seen. Satisfied that no one lurked in the night, he walked into the room, his eyes sweeping over the sparse furniture and unmade bed with disdain.*

*The musty-sweet smell in the room made him suspect that the sweat and bodily fluids of countless men had been left on the thin sheets and threadbare carpet. It was a motel meant for illicit trysts and quick transactions.*

*Doc looked Natalie up and down, wondering if she made a habit of bringing men into the disgusting room in an attempt to fleece them out of money as she was trying to fleece him.*

*"Everyone calls me Doc, now. But let's not waste time with pleasantries. I'm assuming you asked me here to demand money?"*

He noted the cheap red dress she wore and the second-hand purse sitting on the table, as Natalie frowned, wrapping her arms around her body, protecting herself from his disapproving gaze.

"Yeah, things have been rough for me and Vinny," Natalie said, sticking her chin up in a defiant gesture. "The state's taken him cause I can't afford to take care of him."

"What's that got to do with me?"

"You're his dad, that's what. You're the guy that took advantage of me when I was just a kid and then left me knocked up and alone. It's time you did the decent thing. Vinny needs a dad, and yes, we need money. It's the least you can do to make up for...everything."

"You can't prove anything. Why would anyone believe you, a loser who lives out of a cheap motel? Probably a whore, too."

"There are tests now, you know. Tests that can prove what you did. Prove you're Vinny's dad. I think the police might be interested to know you knocked up a minor."

Natalie narrowed her eyes and folded her arms across her chest.

"And your pretty little wife will need to know, too. I think Terri needs to know the kind of man she's married to."

Doc jerked his head back at his wife's name. How did she know?

"Yeah, I know about your wife. I asked my social worker at the clinic about you. She told me some very interesting things about you and Terri."

Doc clenched his fists as he stared into Natalie's defiant eyes. Just when he'd found Terri, a woman worthy of his love, the only one in the whole world that mattered to him, Natalie Lorenzo was threatening to ruin everything.

And from the look on Natalie's face, he knew he wasn't going to be able to convince her to leave him and Terri alone. Why even try?

"I'm sorry," Doc said, and for a minute, he meant it. He didn't want to have to do what he was about to do. But he had to save Terri from the devastation this woman could bring. He had no choice.

"I should hope so," Natalie said, her voice softening. "But as long as you make it right, then I'm willing to forgive you."

"How much will it take to make it right?" Doc asked, his hand moving to the big pocket in his jacket as if he were going to pull out a wad of cash, or maybe a checkbook. Instead, his fist closed around a coil of rope.

"It's not just the money." Natalie turned away, walking toward the table. "Vinny needs a male influence in his life. He needs a father to help him grow into a good man. I have a picture of him here in my wallet -"

Doc moved quickly, pulling out the rope and wrapping it around Natalie's throat before she could understand what was happening. She grabbed at the rope, her fingernails scratching and clawing wildly, gouging deep gashes in her own neck. Blood dripped onto the red dress, spattering the floor.

"I don't want to have to do this," Doc muttered between gritted teeth as he forced her onto the bed, still holding tight to the rope. "But you gave me no choice."

Once Natalie's body had gone limp, Doc sat back and surveyed her still form. Her face was so red it looked almost purple. Suddenly nauseated, he pulled up the bedspread, covering the grisly sight.

He breathed a sigh of relief. Natalie wouldn't be telling tales to anyone now. His secrets were still safe. Terri still loved him. As he left the motel room he furtively looked into the darkness beyond the corridor, fearful of being observed. But he was alone. All was quiet. Everything would be okay.

Doc shook himself, pulling his mind back into the present, knowing that unless he did something soon, everything would *not* be okay. It seemed as though Natalie still had the power to destroy his life from beyond the grave.

He tapped Ace's number into his cell phone with shaky fingers. He needed to tell him about Leo Steele and the man named Barker. And he needed to make sure the men didn't get the chance to talk to Penelope Yates.

# CHAPTER SIXTEEN

rankie Dawson sauntered into the dimly lit bar and surveyed the near-empty room. It was not yet nine o'clock, and the Saturday night crowd wouldn't descend on the bar scene in downtown Willow Bay until closer to midnight. A few of the high-top tables near the front window were occupied with couples and a group of men clustered around a dartboard on the far wall.

A solitary woman sat at the bar, staring down into an empty highball glass. Her jet-black hair was slicked back into a high ponytail, and huge silver hoops hung from her ears. A figure-hugging knit dress revealed an athletic body decorated with a spattering of tattoos.

The woman looked around as Frankie approached the bar, and he immediately recognized Penelope Yates from the public pictures on her Facebook page. She looked older in person than she had in the edited photos, with fine lines etched around her eyes and mouth. She studied him with wary eyes before turning back to her glass.

"You want a refill? I'm buying."

After another long look, her eyes taking in his lanky frame, disheveled hair, and patchy stubble, she shrugged.

"If you're buying..."

Frankie motioned to a short, plump man in a red vest and black pants watching the dart game. The bartender hurried over and produced a toothy smile.

"Hey man, she'll have another...whatever it is she's drinking, and I'll have a bottle of bud light."

"You got it. One whiskey sour and a bud light coming up."

Frankie reached into his front pocket and scooped out his last loose cigarette. He hesitated, then looked over at Penelope.

"You smoke?"

She shook her head, the silver hoops jangling from side to side, then glanced over at him, watching him light up.

"You know those things will kill you, right?"

"Yeah, so will a bus, but I still ride on them if I need to get somewhere."

"That doesn't make sense," she said, but he could see the corner of her mouth turn up in a half-smile.

Frankie relaxed. It didn't really matter if she was laughing at him or with him. If he'd gotten her to laugh, he could get her to talk.

"You live around here?"

Frankie already knew that Penelope Yates lived in a building just around the corner; her condo was on the second floor, Unit 201.

After getting her address off the internet, he'd decided his best bet was an old-fashioned stakeout, so he'd sat on a bench across the street, smoking his way through half a dozen cigarettes. He'd only had one cigarette left in his pocket when she'd walked past him on her way to the bar.

"Yeah, I do live around here. Why do you ask?"

"Looks like an interesting neighborhood."

She turned to face Frankie as the bartender delivered their drinks. Her eyes were an unusual shade of gray, and when she spoke, he caught a flash of straight white teeth, along with the scent of alcohol and something sweet on her breath. An unexpected ripple of attraction ran down his spine.

*No harm mixing a little business with pleasure, is there?*

Frankie took a sip from his bottle, wondering how to ease into questions about her past without arousing her suspicions. Subtlety wasn't his strong point.

"You can skip the small talk, whoever you are," Penelope said, draining a big gulp from her glass. "I saw you skulking around my building earlier. What are you, some kind of stalker?"

An embarrassed flushed spread over Frankie's face.

"Hell no, I'm not a stalker." He straightened his back and looked around to see if anyone had overheard her.

"Then why are you following me around?"

"I'm not...following you."

"Whatever." Penelope rolled her eyes and shook her head. "But whoever you are, and whatever you want, I'm not interested."

"Listen, you got this all mixed up."

Penelope snorted, turning back to her drink, and Frankie suspected the only way he could hope to get information from her, now that she'd busted his cover, was to tell the truth.

*Or I could just crawl back with my tail between my legs and admit I've royally screwed up. Barker would fucking love that.*

But Barker wasn't his real worry. If he messed this up Leo would be disappointed in him. The lawyer had saved his ass more than once, and Frankie couldn't let him down again. This was too important.

"All right, I was following you, but it's not what you think."

"Let me guess, you're a model scout, and I'd be perfect for an assignment you're working on?"

Anger overrode his embarrassment, making his voice hard.

"Yeah, real funny, but the reason I'm here is no joke. You remember a woman named Natalie Lorenzo? You remember what happened to her? Is a woman getting killed funny to you?"

The color drained from Penelope's face. She stared at him with wide, disbelieving eyes.

"Who the fuck are you?"

"Frankie Dawson. I'm working on an investigation for a lawyer by the name of Leo Steele. We want information about Natalie."

Frankie squared his shoulders and took another sip from his bottle. He watched his words sink in, saw Penelope's eyes water.

"I shouldn't even be talking about this."

"Why not? You have something to hide?"

Frankie regarded her trembling hands with curiosity.

*Why the hell is she so scared?*

"I still have nightmares, you know? I've been trying to forget Natalie for the last twelve years, but I can't escape the...the...guilt."

Penelope's hand shook as she drained the remains of her whiskey sour. She looked into the glass, staring at the melting ice with haunted eyes.

"Guilt?"

"Yeah, I'm the one that found her...only not in time. If I'd looked for her sooner...if I'd said something..."

Her words faded away, and she picked up her empty glass and looked toward the bartender. Frankie saw the glass quiver in her hand, and a wave of remorse flooded through him. He shook his head, knowing he was screwing the whole thing up.

*Penelope isn't a suspect, she's a witness. Stop being such a jerk.*

"Hey, it's not your fault some sicko killed her."

"Maybe not, but I knew she was desperate. She needed money for an apartment so she could win back custody of her son."

Penelope swallowed hard and waved to the bartender.

"I just didn't know she'd be desperate enough to start turning tricks again. I mean, she'd been clean for a while. I thought she was going to make it."

Frankie considered her words as the bartender approached.

"Same again?"

"Yeah, man, we'll be sitting over there."

Frankie pointed to an empty table by the window, then steered Penelope across the room before she could protest. He didn't speak again until they were sitting across from each other.

"So, what makes you think Natalie was turning tricks?"

Penelope's pale eyes were bright with tears as she regarded him, searching his face as if trying to decide if he could be trusted. Finally, her shoulders sagged, and she leaned back in her chair with a sigh.

"Well, that's what the cops thought. I just assumed they knew...somehow. Although I was surprised. The last time we spoke Natalie said she'd made up her mind to do the right thing. That she was going to get her kid back. She even said she'd found his father."

The bartender set another glass in front of Penelope, and Frankie waited for her to take a drink. He figured she needed the alcohol to help her deal with the memories. He'd seen the crime scene photos; the horror of what Penelope had discovered in the motel room that night was still fresh in his mind.

"Did Natalie tell you who the kid's father was?"

"No, she didn't want to. She said it was someone I knew, and that she wanted to talk to him first before telling anyone else. I don't think he even knew he had a son."

"So, you never figured out who it was?"

"No, she never had a chance to tell me."

"But she said it was someone you knew?"

Penelope banged her glass on the table in frustration.

"Well, yes, but like I said, I never found out who. Why does it matter anyway? The cops didn't seem that interested back then. Why are you so interested all of a sudden?"

Frankie watched as Penelope looked around for the bartender.

Another drink or two and she'll be too wasted to remember anything.

"Do you remember Helena Steele?"

She inhaled sharply, then turned toward him, her face stricken.

"Why are you doing this?"

"Helena Steele was killed a few weeks after Natalie. And the guy I work for, Leo Steele, he's her son. We think the guy that killed Natalie might have killed Helena, too. We want to find the fucker that killed them."

"Helena Steele was killed by her husband. He went to jail for it."

"And did that make sense to you?" Frankie asked, keeping his voice low, reasonable. "Cause it doesn't make sense to her son."

"I don't want to talk about this anymore."

"Can you think of anyone that might have hurt either Natalie or Helena? Anyone at the community center that was acting weird?"

Penelope shook her head before putting a hand in front of her mouth and squeezing her eyes shut.

"I think I'm going to be sick."

She lurched up from the table and hurried toward the ladies' room, her stiletto heels clattering against the concrete floor. Frankie settled up at the bar, stuffing the receipt for the drinks in his pocket. He'd need it to get Leo to reimburse him for the drinks.

After a few minutes of hanging around outside the ladies' room, Frankie decided he'd have to go in after her. He pushed the door open with one hand and called out in a cheerful voice.

"You need any help in there?"

A terrible retching sound convinced him to quickly close the door again. He leaned against the wall and waited. Finally, the door swung open and Penelope stepped out, her red eyes the only sign she'd been sick. She squared her shoulders and lifted her chin in a defiant gesture that made him smile.

*You go, girl. Nobody puts Baby in a corner.*

"I need to get home. I'm not feeling well."

"I'll walk you. Make sure you get home okay."

Penelope didn't respond, so Frankie followed her out, ready to catch her if she stumbled. He walked behind her down the sidewalk and around the corner. When they got to her building she paused at the front door before punching in her door code and letting him follow her inside.

"I'm on the second floor."

"Yeah, I know. I googled you."

Penelope snorted, shaking her head and trudging up the carpeted stairs with Frankie right behind her.

"You know, you shouldn't let strange men into your building. Especially at night."

"Well, you're right about one thing. You are strange."

It was Frankie's turn to laugh, and he wondered if Penelope Yates had a man in her life. She wasn't wearing a ring, but that didn't mean much.

"Anyone waiting for you up there?"

"No, I live alone, if that's what you're asking."

"A pretty girl like you?"

"Wow, you really do need new material," Penelope said, pulling a key from her purse and fumbling it into the lock. "But I'm an old maid. I don't even have a cat to keep me company, that's how pathetic I am."

"You don't look pathetic to me," Frankie said, staring into her tired, gray eyes. "Far from it from where I stand."

Penelope looked down at her hands, her cocky demeanor falling away as a cautious smile appeared.

"Thanks for walking me home. Sorry I got carried away with the whiskey sours. You may not believe me, but I don't usually drink. At least not anymore. Guess I can't hold my liquor like I used to."

"Yeah, well I'm sorry I upset you. I didn't mean to."

Penelope looked up into Frankie's face, and for one crazy minute, he thought she was going to lean over and kiss him. But then she just sighed and pushed the door open.

"I'll leave you my number. Hit me up if you think of something about Natalie or Helena or the community center. We wanna know anything that can help us track the fucker down."

Frankie felt around in his pockets. The only paper he had was the receipt he'd gotten from the bar. So much for getting reimbursed.

"You got a pen?"

Penelope dug in her purse and handed him a pen. He held the receipt against the door and wrote his name and cell number.

"You think about it and call me. Maybe I can buy you another drink. Only I think next time we should stick to orange juice."

Once the door closed behind Penelope, Frankie realized he still held the pen. He rapped on the door but didn't hear anything from inside. He rapped again, a little louder, and thought he heard a gasp, or maybe a gurgle.

*The poor thing must be upchucking again. Better leave her to it.*

As he turned to leave he saw that the door across the hall was slightly open. A suspicious eye studied him from behind a thick, silver door chain. Frankie waved and offered the woman a cheerful smile. She didn't respond, just kept staring as he backed toward the stairs and bounded down, two stairs at a time.

Once he was on the sidewalk in front of Penelope's building he looked up to see a mass of clouds roll over the moon. Anxiety settled in his stomach as he looked up at the darkening sky. The storm was on its way.

# CHAPTER SEVENTEEN

Ace kept his right arm locked around Penelope's throat, listening for further sounds from the hallway. A rap on the door prompted him to raise the boning knife in front of her face, the five-inch blade glinting in the trickle of moonlight from the window behind him.

Another rap sounded, and Ace tightened his arm, pulling her harder against his chest, making her gasp out an alcohol-scented puff of air.

"Shh....be quiet and I won't hurt you," Ace whispered into her ear, his heart hammering in his chest as he calculated the plan of attack if the man on the other side of the door tried to enter.

He waited until he heard the man's footsteps thudding down the stairs, before pulling Penelope back from the door. A reflection of her panicked eyes stared at him from a mirror on the wall, and his own cold eyes gazed back.

"Remember me?" he asked with a raspy laugh, enjoying the frightened look on her face. Her stunned expression reminded him of another night, and another inconvenient woman that had gotten in the way.

*That nosy bitch never knew what hit her either.*

The remembered thrill of the kill shivered along his body, and he laughed again as he recalled how easy it had been to get away with the murder. He was still smiling when a gleam of light near

Penelope's right hand stopped his heart. He could see in the mirror that she held a ccllphone by her side. The screen emitted a soft glow in the dim room.

*Has she called someone? Is the bitch recording me?*

Rage engulfed him, blurring the room around him and making his temples throb. He released his arm from around Penelope's neck and slammed the phone out of her hand. He watched it skitter across the room and disappear under an armchair before he raised a gloved hand to grip her ponytail and wrench her head back.

Ace kept his eyes on the mirror as he stabbed the point of the thin knife into the side of Penelope's neck and sliced a deep gash across her throat. A torrent of blood spurted into the air, spraying against the wall, spattering the glass, and soaking the protective coveralls he wore over his street clothes. He let the knife clatter to the ground.

Transfixed by the gory aftermath, Ace stood as if frozen until the moonlight from the window disappeared behind incoming clouds; the room fell into darkness. He lowered Penelope onto the floor, dropping her head into the sticky, red puddle that had settled around them, letting her arms fall heavily beside her.

Ace flipped a switch on the wall and the room was suddenly bathed in soft, warm light. He looked down at Penelope's limp body, his gaze lingering on the light gray eyes that stared up in silent horror, before moving downward.

He recoiled at the grisly slash of her throat and the blood-soaked dress, his stomach heaving. Although he enjoyed wielding the ultimate power of life or death, this type of violence, and its gory aftermath, revolted him.

He turned his focus to the discarded knife next to Penelope's outstretched arm and saw that her stiff, clenched fist was clutching a scrap of white paper. He extracted the paper; a name and phone number had been written on the back of a receipt.

*Frankie Dawson. Why does that name seem familiar?*

Ace had heard Penelope talking to a man outside her door as he'd waited for her, armed with the boning knife he'd found in her kitchen. And he'd almost panicked when he'd heard her agree to call the man if she remembered anything more about Natalie and Helena.

But now Penelope was no longer a threat. And if Ace played his cards right, Frankie Dawson, whoever he was, might actually make it much easier to get away with murder. But first, he needed to get away from the scene.

Ace tucked the receipt back into Penelope's hand, then stepped backward. There was no use trying to avoid the puddle of blood at his feet. The blood seemed to be everywhere; his Tyvek booties should mask any identifiable footprints in any case. He left a trail of red smears as he walked to the couch and knelt to feel under it.

The fingers of his glove settled over the hard, slick surface of the phone. The display showed an active connection to *Emergency Services* at the top of the still-glowing screen. Ace ended the call, powered off the phone, and hurried toward the sliding glass door that led to the balcony. He slid the door open and slipped out, looking over the railing at the empty pathway below. A siren sounded in the distance, moving in his direction.

If Penelope Yates' cell phone had been properly registered to her address, an emergency response vehicle could arrive at any minute. Willow Bay was a small town. It didn't take long to drive the ten blocks from the station to her downtown condo.

Ace unzipped the disposable coveralls, ripping them off before removing the protective booties. He stuffed the bloody items into a plastic bag and threw Penelope's cell phone on top of the gory pile before tying the bag shut.

He didn't waste time unfurling the rope ladder he'd used to access the balcony earlier. He just kicked the coiled rope over the edge, threw down the plastic bag, climbed over the rail, and lowered himself down, so that he was dangling over the dry patch of grass underneath Penelope's balcony.

Lights were on in the unit beneath hers, but the curtains were drawn, and no one looked out as he let himself drop the final few feet, landing in a crouched position, ready to fight or run as needed. He paused, looked around, then straightened his back; he was alone in the dark night.

But as he listened he could hear the sirens getting closer. He began to walk toward the alley that would lead him onto Bay Street. From there it would be a quick ten-minute walk to his truck, then a fifteen-minute drive home. With any luck, he'd be home by ten.

*And once I'm home, I'll be home-free. Mission accomplished.*

The nervous tension in his stomach started to fade, and he released another raspy laugh into the night sky as he entered the alley that led toward home. The thought of home made him think about the girl waiting for him there.

She would be pretty hungry by now. If he brought her some food, she'd likely be grateful. Maybe even cooperative. He quickened his pace and began to whistle.

# CHAPTER EIGHTEEN

Nessa had been warned by the responding officers that the crime scene was unusually gory and unusually fresh, but nothing could prepare her for the thick blood spatter on the wall or the sickly sweet, coppery smell that permeated the room.

A heavy metallic aftertaste settled on her tongue and clung to the back of her throat as she pulled up her face mask, positioning it over her mouth and nose while trying not to gag.

She inched into the room, feeling clumsy in the bulky disposable coveralls and Tyvek shoe covers, and waved to Jankowski, who was on the balcony looking down over the railing.

She forced herself to look at the woman sprawled on the floor. Pale, glassy eyes dominated the woman's chalk-white face, which was separated from the rest of her body by the gory laceration that had once been her neck. The woman's arms were splayed out helplessly beside her in a final surrender.

Nessa closed her eyes and stopped before moving further into the scene, unsure if the Thai take-out that she and Jerry had polished off just before the call came in would stay down after all.

"You okay, Nessa?"

Officer Andy Ford was standing guard in the hall, protecting the scene from unauthorized personnel. His worried eyes followed Nessa's progress while keeping well away from the blood and the body in the room.

"She's all right," Jankowski said, and Nessa felt a firm hand descend on her arm and guide her further into the room.

"You took your time getting here."

Jankowski's voice was low in her ear.

"You're lucky I'm here at all. Jerry nearly had a fit when I got called out again."

Nessa didn't mention Jerry's growing suspicion that something was going on between her and her new partner. Jankowski would probably think it was hilarious, but Nessa didn't think the hurt look on Jerry's face when she left was amusing.

And looking at the scene around her, she doubted she would have time to reassure Jerry of her faithfulness any time soon.

The sound of voices and footsteps on the stairs alerted Nessa that the crime scene team had arrived. As she turned toward the door she noticed a piece of paper clutched in the victim's hand.

Before she could lean over for a closer look, Iris Nguyen's slight frame appeared in the doorway. Seconds later the larger, bulkier frame of Wesley Knox appeared behind her.

"Hi Iris, thanks for getting here so fast," Nessa called out, glad to see the chief medical examiner's kind eyes behind the protective glasses she wore.

Nessa had worked with Iris on several homicides in the last year, and she appreciated the small woman's calm, competent approach. Glad for an excuse to back slowly out of the room, Nessa stepped into the hall and turned to Iris.

"Hi Nessa, no problem. I saw Alma Garcia and her team pulling in downstairs. They should be up shortly."

Nessa nodded and breathed a sigh of relief. The cavalry had arrived. They would take care of the blood and the body. But it would be up to her and Jankowski to catch the killer.

*Whoever did this must be a maniac. Or a monster.*

More shuffling on the stairs preceded the appearance of Alma Garcia, Willow Bay's senior crime scene technician. She tucked dark brown curls into her coverall hood as she approached.

"Okay, it looks like the gang's all here," Jankowski said, his voice loud in the narrow hallway. "I'll fill everyone in before you get started."

"Okay, but hurry up, Jankowski," Alma urged, her eyes flashing. "From what I hear this is a fresh scene. The quicker we get started the more likely we can come up with something to help you track down the perp."

Jankowski nodded, and Nessa was relieved he didn't waste time arguing. She agreed with Alma that the clues at the scene might help them track down the killer before he could get too far away.

"Officer Ford and Eddings responded to a 911 call and found the door unlocked," Jankowski said, talking fast. "They could see immediately that the victim had probably lost too much blood to be alive, but they called for backup and an ambulance just to be sure.

The paramedics concurred that the wounds were fresh and that the victim had died before they arrived."

So far the only people that have accessed the crime scene, besides me and Nessa, have been the two responding officers and two paramedics, all of which are still nearby waiting to give samples for elimination purposes.

We haven't had a chance to video the scene or take photographs, but I can tell you already that the perp entered and exited through the balcony, so the area under the balcony will also need to be treated as a crime scene.

I've already sent Officer Eddings down to cordon off the area."

Jankowski looked around at the somber faces as he finished.

"Thanks for the brief, Jankowski," Iris said, her voice quiet. "I'd like to walk the scene and perform my examination of the body in situ. Wesley will be assisting me, and Alma can start recording the scene once I'm done with my initial exam."

Alma nodded and began rummaging through an enormous bag, pulling out equipment and typing in notes on a tablet computer.

"Can I speak to you, Detective?"

Nessa turned to see Andy Ford standing behind her, his freckled face somber. She nodded and stepped back further into the hall, waving for Jankowski to join them.

"You guys will want to listen to the 911 call that came in," the young officer said. "No one spoke on the call, just empty air, but you could hear the sounds of a struggle, and someone coughing or laughing. It's pretty creepy."

"We need to be following up on whatever clues we can find inside and under the balcony."

Jankowski lifted up his face mask and wiped the sweat off his forehead with the back of his gloved hand.

"We need to know if the perp was on foot or in a vehicle, and we need to follow him if at all possible. Listening to a 911 recording without any words isn't likely to lead us to our killer."

Nessa frowned, a question forming in her mind.

"If no one spoke during the call, how did you know where to respond?"

"The phone was registered to a person living at this address," Andy said, his voice matter-of-fact. "A woman named Penelope Yates. I'm guessing she's the woman...in there."

Nessa blinked as she registered the likely name of the victim. It was the same name she'd given to Barker earlier in the day.

*Is the woman on the floor in there the same woman that found Natalie Lorenzo's body? The same woman Barker was planning to track down?*

Jankowski was looking at her with narrow eyes, and she quickly looked away, not ready to share what she knew with her partner. She needed time to think first. To figure out what was going on.

"Thanks for the heads-up, Andy, we'll definitely listen to the 911 call as soon as possible. It could be valuable later on I'm sure. But for now, we need your help taking statements from the neighbors, building residents, and anyone that may have been in the vicinity in the last few hours. Someone must have seen something."

"Actually, the woman across the hall came out when we first arrived," Andy offered. "She said she saw a man hanging around, but I didn't get a chance to ask too much then."

Jankowski crossed the hall and knocked on the door to Unit 202. Within seconds an elderly woman appeared at the door, her eyes ablaze with curiosity.

"Ma'am, I'm Detective Jankowski with the WBPD. We're investigating a serious crime, and I'm hoping you can answer a few questions."

"Certainly, detective. I'm Sarah Myers. I've lived here for the last seven years, ever since my Bernie passed away. He was a good man, God bless him, but then once he found out he-"

"Mrs. Myers, I'm sure you can understand time is of the essence. We need to know what you saw this evening. Officer Fordham said you saw a man in the hall? What time was that, and what did he look like?"

Sarah Myers frowned at the rebuke, apparently not liking Jankowski's brusque tone.

"It was about nine-thirty. I heard voices outside, and I looked out the peephole. Penelope was there with a man. I'd never seen him before."

Nessa's pulse quickened as Sarah Myers' words confirmed the victim was in fact Penelope Yates.

"Can you describe the man you saw?"

Jankowski ignored Sarah Myers' huff of indignation, staring at her with an intense, expectant expression.

"He looked very suspicious to me," Mrs. Myers said, her lips pursing in disapproval. "He was tall and thin with shaggy brown hair. Looked like he hadn't had a proper haircut in years."

"How tall would you say he was?"

"About your height, but much skinnier. Almost bony."

"And his age?"

"Well, it's hard to say. Nowadays even grown men dress like delinquents half the time. But I'd have to say he was in his thirties if he was a day."

"Did you see what he was wearing?"

"Something baggy. Maybe jeans and a shirt. Something dark."

As Jankowski jotted down notes, Iris stuck her head out into the hall, holding a white piece of paper sealed in an evidence bag.

"I think you guys need to see this right away."

Jankowski stared at the bag, cocking his head to read the handwritten name and phone number.

"Frankie Dawson. Now, why does that name sound familiar?"

Jankowski took out his cell phone and used a big finger to tap on the display. After a few minutes, he held up a picture. It was a mug shot of a man with shaggy brown hair.

"This look like the guy you saw?"

Mrs. Myers squinted at the screen, then nodded.

"Yes, that's him."

Nessa leaned over to peer at Jankowski's phone, then frowned.

"What is that?"

"It's a mugshot. Frankie Dawson has been arrested in Willow Bay before, and we need to track him down right away. He's just become our number one person of interest."

# CHAPTER NINETEEN

E den stood by the front window, gazing out into the dark street. She wondered for the millionth time where Kara could be, and if she was okay. The news alerts about the advancing hurricane were growing more ominous, and Eden feared for anyone who would be left on the streets if the storm did make landfall nearby.

Headlights appeared in the distance, drawing closer, before finally turning into the driveway. Eden's heart leapt when she saw Leo Steele step out of his BMW and walk along the front path.

She opened the front door and stepped outside just as he reached the steps; he held a bottle of wine in one hand and a shopping bag in the other.

"I thought you'd never get here."

Before he could respond, she pulled him toward her, raising her mouth to his in a lingering kiss. She sighed in contentment when she felt his lips move against hers.

"If I'd known I was going to get such a warm welcome, I'd have come sooner."

"I've missed you, Leo."

Her whispered words were drowned out by excited laughter as the front door swung open and Hope scurried out ahead of Luke Adams, who carried a bicycle helmet under one arm.

"Oh, sorry, Aunt Eden, I didn't know you were out here."

Hope's blue eyes lit up when she saw Leo standing behind Eden.

"Hello, Mr. Steele. I didn't know you were coming over tonight."

"Yes, I was lucky enough to get a rare invitation from your extremely busy Aunt."

Leo looked over at Luke, who was still standing in the doorway.

"Looks like you and your...*friend*, are making the most of the weekend."

Eden grinned at the protective tone in Leo's voice. He worried about Hope, and, like Eden, he wanted to be sure Luke Adams was good enough for her.

Eden still wasn't sure what she thought about Luke. The boy seemed nice enough, but she knew that appearances could be very deceiving, so she had decided to reserve judgment for the time being.

"Leo, this is my boyfriend, Luke Adams. And Luke, this is my aunt's...*friend*, Mr. Steele."

Leo offered a long hand to Luke, who returned the handshake with easy confidence. The boy's big, brown eyes shifted back to Hope, and she blushed under his scrutiny.

"Sorry, but I gotta go," Luke said. "My mother set an eleven o'clock curfew and I'll be lucky to make it home by then."

Hope followed Luke down to the end of the driveway, waving to him as he climbed on his bike and pedaled away into the dark. She wore a dreamy smile when she walked back up the drive.

"I guess I don't need to ask if you had a good time."

Eden rolled her eyes in feigned exasperation, but inwardly she was happy for her niece.

Hope deserved to be happy. After all she'd been through, an innocent crush on a cute boy her own age might be just what she needed.

Once Hope had gone upstairs to bed, Leo opened the bottle of wine and took a box of dark chocolate out of the shopping bag. He reached back in and pulled out a bag of dog treats.

"I guess Duke is already asleep for the night?"

Eden's eyes shined at him, and she drew him to her for another impulsive kiss.

"Yes, you've arrived a little late for Duke, but I'll be sure to give him these in the morning."

"Make sure you tell him they're from me!"

Eden couldn't stop smiling as they carried their wine glasses to the couch and sat down close to each other.

She liked the warmth of his thigh against hers, and she felt the tension in her shoulders relax as she took a long sip of the smooth merlot.

"I'd ask you how it went at Hope House with Dr. Bellows, but I expect you would have called me right away if you'd found out anything specific about Kara."

"Yes, I would have. Dr. Bellows wasn't forthcoming. And I agree with you that he seems fishy. He knows more than he's willing to say for sure. But he didn't let anything slip."

Eden pushed away a knot of worry in her stomach and willed herself to take another sip from her wine glass.

"I don't want to let Dr. Bellows or anyone else ruin our night."

Leo produced a wicked smile that brought a rush of heat to her face, and she swallowed hard as he leaned toward her and brushed a lock of hair from her cheek.

"Yes, you and I deserved a night off. We need some *alone* time."

"Aunt Eden?"

Eden jumped and slid away from Leo as she heard Devon's small voice behind her on the stairs.

"Yes, Devon, aren't you supposed to be in bed?"

"I couldn't sleep. I'm worried about the hurricane. Is it going to blow our house down? Like in my dream?"

"Don't worry, honey, whatever happens, we'll stay safe, okay? I'm keeping track of the storm, and if it gets too close we'll go somewhere safe. Now get some sleep."

"But I'm too scared to sleep. What if I have another dream?"

Leo put a hand on Eden's knee and squeezed.

"Why don't you go tuck him in, and I'll try to find an update of the storm on the news. I haven't seen the latest report either, so it's best to be safe and check."

Eden led Devon back up to bed, pulling his Power Rangers comforter up to his chin. At ten years old he still had the silky hair and soft, round cheeks of a little boy, and Eden snuggled next to him, wanting to take away all his fear and worry.

She waited until his breathing had become deep and even, before rising from the bed.

As she tiptoed across the dark room she heard Devon whisper, "Be careful, Aunt Eden, the storm is coming. I saw it in my dream."

A shiver worked its way down Eden's back as she descended the stairs. A hurricane was heading their way, but Devon's soft words had stirred an unease that had little to do with the weather.

Leo was sitting upright on the sofa, his wineglass still full on the coffee table in front of him. He'd found the local weather and was watching weather girl, Veronica Lee, in waders and a rain jacket standing in the Gulf as waves lapped at her legs.

"I don't know why they always send some poor reporter out to stand in the storm."

Eden sank onto the sofa beside Leo and picked up her wineglass. He put his arm around her shoulders and drew her closer just as a special news bulletin interrupted the weather forecast.

A reporter stood in front of a building that had been roped off with crime scene tape. She spoke into the camera with grave eyes.

"Breaking news in Willow Bay Tonight. Police were called to this building downtown where a woman's body has been discovered."

The camera panned to a nondescript building where police personnel were attempting to control a growing crowd of onlookers.

"No report yet on the cause of death, and the name of the victim has not yet been released, pending notification of next of kin. But the police have named Frankie Dawson as a person of interest in the investigation. An appeal has gone out from the WBPD to anyone who may know where Mr. Dawson might be."

A picture of Frankie Dawson flashed on the screen, along with the crime hotline number the police had set up to field calls.

"What the hell?"

Leo bolted up from the couch and stared at the television screen in disbelief. Eden rose more slowly beside him, immediately recognizing the man she'd met months before at Leo's office.

"It can't really be him, can it?"

Eden stared over at Leo with worried eyes. She knew how hard Leo had worked to get Frankie's conviction overturned, and now here he was in the crosshairs of the police again.

"Oh, yes it can."

Leo groaned, running a distracted hand through his hair.

"The WBPD is practically famous for jumping to wrong conclusions and persecuting the first person that falls on their radar. I have to go find him. Try to help him."

Eden nodded miserably, watching as Leo rushed to the door. He paused, looking back with a sad smile.

"I guess our alone time will have to wait a little longer. I'm sorry..."

Eden waited until the door had closed behind him and then hurried up the stairs to check on Hope and Devon, overcome by a sudden sense of foreboding. She peeked into Devon's room first.

He was sleeping fitfully, his hands curled into tight fists on the bed beside him, as if ready to fight off the monsters that lurked in his dreams. She closed his door with a sigh and moved down the hall.

Hope was nestled under a fluffy white duvet, her long blonde hair spread over the pillow like a sleeping princess in a fairy tale. Eden watched the gentle rise and fall of her chest, before turning to the window and staring out into the darkness beyond.

# CHAPTER TWENTY

The banging on the door matched the pounding in Leo's skull as he opened one eye and peered around. He tried to lift his head, but a cramp in his neck spasmed painfully, and he let his head drop back onto his desk.

More pounding, and the sound of Frankie's voice calling to him, convinced him to slowly lift his head and stagger down the hall. He rubbed his eyes with one heavy hand and wrenched the door open with the other.

"Where have you been?" Frankie shouted, "Haven't you seen the fucking news? They have a frickin' APB out on my ass."

Leo stifled a yawn, stretching his neck from side to side.

"Yeah, I heard, Frankie. I was driving around most of the night trying to find you. I left about twenty messages on your phone and drove by your house."

Leo walked back toward his office, rubbing his back, which had joined in the chorus of aches and pains caused by sleeping slumped over on his desk for the last few hours. He looked over his shoulder at Frankie, taking in his stunned expression.

"The police were there, too, by the way. Your mother wasn't too happy from what I could tell."

Frankie flopped onto the chair in front of Leo's desk and dropped his head in his hands.

"I crashed over at Little Ray's house. He works nights...lets me hang out there to get away from my mom when she's in one of her moods."

"Well, she was definitely in one of her moods when I saw her," Leo said, turning on the coffee brewer and opening a bag of dark roast. He needed caffeine, and lots of it, to jumpstart his brain after the night he'd had.

"Ray kicked my ass out when he got back from work. Said the cops were after me and my picture was all over the news. I came straight over here."

Frankie jumped up and started pacing back and forth, his hands balled into fists at his side.

"I didn't do anything, Leo, I swear, man. And I don't have a damn clue what the police want with me."

Leo watched the coffee begin to drip into the pot, gratefully inhaling the aroma as it filled the room. He picked up a little remote from his desk and aimed it at the flat-screen television mounted on the wall.

"They found a woman's body last night, Frankie. They haven't released her name yet. They still need to notify her next of kin. She lived in a condo downtown, near Bay Street."

A range of emotions played over Frankie's face as he absorbed the words, then turned to the screen. The woman's murder was the headline story on the Channel Ten Sunday morning news.

Leo could see that a local press conference was in progress outside the Willow Bay City Hall. Mayor Hadley was speaking from a makeshift podium, flanked by the chief of police and the city's media relations officer.

"...our police department has weathered a few storms this past year, but Chief Kramer and his team are doing a fine job. I've authorized them to dedicate whatever resources are needed to solve this terrible crime. I'd now like to bring up Gabriella Jankowski, Willow Bay's media relations officer, to share the latest updates."

Mayor Hadley shuffled back to allow a thin woman in a tailored pink suit to approach the microphone. The woman's hair had been skillfully highlighted and shaped into a modern, asymmetric style that would look right at home on the cover of Vogue. She offered the crowd of reporters and onlookers a perfunctory smile, then cleared her throat.

"Most of the reporters probably know me already, but for anyone new in the crowd, I'm Gabby Jankowski, and going forward you can direct any questions on the progress of the investigation to me."

Gabby glanced down at the podium, reading the prepared statement in a loud, clear voice.

"As of this morning, we have positively identified the victim as Penelope Yates. Ms. Yates was found in her home at approximately nine-thirty last night by an emergency response team."

Shock roared through Leo as he stared up at the screen, his brain trying to make sense of what Gabby Jankowski was saying.

"We are treating the death as a homicide and are searching for a man who was seen leaving her apartment around the time her body was discovered."

Frankie's face flashed on the screen, and Leo recognized the mugshot that had been taken when Frankie had been arrested for armed robbery. Leo had managed to prove Frankie had been innocent of the charges, but the easily accessible mugshot was a permanent record of the accusation.

"Anyone who knows the whereabouts of Frankie Dawson should call the crime hotline number shown on your screen."

Leo pushed on the remote again, and the screen went dark.

He turned to Frankie, who stood frozen in the middle of the room, his face ashen.

"She can't be dead. I just saw her last night. Sure, she was wasted, but..."

"You talked to Penelope Yates last night after you left here?"

"Yeah, I tracked her down to her condo. Waited outside until she left, then followed her to some dive around the corner."

Frankie ran a thin hand through his mop of brown hair.

"I bought her a few drinks and she got hammered, so I walked her back to her place. That was it, man. She went inside and I split."

Leo watched Frankie's face as he recounted the events from last night. His eyes were unguarded, and his words seemed unrehearsed. Leo prided himself on knowing when someone was lying to him. A decade spent as a defense attorney had honed his skill; he felt sure Frankie was telling the truth.

"Did you get a chance to ask Penelope about Natalie or my mother? Did she say anything that might indicate she knew who their killer could be?"'

Frankie stared at Leo in confusion, his forehead furrowing into deep lines over angry eyes.

"What the fuck does that matter now, man? The cops think I killed somebody. I'm a wanted man."

"It matters, Frankie. Did Penelope know anything about Natalie's killer? Could someone at the bar have overheard what you two were talking about?"

A terrible suspicion was growing in Leo's mind, and the coincidence was too strong to ignore. Was the same person who killed Natalie and his mother somehow responsible for Penelope's death, too? Had the killer decided to stop Penelope from talking for good?

\* \* \*

Leo kept a firm hand on Frankie's arm as they entered the police station. The fabric of Frankie's t-shirt was damp with perspiration, and his breathing was becoming more and more shallow as they approached the front counter. The desk sergeant looked up and caught sight of Leo, his eyes widening as he saw Frankie beside him.

"Detective Jankowski is expecting you, Mr. Steele. I'll let him know you're here."

A rush of footsteps sounded beyond the door, and then the door burst open and Jankowski emerged, his face tense and on alert. Nessa followed behind, her tired eyes curious as they landed on Frankie.

"You could have told us you would be bringing Mr. Dawson with you, Steele."

Leo registered the combative tone in Jankowski's voice and sighed. It was going to be a long morning and a very tough sell. Jankowski looked more than ready to play bad cop, so Leo turned to Nessa, who hopefully, as the designated good cop, was in the mood to listen.

"Nessa, my client has willingly come down here to answer any questions you may have. He wants to help you in your investigation if possible."

Jankowski stepped forward and glared into Leo's face.

"If your client is so eager to help, then why didn't he come in last night when we started looking for him? Why make us spend twelve hours hunting for him?"

Nessa stepped forward and put a hand up, her voice weary.

"Let's take this through to the back, guys."

She turned without waiting for a response, heading back down the hall. Jankowski watched Leo and Frankie trail after her, keeping his narrowed eyes on them, before following them into a cramped interrogation room.

"Have a seat over there please, gentlemen. And just to be clear, our conversation is being recorded." Nessa waved up at a camera mounted in the corner and smiled. "We want to be sure we do this by the book."

"Yeah, we want to make sure this sticks when we get to court," Jankowski added, pulling up a metal chair across from Frankie.

Leo ignored Jankowski and directed his words at Nessa.

"My client is prepared to provide a full statement of his activity and whereabouts last night. You already have his fingerprints and DNA in the database based on his last *wrongful* conviction."

Leo didn't want to resort to threats so early in the day, but he knew the possibility of another scandal in the press was something everyone in the department wanted to avoid. He'd gotten Frankie a decent settlement after he'd proven the police's negligence and shoddy work had resulted in Frankie spending time behind bars for a crime he hadn't committed.

Nessa didn't react to Leo's subtle threat. She spoke in a calm voice, looking into Frankie's eyes.

"Frankie Dawson, I'm Detective Nessa Ainsley and this is Detective Simon Jankowski. We're looking into a homicide that occurred last night. I'm sure you've heard on the news that Penelope Yates was murdered in her condo. Can you tell us where you were between nine and ten last night?"

Frankie drew in a deep breath. He glanced over at Leo, and Leo nodded, fighting his instincts to advise his client to remain silent.

Leo knew it was a gamble, but he and Frankie had decided to tell the police everything that had happened, even though it placed Frankie at the center of the crime. If they tried to leave out any of the facts that appeared to incriminate Frankie, it could raise doubt as to his whole story if found out later, and worse, it could prevent the police from finding the real killer, who was still out there, perhaps ready to kill again at any time.

"I went over to Penelope's place around nine or so," Frankie said, his voice hoarse, his hands fidgeting without the usual cigarette to keep them busy. "I sat on a bench outside her place waiting for her to pass by. When she did, I followed her to a bar around the corner."

"So, you admit you followed her?" Jankowski asked, and Leo thought he heard a hint of disappointment in the bulky detective's voice.

"Yeah, I'm working on an investigation for Leo. He wanted me to ask Penelope some questions about two cold cases. She was the one who had found one of the bodies."

"Which cases?" Jankowski snapped. "And why would you think Penelope Yates would have information?"

Leo watched as Nessa dropped her eyes and bit her lip. She'd told Barker about Penelope's link to both cold cases. Apparently, she hadn't shared that detail with Jankowski yet.

"I'm just the investigator, man," Frankie said, leaning back in his chair and putting his hands up in mock surrender. "You'd have to ask the big guy there about the details. All I know is Leo asked me to talk to Penelope, and I did."

"So, you talked to Penelope at the bar, and then what?" Nessa asked, not looking at Jankowski.

"She got really upset thinking about the murders. Said she felt guilty she couldn't save Natalie. So, I bought her a few drinks and she ended up getting sick."

"Yeah, we've already figured all this out," Jankowski growled. "Witnesses have placed you at the bar, and the bartender said you kept encouraging Penelope to order more drinks. So, once you left with Penelope, what happened?"

"I walked her home and left her at the door. Oh, and I gave her my number in case she wanted to talk more. I mean, about the cases. That was it. She closed the door, and I split."

"Where did you go after that?"

"I went to my buddy's house. He has a trailer off Old Shepard Highway. Lets me chill there while he's at work. I guess I crashed. Didn't wake up until my friend was shaking my ass this morning."

"We'll need your friend's name and address," Nessa said. She glanced at Frankie's rumpled shirt. "These the same clothes you were wearing last night?"

"Yeah, sorry, do I stink? I didn't have time to change."

"We'll need to take the clothes for testing. In fact, if you'll agree, we'd like to have our techs examine you and run some tests."

Jankowski was brooding next to Nessa, his head cocked as if he didn't believe a word Frankie had said.

"Yeah, and how about a lie detector test, Frankie?" Jankowski asked with raised eyebrows. "You up for that?"

Frankie looked over at Leo, who shrugged. Every fiber of his being was telling him to advise Frankie to refuse the lie detector test. He didn't trust the department, and he didn't trust their tests. But if he said no, they would continue to try to pin the murder on Frankie, instead of going after the real killer.

"Okay, Frankie, if you feel comfortable, go ahead with the test."

Frankie stood and nodded.

"Yeah. I'm good. I didn't do anything, and Penelope seemed like a really cool chick. I wanna find the fucker that did this. So, I'll take whatever tests you can throw at me."

Nessa stared over at Leo with a frown.

"And you are okay with this, as his legal counsel? You agree that he should take a lie detector test?"

"It's his decision, but if it will help eliminate Frankie so that you can concentrate on finding the person who did this, then I agree."

Jankowski left the room, coming back in minutes with a man who Leo recognized as Marc Ingram, the detective that had partnered with Barker on the Lorenzo investigation.

"Frankie, you can follow Detective Ingram. He'll get you set up for the lie detector test."

Jankowski turned to Ingram, who sported a short blonde crewcut over a thin, pinched face.

"Get him set up and I'll join you all shortly."

Frankie trailed Ingram out of the room, his tall, lanky body a stark contrast to Ingram's thin, wiry frame.

When the door had closed behind them, Jankowski spun back to Leo and Nessa.

"Okay, the video is off. Now can the two of you tell me what the hell is going on?"

Nessa leaned back in her chair and huffed.

"I told Barker yesterday that Penelope Yates was mentioned in the files for two old homicides. He shared that information with Leo. Leo shared that information with Frankie, and now here we are."

Jankowski glared at Leo, his fists waving by his side.

"So, you pressure Nessa into getting you this information? Why? What the hell did Penelope Yates have to do with anything?"

"She was a common link between two homicides that occurred two weeks apart in 2006. The only two homicides that year. She had contact with both victims through the old community health center. We wanted to ask her about those cases."

"And the cases are...?"

"The Natalie Lorenzo homicide and the Helena Steele homicide."

Jankowski frowned, and Leo could see him trying to put together the pieces. Leo stood and put both hands on the table between him and Jankowski, his voice loud in the small room.

"Penelope may have known the person who killed my mother. I think that same person killed Natalie Lorenzo. We asked her about the cases and now Penelope is dead. Seems like a pretty big coincidence to me."

"What are you saying, Leo?"

Nessa's eyes were wide in her pale face. Leo thought she looked like she hadn't slept all night.

"I'm saying that whoever killed Natalie and my mother may have also killed Penelope Yates."

"Well, for now, Frankie Dawson is our prime suspect," Jankowski said, moving toward the door. "And nothing you've told me changes my mind about that."

"You don't have enough evidence to charge him," Leo said, his quiet voice stopping Jankowski's hand on the doorknob. "When you test his clothes and give him a physical, you won't find anything. And I believe Frankie when he says he never even went inside Penelope's condo. So, there won't be any evidence placing him at the scene. All you've got is circumstantial, and he can explain all that away."

"So, you're going to try to get him off? Let a killer go free?"

Leo fought back an angry response at Jankowski's accusation.

"No, I'm going to try to find the real killer. Something you and this department could never do for Natalie Lorenzo or my mother. I'm not going to let you pin the murder on the first poor guy that you can find like you did to my father."

Nessa stood and put her hand on Leo's arm.

"Leo, we want to find the right perp, too. But we have to look at all possibilities. Frankie was at the scene. Or at least right outside. We need his cooperation to solve this, and it sounds like he has information that can help us."

"If you want to find the killer, you need to find out who would want to silence Penelope Yates. She was the only person who has admitted to knowing both Natalie and Helena. The only one we know who might have been able to lead us to the person who killed them."

"Maybe Frankie killed them all," Jankowski said, jerking the door open. "Maybe he killed both women and was in the perfect position to silence Penelope."

Leo watched the door close behind Jankowski, before turning to Nessa, his heart sinking at the look of doubt in her eyes. She was the only chance he had to get someone on the force to help him find his mother's killer.

"Nessa, please listen to me. Somehow the killer knew we were on to the connection with the community health center, and that we had identified Penelope Yates as someone who could possibly help us. He must have killed Penelope to stop her from giving us incriminating information."

Nessa shook her head and sighed.

"I don't know, Leo. I'm already going to be in hot water for giving Barker the information on Penelope Yates. If I go running around on a wild goose chase and it doesn't pan out, I just might be kicked off the force altogether."

"Well, if you don't find out who killed Natalie and my mother, Penelope's killer will still be out there, free to kill again."

# CHAPTER TWENTY-ONE

Kara stared up at the little window through bleary eyes, trying to determine if the light through the bars was getting stronger. She wasn't sure what time it was, but she figured she'd been in the room for at least twenty-four hours. That meant it was already Sunday morning, and Anna was probably wondering why she hadn't called yet.

The grumbling from her stomach reminded her that she hadn't eaten since the previous morning. The hospital had provided a tray with lumpy oatmeal, half a grapefruit, and a carton of milk. Kara now regretted that she'd taken only a few unenthusiastic bites before pushing the tray away.

She thought of the sandwich Ace had brought up to the room the night before. She'd been huddled on the bed, half asleep when he'd suddenly been standing at the door, holding a white paper sack from Bay Subs and Grub.

"You gettin' hungry?"

Her throat had been too dry to answer at first, so she'd just nodded, keeping her eyes trained on the big man, afraid of what he might do.

When Ace had stepped forward, she'd instinctively tensed her muscles, preparing to defend herself, looking for his soft spots; he'd paused and lifted his hand to his cheek, tracing his finger along the pink scratch mark still healing there. He'd narrowed his eyes at Kara.

"You try anything stupid and I'll leave you here to fend for yourself. Won't come back until you're just shriveled up bones."

Kara's blood had run cold at his words, but before she could respond, Ace's phone had buzzed. He'd read the text message with eager eyes, looking up with a smirk.

"Looks like the shit's really hitting the fan downtown."

"Are they looking for me? Does my sister know I'm gone?"

Ace had laughed at that, the raspy chuckle sending chills down her spine.

"I think after tonight they'll have more important things to do than search for some runaway drug addict."

More buzzing on his phone had prompted Ace to curse and glare over at Kara, frustrated desire clear in his eyes.

"Looks like I'm gonna have to go take care of some unfinished business. But don't you worry, I'll be back soon."

He'd stomped toward the bed and thrown a little baggie of pills onto the mattress beside her.

"That'll keep you for now."

Kara had watched him leave with relief, not realizing until after he'd gone that he hadn't left the sandwich. She'd been too scared to feel hungry then anyway, but now her stomach ached at the thought of food. With the sun rising higher in the window, she figured Ace had been gone for close to twelve hours.

*Maybe he's decided to leave me in here until I'm just bones like he said he would. Maybe I'll die in here without anyone ever knowing.*

She looked at the pills on the bed and picked up the little baggie, wondering what they were.

*Probably the same stuff Dr. Bellows gave me at the hospital. He's probably hoping I'll pass out, so I won't be able to fight back.*

The thought of swallowing the pills made Kara think of water, and she was suddenly overcome by thirst. She'd realized the previous evening that the chain on her shackle allowed her to step about ten feet away from the wall. Long enough to reach a tiny alcove that functioned as a crude bathroom, where a rusty water spigot on the wall emptied into a floor drain next to a toilet.

Kara made her way to the alcove, moving slowly to prevent the metal from rubbing against her already sore ankle, and turned on the spigot. A stream of water trickled out, and she leaned over, letting the cool, fresh water flow into her parched mouth.

With her thirst quenched, she shuffled into the middle of the room, as far as the shackle would permit, and stared at the photos on the far wall. Questions flooded her mind.

*What happened to you...and where are you now?*

She studied the girls in the pictures, wishing she knew their names, hating that Ace had given them only numbers, taking away their identities. Sadness seeped through her at the thought that now she too could only know them as numbers on a wall. She would never know the lives they'd lived or the people they'd loved.

Girl one stared out from her picture with scared eyes. Her straight, light brown hair had been parted in the middle and fell to her shoulders. Her cheeks and lips were full, and the white dress hung on smooth round shoulders. Kara tried to see what it was that had made Ace notice the girl.

"You look so normal," she whispered to the picture, breaking the stillness of the room. "What was it about you that made him choose you first? What started it all?"

Kara turned her attention to the second photo, taking in the girl's short blonde hair and kind, blue eyes. A light spray of freckles covered her pale cheeks. But she looked nothing like the girl in the third photo, whose short brown hair curled around a long, thin face.

Kara stared at the girl under the number four with growing dismay. The petite girl's blonde braid was disheveled, and she had a dazed look in her light green eyes. By the time Kara studied girl five, an unsettling truth had emerged.

*There is no rhyme or reason for what he's doing. He doesn't have a type. Any girl will do. It's all just random to him. It's just some sort of sick potluck.*

Girl five was unusually pretty, with silky black hair and startlingly blue eyes. She was tall and graceful, and her eyes held both fear and anger. Kara imagined girl five hadn't surrendered easily.

*She looks like a fighter...like me.*

Girl six had chestnut waves and big, brown eyes that stared blankly toward the camera as if she were in shock. The final picture showed a delicate girl with long red hair in a small, pale face. She had her thin arms wrapped around her body as she sat on the bed, offering comfort to herself.

Kara considered the long red hair in photo seven, then turned and walked back to the bed. She knelt next to the frame and gently reach out a finger. A thin red hair was entangled around one of the bolts. She'd noticed it earlier but hadn't connected it to the girl who had been in the room before her until now.

The presence of the now-gone girl seemed to fill the room as Kara rocked back and forth on the ground, trying not to cry, not to give in to despair.

*That's what he wants. He wants me to give up. And then he'll do to me what he's done to all of them.*

Anger simmered at her realization that Ace would turn her into girl eight and that the girl after her might someday look at her picture, wondering who she was and what had happened to her.

*I can't let that happened. I can't let him do this to anyone else.*

Kara pushed herself onto the mattress and looked down at her ankle in frustration. If only she could get the shackle off, maybe she could find a way to pry open the door or break the glass in the window. But with the shackle securely fastened, she was helpless to escape.

Gritting her teeth and closing her eyes, Kara pushed down on the cuff around her leg with both hands, and wrenched her leg up, trying to force it out of the shackle. Pain seared through her, making her cry out in agony. Fighting back the waves of dizziness that threatened, she twisted her foot back and forth, trying to wedge it through the circle of metal.

The thin skin around her ankle split and began to bleed, fresh blood making the cuff slippery in her hands as she continued to pull and struggle against the restraint. Tears streamed down her face as she looked at the raw, ruined flesh that now hung in strips and tatters around her ankle.

*I've got to break the bone. It's the only way I'm going to get free.*

But the stabbing pain radiating up her leg was getting worse, and waves of nausea rolled through her. She fought to stay upright on the bed. Her eyes fell on the little bag of pills. The pain would be too much for her to handle without some help.

Shaking two of the little pills out of the bag, Kara put them on her tongue, wincing at the bitter taste as she swallowed them dry. Her foot hurt too much to walk to the water spigot for a drink. She'd wait until the pills kicked in, and then she'd try again to get free. If she took enough pills, maybe the pain would be bearable.

But a little voice spoke in the back of her head.

*How will you open the door? How will you run with a broken foot?*

The words echoed in her head as she fell back on the bed, the room swirling into darkness around her.

# CHAPTER TWENTY-TWO

**N**essa braced herself as Iris Nguyen pulled down the crisp, white sheet, revealing Penelope Yates' face, her skin now a sickly gray. The dead woman's eyes were open in an accusatory stare that unnerved Nessa. She knew it was foolish to think Penelope would blame her, but deep-down Nessa suspected that the poor woman would still be alive if she hadn't told Barker about her connection to the Lorenzo and Steele cases.

"I think we're ready, Nessa. Wesley will assist me, and he'll be recording the autopsy notes."

The young forensic technician nodded a greeting to Nessa. His eyes smiled at her from behind his protective mask. He clicked on the handheld recorder and gave a thumbs up to Iris, who began to speak in a calm, deliberate voice.

"The body is that of a well-developed, well-nourished white female measuring sixty-eight inches and weighing one hundred thirty-two pounds. General appearance is consistent with the victim's age of forty years. Lividity is fixed in the distal portions of the limbs. The eyes are open. The irises are gray; corneas are cloudy with no evidence of petechial hemorrhages."

As Iris continued to describe Penelope's physical features, Nessa resisted the urge to look at Penelope's eyes again, wrestling with the irrational fear that the woman would be looking back at her. She forced herself to focus on Iris' voice as the pathologist folded the sheet back to reveal the lacerated throat and bare shoulders.

"...sharp force injury to the right side of neck, transecting right internal jugular vein. Injury begins on the right side of the neck, at the level of the mid-larynx, over the right sternocleidomastoid muscle, measuring three inches in length."

Nessa felt her stomach lurch as Iris described the grotesque injuries laid out so pitifully before her on the sterile white sheet. She struggled to keep down the potful of coffee she'd downed in her efforts to stay awake this morning after pulling an all-nighter.

"...hemorrhage along the wound...transection of the left internal jugular vein...dark red hemorrhage in the adjacent subcutaneous tissue..."

Nessa's feet started moving before her mind registered that she was going to be sick. She made it to the stainless-steel sink just in time to spew up what felt like a gallon of warm, brown liquid. Wesley stood behind her, holding a clean towel when she turned around.

"Don't worry about it, Nessa, it happens to the best of us."

"I hope you didn't get that little episode on tape," Nessa said, her cheeks flushed and sweaty.

Wesley just laughed and went back to stand beside Iris, who stood waiting over Penelope's body, nonplussed by Nessa's reaction. She continued to dictate notes, Wesley close behind her with the recorder, Nessa hovering a few feet away. Finally, Iris turned to Wesley and motioned for him to stop the recorder.

"We still have some wrap-up to take care of, but you don't need to stick around for that. I think I can call cause of death at this point."

Nessa nodded, trying not to show her relief that the ordeal was over. Iris stepped away from the table, pulling down her face mask.

"The manner of death is clearly homicide. Although it is possible for someone to commit suicide by cutting their own throat, I found no evidence at the crime scene to support that theory, and there are clear indications on the body that the injury was not self-inflicted."

Nessa's eyes widened, surprised by the notion someone could actually cut their own throat. She'd never even considered the possibility.

"I found no hesitation marks on the neck, and the injury was perpetrated by someone using their left hand. When I notified Penelope's mother about her death, I verified that Penelope was right-handed."

Nessa nodded, glad that Iris hadn't jumped to conclusions and was investigating all possibilities. She knew from experience that if they ever did get the killer into a courtroom, the defense would try anything, even accusing the victim of cutting her own throat, to get their client off.

"Cause of death was exsanguination, or in common terms, massive blood loss," Iris continued. "The perpetrator cut her throat, slicing the jugular, so she bled out quite quickly."

"Sounds as awful as it looks," Nessa said, her mind whirring at the words Iris had used to describe the cause of death. She'd seen those words recently, in the old case files she'd gone through for Barker.

"Iris, are you able to access the autopsy files from 2006?"

"Yes, of course. Why do you ask? Is this homicide linked to an earlier case?"

Nessa hesitated, not wanting to drag Iris into the mess she'd created, but knowing she had no choice. She had to find out if whoever had killed Penelope Yates might have been responsible for the murder of Natalie Lorenzo or Helena Steele.

"I'm not sure, but we've received a tip that two murders in 2006 might be related to the death of Penelope Yates. One of the 2006 victims was Helena Steele. Her throat was also cut."

Iris looked over her shoulder at the table, then back at Nessa.

"Let me finish up here, and then I'll pull up the files for you. You can wait in my office if you like."

* * *

Nessa listened to Jerry's recorded greeting again before hanging up without leaving a message. He must still be sulking. She'd gotten home from the crime scene at three o'clock in the morning and left again before breakfast to attend the autopsy. Safe to say Jerry wasn't a happy camper.

Struggling to keep her eyes open, Nessa looked around the small, cozy office. Iris had furnished the space with a simple oak desk and matching credenza. The polished desktop was clear of the papers, files, and clutter that routinely collected on Nessa's desk, holding only a laptop computer and docking station.

Two picture frames stood on the credenza and Nessa leaned over to study them, suddenly curious about the medical examiner's personal life. Iris had lived in Willow Bay for the last two years, but Nessa still hadn't met her family or had an opportunity to socialize with the quiet woman who always seemed so serious and composed.

*Why would a talented woman like Iris move to a small town like Willow Bay? Was she running away from big-city crime like me, or was it something else that brought her here?*

A man in a loose white shirt, jeans, and sandals gazed out from one of the photos. He was standing on the beach, a shy smile playing around his lips, his hands shoved awkwardly into his pockets. Nessa recognized Iris' warm brown eyes and dark, glossy hair.

*Her father? Maybe an older brother? Whoever he is, he's earned a place of honor in her office; he must mean a lot to her.*

The other framed photo showed Iris in a graduation cap and gown. She beamed at the camera, one hand holding up a roll of paper with a red ribbon, the other hand draped over the shoulder of a woman even shorter than Iris, who Nessa estimated to be no more than five feet, two inches tall.

Nessa jumped when Iris suddenly opened the door, feeling a little guilty, as if she'd been searching through the desk drawers instead of looking at a few framed photos on display.

"Nice pictures. Those your parents?"

Iris nodded, her eyes resting on the man with the shy smile.

"Yes, my father loves the beach," Iris said, sitting in the desk chair and switching on the laptop. "That's one of the reasons he and my mother moved to Tampa after he finished medical school."

"He's a doctor?"

"He was. He's...retired now." Iris looked at Nessa, her expression grim. "He has Alzheimer's. It's hard for him, and for my mother."

"I'm sorry to hear that, Iris. I bet it's hard on you, too."

Iris shrugged, but Nessa saw her swallow hard as she answered.

"Yes, it's hard to see him losing...himself. I moved to Willow Bay so I could be close to them. This was the closest city to Tampa that had a position available. I was very lucky to find it."

A flicker of shame flashed through Nessa.

*Well, now you have your answer as to why she's here, Nessa.*

Iris cleared her throat, turned to the computer, and rested her hands on the keyboard.

"Let me pull up those files. You said 2006?"

"Yes, in May. Natalie Lorenzo and Helena Steele."

Iris raised her eyebrows as Nessa said the names but kept typing.

"Okay, I see Natalie Lorenzo's autopsy file."

Nessa kept her eyes on Iris' face as the medical examiner read through the details of the report. Iris grimaced and shook her head.

"What is it?" Nessa asked. "Is something wrong with the file?"

"No, it's fine. I just get frustrated when I look through some of these older files. The previous medical examiner wasn't very...thorough. His notes are sometimes hard to decipher."

Iris turned the monitor to show Nessa the scanned copy of the official death certificate. Sloppy, handwritten notes filled several boxes, above the signature of Archibald Faraday, Chief Medical Examiner. Nessa wrinkled her nose.

"Oh yes, I remember him," Nessa said, recalling the old man that had been so difficult to work with, wishing she knew Iris well enough to tell her how she really felt.

*I sure am glad that old bastard finally retired.*

"I hate to talk ill of people," Iris said, a blush rising in her cheeks. "But...suffice to say it doesn't seem as if he was concerned with doing a high-quality job. I'm not sure he was properly trained."

"Talk as much as you want, Iris. The old guy was a real piece of work. Rude to everyone but the chief and the mayor."

"Yes, that's what I've heard from my team," Iris agreed. "They weren't exactly sad to see him go."

Archie Faraday's dour face flashed through Nessa's mind. He'd been the chief medical examiner when she'd first moved to Willow Bay. His family had helped establish Willow Bay at the turn of the twentieth century, and he never let anyone forget it.

"If you look up *Good Old Boy* in the dictionary, you just might see Archie's picture," Nessa said, shaking her head in disgust. "Along with the mayor, the chief, and practically everyone on the city council."

"I certainly got the feeling that he wasn't too happy to be turning over the reins to a woman, and a Vietnamese woman at that," Iris replied, and Nessa thought she saw a shadow of anger in her eyes.

"Well, we're all glad you're here now. We need someone like you to help us solve the tough cases."

Iris dropped her eyes back to the computer screen and sighed.

"Okay, here it is...Natalie Lorenzo's manner and cause of death listed as homicide by ligature strangulation. The notes in the report indicate signs of sexual assault."

Iris frowned at the screen, then looked up at Nessa.

"This doesn't seem to fit with the Penelope Yates case."

Nessa felt doubt creep in as she watched Iris' fingers tap out more words on the keyboard.

"Okay, I've got Helena Steele's file open."

Iris studied the file, her eyes widening as she read.

"Archie Faraday again, so not much to go on, but he does list the manner of death as homicide, and the cause of death exsanguination due to a cut throat."

"Does it say if the injury was inflicted by a left-handed perp?"

Nessa held her breath, knowing the answer wouldn't prove anything but would shed light on the theory that all three murders were linked.

"No, it doesn't include the details needed to determine that," Iris said, her mouth set in an angry line. "This is pretty basic stuff. It's outrageous that Faraday was allowed to submit this type of inadequate report."

Nessa let out the breath she'd been holding.

"So, there's no way we can tell if the killer was left-handed?"

"Let me try one more thing."

Iris browsed through a library of folders, finally double-clicking on one. A collection of thumbnail images appeared, and she scrolled through the autopsy photos, stopping on a close-up picture of Helena Steele's throat. Nessa instinctively turned away from the grisly wound as Iris bent closer to the screen to view it.

"If I had to give an opinion based on this photo alone, I'd say the wound was very likely inflicted by a left-handed perpetrator. See the sharp-force entry to the right side of the neck?"

Nessa looked at the photo, nodded weakly, then looked away.

"That's where the perpetrator stuck in the knife before drawing the knife back to the left, slicing the throat. It's indicative of an attacker coming up behind a victim and using their left hand to cut the victim's throat."

Nessa's head began to ache as she absorbed the information. Questions flooded in.

*Was Helena Steele's husband left-handed? Did anyone even think to check that the man they'd convicted could have committed the crime?*

She knew she should be excited to have uncovered a lead that might help her find Penelope Yates' killer, but for the moment she felt only fear. The information she had might end up revealing the police department had convicted an innocent man, and that they had allowed the real killer to go free, and to kill again.

# CHAPTER TWENTY-THREE

Terri Bellows looked out of her office window trying to catch sight of the sky. She'd been keeping a watch on the weather forecast and was getting worried about the tropical storm that was showing every sign of strengthening into a full-fledged hurricane in the next twenty-four hours. The storm was barreling toward the Gulf of Mexico with a predicted landfall on Florida's west coast, although no one knew for sure how close the storm would come to Willow Bay.

A metallic blue Prius slowed down in front of the house, then pulled alongside the curb. Terri watched a big man in baggy pants and a sports coat step out of the car. He took a minute to survey the house from behind dark sunglasses before walking up the driveway. A loud rap on the door caused Terri to start rolling. She maneuvered her wheelchair through the office door and down the hall.

"Who's there?"

Doc had warned her not to open the door to strangers, especially after the spate of murders in the last year, but the man didn't look like a criminal. Of course, he could be a door-to-door salesman trying to talk her into buying something she didn't want or need, but something about the way he'd studied the house as if scoping out the place, made her think he must be someone official.

"Hello, Mrs. Bellows? I'm Peter Barker." The man's voice was firm but polite. "I'm hoping to speak to your husband. Eden Winthrop told me I might be able to find him here."

Terri smiled even though Barker couldn't see her through the door. If the man was from the Mercy Harbor Foundation he must be harmless. She opened the door and pushed back her wheelchair to allow the man to step inside.

"Hi there, I'm Terri Bellows."

She held up a small, soft hand.

"And I'm Pete Barker, but everyone just calls me Barker."

Barker took the offered hand and gave it a gentle squeeze.

"Nice to meet you, ma'am. I'm hoping to speak to your husband. Is he at home?"

As he spoke, Barker's eyes peered further into the house, and Terri blushed in embarrassment.

"Forgive me for being rude," Terri said, waving Barker past her and into the living room. "Please, come on in and make yourself comfortable. Doc isn't here, but I so rarely get to meet anyone from the foundation, it would be nice to have a chat."

"Will your husband be back soon?"

Terri wished she knew the answer. Doc had gotten a call from Ace early that morning and had left to meet his old friend. He'd been gone for hours without a word and had promised to bring back plenty of sandbags and any supplies needed to ride out the storm.

"Doc went out to help a friend, and then he's going to round up supplies ahead of the storm." She smiled up a Barker, but he didn't smile back. "You work with him at the foundation?"

"No, but I am working on something for Ms. Winthrop and was hoping Dr. Bellows could help answer a few questions about the community health center where he used to volunteer."

His reference to the old center surprised her. She sat up straighter in her chair and cocked her head.

"Wow, that's a blast from the past. What did you need to know about that old place? I volunteered there as well before my...my accident."

Barker cocked his head as if considering the idea.

"You volunteered there, too?" He finally offered her a smile. "Is that where you met your husband?"

"No, but we did volunteer there together soon after we met. He'd just moved to town after his residency, to open his practice. I was visiting a friend. The rest is fate."

"He must be pretty dedicated to volunteer work." Barker raised his eyebrows as if impressed. "I mean, to be in the midst of opening his own practice, and still have time to search out volunteer opportunities."

"Yes, he's very community-minded. But he had worked at the community center when he was here before."

"Before?" Barker looked interested.

"Yes, Doc came to Willow Bay after he left the military. One of his air force buddies grew up here, so Doc came to visit and ended up doing some volunteer work at the community center. That was before he was a real doctor, before med school. Although he had been a medic in the service."

"Really? Wow, your husband gets around."

Terri narrowed her eyes at Barker, suddenly feeling as if he was mocking her. His comments about Doc were all complimentary, but something about his demeanor suggested he wasn't being sincere.

"So, you volunteered at the community health center with your husband back in 2006? What did you do there?"

Terri nodded, relieved that Barker hadn't asked another question about Doc.

"Yes, we worked there together right up until my accident. I was a nurse practitioner, specializing in women's health. I still am, I guess, although I don't practice anymore."

Terri felt the blush rise in her cheeks again. She hated that she sat at home all day when she knew she could be out in the world making a difference. But Doc worried too much. He wouldn't allow it, as he'd said many times. He wanted to keep her safe at home.

"So, you've been in the wheelchair how long?"

Terri counted backward in her head, finding it hard to believe it had been twelve years since she'd woken up in the hospital, paralyzed from the waist down and unable to remember what had happened. Before she could reply to Barker, the front door banged open and Doc's angry face appeared in the hall.

"What the hell are *you* doing in my house?"

Terri blinked in surprise at the rage in her husband's normally quiet voice.

"Doc, honey, this is Peter Barker. He said Eden Winthrop sent him. He was just waiting for you to get home."

"And he can show himself out," Doc spat, striding to the door and opening it wide. "My wife isn't well enough to have visitors, so please leave. Now."

Barker turned toward Terri and nodded.

"Thank you for the chat, Mrs. Bellows. I hope you start feeling better real soon."

Terri had to bite her lip to stop herself from replying that she was feeling just fine. She glanced at Doc's face, confused and scared.

*No, best not say that. Doc wouldn't like that at all.*

Doc watched Barker walk out the door with narrowed eyes, his chest heaving in and out as if he'd just come back from a run. Once the door closed behind the man, Doc turned to Terri.

"Why in the world would you let that man into our home, Terri? Are you really that stupid? Haven't you listened to anything I've told you all these years?" Spittle flew from his mouth as he yelled. "You can't go letting in strangers. You can't put yourself in harm's way."

Fear washed through Terri at the fury and disgust evident in Doc's words. The red flush to his face and the feral gleam in his eyes made her head spin. A faraway memory flashed through her mind: another day when she had seen Doc screaming in rage. A wave of nausea made her grip the armrests of her chair to steady herself.

"Okay, Doc, I hear you," she muttered, trying not to be sick as she pushed toward the kitchen. She needed to get away from him, and she needed a drink of water.

She steered the chair past the stairs that she no longer used, glancing up into the dark rooms above. Resentment burned in her chest as she thought of everything those stairs had taken away from her. Now she couldn't even have the satisfaction of stomping away from her husband when he was acting like an idiot. She just had to roll away in defeat.

A firm hand on the back of her chair stopped her just before she reached the kitchen. Terri looked around, tears streaming down her face; she saw that Doc was crying, too. He circled the chair, knelt in front of her, and laid his head on her lap.

"I'm sorry, Terri. I'm so sorry. I just want to protect you."

Terri looked down at Doc's heaving shoulders and ran a gentle hand through his hair. When Doc raised his head to wrap his arms around her, she allowed herself to relax against him.

*What else can I do? He's all I've got left.*

# CHAPTER TWENTY-FOUR

I t was noon on Sunday before Anna Stanislaus finally returned Eden's phone call. Kara had gone missing from the hospital more than twenty-four hours before, and no one at Hope House had seen or heard from her since. Eden's heart jumped when she saw the hoped-for number on the phone's display. She stepped out onto the back porch and tapped on the screen to accept the call.

"Hello, Anna?"

The woman's soft response was drowned out by the sound of a child crying. Eden heard rustling in the background and then the woman's pleading admonishment.

"Niko, be quiet, let Momma talk."

More fussing, and then Anna's voice close to the phone.

"Hello...are you still there?"

"Hello, Anna? This is Eden Winthrop. I'm with Hope House, the recovery center where your sister, Kara, has been staying."

"Yes, I know. I got your message. Has Kara been found yet?"

The question ended Eden's hope that the young woman had made her way back to Orlando, and the truth settled into Eden's stomach with cold certainty: Kara was officially a missing person.

"No, I'm sorry, Anna, but we still haven't heard from Kara. She left the hospital yesterday morning and no one here knows where she could have gone. I was hoping she'd gone to see you."

When Anna didn't respond right away, Eden gave her time to digest the unwelcome news that her sister was missing.

The quiet on the other end of the phone was soon interrupted by a high-pitched squeal, and the sound of something banging. Finally, Anna cleared her throat.

"I can't think where she would go. She has no one else. At least, not that I know of."

Anna's voice was hesitant, unsure.

"Why was she in the hospital? Was she sick?"

"She'd had an accidental overdose. We aren't sure what she took, or how she got the...drugs."

Eden winced at the words, knowing it sounded as if Kara had relapsed, and she rushed to explain.

"But, I'm sure it was an accident. Kara told me on Friday that she was determined to get straight so that she could return to Orlando and help you and Niko."

"I don't understand what's happened," Anna murmured. "Everything was fine six months ago, and then..."

Eden waited, but Anna had drifted away. The baby was fussing, and Anna responded with the soft, low soothing words that seem to come naturally to new mothers.

"Momma's here, Niko. Momma's right here. That's a good boy."

Finally, Anna returned to the phone.

"I have to work the late shift today, but maybe Niko and I could drive down tomorrow. I could call in sick. We could look around the town and see if we can find Kara."

"No, that's the last thing Kara would want."

Eden remembered Kara's panic at the thought of Anna driving all the way to Willow Bay because of her.

"Kara wanted to help you and Niko. She wouldn't want you to worry. I've reported the situation to the police, and I have some friends helping to search as well."

"The police? Won't they arrest Kara if they find out she overdosed? She was allowed to go to Hope House instead of jail. Will the police take her to jail?"

Eden wanted to assure Anna that Kara wouldn't be in trouble when she was found, but she wasn't sure herself. If the girl had run away to get high, or to avoid rehab, and the police found her first, Eden wasn't sure what would happen.

"I'll do everything I can to make sure that doesn't happen," Eden said, promising herself she'd find a way to get Kara back into Hope House when she was found. "But first we've got to find her."

"I have to go. I need to drop off Niko at the sitter's and be at work soon. But my day off is Tuesday. If you don't find Kara by then, I'm driving down there, whether Kara will like it or not."

Eden recognized the grim determination in Anna's soft voice. She knew that feeling better than anyone else.

It had been the same feeling that had driven her to try to save her sister, Mercy, from an abusive husband. The same protective instinct that had compelled her to kill in order to save Mercy's children.

*No use trying to talk her out of coming to find her sister. I wouldn't listen if it was my sister, so why should she?*

"All right, but please keep in touch, Anna. You can reach me at any time. If Kara calls you, please let me know. And if I hear from Kara, I'll contact you right away."

Eden held the phone in her hand after the call had ended.

*There has to be something more I can do.*

She thought for a minute, then dialed Reggie's number. Her friend answered on the third ring, already talking.

"No, I haven't heard from Kara, and yes, I'm worried, too."

"I can't just sit around and wait for something terrible to happen."

Eden's tone was defensive.

"I know first-hand that it's dangerous to wait for the police to handle things around here."

Reggie sighed and made a noise that Eden took for agreement.

"I'm calling you to ask if Dr. Bellows is scheduled to run any sessions at Hope House today. I'm convinced he knows something, and I want to try to talk to him again."

"I don't think that's a very good idea, Eden. Besides, we don't hold sessions on Sundays, so he won't be at Hope House in any case. He won't be there until Tuesday."

"Then tell me his home address."

Eden wasn't going to give up that easily, and she certainly wasn't going to wait until Tuesday to speak to him. The self-important doctor was hiding something, and she was going to find out what he knew.

"You can't go around confronting people, Eden," Reggie pleaded, sounding worried. "For one thing, it isn't safe."

"I thought you said that Dr. Bellows was a charitable, respected member of the community. What's the harm of me stopping by for a friendly chat? Are you worried he'll be offended?"

"I'm not worried about him, Eden, I'm worried about *you.*"

Eden felt tears threaten as she struggled to think of something to say. Reggie just didn't understand. She hadn't lost someone to violence. She hadn't seen the pitiful ruins of a young girl left to fend for herself.

She didn't have to live with the nightmares.

"I'm not the enemy you know. I'm just trying to keep you safe."

"What's his address, Reggie?"

"Eden, please don't do this."

"Fine, if you don't want to tell me, I'll just look in the foundation's records."

"Okay, I'll text you the address. But don't say I didn't warn you."

After she'd disconnected the call, Eden felt guilty for taking her frustration out on Reggie. The kind woman had been a godsend, and Eden knew she'd be lost without her.

*I'll apologize to Reggie the next time I see her, but first, I need to pay Dr. Bellows a visit.*

\* \* \*

Eden drove to the exclusive Grand Isles Estates lakefront community, turning down a winding road that led to the Bellows house. Spanish moss hung heavily from ancient cypress trees, blocking out the afternoon sun, and casting gray shadows on the houses below.

She parked her white Expedition by the curb and hurried up the walkway, eager to knock on the door before she lost her nerve.

But no one responded, and after several seconds she knocked again, becoming impatient to ask Dr. Bellows and his wife exactly what they'd seen at the hospital the previous morning.

After further silence from inside, Eden circled around to the side of the large two-story, colonial house.

The door to the garage was closed, and a large wooden fence blocked her from going into the backyard. She tried pushing on the gate, but it was firmly locked.

She began to walk back toward the front and noticed that decorative glass panes ran across the upper part of the garage door.

Eden looked around to make sure she wasn't being watched. Seeing no one, she approached the door and stood on her tiptoes, peering into the dark garage, glad for once that, at five feet ten inches tall, she'd inherited her father's height.

Her mood soured when she saw that the big blue van was not in the garage. Dr. Bellows and his wife were not at home. Her questions would have to wait.

Eden trudged back to her car with a heavy heart. She drove past the thick, gnarled trunks of the cypress trees, emerging from their oppressive shade to see puffs of clouds on the horizon, drifting in from the Gulf. Thoughts of the approaching storm made Eden frown.

*Will the storm hit Willow Bay? If so, will we find Kara before it does?*

# CHAPTER TWENTY-FIVE

Wind gusted through the Sacred Heart Cemetery, rustling the calla lilies in Barker's arms, and covering the headstone with dead leaves. He knelt and put the flowers into the bronze vase, before brushing the leaves aside to reveal the name etched into the marble: Caroline Ferguson Barker, Beloved Wife and Mother.

"That's better," Barker said, keeping his voice low but cheerful. "All clean now, baby. Just the way you like it."

He sat back on his heels and looked around at the other graves. Most were covered with leaves and debris that had blown in from the forest beyond the wooden fence, where palm tree fronds shivered in the wind as they towered over a motley collection of cabbage and scrub palmettos.

Sacred Heart was the oldest cemetery in Willow Bay, and its age showed in the cracked wooden fence and overgrown lawn. But Caroline had thought the place had character, and an interesting past which went all the way back to the town's founding, unlike the carefully manicured Bay Haven Memorial Park on the other side of town. She'd made all the arrangements herself, and now here she was, part of the town's history.

"You always did manage to get your way in the end."

Barker studied the marble headstone, pretending everything was all right, just as he did most Sundays, but this time his mind wouldn't play along. A little voice kept asking him what Caroline would say if she could see him there alone at her grave.

*Where's Taylor? Why isn't she with you? Why hasn't she come to see me?*

They were questions he didn't want to answer. What could he say to himself or to his wife's memory that would make sense? Did he even know the truth?

*Taylor left. She doesn't want to see me. She doesn't want to remember.*

Barker kissed the tips of his fingers and touched them to the cool marble next to Caroline's name. He held them there for a long beat, wishing everything had happened differently. Wishing he could do it all over again. Slowly he stood and walked across the lawn, toward the overgrown path that led to his car.

He sat in the blue Prius and stared out at the cemetery, the graves and the trees replaced by visions of Caroline, gone now for three years, but still so vivid in his mind. Caroline on their wedding day, stunning in white satin. Caroline in the car as they brought baby Taylor home from the hospital. Caroline dry-eyed and stoic after finding out the cancer had returned. Caroline in their bed, that very last night.

He shook himself and dried his eyes.

*Three years of grieving is long enough, Barker.*

But somehow he didn't believe it. How could twenty-five years of marriage be forgotten in only three years of mourning? The math didn't work. Forgetting didn't work. Nothing seemed to work without Caroline. But he had no one to blame but himself.

At least that's how Taylor had seen it, and her accusing words still stung after all this time.

"You caused Mommy's cancer. Always smoking like a chimney around us. I'll be dead next, and it'll be all your fault."

He knew she'd been hurting; he thought she hadn't really meant it. But his daughter had been gone without a word for more than two years now. Enough was enough. It was time for him to stop grieving and sulking, and time for Taylor to come home.

*Now I just need to find her and tell her.*

Barker started the car and pushed on the gas, steering the car along the narrow, winding road that snaked through the cemetery. As he neared the front gates, he noticed a small figure seated on a bench next to a gray marble lawn crypt. The woman's silky white dress complimented her smooth, ebony skin.

Barker blinked in recognition.

*Isn't that Eden Winthrop's friend?*

His car's brilliant blue exterior – the only splash of color in the cemetery other than the flowers among the graves – must have drawn the woman's attention, because she glanced over, before turning back to the grave and bowing her head.

Barker tried to catch a glimpse of her in his rearview mirror, but a large weeping willow was in the way.

*I'm sure that was Reggie. I guess she's lost someone, too.*

Reggie's thin shoulders and bowed head stayed with Barker as he drove home. He told himself that the knowledge that someone else was grieving should make him feel even worse, but somehow it comforted him. He wasn't the only one caught up in the past. He wasn't the only one that spent the weekends socializing with the dead.

\* \* \*

Barker sat at his dining room table writing notes onto a stack of index cards. He'd stopped to buy the cards at Bayside Market on his way home from the cemetery, determined to map out all possible links between Natalie Lorenzo and Helena Steele.

His father had taught him to use index cards to walk through a case. Each clue or fact would go onto a card, as would each suspect, location, and open question. The cards provided a way to visualize and sort the information collected in different ways.

Barker's phone buzzed in his pocket just as he wrote *Community Health Center* on one of the cards.

"Hey, Leo, what's up?"

"I'm guessing you haven't seen the news?"

"The news? No, I make a point never to watch Sunday morning news," Barker replied, still moving the cards around on the table. "Too many politicians telling too many lies. Besides, I have a standing date on Sunday mornings."

"Well, you might want to catch up on the headlines. There's been another murder in Willow Bay, and the police have named Frankie Dawson as their number one suspect."

"You're messing with me, right?" Barker sputtered. "This is a joke?"

"If it's a joke then you haven't heard the punchline yet."

Leo didn't sound even slightly amused.

"I don't think I want to hear this."

"The woman that got murdered? Her name is Penelope Yates."

Barker drew in a breath and held it, trying to understand what he was hearing.

"The same Penelope Yates that Nessa told me about yesterday? The same woman that Frankie was going to track down?"

"Yep, that's the one. I don't have all the details of the murder yet, but the police think Frankie might be involved."

"And what does Frankie say?"

"He denies it," Leo said, sounding tired. "Says he met Penelope at a bar, but he left her at home and alive."

"Has he been arrested?" Barker asked, still dazed by the thought of Frankie being accused of murder. The guy could be a jerk, but he wasn't a killer. Anyone could see that.

"No. I talked him into going into the station for a voluntary interview, but they haven't provided me with any of the evidence yet."

Barker thought for a minute.

"They probably won't share the details with you and Frankie unless they charge him. Then they'll have to."

"Yeah, I know how they operate," Leo snorted, his disdain for the police clear in his voice. "So, I'm hoping you might be able to get some details from Nessa."

"Oh, man, poor Nessa," Barker groaned. "She's the one that gave me the Penelope Yates connection. I bet she's freaking out about all this."

"Poor Nessa? I'm more worried about Penelope Yates, who is dead, and Frankie Dawson, who is being falsely accused right now. I'm sure *poor Nessa* can take care of herself."

"Calm down, Leo. I'm just saying none of this is Nessa's fault, and she's going to be left holding the bag. I feel for her. But you're right, we need to focus on proving that Frankie didn't do this."

"I'm glad to hear you say that, Barker. I know you and Frankie don't always get along, but it's good to know you've got his back."

"This isn't about having Frankie's back, Leo." Barker shook his head in frustration. "Don't you get it? It's about making sure that whoever did kill Penelope Yates is caught before they can kill again."

Leo went silent, and Barker wondered if he was counting to ten, trying to stop himself from lashing out. Barker used the technique himself when he started getting out of control.

"You're right, Barker. Finding out who killed Penelope has to be the top priority because I'm convinced that whoever killed her has killed at least twice before and won't hesitate to kill again."

Barker frowned, looking down at the index cards spread out in front of him. Penelope Yates' name was already written on one of the cards he'd put in the witness pile. Barker picked up the card with Penelope's name and placed it on top of the cards listing Helena Steele and Natalie Lorenzo. She was one of the victims now.

"Okay," Barker agreed. "I'll call Nessa."

# CHAPTER TWENTY-SIX

The faded pick-up truck turned onto the dirt road, emitting the usual rattles and groans as it lumbered toward the old dairy farm. Ace had neglected to fill in the inevitable potholes and ruts that had formed over the years, and the road was uncomfortable to navigate in any vehicle, much less an old truck with worn-out shocks.

But that was the way Ace liked it. He didn't want anyone from town snooping around. His old truck was the only vehicle that should be on the dirt road, and he only drove it out to the farm and back. In town, he drove a shiny, well-maintained car that hummed so smoothly no one could hear it coming.

As Ace approached the stable, the sun glinted off the tin roof, reflecting onto the windshield and causing Ace to lift one callused hand to block the glare. He climbed out of the truck and strode to the stable, opening the doors to reveal the hardpacked floor and empty milking stalls just as he'd left them.

The dirt floor in stall seven was undisturbed. He walked in and stood in the middle of the stall, remembering the girl safely buried only a few feet below him. Heat rose in his veins as he remembered the smooth, pale skin and scared blue eyes. He pulled his cell phone out of his pocket and opened his photo app. The last picture he'd taken popped up on the screen.

There she was, the fairy tale princess he'd kept in the tower. Only he hadn't been a prince, and she hadn't lived happily ever after.

*No prince charming for you, princess. Just the ugly frog.*

He chuckled, but the laugh was forced. He was feeling moody again. Coming out to the old place could do that to him. The memories he had there were a mix of good and bad. Some days the bad ones seemed to take over. Sometimes the old farm made him think about his father, and that could ruin his mood for the rest of the day.

*Pop was a mean, old bastard, but he taught me how to be tough.*

The lessons Ace had endured on the farm were just blurred memories now, but he knew they'd hardened him and had prepared him for the life he'd led. His mental toughness and self-sufficiency had seemed a perfect fit for the military, where he'd excelled at first, eventually being stationed in Germany, where he'd been lucky enough to meet Doc.

Doc had been a medic, which meant he'd had easy access to strong sedatives and pain killers, and he hadn't been squeamish about using them for clandestine recreational purposes. Ace smiled at the memories.

*Doc and I sure had fun while it lasted. Like the song says, nothing'll stop the US Air Force!*

Of course, that was before he'd run into trouble. Back before he'd learned to bury the evidence of his indiscretions.

Ace shook his head, trying to clear away the unwanted images. He preferred to think of his hasty return to the states as a minor bump in the road that led him to his true calling, as opposed to a dishonorable discharge. And nobody in Willow Bay knew what had happened. It was his little secret. Just like the princess buried beneath him.

Ace dropped his phone back in his pocket and heard a faint clink. He stuck his big hand in and felt around, feeling the cool metal of the gold cross Doc had given him. He pulled it out, dragging the thin chain with it. He looked closely at the girl's necklace, wondering how much it was worth. The cross was small, and the chain thin, so it probably wouldn't bring in much, even if he could risk selling it.

The feel of the necklace in his hand made him think of the girl who had worn it. Ace knew she'd be waiting for him in the room above the garage. But the thought didn't bring the usual satisfaction. This time there was too much going on to enjoy the hunt and the thrill of the capture. This time there was too much at risk to fully enjoy his new prize.

His eyes moved to stall eight, and his pulse quickened at the thought of completing his collection. When he'd first started the mission with Doc, all the stalls had been empty, and the challenge of filling them had been intoxicating.

Back then he'd known the game of hunt, capture, and kill would go on for years before all eight stalls were full, and the mission was complete. He hadn't thought about the end.

But the last ten years had gone quickly. Although he and Doc had been patient, waiting for the perfect risk-free targets, stopping to take breaks when the risks became too much, the game was almost over. He looked again at stall eight.

*What's next? Another mission? Another partner?*

A buzz from Ace's pocket brought him back from his memories. He once again pulled out the phone. The text message was from Doc, and Ace rolled his eyes in frustration. More panic. More problems. Doc was in trouble again.

*Maybe it's time to get a new partner.*

It wasn't the first time the thought had crossed his mind.

Although Doc had played his agreed part to the best of his ability, Ace knew that Doc wasn't tough, that he hadn't been raised to be hard like Ace had been. While Ace had never even met his own mother, Doc had been raised by a coddling woman who rushed to meet his every need. If Ace was honest with himself, he'd say that Doc was weak.

*But he's the one that can get the girls.*

Ace couldn't deny that Doc's bland appearance and soft voice allowed him to fly under the radar with women. Doc seemed harmless, or even helpful, most of the time. Women in need gravitated to him, while Ace's rough features and gruff personality put most women on guard.

As a teenager Ace had sensed that the girls at school feared him. They didn't tease him or make fun of him, but they stayed away. Sometimes he'd catch a girl staring at him with nervous eyes. He'd come to realize they were scared of him; scared in the way a rabbit is instinctively scared of a fox.

And Doc had proven himself to be a good partner; he was loyal and grateful for the many times Ace had risked life and livelihood to save Doc from certain ruin. The first time had involved a mishap in Germany. Either Doc had misjudged the dosage, or the local girl had an unusually high tolerance to the drugs. Either way, the girl had regained consciousness sooner than expected and had run from the room yelling for help.

Although Ace and Doc had quickly decamped back to base, the room had been booked in Ace's name, and the German federal police quickly tracked him down. But Ace had denied any wrongdoing and claimed that no one else had been involved with the assault. Ace hadn't been able to save himself, but he'd kept his mouth shut, and Doc had stayed in Germany while Ace had flown home in disgrace.

After Doc's enlistment had ended, he'd left Germany with an honorable discharge on his record, making his way to Willow Bay. He'd wanted to visit Ace before med school started and, thanks to Doc's volunteer work at the community health center, they'd once again had access to the drugs that provided opportunity for more illicit adventures.

And while they thought they'd been careful that summer and had assumed they'd gotten away with their misbehavior, it wasn't until Doc had returned years later to set up his private practice in Willow Bay that they'd been confronted with the truth.

Ace could still see the panic in Doc's eyes when he'd come begging for help. A woman from the past was threatening to tell Doc's wife everything. About the assault when she'd been a teenager. About the son she wanted him to provide for.

Doc had said he'd made a terrible mistake, and so Ace had stepped in and fixed it once again. But this time it was different. This time, to protect Doc, he'd had to become a killer. It had been his first kill, and he still relished the memory.

*Helena Steele never suspected anyone was in the house. She came home from work, ate a solitary dinner, and padded up the stairs to take a shower. Ace watched her enter the bedroom from his hiding spot in the closet. He saw her remove her work clothes and walk into the bathroom wearing just her bra and underwear. He had to admit she was a fine-looking woman; the kind of woman that had never given him the time of day.*

*Once Helena turned on the shower, Ace crept out of the closet and slid under the bed, careful not to cut himself with the boning knife he'd pilfered earlier from the knife rack downstairs. Ace had been in the house for hours, rifling through the family's possessions, hoping to find a gun. The best he could come up with was the knife. He'd also impulsively pocketed a sterling silver bracelet he'd found in a dainty jewelry box on the dresser; it would make a good souvenir.*

*The jarring ring of the phone prompted Helena to turn off the water. Ace lay utterly still under the bed as she entered the bedroom, her bare feet whispering against the carpet as she crossed the room. He was mesmerized by the one-sided conversation, enjoying the soft intimacy of her voice as she spoke and paused, laughed and paused.*

"Hi, honey...yes, I heated up the lasagna...uh-huh...just got out of the shower...how was your day...that's nice...okay, no hurry...I won't wait up...drive safe...love you, too."

His excitement built as Helena performed her final bedtime routine. He relished knowing that he had the power to decide how long she lived, and when she would die. By the time she turned the lights out, he was shaking with anticipation. The sound of her steady, even breathing was his cue to slip out from beneath the bed.

The glow of the bedside clock provided just enough light for Ace to see Helena's long, dark hair spread out on the pillow. Her face was pale and almost ethereal as he stood over her, wishing she were awake so he could see the fear enter her beautiful eyes. But her husband would be home soon, and he needed to complete his mission and leave undetected.

He raised the boning knife high in his left hand, ready to stab down in a dramatic arc when the phone rang again. Helena's eyes blinked open, immediately focusing on the glint from the knife above her. Ace hesitated then brought his hand down, but she'd already rolled to the side.

Perhaps it was survival instinct that made her move so fast. She was up and halfway off the other side of the bed before Ace caught her, wrapping his big hand in her thick hair and ripping her head back against his chest. The sharp point of the knife sunk into the soft flesh of her neck; a swift cut to the left turned her scream into a gurgle. Blood squirted and gushed, painting the once white room a garish crimson.

Ace dropped Helena's lifeless body onto the bed, glad he'd thought to pull on protective coveralls before he'd entered the house. In his line of work, he'd become well-acquainted with blood, only he usually didn't have to deal with such hot, fresh blood. And so much of it.

He knew he needed to leave. Knew her husband would be home soon. But he wanted to remember her. Needed to have more than just a token of his first kill. He unzipped his coveralls and reached into his pocket for his phone. The flash lit up the room, allowing him to see the woman clearly for the first time since he'd entered the house. The sight of her dark staring eyes, *now blank and devoid of life, thrilled him to his core. The unattainable woman who would have never looked at him twice in the street could never look at any man again. In the end, he had won, and the victory was sweet.*

The patch of light shining in through the stable door suddenly dimmed, and Ace blinked, the memories fading, a massive cloud moving over the sun.

*Storm's on the way. There'll be work to do.*

Ace needed to go home and prepare the house for the storm before it was too late. After he boarded up the windows and put sandbags by the doors, he'd figure out what to do about Doc, and about girl eight.

He knew he should take time to enjoy the girl; she might be the last one, at least for a while. But there were too many people in Willow Bay asking too many questions. It wouldn't be smart to have her above the garage much longer. Especially with the storm coming and crews out searching for people needing help.

No, if the path of the storm veered toward Willow Bay, he'd have to bring the girl to the stable. And once she was safely put to rest, he'd need to tell Doc that their mission was finally over.

# CHAPTER TWENTY–SEVEN

Leo rubbed his eyes and yawned as he knocked on Barker's door. Before leaving the office he'd taken out the backup shaver and hair gel he kept in his desk for emergencies, and he now appeared refreshed and immaculately groomed. But the lack of sleep and stress had sapped his energy; mentally he was shattered.

"Door's open!"

Barker's yell reverberated down the hall, prompting Leo to shake his head as he twisted the doorknob.

"Yes, it sure is, Barker," Leo called out, stepping into the hall and looking around. "Don't you know a killer is on the loose in Willow Bay?"

"I'm in here."

Leo followed the voice to the dining room, where Barker sat with his laptop computer open and a table full of index cards spread out around him. The blinds were closed, and only one of the bulbs in the overhead light fixture was working.

Leo strode to the window and opened the blinds, letting in a flood of sunlight and making Barker recoil as if he were Dracula emerging from his coffin.

"Do you always leave your door unlocked?"

"No, not always. But I'm hoping the killer will see that the door is open and just walk on in," Barker muttered, not taking his eyes off the cards. "It's easier that way."

Leo waited for Barker to look up, but the big man kept his head down and his eyes on the table. Finally, Leo couldn't take it anymore.

"What did you find out at Dr. Bellows' house? Would he talk to you? Did he admit anything?"

Barker sighed and leaned back in his chair, looking up at Leo with red, tired eyes. He cocked his head as if trying to remember.

"Dr. Bellows wasn't home when I got there, but his wife let me in. She seems like a nice lady."

"What did you ask her? What did she say?"

"Calm down, Leo, I'm trying to tell you."

Barker stretched his arms and then his back, which produced a cracking sound that made Leo wince.

"Mrs. Bellows was kind enough to tell me that her husband was a volunteer at the community health center in 2006. She volunteered there as well."

"Did you ask her about Natalie, or my mother?"

"No, I didn't get the chance. Dr. Bellows came home and threw a fit. Kicked me out before I could ask more questions."

Leo felt his shoulders slump. All the adrenaline that had coursed through his veins with the hope Barker may have found another lead suddenly drained away.

"Don't look so down. I did manage to get some new information that might mean something. I'm sitting here trying to figure out what though."

Leo looked over at the cards Barker was studying. He saw that Barker had written *Community Health Center* on one of the cards. Other cards seemed to include years. He'd written *1994* on one, and then *2006* on another.

"What does 1994 have to do with this?" Leo asked, looking up at Barker.

"That's the year Bellows came to Willow Bay for the first time, just after he got out of the military, and just before med school. He volunteered at the Community Health Center then, too."

"So, you think Bellows may have met Natalie or my mother when he came to Willow Bay in 1994?"

Barker shrugged and picked up the 1994 card and placed it next to Natalie Lorenzo's card. He thought for a minute, frowning in concentration.

"I'm not good at math, but based on Natalie Lorenzo's date of birth, I have her at only sixteen in 1994."

Leo nodded, following Barker's train of thought.

"Could she have been hanging around at the community health center back then? Maybe met Dr. Bellows?"

"That's what I'm wondering," Barker said.

He pointed to another card that lay by itself on the edge of the table. Leo bent over to read the name that Barker had written.

"Vinny Lorenzo?" Leo glanced over at Barker. "What's Natalie's son have to do with this?"

"He was born in 1994."

Leo stared at Barker with wide eyes. A chill crept up his spine as he considered the implications.

"Bellows was already a grown man in 1994, a respected veteran and volunteer. If he'd gotten a teenager pregnant, he'd be in big trouble with the police, wouldn't he?"

"He would be if they found out about it. But it doesn't look like they did. When Natalie died, Vinny was declared an orphan." A shadow fell over Barker's eyes. "I'm the one who told the kid his mother had been killed. I remember that day clearly. I guess you could say it stayed with me."

Leo heard something in Barker's voice that kept him quiet. He waited for Barker to continue.

"Vinny told me he didn't know who his father was. His mother had never told him. But at that point, the kid was only twelve years old. Natalie was probably trying to protect him from the truth."

"So, maybe when Bellows moved back twelve years later, he found out about his son," Leo said, warming to the theory. "Maybe she threatened to go to the cops, and he panicked and killed her."

"It sounds as good a motive as any. But how do we prove it? We don't even know for sure that Bellows is Vinny's father."

"There's one sure way to find out," Leo said. "DNA doesn't lie."

"You think Dr. Bellows is going to volunteer to give us a DNA sample? You're crazier than I thought."

Leo gave Barker a thin smile.

"Who said I'm going to ask him to volunteer it? There are plenty of ways to get DNA."

Barker crossed his arms over his chest and stared down at the index cards. He picked up his pencil and wrote a question to add to the pile: *Is Bellows Vinny's father?*

Leo stared at the words, knowing the question would need to be answered before they could present the far-fetched theory to the police. Circumstantial evidence was never as convincing as DNA.

Leo let his eyes fall on his mother's name, and a disturbing thought floated through his mind.

*If Bellows killed Natalie to silence her, where does that leave my mother's case? Why would Bellows kill my mother?*

"My mother didn't start working at the community health center until 2002," Leo said, almost to himself. "She may not have even met Bellows."

Barker looked up in surprise.

"So, now you're thinking the two cases *aren't* connected?"

Leo shook his head, not wanting to give up on the idea that he could find his mother's killer by following the clues in the Natalie Lorenzo case."

"I don't know. It seemed to make sense that a serial killer on the loose in Willow Bay may have chosen two victims he'd encountered at the community center. But if Natalie's murder wasn't a random attack, if there was a personal motive, then the connection starts to fall apart."

Barker cocked his head and frowned down at the index cards.

"It still seems strange. Too much of a coincidence to give up on so easily if you ask me."

Leo nodded, his face grim.

"When you looked through the files at Nessa's house, did you see Adrian Bellows listed as one of my mother's co-workers at the community center?"

Barker shook his head.

"I don't remember seeing his name in either file. And I don't remember talking to him as part of the Lorenzo investigation, but maybe Ingram handled that interview. I can ask him."

"If the investigators talked to Penelope, you'd think they would also talk to the other people that worked or volunteered there."

Barker nodded in agreement. He picked up a blank card and wrote *Did Ingram or Vanzinger talk to Bellows?*

"Who's Vanzinger? Why does that name sound familiar?" Leo asked, reading the card upside-down.

"He was Reinhardt's partner back then. He worked your mother's case. I'm sure you must have met him."

Leo tried to think back to the nightmarish days after his mother's body had been found. So many people had spoken to him, so many pitying faces had stared at him.

"I don't remember him," Leo finally said, but he had a vague image of a man's face in his mind. The man's weathered skin and chapped lips had left the impression of an outdoorsman.

"Tucker Vanzinger grew up in Willow Bay and joined the WBPD right out of school. Was in uniform for quite a while before moving up to detective. He'd been working in the Violent Crimes Unit for a year or so when he and Reinhardt got called out to your mother's...scene."

Leo felt Barker's eyes on him, but he kept his eyes on the table, his face impassive. He couldn't afford to get emotional every time his mother's murder was mentioned. He needed to focus on finding her killer. Only then could he allow himself to give in to the grief. And maybe then he'd be able to find some sort of closure.

"A few weeks later Vanzinger just up and quit," Barker continued. "Disappeared from Willow Bay before the case had been closed."

Leo bent down and wrote *Tucker Vanzinger* on one of the cards and placed it on the table in front of Barker.

"He's got to know something about my mother's case. Something that made him quit the force."

Leo walked to the window and looked out, trying to hide the frustration that was taking hold.

"Well, the case was Vanzinger's first violent homicide. Maybe he couldn't handle it," Barker said, his voice cautious. "Or maybe he'd had issues with Reinhardt."

Leo stiffened at the name of the dirty cop that had tried to kill Nessa. The corrupt detective had been capable of trafficking young girls, dealing drugs, and working with an organized crime syndicate to pay off gambling debts. Leo was sure Reinhardt would have been capable of covering up a crime or sending an innocent man to jail.

The thought brought a lump to Leo's throat; he swallowed hard. How could anyone have believed his father had been a killer? The naked agony on his father's face that night had been too real and too raw to fake. Ken Steele had been devastated. He'd never gotten over losing Helena, and he'd eventually decided he didn't want to be in a world without her.

"My father killed himself in jail after being falsely convicted," Leo said, wanting Barker to hear the truth, needing to say it out loud. "And I'm going to find the real killer. I'm going to clear my father's name, and I'm going to avenge both my father and my mother."

"I hear you, Leo, and I want to help."

"Then help me find Vanzinger. He must know something. Maybe he even knows who the killer is. If Reinhardt let the killer go free, or if he just didn't chase up the case properly, maybe Vanzinger will know. Maybe he'll want to help us make things right."

Barker looked doubtful, but he nodded.

"I'll see what I can do. I think he and Jankowski were close back when they were both in uniform. I'll ask him to help."

Leo rolled his eyes at the mention of Nessa's partner. He wasn't sure he trusted the beefy detective. The guy always looked pissed off, unless he was looking at Eden. An unfamiliar wave of jealousy washed through Leo, but he pushed it away. He didn't need any more distractions. He needed to be sharp and focused.

"Fine, ask him about Vanzinger, but I don't want to involve Jankowski further unless it's absolutely necessary. I'm not sure we can trust him."

Barker looked ready to protest, but then shrugged and nodded when he saw the stubborn set to Leo's chin.

"I've got to go," Leo said, walking to the door. "I want to check in with Eden to see if she's heard anything from Kara Stanislaus. And I need to prepare. Frankie's being questioned again at nine o'clock tomorrow morning. No need to get up. I'll let myself out."

He turned and walked out, leaving Barker surrounded by his growing stack of clues and questions.

# CHAPTER TWENTY-EIGHT

The sky was starting to spit rain as Frankie stood outside the Willow Bay police station waiting for Leo. He pulled the hood of his sweatshirt up over his head and stuck one of his hands in the front pocket of his faded jeans. The other hand held a lit cigarette to his mouth. He inhaled deeply, hoping the rush of nicotine would help calm his jittery nerves, but instead he started coughing and sputtering. He looked up with red eyes just in time to see Leo exit the parking garage and walk toward him.

"It's almost nine, man, where the hell have you been?"

"This is a first." Leo patted Frankie on the back and guided him toward the station entrance. "You're on time for once and I'm the one running late."

"Hold on, man, I'm not done with my smoke."

Leo snorted and plucked the cigarette out of Frankie's mouth. He chucked it into the receptacle by the door as he entered the station. Frankie stared after him with narrowed eyes, tempted to walk away.

"I don't need this crap, Leo," Frankie said, following the lawyer inside and pushing back his hood. "I'm in this mess because I was trying to help your ass."

Leo sighed and looked over, motioning for Frankie to be quiet. He greeted the desk officer in a friendly voice.

"Good morning, Officer Eddings. We're here to see Detective Ainsley. We've got an appointment at nine."

The young cop in the uniform turned away to use the phone, and Leo faced Frankie, raising his hand in a placating gesture.

"Don't worry. I'm sure when we have a chance to go through all the facts with them they'll have to admit you didn't kill Penelope."

"I hope you're sure enough to bet my life. Cause Florida's got the damn death penalty. If they don't believe me I could end up riding Old Sparky."

"Florida doesn't use the electric chair for executions anymore. Unless you specifically request it," Leo said, his voice matter-of-fact. "Now it's lethal injection, but I'm not sure which drugs they use."

"That's real reassuring, man. Thanks for nothing."

Frankie looked toward the doors, wondering if he had time to get through them before the detectives showed up. He felt Leo's hand on his arm and turned to see Nessa waving them into the back.

"Good morning, gentlemen," Nessa said, her southern drawl reminding Frankie of his mother's family up in Memphis. "We're gonna be in the third room on your left."

Frankie's heart sank when he saw Detective Jankowski waiting for them inside the little room. The brawny detective didn't smile as Frankie sat down, and he maintained a sullen eye contact that quickly turned into a staring contest.

Leo broke the silence just as Nessa joined them at the table and opened up a notepad.

"Frankie wants to clear this up quickly and be on his way." Leo looked at Nessa and raised his eyebrows. "A hurricane warning was issued last night. Coastal evacuations have already started. He'll need to help his mother secure her home and prepare to leave if needed."

"That's assuming he'll be leaving here today at all," Jankowski said, frowning at the lawyer and leaning forward to prop both his elbows on the table. "And that's a pretty big assumption."

"You don't think the results of the lie detector test prove he's telling the truth and clears him of any wrongdoing?"

"How did you get the results?"

Jankowski turned to Nessa, clearly aggravated.

"Did you share the results with him? Was it your buddy Barker?" Leo interrupted, clearing his throat and raising his voice.

"No one told me the results. But I'm one hundred percent sure Frankie couldn't have killed anyone. I know the results prove that."

"Lie detector tests aren't conclusive proof," Jankowski insisted, but Frankie thought he saw doubt in the detective's eyes. "We still need to understand why he was there, and what happened."

Frankie opened his mouth to respond, but Leo stopped him.

"As I said yesterday, he went to talk to Penelope because I asked him to. He's helping me investigate the old Lorenzo and Steele cases, and Penelope Yates came up as a possible link."

Jankowski crossed his thick arms over his chest and leaned back in the metal chair.

"Refresh my memory. How was she linked to the cases?"

"Penelope worked at the old community health center with my mother. They were both social workers. Around the same time, Natalie Lorenzo enrolled in one of the center's treatment programs."

Jankowski looked over at Frankie, his face tense.

"So, you talked to Penelope. What did she tell you?"

Frankie cleared his throat, tried to wet his dry lips.

"You got some water?"

Nessa stood and left the room. Within minutes she was back carrying a Styrofoam cup of water. She set the cup on the table and looked at Frankie with an encouraging nod.

"What did Penelope tell you, Frankie?"

Frankie sipped the water. He looked at Nessa, keeping his eyes on hers, noticing for the first time how blue they were.

"She didn't say much," Frankie admitted, wishing he had more to tell them. "She busted me for following her to the bar. When I asked her about Natalie she got all upset. Started chugging whiskey sours."

"Why was she upset?" Nessa asked. "Did she say?"

"She felt guilty she hadn't gotten to Natalie in time to save her."

Frankie remembered the tears in Penelope's bright gray eyes, and the words she'd used.

"She said she still had nightmares about it."

Something clicked in Frankie's mind; something else Penelope had told him.

"Penelope didn't believe Natalie had been turning tricks, even though that's what the cops told her. She said Natalie was getting straight and had found her kid's father. She was going to hit the guy up for money so she could get the kid back."

Leo inhaled sharply and turned to Frankie.

"You never told me that."

Leo's eyes were intense as he searched Frankie's face.

"She told you Natalie was going to confront her son's father? That she knew who he was? Knew where he was?"

"Yeah, but Penelope said that Natalie wouldn't tell her anything about the guy. It was some big secret I guess."

Nessa leaned toward Leo, her brow furrowed.

"What's going on, Leo? What does all this mean?"

"It doesn't mean anything," Jankowski said, banging his hand on the table. "They're just trying to come up with an *alternative theory*. Someone else to blame. Don't you know that's how defense attorneys work?"

"No, it means that whoever killed Natalie might have killed Penelope to try to shut her up," Leo said, not looking at Jankowski. "And if Natalie was threatening to expose the man who fathered her son, he could be a suspect. Especially since she was only sixteen when she got pregnant. If he was an adult he'd have a lot to lose."

Frankie watched Nessa's face, suspecting she was his only hope of walking out of there a free man.

"So, if your theory is correct, how are we supposed to figure out who this man is?"

Nessa's question prompted Jankowski to stand and push his chair back in frustration; she ignored him, keeping her eyes on Leo.

"Do you have any idea who this man could be?"

Leo also stood, and this time he aimed his words at Jankowski.

"As a matter of fact, I do. We've identified a man who worked at the community health center when Natalie got pregnant. He then returned as a volunteer twelve years later, just before she was killed."

"Does this man have a name?" Nessa asked, her pen poised over her notepad. "Is he still in town?"

"His name is Dr. Adrian Bellows, and he owns his own private practice in Willow Bay. He also volunteers at Hope House."

It was Frankie's turn to stare over at Leo. His mind was reeling.

"You didn't tell me that, man! This doctor guy is Vinny Lorenzo's father? You think he's the one that killed Penelope?"

Jankowski spoke before Leo could respond to Frankie's question.

"Is this the same Dr. Bellows that Eden Winthrop has accused of being involved in Kara Stanislaus' disappearance?"

Frankie gaped at the detective, his eyes wide.

"Wow, this doctor dude must really get around."

"Yes, he's the one," Leo said. "I spoke to him on Saturday, but he denied even knowing Natalie or my mother."

Jankowski stared at Nessa, as if trying to gauge her reaction to the unexpected news, then turned back to Leo.

"Did you ask Dr. Bellows if he knew Penelope Yates?"

Leo thought, then shook his head. Jankowski pointed his finger in Frankie's face.

"Did you ask Penelope if she knew Bellows?"

"Nah, I never heard of the guy until today," Frankie admitted. "But I did ask her if she knew anyone who'd want to hurt either Natalie or Helena. She couldn't think of anybody, but she was pretty wasted by then, so I gave her my number and told her to call me if she remembered anything."

Frankie felt a little queasy at the memory of the almost-kiss at Penelope's door. Maybe if he had tried something she'd still be alive.

*Or maybe I'd be over there in the morgue with her.*

He looked over at Leo wondering if it was the right time to ask for reimbursement for the drinks he'd bought Penelope. But the look on Leo's face told him it wouldn't be good timing.

Leo had locked eyes with Jankowski and the two men stood toe to toe in the little room; the tension between them thick in the air. Finally, Jankowski spoke, his voice a low growl.

"Your client is free to go. For now. But I'd advise him not to leave town. He's still a person of interest, and the last person to see Penelope Yates alive."

"Uh, technically whoever killed her was the last person to have seen Penelope alive," Frankie said, standing and inching toward the door. "And I hope you guys find him soon because he sounds like a sick fuck."

Leo followed Frankie to the door, turning back to speak to Nessa.

"Talk to Adrian Bellows. Ask him about Natalie and Penelope. Request a DNA sample and see if he's Vinny Lorenzo's father."

When Nessa didn't answer, Leo shook his head and sighed.

"Don't just sit on this, Nessa; other women could be killed. Their blood will be on your hands."

Frankie heard only silence as the door closed behind him.

# CHAPTER TWENTY-NINE

Tucker's Truck Stop was too far off the interstate to be convenient for people traveling southwest to the beaches or northeast to the theme parks. But the hurricane had caused a run on every gas station and convenience store in the area, and the parking lot was jam-packed with cars, buses, and RVs as locals and tourists hurried to get enough gas and supplies to see them through the worst of the impending storm.

Jankowski circled the parking lot a few times before spotting an empty space under the battered *Truck Repairs Here* sign. He parked his black Dodge Charger and climbed out, narrowly avoiding being run over by a lifted pick-up truck with oversized wheels. The driver of the truck continued talking into a cell phone as he barreled out of the lot, ignoring Jankowski's extended middle finger.

His phone buzzed in his pocket, and he winced when he saw Gabby's number on the display. Tempted to ignore his ex-wife's call, he sighed and swiped, determined not to let her get under his skin.

"What do you want, Gabby? I'm busy."

"This isn't a social call, Simon," Gabby said, her voice dripping with disdain. "I need to know where you're at with the Penelope Yates homicide investigation. Mayor Hadley is asking, and the press is hounding me for an update. I want to send out a press release before we evacuate city hall."

"The investigation is ongoing, and we've questioned a few leads, but nothing concrete yet."

Jankowski tried to keep the resentment out of his voice. It was hard having a wife that cheated on you with her twenty-year-old personal trainer. It was even harder to then have to maintain a professional relationship with her after she became your ex-wife.

"Mayor Hadley's not going to be happy," Gabby said as if Jankowski cared what the pretentious old politician thought. "And the press is going to keep beating on the door until we give them something to run with."

Jankowski cared even less about the Willow Bay press corp.

*Every last one of them would trade their own kidneys for a juicy story.*

"Well, that's all I've got for now, so they'll have to live with it," Jankowski muttered, looking around the busy lot. "I'll call once we have more news to share, but it'll be after the hurricane passes by, so don't hold your breath."

He disconnected the call and stuffed the phone back in his pocket, angry with himself for letting Gabby get to him. After everything that had happened, she still had the power to mess with his head and ruin his day.

"Well, if it isn't Detective Simon Jankowski. What brings you slumming out to the boonies today?"

Jankowski turned at the sound of the deep voice behind him. A tall man with a thick crewcut and a two-day beard stood with his hands on his hips. He didn't look happy to see Jankowski.

"Tucker Vanzinger! It's been way too long. How's it going, man? You enjoying the easy life out here?"

Tucker looked down at his mechanic coveralls and sturdy work boots, then back up at Jankowski.

"Yeah, Jank, I'm living the dream. Now, what do you want? There's a hurricane coming and the folks around here are going batshit. I don't have time for chitchat."

Jankowski winced, hurt by Tucker's tone. They'd been close once. Had ridden patrol together for over a year back when they'd first been on the force.

*Guess a decade fiddling around under the greasy hood of a semi-truck would make anyone bitter.*

Jankowski held his breath as he watched an eighteen-wheeler skim by a young couple carrying bags of groceries and pushing a toddler in a stroller. The truck whooshed past the family with only inches to spare. Jankowski released his breath and turned to Tucker.

"I know you're busy, Tuck, but we need to talk."

Vanzinger snorted, checked his watch, then shook his head.

"You've got some nerve showing up after...how many years? Saying you want to talk? What the hell do we have to talk about, Jank?"

"Come on, man, that's not fair. So, we fell out of touch for a few years. That doesn't mean we aren't still friends, does it?"

"I don't have to ask my real friends if we're still friends, man."

Jankowski put a hand out, gripping Vanzinger's arm.

"We might not wear the same uniform anymore, but we're still brothers in my book. It's just...well, a lot of shit has happened in the last year or so."

Vanzinger swiped a rough hand through his hair before checking his watch again. Letting out a deep sigh, he met Jankowski's eyes for the first time.

"Is Gabby okay?" Tucker asked, the aggression in his voice gone, replaced by a reluctant concern.

"Yeah, she's doing pretty good, now that she's got half my money and a new boyfriend half her age."

Jankowski tried to keep his voice light, but the words stung.

"How about you? You seeing anyone?"

"Here and there, but nothing special. I keep to myself most of the time. Try to keep out of trouble."

"I hear you. We can't raise hell forever," Jankowski said. "Gotta grow up sometime."

"So, what do you want, Jank? What's happened to bring you out in this direction when everybody else is running the other way?"

The fatigue in Vanzinger's voice made Jankowski take a closer look at his old friend. Tucker Vanzinger had been a sharp, energetic detective when he'd been with the WBPD, but the man standing in front of Jankowski now had become weathered and reserved. Time had etched fine wrinkles into Tucker's once unlined face and had dimmed the light in his now-guarded eyes.

Jankowski resisted an urge to ask Tucker what had happened.

*The years haven't been kind to you my friend, have they?*

Jankowski's phone buzzed again, but he ignored it.

"I wanted to ask you about a case you worked on," Jankowski said, knowing he needed to stop reminiscing and focus on the task at hand. "Your last case, actually."

Vanzinger grew still at the words, then dropped his eyes to his watch. He bit his lip and shook his head in frustration.

"Sorry, man, but the roads around here are going to be flooded whether we get a direct hit or not," Vanzinger said, stepping back. "And most of the power lines will go down, too. The governor's declared a state-wide emergency and called out the Guard. I need to report to the base, not stand here talking."

Jankowski saw Vanzinger take another step back, and he reached out and pulled the big man out of the path of a Jeep full of teenagers.

"Watch out, Tuck. A guy could get run over out here."

Vanzinger didn't notice his brush with death. He seemed too intent on getting away from Jankowski and his questions to care.

"I don't have time to drudge up old cases that have been solved and closed. It's been a dozen years since I left the force. I'm done with all that."

"Someone else has been killed," Jankowski said, raising his voice over the rumble of two motorcycles pulling into the lot. "A woman named Penelope Yates. She was interviewed during the Steele case. On Saturday her throat was slit, just like Helena Steele's had been."

Vanzinger paused, and Jankowski watched as his big hands curled into fists. Seconds ticked by as Vanzinger remained silent.

"Did someone send you here?" Vanzinger finally asked.

"If you're asking me if this is an official visit, then, no, I'm not here in an official capacity, and this isn't on the record. But I thought you might have some information we need. I wanted to talk to you before..."

"Before what?" Vanzinger demanded. "Before you haul me down to the station for questioning?"

"No, before we start going off on a wild goose chase. I'm not convinced this new homicide is even linked to the Steele case. I just want to hear more about what you and Reinhardt found out. Hear your side of the investigation."

"It's all on the books," Vanzinger said, but he didn't meet Jankowski's eyes. "There was a trial. All the evidence was released. What more can I tell you?"

Jankowski's phone vibrated again, and this time he slipped it out of his pocket and glanced at the screen. Nessa wanted to know where he was and what he was doing. He thumbed back a message.

*Missing me already?*

Without waiting for a reply, he tapped out another message.

*Running down lead on Yates case. Be back soon.*

He dropped his phone in his pocket and looked up at Vanzinger, who was staring out toward the east, jaw clenched, hands flexing and unflexing by his sides.

"I haven't had a chance to review all the files, but I know you and Reinhardt arrested the victim's husband, and he was sent down for twenty-five to life."

Jankowski paused, giving Vanzinger an opening to say something if he wanted to, but he just stared into the sky, as if made of stone, so Jankowski continued.

"It's just that some people are asking questions. They think maybe you got the wrong man. They think the real killer may still be out there."

Vanzinger didn't react, so Jankowski bulldozed ahead.

"So, what do you think, Tuck? Was the wrong man convicted? Any chance the same perp was involved in this new homicide?"

Vanzinger shook his head and glared over at Jankowski.

"I may not be on the force anymore, but I'm not a damn stoolie."

"What's that supposed to mean?"

Vanzinger just shook his head, his mouth grim.

"I hope you're not saying what I think you are." Jankowski felt the blood drain from his face. "Are you saying that you've kept quiet to protect the department? Is that why you left? Because you'd gotten mixed up in some sort of cover-up?"

"I stuck to the code, that's all. Didn't have a choice anyway."

Jankowski grabbed Vanzinger's arm again.

"Was it Reinhardt? What did he do?"

"Does it matter now? Reinhardt's dead and I'm off the force. We've paid for whatever we may have done."

Jankowski felt anger rising at the stubbornness he saw in Vanzinger's face. The man was hiding something. Knew something about the person who had killed Leo Steele's mother. But he wasn't willing to reveal what he knew without a fight.

"You are fucking kidding me, right?" Jankowski sputtered, not caring if the throng of people in the parking lot around him overheard. "Another woman has been killed, and you're thinking everything's been settled? If Helena Steele's killer is still out there I need to know. I need to stop him."

Vanzinger's shoulders sagged as he looked at Jankowski.

"I don't know who killed Helena Steele," Vanzinger said, his voice defensive. "I don't know if the man we convicted was guilty or not. All I know is that certain evidence was ignored. Some witness statements were lost. When I questioned Reinhardt, he threatened me. Said I didn't know who I was dealing with and that I'd better learn to keep my mouth shut."

"And so you just ran away? You left the force to hide out here?"

"That's not how it was." Vanzinger looked like he wanted to say more but couldn't. "I've got to go. Look around; the sky is falling."

"But what about the new homicide? What am I supposed to do?"

"I've gotta report to my guard unit before it's deployed."

Jankowski searched Vanzinger's eyes to see if the man he used to know was still in there somewhere, but his face was inscrutable.

"Come on, Tuck. You've got to deal with this."

Slowly Vanzinger nodded.

"Yeah, maybe you're right. I always figured the past would come back to haunt me eventually. Looks like the ghosts I thought were buried a long time ago are calling me back to Willow Bay."

"So, you'll come back and answer our questions? Help us figure out what's going on?"

"Yeah, after the storm I'll come home. I'll clean up my mess."

Vanzinger smiled then for the first time as if a weight had been lifted off his shoulders. He walked toward the truck stop, then stopped and called back to Jankowski.

"If you need rescuing during the storm, you know who to call!"

Jankowski climbed into the Charger. As he pulled out of the lot, he wondered what he should tell Nessa when he got back. If she found out he was hiding information again, he really would need rescuing.

# CHAPTER THIRTY

Doc backed the big van out of the garage and onto the street. Rain streamed through the canopy of cypress trees, causing the heavy Spanish moss to sway and sag above him as he drove out of Grand Isles and headed toward downtown. Once he was on the open road he took out his cell phone, dialed Ace's number, and waited, the panic rising again in his chest.

"What's up, Doc?"

A wave of relief washed over him as the gruff voice sounded in his ear. Ace would know what to do. He would fix everything, just like he'd always done before.

"I'm worried, Ace."

"You're always worried, Doc." Ace's voice held an edge of irritation. "What's happened now?"

"That guy Barker showed up at my house yesterday."

"Barker? What the hell did *he* want?"

Doc fumed at Barker's audacity. The big man had dared to go to *his* house and accost *his* wife with invasive, personal questions about their past.

"He talked to Terri. Asked her questions about the community health center. Luckily I got home before he could do too much damage."

"What do you mean by *too much* damage? Did he say something that made Terri suspicious? Is she asking questions now, too?"

Doc didn't like the menacing tone in Ace's voice. Ace could be paranoid. If he thought Terri was a liability, it would be dangerous.

"Of course not. She trusts me completely...always has."

Doc felt his pulse quicken at the lie. A shiver rippled through him as he imagined Ace discovering the truth about Terri's accident. He needed to say something that would steer Ace's attention toward someone other than Terri.

"Eden Winthrop also came nosing around yesterday."

Ace cursed, huffing into the phone, his patience wearing thin.

"Well, what did she want? More questions about the girl?"

Doc paused, distracted by Ace's reference to Kara Stanislaus as *the girl*. Ace had always refused to speak the names of the girls he'd collected, calling them only by the number he'd assigned to them.

Doc was reminded again how paranoid Ace was about getting caught. If he thought anyone might overhear them...

"Doc, you still there? What did the Winthrop woman want?"

"I assume she wanted to ask about...about Kara...again, but I'm not sure. Terri and I weren't home. The security camera at the front door picked her up. That's how I knew she'd been here."

Ace was silent. When he spoke again, his voice was stone cold.

"Did Terri ask why Eden Winthrop was there?"

Doc's heart skipped a beat at the words.

"No, she didn't even realize the bitch stopped by," Doc quickly assured Ace. "She never checks the security feed."

"Okay, then there's nothing to worry about," Ace said, his voice back to normal. "I'll take care of Eden Winthrop."

But after Ace had disconnected the call without saying goodbye, Doc was uneasy. He replayed the conversation in his mind.

*He's worried about Terri. He thinks she suspects something.*

Of course, Terri had no idea about the covert mission he and Ace had started over a decade before. She had no clue that Ace collected girls, and that Doc was his wingman. Doc had always tried to protect Terri from that part of his life.

A small, cold voice in the back of his head asked the question he tried never to think about.

*What if her memory comes back? What if she remembers the accident?*

Doc turned into the clinic's parking lot and turned off the engine. Rain battered against the van, beating out a frantic rhythm on the windshield, but he stared into the downpour with unseeing eyes, his mind dragging him back to the night Terri fell.

*Doc thought the house was empty. Terri was working the second shift at Willow Bay General Hospital and wouldn't be home until after eleven o'clock. No need to keep his voice down as he called Ace to ask for an update.*

*Although Natalie Lorenzo's murder at the beginning of May had generated only a few articles on page four of the Willow Bay Gazette, the story of Helena Steele's murder had been picked up as a headline in all the local news outlets.*

*Doc had seen Helena's picture on the front page of the Gazette that morning, and she'd stared out at him from Channel Ten's nightly newscast that evening. Doc was beginning to worry that Ace may have made a mistake.*

*He'd killed Helena Steele to shut her up, but her death was now garnering the attention of the whole community. The police and the reporters were asking questions, interviewing practically everyone in town, and there was no telling what they may find.*

*"I'm getting worried," Doc said as soon as Ace picked up. "The news is everywhere. What if someone saw something? What is someone talks?"*

*"Calm down, Doc. No one saw anything, and the husband's going down for the homicide. I've made sure of that."*

*"How can you be sure they'll charge her husband?"*

"Trust me. It's all going to work out just the way we planned."

Doc felt the tension begin to fade away. Ace had that effect on him. He could always make things right, no matter how bad Doc had screwed up. A rush of remorse and gratitude filled Doc's chest.

"I'm sorry, Ace. I know I caused all this. If I'd talked to you before killing Natalie you would have taken care of it. You could have figured out some other way, and neither of us would have blood on our hands. I should have trusted you."

"Yeah, you should have." Ace didn't sound mad. "But what's done is done. Now we just need to lay low until hubby is charged."

"You really think Ken Steele will be arrested? Won't they need evidence to convict him?"

"They'll find what they need to find. As I said, I'm handling it."

Doc nodded into the quiet room, trying to reassure himself that Ace was right. Then another question popped into his head.

"But what about Penelope Yates? What if Natalie told her more than what she let on? What if she knows the whole story and Helena's murder scares her into coming forward?"

"I've already talked to that crazy bitch. Told her I'd get her locked back up in the psych ward if she tried to stir up any trouble. With her mental history, no one would believe her anyway."

"But what if she raises suspicions? Can we afford the risk?"

There was silence at the other end of the line, and Doc wondered if his nagging and worrying had gone too far.

"Penelope Yates won't be a problem, and besides, we can't risk another homicide now. One more woman ends up dead in Willow Bay and the feds will be crawling all over. Best to bide our time."

A creak of the stairs made the hairs on the back of Doc's neck stand up. He looked over his shoulder and saw a shadow move.

"I've got to go, Ace. I'll call you back."

He hung up without waiting for a reply and charged out to the landing. Terri stood at the top of the stairs, her dark eyes huge in her ashen face.

*"What did you hear, Terri?"*

*Adrenaline pumped through Doc, turning his words into a hoarse scream as he stared into Terri's frightened eyes. His face burned red with anger and fear as he reached for her.*

*He had to make her understand. Had to keep her from running out.*

*Terri flinched and screamed in terror. She jumped back, frantic to get away, misjudging her distance from the top step. As she toppled backward Doc covered his eyes, not wanting to see her fall. He heard a terrible crack as Terri came down hard on the mahogany banister, the force of her fall propelling her up and over.*

*Her head landed with a final thud on the living room's hardwood floor, and then all was still.*

*"Terri!" Doc called out.*

*His anger had disappeared over the banister as quickly as Terri had, and he hurried down the stairs and hovered next to her sprawled body.*

*"Terri, can you hear me?"*

*Terri didn't respond, but Doc could see the slight in and out movement of her chest that meant she was still alive.*

*He thudded back upstairs to pick up his phone where he'd dropped it. One tap and he'd be on the phone to 911. An ambulance would come to save her. She might make it.*

*Doc hesitated. What if Terri had heard everything he'd said to Ace? What if she woke up and told the police? What if she decided to leave him?*

*Doc descended the stairs slowly, trying to think through the possibilities. What should he do? Could he really let Terri die? He knelt beside her and smoothed back a dark strand of hair from her face.*

*She was the only person he'd ever loved. The only one who had truly loved him back. No matter what happened he had to save her. He had to protect her. And if she survived, he promised himself he would never look at another woman again. If he didn't lose her, he would spend his life making it up to her. She would be his everything.*

*With a firm finger, he pressed 911.*

Doc blinked into the glare of oncoming headlights. A car approached, and then passed the clinic without turning in.

It was time to go. No use sitting there stewing on the things that couldn't be changed. He'd been lucky really.

While Terri had suffered a thoracic spinal cord injury, which had left her in a wheelchair, as well as a traumatic brain injury, which had taken away large chunks of her memory, including the events surrounding her accident, she had survived.

She was still with him, and their marriage was stronger than ever.

In a way, her accident had been a blessing. It had been a wake-up call. He'd kept his promise. No more womanizing. No more playing away. Of course, Ace hadn't liked it. He wasn't able to hunt the way he wanted without Doc and his drugs. But they'd found a compromise.

Doc would supply Ace with a certain kind of woman whenever an opportunity presented itself. What Ace did with those women was not Doc's concern.

Why should he care as long as Ace made sure the women never came back to tell tales?

All he had to worry about was Terri.

The other women were not his responsibility. They lived degenerate lives and wasted the healthy bodies they had been blessed with.

They didn't appreciate the independence that Terri no longer enjoyed. He felt no pity for the eight women he'd turned over to Ace.

*They deserved what they got.*

But he did worry about Terri. Sometimes he suspected her memory may be coming back. She'd give him a strange look, almost as if she were afraid of him, which was ridiculous.

Melinda Woodhall

If only he could tell her that everything he'd done had been to protect her and their marriage.

She was the only one he'd ever loved. He would do anything, had even killed, to protect her, and he wouldn't hesitate to do so again if needed.

# CHAPTER THIRTY-ONE

E den heard a television blaring inside the house as she once again stood on the Bellows' front porch. Veronica Lee was warning residents that strong winds, heavy rain, and local flooding should be expected for the next twelve to twenty-four hours as the hurricane plowed through the Gulf of Mexico, heading straight for the Florida coast. The eye of the storm was projected to make landfall just north of Willow Bay.

Eden knocked twice and waited. The noise from the television abruptly stopped, and the blinds moved at the big bay window. A woman's face looked out at Eden, then disappeared.

"Mrs. Bellows? It's Eden Winthrop. I need to speak to you."

Eden waited, hoping to hear the rattling of the door chain, but there was only silence from the big house.

"Please, Mrs. Bellows, a girl is missing...and the hurricane is coming. I need your help."

Finally, the door swung open. Terri Bellows looked up from her wheelchair, cheeks flushed and eyes cautious.

"I'm sorry to be a pest," Eden said, inching her way past Terri and into the foyer. "But I'm getting a little desperate."

"No problem, Ms. Winthrop." Terri closed the door behind Eden. "It's just that my husband told me not to let anyone in when he's gone...but I'm sure he didn't mean you."

Eden wondered why Bellows didn't want his wife to let anyone into the house. Her work with abused women at the Mercy Harbor Foundation had taught her that a man who claimed to be protecting a woman by isolating her, was usually trying to control her.

*Is Bellows an abusive husband, or does he have something else to hide?*

"Well, I do appreciate it," Eden said, pasting on a smile. "You see, a young woman from Hope House has gone missing, and I'm hoping your husband may know where she is."

A confused frown appeared on Terri's face.

"Is it the girl he saved? The one that overdosed?"

"Yes, she's the one," Eden agreed. "Her name is Kara Stanislaus, and she's been gone for over forty-eight hours now. With the storm coming I'm getting pretty worried."

"And you think Doc knows where she could have gone?"

"Doc?" Eden blinked, then smiled. "Oh, is that what you call your husband?"

"Yes, all his friends call him Doc. I think the nickname started even before he was a real doctor, back when he was just a medic in the air force."

Terri wheeled into the living room, motioning for Eden to join her. She came to a stop under a framed photo on the wall.

"There he is in his uniform." She smiled up at the picture. "He was so young and handsome. I wished I'd gotten the chance to know him then. He served overseas you know, at an Air Force base in Germany. That's where he met Ace."

"Who's Ace?" Eden asked, studying the picture of the young Bellows, dressed in a dark blue uniform and service cap.

"Ace is the reason Doc moved here. They met in the military and just hit it off. Once Doc was discharged, he came back to Willow Bay to visit Ace. Then after his residency, he'd wanted to move back here and open up his practice. He says he fell in love with the town, but I think he just wanted to be near his buddy."

A gust of wind rattled the window next to them and Eden flinched. The storm was near. She needed to find Kara.

"It sounds like Doc enjoys helping people, so I'm hoping he can help me find Kara. Or maybe you've seen her? She was at the hospital on Saturday around the same time you were there. Then she just disappeared."

Terri looked blank. Once again the frown appeared.

"I wasn't at the hospital on Saturday. In fact, I didn't leave the house all day. Doc was pretty busy."

Terri seemed sad as she remembered. Then her face lit up.

"But he did find time to take me for a drive Sunday afternoon. We even stopped for lunch at that new café on the corner of Hyacinth and Main. Their butternut squash soup was absolutely delicious."

Eden stared at the woman in dismay, not sure if she understood the seriousness of the situation.

"Mrs. Bellows?"

"Please, call me Terri. And may I call you Eden?"

"Yes, of course. But I really need to ask-"

"You know I've read all about you and the River Girls killer in the paper. I do admire you." Terri's words spilled out in a nervous rush. "You must have been very brave to have saved those girls."

"Thank you, I just did what any concerned citizen would-"

"I was so proud when Doc told me he was going to volunteer at Hope House."

Terri didn't seem to notice that Eden had spoken.

"He does love working with the girls there. He should be home soon, you know."

Eden considered Terri's nervous eyes and the way her hands kept fidgeting with the skirt of her white dress.

The woman was definitely scared of something, or someone.

"Doc wanted to check on the clinic before the hurricane hits. He's so considerate. Always thinking of others."

Terri suddenly wheeled her chair around.

"I just remembered I was clearing lunch off the table when you knocked."

"Oh, well, let me help you. Is it this way?"

Eden followed Terri down the hall, furtively looking into each room as they passed.

The dining room table had been set for lunch. One plate held a half-eaten sandwich and a few potato chips.

"Doc didn't finish his food." Terri tutted as she wheeled toward the plate. "He hasn't had his usual appetite lately."

"I'll get that for you."

Eden scurried around and picked up the plate with one hand, then used the other to collect the napkin and glass next to it. She carried the dishes into the big kitchen, putting the plate into the sink. Terry pushed through the door behind her just as Eden wrapped the napkin around the glass and dropped it into her purse

"So, you worked at the old community health center with Doc?"

Eden turned to face Terri.

"Did you know either Natalie Lorenzo or Helena Steele?"

Terri looked down at her lap, fingers still twisting her dress.

"I'd met Helena Steele."

She spoke softly, not looking up.

"But I didn't really know her. She was...gone soon after I started volunteering there. It was very sad for everyone involved."

"What about Natalie Lorenzo. Did you meet her, too?"

A pained expression passed over Terri's face. She clutched at her head and rocked back and forth. Eden crossed to her and put a soft hand on her arm. Her skin was cold and clammy, and she was shaking like a leaf.

"Are you okay, Terri? Do you need an ambulance?"

"No, it's just one of my episodes," Terri managed to say, still holding her head. "I had a TBI...a traumatic brain injury...some years ago. Sometimes it acts up. I think I need to rest now."

"Yes, that's a good idea," Eden said, suddenly eager to leave. "I'll come back later when Doc is home. Good luck with the storm."

\* \* \*

Pat Monahan's desk was empty as Eden passed, and she assumed the paralegal must have gone home to secure her house and collect her pug, Tinkerbell, before evacuating further inland.

Leo sat with his legs propped on the desk, talking into the phone. He smiled when he saw Eden enter, and dropped his legs to the floor.

"Gotta go, Barker. A very welcome visitor just stopped by."

He dropped the phone on the desk and rose to pull Eden to him. She inhaled the heady scent of his cologne and allowed herself to lean against his chest for a few, blissful minutes. Then she pushed back and looked into his tired eyes.

"I have something for you."

Leo raised an eyebrow and produced a wicked smile.

"Is it what I hope it is?" he teased, taking her hands in his and trying to pull her back toward him. "After all, we are all alone here."

"Stop messing around, Leo," she said but softened the words with a smile. "This is important."

Eden reached into her purse and pulled out the glass she'd wrapped in the napkin. She set it carefully on the desk in front of Leo, watching his handsome features settle into a puzzled frown.

"I stopped by Dr. Bellows' house and talked with his wife," Eden said, hoping he wouldn't be irritated that she'd gone on her own. "Although Terri Bellows didn't share any useful information, I did manage to get this."

Leo reached for the glass, but Eden put out a hand to stop him.

"Don't touch it, Leo. Dr. Bellows' fingerprints should be on that glass. If we give it to Nessa, maybe she can compare it against the prints they found at Natalie Lorenzo's crime scene."

Leo bent to stare at the glass, then smiled up at Eden.

"I like the way you think."

Eden returned the smile, already dialing Nessa's number.

# CHAPTER THIRTY-TWO

L eo almost missed Nessa as she ran past him in the street. The hood of her yellow rain slicker had been pulled up, hiding her trademark red curls and disguising her as just another citizen trying to escape the city before all hell broke loose. But at the last minute she glanced up, and Leo caught a glimpse of pale blue eyes puffy with exhaustion.

"Nessa? Hey, wait up!"

Rain sluiced down the bright yellow PVC jacket as Nessa whirled around and squinted through the rain. Leo huddled under a large, black umbrella, his expensive shoes and the pants of his custom-made suit drenched.

"Leo? What the hell are you doing out here in this weather? You aren't thinking to ride out the storm in town, are you?"

Her voice blew away in a gust of wind and Leo motioned that he would follow her into the parking garage.

Once they were both safely under the heavy concrete roof of the garage, Nessa pushed back her hood and watched Leo close his umbrella. She turned tired eyes up to him, not bothering to hide her impatience.

"Okay, so what's more important than a natural disaster?"

"I need your help, Nessa."

Leo lifted up a plastic bag he'd tucked under his arm.

"I've obtained an item that belongs to Dr. Bellows. His fingerprints are clearly on it, and I want you to compare them to the prints found at the Natalie Lorenzo crime scene."

Nessa's eyes suddenly looked less tired, and Leo thought he saw a flash of interest. But then she shook her head in frustration.

"We can't test something that hasn't come into our possession through the proper channels, Leo. You know that."

She looked around the dark garage as if worried someone might be lurking in the shadows listening. She lowered her voice.

"And the object, whatever it is, obviously hasn't been protected through a documented chain of custody. Even if I wanted to test it, it wouldn't stand up in court."

"I don't give a damn about it standing up in court right now," Leo said, not caring who might hear. "I just want to know who killed Natalie Lorenzo, and if that person also killed my mother. I have a right to know."

Nessa's eyes softened but again she shook her head.

"The whole city is closing up to brace for the hurricane. It's essential personnel only right now, so I'm not even sure Alma or her team would be able to help."

Leo let out a frustrated breath, looking out at the sheets of rain around them with angry eyes.

"As soon as the storm passes I'll think of a way to get the item tested," Nessa said, although she didn't sound confident.

"I can't wait anymore, Nessa. I've waited twelve years already. Please, at least ask Alma if she'll stay and compare the prints."

When Nessa still looked unsure, Leo decided he had no choice but to pull out his secret weapon.

"Please, Nessa, have you forgotten so soon that I risked my life to save you?" Leo arranged his features into a forlorn expression. "Can you really refuse me a simple request to compare these prints?"

Nessa rolled her eyes and crossed her arms over her chest.

"You're really gonna use the old guilt trip on me?"

"You owe me, Nessa. Besides, if Adrian Bellows is linked to Natalie's murder, that gives you a possible motive for him killing Penelope Yates. Don't you want to know if he's a killer?"

Nessa sighed and reached for the plastic bag in Leo's hands.

"Do I dare ask how you got this?"

Nessa peeked in the bag but didn't reach in to touch the glass.

"Let's just say a mutual friend of ours got it right off the saintly doctor's dining room table."

Nessa looked impressed, then stuck the bag under her raincoat and pulled her hood back up. But before she turned to go, she stopped and stared at Leo.

"Was Pete Barker involved in obtaining this?"

"No, Barker didn't take this. But he is working with me, and he does know we have it. Why?"

"Barker doesn't need to get in any more trouble, Leo. He's still recovering from his heart attack, and..."

Nessa's voice trailed off as if she had been about to say something she shouldn't say.

"And what, Nessa? Is there something about Barker I need to know?"

"Well, he tries to hide it, but he's still a mess over losing his wife to cancer a few years back. He really went off the deep end when it happened, and then after Taylor just up and ran off...well, it really tore him up."

"Who's Taylor?" Leo asked, realizing he'd never talked to Barker about his family, and knew next to nothing about the retired detective's personal life.

"She's his daughter."

"He never mentioned having a daughter. Does she live in town?"

"That's the problem. Barker doesn't know where she lives. Taylor took off after her mother died, and Barker seems to think she blames him for her mother's death."

"Ouch. That must hurt. Might even explain his heart attack."

Leo knew the excruciating pain of losing a parent, and he'd suffered through years of people blaming his father for his mother's death. Like Barker, he'd lived through the agony of losing his whole family. Empathy for Barker rushed through him.

*Barker's helping me track down the man who ruined my life when his own life has just been shattered. And he's never said a word.*

"It must be hard for him not to know where his daughter is."

Leo was reminded of Kara Stanislaus and her family. They too would be worrying and waiting for a girl that may never return.

"How old is Taylor?"

"She's probably in her early twenties by now," Nessa said, cocking her head. "I'm pretty sure she'd just turned eighteen when Caroline, Barker's wife, got sick. The cancer took her within a year of diagnosis, the poor thing."

Nessa put a hand on Leo's arm and squeezed.

"Just take it easy on him, Leo. He may act tough, but he's really a softie. And he means a lot to me."

Leo nodded, glad that Barker had a loyal friend in his corner.

A loud crack startled them as a branch from the ancient elm tree outside the garage splintered onto the pavement. Nessa looked at the gnarled branch with wide eyes.

"I better get going on this." She held up the plastic bag. "I guess the sandbags will have to wait a little longer. Jerry won't be happy."

"Thanks, Nessa. I really appreciate it."

"I'll get this to Alma...if she's still here."

"If the prints come back showing Dr. Bellows was at the scene, will you be able to get a warrant to search his house and vehicle?"

Leo asked, impatient to get Bellows off the street. "And will you bring him in for official questioning?"

Nessa bit her lip and shrugged her shoulders. The dejected look on her face didn't give Leo much Hope.

"The chief's determined to do everything by the book now, so it may not be easy to convince him that this evidence is viable, but I'll do what I can."

"I just hope that's enough," Leo murmured as Nessa ran back toward the police station.

He kept his worried eyes trained on her yellow rain slicker until it disappeared into the torrential downpour.

# CHAPTER THIRTY-THREE

Alma Garcia had no intention of evacuating her crime scene lab during the hurricane, or so it seemed to Nessa as she walked into the cold, sterile room and looked around. The long, white counter on the far wall held a collection of neatly arranged packages. Alma stood over the counter, a boning knife in one gloved hand, as Nessa approached, her eyes drawn to the blade.

"Were you able to confirm that's the murder weapon?"

Alma nodded, and Nessa watched the five-inch blade disappear into a big paper evidence bag. She blinked away the images that came to mind: the gruesome, gaping neck wound, the blood-splattered walls, the dead, gray eyes staring at her in silent accusation. It seemed surreal that the knife, now safely wrapped and sealed, had been used to slit a woman's throat only the day before.

"Any surprises or smoking guns in all this stuff?"

"The only surprise is how little the evidence is revealing so far," Alma said, her forehead furrowing in frustration. "No fingerprints, hair, or viable DNA samples so far. It even appears as if the perp had some type of cover over his shoes."

"He left nothing behind, and wore protective booties?" Nessa found herself frowning along with Alma. "Sounds like our killer was very careful. Maybe too careful to be a civilian."

Alma glanced up at Nessa and raised her eyebrows.

"You think someone in law enforcement had something to do with this homicide?"

Alma didn't sound as shocked by the theory as she might have been before Detective Reinhardt had been outed as a dirty cop. He'd committed a variety of crimes, including the attempted murder of a fellow detective. Nessa had been a victim of Reinhardt's depravity, and everyone on the force had lost something that would be very hard to get back: the trust of their fellow officers and the respect of the community.

"Well, it's definitely someone who knows how to cover his tracks," Nessa said, not wanting to sound paranoid.

*Can't let people think I'm crying dirty cop just because I got shot.*

Alma picked up another package, then looked over at Nessa.

"Was there something else, Nessa? Is that something for me?"

Alma nodded at the plastic bag under Nessa's arm.

"Oh, uh...yes," Nessa said, holding out the bag to Alma. "I'm hoping you can do me a favor and see if you can get any prints off this glass."

Alma stared at Nessa.

"Where did you get that?"

She didn't reach out to take the bag.

"I got it from a trusted source," Nessa said, still holding out the bag. "Someone who's trying to track down Natalie Lorenzo's killer."

"Someone outside the department, I'm guessing?"

Nessa nodded and laid the bag on the counter.

"I know anything you find won't hold up in court, but it could help guide us in the right direction. We think Natalie's killer may have also killed Penelope Yates."

Alma considered Nessa's words, then cocked her head.

"Vinny Lorenzo's prints were collected at Natalie Lorenzo's crime scene. But now we know he was there trying to find his mother. He wasn't the one who killed her, right?"

Nessa nodded, not sure where Alma was heading.

"Well, if the prints on this glass match other prints from the Lorenzo scene, it won't necessarily prove that the person who matches the prints is the perp, either."

Nessa scratched her head, wondering if the lack of sleep was finally proving too much. She took a deep breath and tried again.

"I'm not saying this proves anything, Alma. And the results won't be used to convict anyone. It's just a hunch anyway, but I'd hate to ignore the hunch and then find another dead body."

"So, whose prints are these?"

Alma finally picked up the plastic bag and peered inside.

"This isn't from someone in the department, is it?"

"No, it isn't. I promise. The prints on the glass belong to a doctor at the community health center where Natalie visited before she was killed. If the prints don't match, we can save some wasted time. If they do match, then we can look into him more closely."

Alma sighed and shook her head.

"Okay, I'll do it, but if Chief Kramer finds out we'll both end up on his shit list."

"I hear you, Alma. I'll go by Kramer's office and fill him in after I leave here. I think I can persuade him to let you test it so long as we don't try to submit it as evidence."

Alma looked doubtful, but she just nodded and reached for the next evidence bag in the pile. She read the label, then reached in and pulled out a small USB memory stick

"You might want to listen to this before you leave, Nessa."

"What's on it? Files from Penelope's computer?"

"No, actually. This is from the emergency response team. They were kind enough to download the 911 call on this memory stick so that we can keep a copy with the rest of the evidence."

"How sweet," Nessa said, fighting back the unease that gripped her at the thought of listening to Penelope's murder.

Nessa watched as Alma crossed to the computer and inserted the stick in the USB slot. She moved the mouse and clicked. The emergency operator's voice sounded out clear and loud.

*"You've reached 911. What's your emergency?"*

The response was a frantic rustling, followed by an inaudible whisper and a raspy laugh. Then more rustling and the sound of the phone falling. Again, the operator tried.

*"This is 911. Are you calling to report an emergency?"*

Now the sounds of a muffled struggle could be heard: gasps, a terrible gurgling, followed by a heavy thud. Silence, then the soft padding of footsteps before the call was disconnected.

Nessa turned to Alma.

"Did you hear the whisper? Could you understand what he said?"

Alma shook her head and began moving the mouse around and typing on her keyboard.

"No, I couldn't really hear it, but I've got a program that will remove the background noise and enhance the audio."

After a few more minutes of clicking and typing, Alma looked up.

"Okay, let's try it again."

This time the whispered words were clear enough to understand, and they raised goosebumps all along Nessa's arms.

*"Remember me?"*

Alma stared at Nessa in horrified silence.

"It was someone she knew," Alma said in a low voice.

"Someone she wasn't expecting to see or hasn't seen in a while."

"Could be someone like that doctor," Alma suggested, looking at the plastic bag that held the glass. "Someone she worked with twelve years ago."

Nessa nodded slowly, then headed toward the door. She needed to find Chief Kramer and get his buy-in. She had a feeling she was going to need a warrant before the day was through.

* * *

The lobby of the police station was buzzing with activity as Nessa hurried toward Chief Kramer's office. All essential duty personnel had been instructed to prepare for a direct hit.

The hurricane had gained strength, with reported sustained winds of up to one hundred and thirty miles an hour, and no one was sure exactly where it would make landfall.

The city's hotline had already taken a dozen calls from citizens reporting downed trees and flooded streets, but the worst was yet to come. Nessa charged down the hall toward the executive offices, then stopped short when she saw that the lights were off in the corner office Chief Kramer had occupied ever since Nessa had joined the force. He was usually there when she arrived in the morning, and still there when she left at night.

*Only a natural disaster can get Kramer out of the office before five.*

She spun around and made her way back to her desk, feeling deflated and fatigued. The picture of Cole and Cooper on her desk brought the sting of tears to her eyes.

*The poor kids are probably scared to death.*

Impulsively she picked up the phone and called home, resolved to face Jerry's wrath so that she could reassure the boys that everything would be okay.

"Hi, Mom!" Cooper's high-pitched greeting sounded far away. "Are you in the hurricane?"

"No, honey, I'm still at the station." Nessa couldn't help smiling. "And I'm safe."

She heard scuffling in the background and then Cole's voice.

"Mom? When are you coming home? I thought you were gonna bring sandbags. Dad's madder than a-"

"I get the idea, Cole. Just put your daddy on the phone."

"He's outside putting boards on the windows."

218

"Well, once he comes back inside you tell him I called and that I'm going to bring those sandbags home real soon."

"Okay, mom. I gotta go. I've almost reached the next level."

"See you soon, honey. Love you."

But Cole was already gone. Nessa stared at the phone, stuffed it into her purse, and slung the purse over her shoulder.

*Time to get those stupid sandbags.*

She stomped out to the lobby and was pleased to see Mayor Hadley, Chief Kramer, and several of the other town leaders gathered by the front doors. By the way they were laughing and slapping each other on the back, Nessa would have thought they were heading out to a Friday night football game instead of a press briefing about the big, bad hurricane that was pounding on the door of their little town.

*Little town, little town, let me come in.*

Nessa looked around at the brick walls inside the lobby and swallowed hard, hoping the foundation of the building was made of something stronger, preferably steel and concrete.

*Otherwise, the storm just might blow this old house down.*

She hovered just behind Kramer, waiting for a break in the conversation so that she could ask him about the fingerprints, and about questioning Dr. Adrian Bellows. But one of the old men in the group kept talking and going on about the old days.

With a sinking sensation, she realized the old man was the previous medical examiner, Archie Faraday. She was tempted to creep away, but Archie looked over Kramer's shoulder and caught her eye. He produced a lukewarm smile and kept talking.

*Oh no, you don't ignore me, you old windbag.*

Nessa tapped Kramer firmly on the shoulder, and he looked around, then turned to face Nessa.

"Everything okay, Detective Ainsley?"

He kept his deep voice low, perhaps reluctant for any nearby reporters to get a scoop.

"Are you and Jankowski making progress on the Yates case?"

"Actually, we do have a hot lead we want to follow up on right away, but I need your okay since it's not strictly by the book."

Nessa noticed Archie Faraday straining to listen, and she purposely lowered her voice. Kramer leaned in, stooping over to listen intently as she explained the situation with the glass, the fingerprints, and her suspicion that Bellows might be involved with the Lorenzo murder as well as the Yates homicide.

"Isn't that the same man you brought to my attention on Saturday?" Kramer asked in surprise. "Now you're saying you think he's killed two women?"

Faraday moved closer, his eyes bright with curiosity.

"I don't mean to eavesdrop, but are you saying you've identified a suspect in the recent murder?"

Kramer looked over at Faraday with irritation, but he nodded and turned back to Nessa with grim eyes.

"Check the prints. If they come back matching, bring him in."

Relief flooded through Nessa and she spun on her heel, eager to give Alma the good news. But she'd have to call her from the car. She needed to see if the city had any more sandbags available. It might already be too late.

The rain pelted her as she pushed through the lobby door, and before it could close behind her she heard a raspy laugh that turned her blood to ice. She paused, holding the door open, letting in a swirling gust of wind and rain, and looked back at the crowded lobby.

A sea of familiar faces looked back, their attention drawn to the open door and the fury of the wind.

"Sorry," she called out, taking one last look around the big room. "Y'all stay safe now."

As the door swung shut behind her, Nessa shook her head and rubbed her eyes, trying to convince herself she was hearing things.

*You're just tired, Nessa. You know all those folks; no one there is a killer.*

# CHAPTER THIRTY-FOUR

oc knew something was wrong as soon as he pulled into the driveway. All the blinds in the house were drawn, even the ones upstairs. He couldn't remember closing them when he'd left after lunch, and Terri couldn't have closed them on her own.

Not wanting to waste time pulling into the garage, Doc brought the van to a jerking halt on the driveway and jumped out, oblivious to the rain and wind that pelted him as he ran to the front door. He grabbed the doorknob and twisted, expecting it to be locked, but it turned smoothly in his hand, causing his heart to drop.

*This is all wrong. Terri would never leave the door unlocked.*

Doc stepped into the hall, listening for the sound of Terri's wheelchair rolling toward him over the hardwood floor, but only an eerie silence greeted him.

"Terri?"

A gentle creak on the stairs lifted the hair on the back of his neck. Someone was in the house. Someone that wasn't in a wheelchair.

"Who's there?"

The house was quiet. Perhaps the sound on the stairs was just the big house reacting to the raging wind outside.

Doc moved further into the hall and looked over into Terri's office. He breathed a sigh of relief. Terri's wheelchair sat facing the desk. Her head was slumped, and it looked like she was wearing some sort of plastic hood. Had she gone out in the rain?

"Terry, honey? You okay?"

He walked in to stand beside the desk and looked down at his wife. A silent scream built and stuck in his throat. He stared in horror at Terri's open, staring eyes, the pupils grotesquely dilated behind the clear plastic bag. He automatically reached out and put a shaking hand on her wrist. The skin was cold to the touch. No pulse, no life moved under the alabaster skin.

"I'm sorry, Doc. I know how much you loved her."

The scream finally burst forth as Doc spun around to face Ace, who wore blue hooded crime scene coveralls and gloves. Protective shoe covers completed his outfit.

"But there are too many people asking questions, so I had to make the tough call. It's time to abort the mission."

Doc dropped his eyes to see what Ace was holding; he shook his head and stepped back when he saw the gun. It was the little Ruger handgun he kept under the bed. Terry had hated it, but he'd insisted. They needed to protect themselves from the bad guys, didn't they?

"Ace, what have you...done? Why would you hurt Terri?"

"It's nothing personal, Doc."

Ace stepped closer, holding the gun higher.

"But it's time to erase the evidence. Time to tie up loose ends. Terri was a potential risk to my freedom. So are you."

Doc's knees buckled and he leaned against the desk for support. He bowed his head, trying to catch his breath, and saw that a blank sheet of notebook paper had been placed on the desk in front of Terri. A ballpoint pen sat neatly beside it.

Ace followed Doc's gaze and smiled.

"You know what that is?"

Doc didn't respond, he just stared mutely at the blank paper, shock setting in, his limbs starting to shake.

"That's going to be your suicide note."

Doc's legs finally gave out and he collapsed at Terri's feet, which had remained undisturbed on the padded footrest during the attack. He laid his head in Terri's lap and pulled her limp hand to him, wanting to feel her hand in his hair. Wanting to feel her comforting him and telling him that everything was going to be okay.

He closed his eyes when he saw that Terri's fingernails were torn and coated with blood from her desperate struggle to remove the bag.

"You have any last words you want me to add in there?"

A raspy laugh sounded over Doc's head and for a minute he let himself imagine this was all a bad joke. That Terri would sit up and rip the bag from her head, and Ace would pound him on the back and tell him to stop freaking out.

"Okay, then I'll just add in what I think you'd want to say."

A conspiratorial tone entered Ace's voice.

"You know, how you couldn't live with what you've done. How you took Terri with you so she wouldn't be alone. By the time I'm done the folks around here will think you're some kind of martyr."

Doc heard Ace's words as he burrowed further into Terri's lap, but didn't lift his head.

*This isn't real. It's just a bad dream. I'm going to wake up and Terri will be fine, and everything will be back to the way it was before.*

A strong hand settled around Doc's hand, forcing it around the hard metal grip of the gun. It felt strange to be holding the gun in his left hand.

"Doc, I just want to say I appreciate everything you've done."

A somber tone had entered Ace's voice.

"You've been a good partner. I've enjoyed our mission."

The words filtered through to Doc's brain, but he didn't try to understand them. He didn't want to think about Ace and his mission. He didn't want to think about the girls he'd taken, or what Ace might have done with them. The girls weren't his responsibility. Only Terri was. She was the only one that had mattered. And now she was gone.

A slow rage began to build inside Doc at the injustice of it all. He'd only been trying to protect Terri. He hadn't wanted to kill anyone. He hadn't wanted to kill Natalie. He hadn't wanted Helena Steele to die.

But what else could he have done? They were going to tell everyone. They were going to ruin everything. He'd had no choice but to stop them.

"I wish there was some other way, but there's not."

Doc tried to pull his hand back, but Ace was close behind him, holding him down, forcing the gun up.

"Don't make me do this the hard way, Doc. Be a man about it."

The hard metal of the gun rested against Doc's left temple, and he squeezed his eyes shut even tighter.

*Why resist? Without Terri, nothing matters anyway.*

Ace tightened his finger on the trigger, and Doc's world exploded into darkness.

# CHAPTER THIRTY-FIVE

**B**lood seemed to be everywhere. It coated the front of Terri's white dress, dripped from the plastic bag, and pooled on the desk. Ace had even felt a light spray of back spatter sting his eyes, which were the only part of his body not covered by the protective gear. He blinked and squeezed his eyes shut until the stinging had subsided.

When Ace looked around again he saw bright red streaks had splashed across the paper he'd hoped to use for the suicide note. Reaching out a bloody glove, he opened one of the desk drawers and pulled out a fresh sheet of paper and another pen. He hesitated, then determined the desk was too messy to use. The kitchen table would be a better idea.

But he didn't have long. The detectives would come by soon wanting to question Doc, and Ace needed to be gone before they arrived. With any luck, they would find the bodies, read the note, and close a handful of open cases all in one afternoon. Everyone would win, and then Ace could decide what he was going to do next.

*But first things first. I gotta check the scene. Can't afford any mistakes.*

He studied the position of Doc's body, which was splayed awkwardly on the floor, having been propelled sideways by the force of the 9mm bullet. Ace was glad to see that the Ruger was still clutched in Doc's hand. The firearm was registered in Doc's name, and Ace knew that once they tested Doc's arm for gunshot residue they would have to conclude that only Doc could have pulled the trigger.

*And the note will be the final touch. No way they can see all this and not call it a murder-suicide. It'll be open and shut, case closed.*

Ace took a step toward the kitchen, then stopped when he saw that his protective shoe cover had left a bloody smear on the floor where he'd been standing. He surveyed the rest of his body and realized that he needed to remove all traces of blood before moving through the house. Otherwise, he might leave behind evidence that someone else had been in the house when Doc and Terri had died.

The shoe covers slipped off easily, but the blue coverall was harder to remove. After a few minutes of tugging and pulling Ace stood in his street clothes, the protective gear rolled into a bundle under his arm.

He decided that he would throw the bundle into the Willow River on his way home; the acidic water would dissolve the disposable material and destroy any evidence that he'd ever been in the house.

Satisfied that the bodies and the scene had been arranged just as he'd planned, Ace sat at the kitchen table and smoothed out the blank page in front of him. He picked up the ballpoint pen and began to write:

*To My Family, Friends, and Community:*

*If you're reading this note, then you must have found me and Terri. Let me start off by saying I'm sorry it had to end this way. I didn't set out to hurt anyone, and the last thing I wanted was to let everyone down. But somehow everything just got out of control, and I ended up doing some terrible things that I deeply regret, and which I can no longer live with. I've taken*

*Terri with me so that she won't have to struggle in this cruel world alone.*

*I have prayed to be forgiven for the evil I've done, and I have faith that Terri and I will be going on to a better place together. In the spirit of repentance, I hope that the following confession will allow some of you to find closure and peace.*

*I'm ashamed to say I've taken the lives of several innocent people in a misguided attempt to protect myself and my wife. In 1994 I had a sexual relationship with Natalie Lorenzo, who at that time was a minor. Twelve years later Natalie claimed that I was the father of her son and demanded that I tell my wife and provide support for the boy. I panicked and ended up killing Natalie in a fit of rage.*

*Two weeks after Natalie's death, a woman named Helena Steele approached me and said she knew that I was the father of Natalie's child and that Natalie had asked her opinion about seeking child support. She threatened to go to the police. Again, I panicked and killed Helena Steele to stop her from exposing my secret. I had selfishly tried to protect my wife from finding out what I'd done and hoped never to be discovered.*

*For twelve years I lived with my guilt, trying to make amends by caring for my disabled wife. I hoped my terrible past was behind me. Then recently an investigation into these crimes was reopened. I was questioned and grew nervous, and in my anxiety, I accidentally supplied a patient at Hope House with the wrong medicine and she was hospitalized. Once I figured out what I'd done, I went to the hospital to apologize and explain my mistake to the girl, but she became hysterical and threatened to report me to the police and have my medical license taken away. I panicked, tried to silence her, and ended up killing her. I buried her body where it will never be found.*

*After that I was paranoid, thinking everyone was out to get me. When I heard that Penelope Yates had been talking to investigators, I thought the only way to keep her from sharing any information she might have about me and Natalie was to kill her. I wasn't thinking straight, and I went to her apartment and did what I felt I had to do.*

*Later I came to my senses and realized how stupid and selfish I'd been. At that point, I realized that there was only one way out of the mess I'd created. And only one way to prevent my wife from finding out about the terrible things I'd done to protect her.*

*I hope in heaven my lovely Terri will forgive me, and I pray that all of you will find it in your hearts to forgive me, too. My final request is for Terri and me to be cremated and for our mingled remains to be scattered in the ocean.*

*Farewell to all,*
*Dr. Adrian Bellows*

Ace read through the letter several times, proud of the job he'd done. He'd managed to neatly tie all the open investigations together in one straightforward confession. It would be easy to convict Doc posthumously and close the cases without Ace's involvement ever being discovered. If all went as planned, he would be in the clear. All he had to do was finish with girl eight, and he could start over again. Come up with a new mission.

After propping the suicide note on the kitchen table, Ace headed for the back door, careful to take the bundle of evidence with him. A loud knock on the front door stopped him just as he reached for the doorknob.

He froze, unsure what to do, then crept back down the hall and peeked through a slit in the blinds. Eden Winthrop stood on the doorstep, huddled under an umbrella, her long blonde hair blowing frantically in the wind as she knocked again on the door.

A wild rush of anger surged through Ace, and it took every bit of self-control he had not to rip open the door and strangle the woman right there on the front stoop.

*Hasn't the bitch already caused enough trouble? Isn't it really her fault that Doc and Terri had to die?*

But Ace knew he was close to settling everything to his satisfaction. If he gave in to his anger and killed Eden, the whole murder-suicide scenario would fall apart. Besides, the storm was getting stronger and he still needed to get the girl in his garage out to the farm. It was too risky to hold her in his house any longer.

One more dirty deed and the mission would be over.

# CHAPTER THIRTY-SIX

Eden struggled to keep the umbrella steady as she knocked on the door. No answer. She looked back at the blue van parked at an angle in the driveway. Dr. Bellows had to be home. So why wasn't he opening the door? Would he really refuse to let her in out of the wind and rain?

*He will if he has something to hide.*

She looked at the windows on the ground floor and noticed that all the blinds were closed. She stepped back and looked up, seeing closed blinds on the second floor as well. Perhaps they really weren't home.

Maybe Dr. Bellows and his wife had already evacuated in another vehicle and left the van behind.

After giving the front door a long, frustrated glare, Eden splashed back to the Expedition and climbed in. But she didn't start the engine; something didn't feel right.

Duke's head appeared in the rearview mirror, and Eden turned around to stare into his doleful eyes.

"You should have evacuated with Barb and the kids, Duke. Staking out Dr. Bellows' house is going to be pretty boring."

*And dangerous if the hurricane stays on the same path.*

Duke stared back, then curled up on the back seat and put his head on his paws, as if making a point that he wasn't going anywhere.

Eden had packed Barb and the kids into the older woman's big Buick, and they were already halfway to Orlando, where they planned to spend the next few days hunkered down with Barb's son and daughter-in-law.

Barb's dog, Lucky, had gone with them, and the Yorkie's tail had wagged nonstop as they'd loaded up the car. But Duke had refused to get in, no matter how much Hope coaxed, or Devon begged.

Finally, Eden had sighed, and agreed that perhaps Duke would be happier staying with her while she made one last effort to track down Kara before the brunt of the storm hit town.

The idea of Kara out on the streets, fending for herself all alone, stopped Eden from leaving town before she'd done everything she could to find the missing girl.

Eden thought of the promise she'd made to Kara's sister earlier that day. Anna Stanislaus had called to say that she and little Niko were heading to Willow Bay to look for her sister, hurricane or no hurricane.

Eden had only been able to convince the young mother not to drive down in the storm by promising that she would keep looking for Kara as long as the weather permitted.

And the heavy rain and blustery wind hadn't stopped her so far, but she was at a loss as to where to look next. If Dr. Bellows had already left town, what was her next move?

She stared defiantly at the windows of the silent house, impatient to do something other than wait around for Dr. Bellows to appear. Her eyes rested on the big blue van, and she wondered if the gold chain she'd seen might still be inside, perhaps under the seat.

*It couldn't hurt to have a look, could it?*

Before she could talk herself out of it, she opened the car door and stepped back into the rain. She held up the battered umbrella and began sloshing through puddles of water toward the van. Once she reached the van she again turned to the big house to see if anyone was watching. The house was still quiet, still closed up; nothing moved in the windows.

As Eden leaned forward to peer into the front passenger side window, she saw with surprise that the door was unlocked. Her eyes flicked to the console; the keys were still in the ignition. Heart racing, she opened the door and pulled herself up and into the passenger seat of the van. She looked down at the floor.

No gold chain, no cross. She slid her hand along the carpet and under the seat. Nothing.

Her eyes studied the interior of the van, not sure what she was hoping to find. They stopped on the satnav display and lingered. What could it tell her about Dr. Bellows' activities? She turned the key in the ignition. The radio blasted out an update on the storm's coordinates, and the engine began to purr.

Eden reached out a finger and began tapping on the satnav display. Within minutes she was staring at all the locations that Doc had driven to on Saturday, the day Kara had gone missing from the hospital. She saw that Doc had been at the hospital around the same time she'd arrived.

*Terri told me she hadn't been at the hospital on Saturday, and that she hadn't left the house all day. So why were you there, Dr. Bellows?*

Eden scrolled down to see that after leaving the hospital he'd driven to 3278 Ironside Way, a residential address about ten miles west of downtown.

*Where did you go, Doc? And who did you have with you?*

Eden pictured Dr. Bellows driving away from the hospital. She could have sworn she'd seen a figure in the passenger seat of his van. Could it have been Kara? Could Dr. Bellows have taken her to the house on Ironside Way?

*There's only one way to find out.*

Eden opened the door of the van and scurried back to her SUV, heedless of the ankle-deep puddles all around. Once back inside the car, she considered her plan of action, then dialed Nessa's number before she lost her nerve. She rehearsed what she would say as the phone began to ring.

*Nessa, will you go to an unknown address to search for a doctor who may or may not know something about a girl who may or may not be missing?*

But after four rings the voicemail picked up and Eden realized she'd have to leave a message.

"Nessa, this is Eden. I'm sure you're busy with the storm and...well, everything, but I think I may know where Dr. Bellows took Kara Stanislaus. I have an address...it's 3278 Ironside Way."

She paused, knowing that once she hung up she would have passed her responsibility to find Kara over to the police. After that, she would only be able to sit and wait for a call that might never come.

Eden was surprised to hear herself saying, "I'm going to go by there now to check it out. Please, call me when you get this."

Already regretting her impulsive decision, Eden started the engine and backed out of the Bellows' driveway.

Standing water in the road hinted at the flooded streets to come, and the wind gusted through the massive branches of the overhanging Cypress trees, making the long ropes of Spanish moss dance overhead. As debris began to fall and water began to rise, many streets would become impassable. There was no time to waste. If she was going to make it to the address in Bellows' satnav, she'd have to get going.

*It's probably just a wild goose chase anyway.*

But as she drove onto the highway and headed east toward Ironside Way, she found herself holding her breath, filled with both a tentative hope and a nagging fear of what she might find when she arrived.

# CHAPTER THIRTY-SEVEN

ankowski walked back into the office just as the phone on Nessa's desk started to ring. He dropped his backpack and looked over at the blinking light. The call was coming in from an internal number. Someone in the building was trying to reach Nessa.

"Hello, this is Jankowski, and no, Nessa's not here right now."

"Oh, hi, this is Alma. I needed to speak to Nessa. Do you think she's already left for the day, or is she on duty for the duration?"

Jankowski scanned the office. Nessa's purse was gone but her laptop still sat open on her desk.

"It looks like she's gone out, maybe had to run an errand, but her computer's still here so I think she'll be back. Can I help?"

"I managed to lift a print from the glass she dropped off earlier."

Alma's voice was high-pitched with excitement.

"And it's a perfect match with an unidentified print collected from the Natalie Lorenzo scene."

"Okay, that's great news," Jankowski replied, struggling to hide his confusion. "So, the print at the scene definitely matches the print on the...the glass?"

"Yeah, I was shocked, too," Alma said, her words spilling out. "When Nessa brought me the glass I thought she was really grasping, but she was right. Looks like this doctor guy must have been at the Lorenzo scene after all."

Jankowski waited for his mind to catch up.

*What glass did Nessa give to Alma? Could the doctor Alma mentioned be Dr. Adrian Bellows? Had Bellows been at the Natalie Lorenzo scene?*

"Of course, just because he was at the scene, it doesn't prove he's the perp."

Alma's initial excitement gave way to concern.

"And without having a warrant or documented chain of custody on the glass, the fingerprint won't help you in court. If it gets that far, I mean."

"Right, I think I understand," Jankowski said, although he wasn't sure what was going on, other than his partner had failed to tell him about crucial evidence she'd obtained without a warrant in a murder investigation and had gone behind his back to get that evidence tested.

"So, you'll let Nessa know?"

"Absolutely. In fact, I'm going to hunt her down right now."

But as soon as Jankowski had hung up, the phone lit up again, this time with a call from an external number.

The caller ID displayed a number that Jankowski recognized. It was Nessa's home number.

"What are you doing at home, Nessa?" Jankowski said, his voice curt. "Based on your texts I thought you'd be here waiting."

The was a slight pause on the other end, then Jerry Ainsley cleared his throat and spoke in a quiet voice.

"Nessa's not home yet, Simon. And she's not brought the sandbags by either. The boys and I are getting pretty worried since she's not answering her phone."

Jankowski heard anger behind Jerry's calm words.

*Sounds like there's trouble in paradise to me.*

But his irritation with Nessa for going behind his back overrode any empathy he might have for her domestic problems.

"Sorry to say, Jerry, but it looks like your wife may be keeping both of us in the dark. Seems she likes having secrets."

Jankowski shook his head and sighed, then forced himself to calm down. Maybe Nessa had a good explanation. He shouldn't be taking out his frustration on poor Jerry anyway.

"Look, I'm sorry, Jerry. I shouldn't have said that. I'm sure Nessa is fine and that she'll be home soon."

But Jerry had already hung up. Jankowski cursed into the empty room. This was all Nessa's doing. He needed to find her and make her tell him everything she knew. He took out his phone and tapped in a text.

*Prints on glass match prints at Lorenzo scene. We need to talk to Bellows. Call me as soon as you get this.*

He thought for a minute, then got up and shut the door. This discussion called for privacy. He tapped on a number he hadn't expected to call so soon. A deep voice answered after the first ring, but the sounds of traffic and wind made it hard to hear the words.

"Hey Tucker, it's me," Jankowski called out, raising his voice as if the noise was coming from his end of the line.

"What's up, man?" Vanzinger's voice broke in and out as he yelled to be heard over the ruckus around him. "My unit's headed over to the coast. We're on standby to run rescue. You okay?"

"The shit's going to start hitting the fan here very soon. The Lorenzo case is blowing up, and it looks like the Steele case may be connected. Once the press finds out we screwed this up...well, you need to get your head straight. Be ready to answer questions."

Vanzinger didn't respond right away, and for a minute Jankowski thought the connection had dropped.

"You still there, Tucker?"

"Yeah, I'm here."

Vanzinger's voice sounded grim.

"But, listen, Jank, this whole thing, it's way worse than you think. If I come forward, I'll be putting my life on the line. And anyone who tries to help me will be at risk, too."

"Whatever it is you know, you have to come clean," Jankowski said, wondering even as he said it if he knew what he was doing. "People are getting killed. You have to make this right."

"I know. I'm just warning you, it's not gonna be easy."

"Nothing ever is, man. Nothing ever is."

A voice on a megaphone sounded somewhere behind Vanzinger. Jankowski could hear a man shouting orders.

"Gotta go, Jank. I'll keep my phone on as long as I can, just in case anything comes up before this storm blows through."

"Okay, Tucker. Thanks."

"And Jank?"

"Yeah?"

"Be careful."

The line dropped and Jankowski found himself replaying Vanzinger's words over in his head.

*It's way worse than you think. I'll be putting my life on the line.*

He wondered what could be worse than convicting an innocent man and letting a killer go free to kill again. A sudden knock on the door made him jump up.

"Yeah, come in."

The door opened and Gabby Jankowski stepped into the office, yesterday's pink suit replaced by a forest green blouse and dark, slim-fitting jeans that accentuated her long legs.

"Are you taking a nap in here, Simon?"

Gabby's voice had the same effect on Jankowski's nerves like fingernails on a chalkboard.

"What I do is no longer your concern, Gabby. But if I didn't know better I'd think you were trying to find excuses to see me."

"Dream on, Simon. That boat has already sailed long ago."

"So, what do you want?"

"Well, I thought you'd be out there sandbagging or doing something helpful, instead of slacking off, but in this case I'm glad."

"And why is that?"

"Because our house needs to be secured ahead of the hurricane, Simon, and I'm too busy to take care of it myself."

Jankowski raised his eyebrows in disbelief.

"You're living in that house with your new boyfriend, for fuck's sake, Gabby. You think I'm going to come around and make sure you both stay safe and cozy?"

Gabby rolled her eyes at his comments.

"No need to be vulgar, Simon. And until we sell the house, you have just as much responsibility to take care of it as I do."

The familiar rage started to simmer in Jankowski's chest, but he forced himself to keep his voice steady, keep his face neutral. He didn't want to let Gabby see she'd gotten under his skin.

"You seem to have enough time to come here and bother me. Why not use that time more wisely. Go get some sandbags. Board up some windows. Maybe get your boy toy to help you."

"Actually, Bodhi already evacuated. He went with his mother to Ft. Lauderdale. They have family there."

"So, he's run off with mommy and left you to fend for yourself?"

Jankowski shrugged and shook his head.

"Sounds like young Bodhi's got his priorities straight, as do I. I'm not leaving here to haul sandbags to your house. There's a homicide investigation on and I've got a job to do."

Gabby narrowed her eyes and put both hands on her slim hips.

"Why do you always have to be such a jerk?"

Gabby spun around to leave, then stopped and looked over her shoulder, her pretty face twisted into an ugly sneer.

"And you wonder why I found another man to make me happy."

"Whatever your reason, you did me a favor, now get out."

Jankowski slammed the door shut, blocking out all thoughts of his ex-wife and her petty insults. He needed to find Nessa, and they needed to question Dr. Bellows before it was too late.

# CHAPTER THIRTY-EIGHT

Barker hefted the last of the burlap sandbags up and into the trunk of Nessa's Charger, his arms trembling with the exertion. Each bag weighed about thirty pounds, and Barker hadn't done much heavy lifting since his heart attack. He wiped sweat off his forehead with the back of a gritty hand, trying not to let Nessa see how much the exertion had taken out of him.

She'd called him in a panic after discovering the city distribution center had run out of sandbags, and that all of the home improvement stores in the area had closed due to the severe weather. The town was hunkering down, and Nessa was totally unprepared.

Luckily Barker still had a shed full of sandbags left over from the previous hurricane warning. That hurricane had suddenly shifted course and Barker had been left with a mountain of sandbags he didn't need; he readily agreed to share his supply with Nessa. She had raced over, hoping to drop off the bags at home and be back to the station before anyone found out.

"The chief's ordered all essential personnel to remain on duty and be ready to respond to emergency call-outs," she told him, adjusting the hood of her yellow slicker.

Rain spewed down from the gray mass of clouds above them, and Barker raised weary eyes to the sky, wondering how the Calla Lilies in the cemetery were holding up. He imagined the petals would likely be torn apart and scattered in the wind by now.

Nessa's phone vibrated and buzzed in her pocket for about the tenth time since she'd arrived, and this time she took it out and glared at the screen.

"Jerry, again. He's pissed that I haven't gotten these bags home already. I'll call him back once I'm on the road."

Barker shook his head and sighed.

"He and the boys are probably worried, Nessa. It's kind of shitty to just ignore the call."

"I'd say he's acting more jealous than worried," Nessa said, her voice defensive. "He's got some crazy idea in his head, and I don't have time to deal with that right now."

Before she could say more her phone buzzed again.

"Holy cow! I knew it!"

Nessa looked up at Barker with wide eyes, her face a mixture of excitement and disbelief.

"The fingerprints on the glass match the print from the Lorenzo scene. Dr. Bellows was at the motel that night. He really could be the man who killed Natalie...or at least he might know who did."

Barker digested the information as Nessa slammed the Dodge's trunk shut and sloshed through expanding puddles of muddy water to the driver's side door.

"I've gotta go. I need to get back to the station."

She backed into the road and accelerated toward town, her tires spraying water in her wake, not bothering to say goodbye.

The phone was in Barker's hand before the red glow of the Charger's taillights had disappeared around the corner. By the second ring, he was already running for his Prius

"Leo? The prints match. Bellows was at the Lorenzo scene. I can meet you at his place in ten minutes."

\* \* \*

The BMW pulled into Grand Isles Estates just ahead of Barker, spraying up a sheet of rainwater that coated the Prius with a soupy mixture of leaves and mud.

Barker was relieved to see Dr. Bellows' van parked on the driveway in front of the house. He pulled in behind Leo, then cursed when he saw Frankie emerge from the passenger side of the BMW.

"Why'd you bring him, Leo? He's a suspect in an ongoing murder investigation."

"Exactly. Frankie's been accused of a murder that he didn't commit," Leo agreed, his voice hard. "So, he has a vested interest in finding out who did it, and I think Bellows is just the man to talk to."

"Don't worry, Barker, I'll let you and Leo do all the talking."

Frankie flashed an innocent smile and began trudging through the rain after Leo. Barker had no choice but to follow behind, his regret at calling Leo growing with each step.

*I should've waited for Nessa instead of involving these two hotheads.*

Both Leo and Frankie were emotionally invested, and neither had police or security training. If Bellows decided to greet them with a shotgun, the men would be woefully unprepared to deal with the situation. Barker put his hand on the outline of his gun. He was suddenly glad he'd holstered it under his raincoat before getting out of the car.

"Let me handle this," Barker said, pushing his way in front of Leo and blocking the front door. "You two stand back for now."

He knocked firmly on the door and called out, "Dr. Bellows, we'd like to speak to you. We just have a few questions."

No sound from inside.

Frankie cleared his throat.

"Um, can I make a suggestion?"

"No, just stand there and stay quiet," Barker said, knocking again and glaring over his shoulder at Frankie.

Leo leaned forward to knock as well, his impatience palpable.

Barker stepped off the front stoop and walked to a big bay window that faced the street. Leo followed him and they tried to peer in, but the blinds were drawn, blocking any hopes of seeing inside.

"Uh, guys, the door's unlocked."

Barker looked over just in time to see Frankie disappear into the house. In his haste to get inside, Barker slipped in the mud and almost went down, but Leo grabbed his arm and helped him regain his balance. With slippery, eager feet they scurried over to the door and followed Frankie inside.

"Frankie?"

Leo's deep voice seemed to echo down the hall, and Barker felt a chill make its way up his spine.

"I'm in here, guys," Frankie called out from a room off the hall, his voice weak and unusually high-pitched. "You better get in here."

But before Barker could make it into the room, Frankie staggered out and ran for the front door. He knelt and stuck his head out into the rain, retching out strings of bile onto the soggy doormat.

Barker stared back at Frankie, then lifted his eyes to Leo, who stood frozen in the hall. Wordlessly they walked toward the doorway, both somehow knowing what they would see, but still unprepared for the bloody scene spread out in front of them as they entered.

Dr. Bellows was splayed on the floor, blood and brains painted in gory streaks all around him. Terri Bellows sat cold and stiff in her wheelchair, her face trapped in a horrified grimace behind the plastic bag. Barker inched into the room and saw that Bellows clutched a small gun in his left hand. He wanted to turn his eyes away but couldn't.

"Looks like a murder-suicide," Leo muttered, instinctively putting a hand over his nose and mouth to block the nauseating smell that had already permeated the room.

His words struck a memory in Barker's mind. Another scene five years earlier. Barker had responded to a 911 call. Mercy Lancaster and her husband, Preston Lancaster, were dead. Eden Winthrop had come by to check on her sister and found the bodies. It looked like a murder-suicide. Except Eden had blood on her hands. Except the angle of the bullet that hit Preston wasn't right.

"Barker, you okay?"

Leo's voice brought Barker back to the current day. The current blood bath. Five years had passed, but here he stood, still surrounded by death and carnage.

"Yeah, I'm good. Just trying to think what we should do."

"Well, I know enough to know we shouldn't mess with the scene," Leo said, backing out of the room.

"Maybe we should look around the house for other victims?" Barker suggested.

"Good idea," Leo agreed. "Kara Stanislaus is still missing."

Leo strode further down the hall, and Barker followed close on his heels, his hand on the butt of his weapon, ready to pull and shot if someone jumped out at them from the shadows.

But the kitchen was empty. The clean floors and counters showed no sign of a struggle. No blood or gore stained the walls or floors.

"Look at this," Leo said, crossing to the kitchen table.

Barker looked over his shoulder and began to read. By the time he'd scanned the page his pulse was racing, and he looked over at Leo with worried, empathetic eyes.

Leo's back was stiff and straight, but Barker could feel him trembling.

"Your mother..." Barker tried to say, but his throat tightened and closed up.

"Yes, that bastard in there killed my mother," Leo gritted out between clenched teeth. "He killed her to stop her from going to the police."

"Looks like he's been...busy," Barker said, scanning the note again, trying to make sense of it all.

Could the prissy doctor have really done everything he'd confessed to in the letter? Could he really have killed all those women on his own and gotten away with it all these years? It was hard to believe, and Barker knew that scenes could be staged, and evidence planted. He flinched as Frankie's voice sounded from down the hall.

"The cops are here."

# CHAPTER THIRTY-NINE

The girl was asleep on the bed when Ace entered the room for the last time. He stared down at her raw, swollen ankle, still firmly enclosed in the cuff, and shook his head. Some of the girls never learned to accept their fate, although in a way he actually admired the stubborn ones. And he had to admit it was more satisfying to break the spirit of a tiger than a lamb. Of course, in the end, it didn't matter. They all went into the ground eventually, no matter how fiercely they had fought to stay alive.

Ace picked up the empty bag that had held the fentanyl. It was on the floor, having been discarded once the girl had swallowed the contents in a vain attempt to stop the pain.

*The pills should keep her under for the drive out to the farm.*

If they didn't, he would take care of her the old-fashioned way. He flexed his fingers and imagined them squeezing the tender flesh of the girl's throat.

*There won't be so much blood that way, and it'll be something new.*

Pulling a metal key from his pocket, he slipped it into the lock on the bottom of the ankle cuff. The key turned smoothly, and the shackle clattered to the floor. He kicked the shackle out of the way and pulled the girl's limp body off the bed and onto the tarp he'd spread out on the floor below.

A soft grunt escaped Kara's lips when she hit the ground, but she didn't move as Ace rolled the tarp and dragged it to the door. He hesitated, wondering if he should check the vicinity once more before bringing her downstairs, but then decided it wasn't worth the extra time. Who would be out in this weather nosing around?

He heaved the heavy bundle up and into the back of the truck, then adjusted the tarp over the girl and rolled the truck bed cover down. He surveyed the end result, satisfied that girl eight was ready for the drive out to the farm and pushed the remote to open the garage door. As the door slid up, he saw movement out of the corner of his eye. His breath caught in his throat, and for a minute he wondered if he was hallucinating.

A white Ford Expedition had pulled into the driveway, and a tall, blonde woman climbed out. She popped open an umbrella and held it over her head as she looked around. She turned to let a golden retriever hop down after her.

*How the hell did Eden Winthrop find me?*

Stunned into momentary indecision, Ace hovered inside the garage, not knowing what to do, unsure if she was alone. He watched her approach the front door to the house and knock, before turning a curious face toward the garage. His fear soon turned to anger. He would have to put a stop to the woman's meddling now before she could do any more damage.

Ace leaned in and opened the truck's glove box. He slid the little Ruger out and cradled it in his hand. It perfectly matched the gun he'd used to shoot Doc earlier that afternoon. He'd recommended the model to his late-partner in crime just the year before. He was tempted to laugh at the thought.

*I made a good choice. Just look how handy they've been.*

But as he stood and quietly closed the truck's door behind him, his eyes fell on a cabinet by the door leading to the stairs. He'd almost forgotten that he'd stashed a clean white cloth and a bottle of chloroform in the cabinet. He'd planned to use it only in the event of an emergency, thinking it would come in useful if one of the girls escaped. And now, after all these years, he finally had a reason to use it.

Keeping one eye on the open garage door, he crept to the cabinet and took out the bottle. He looked at the clear liquid inside with some trepidation. He'd never tried it on anyone before. How much was enough? How much would be too much?

He didn't want to kill the woman right away. He needed to find out how much she knew, and who she'd told, first. Then he could get rid of her. He could put this whole mess behind him before it got out of hand.

A blonde head bobbed into sight beyond the roof of the truck, and Ace heard the dog give a low bark.

"What's wrong, boy? Is the rain bothering you?"

The woman's soft voice was soothing, but the dog barked again, and Ace tightened his hand around the Ruger. Dogs had never liked him, and he had never been too fond of them either. They always stared at him suspiciously and growled or barked, and he never missed the opportunity to give a kick to any flea-bitten mutt that got in his way.

"Do you see something, Duke?"

Eden stepped into the garage and lowered her umbrella. Rain dripped around her as she stared into the shadows.

"Hello, is anybody in there?"

Ace crouched behind the truck, knowing the dog would sniff him out, knowing he didn't have a chance to get by her without being seen. He watched as Eden turned her head back toward the house, perhaps wondering why no one opened the door since a truck and a big shiny car sat in the garage. Didn't that indicate someone must be at home?

Knowing he may never get a better chance to take her by surprise, Ace tipped the chloroform into the rag and sprang up behind Eden. Her scream was stifled by Ace's big hand in the white cloth. She grabbed for the cloth and tore at his hands, but he held tight, his rage and hate numbing the searing pain inflicted by her nails as she clawed him and kicked backward, aiming for his shins.

Suddenly, the dog appeared behind him, growling and snarling as he snapped at Ace's legs. Ace raised a thick work boot and kicked hard at the dog's head, his arms beginning to tire as the woman continued to struggle against him.

Just when he began thinking he must have badly misjudged how much chloroform to use, Eden's body slackened, going limp in an instant. Ace let her drop to the floor just in time to meet the dog's charge head-on.

He threw the golden retriever back against the garage wall and grabbed for his gun, raising it toward the dog with weak, shaky hands. He squeezed off a shot that ricocheted against the wall, prompting the dog to scurry out the door and into the rain.

Ace lunged out into the storm, aimed the gun at the dog's retreating tail, and pulled the trigger. Not waiting to see if he hit his mark, Ace hustled to the truck and rolled back the bed cover. Using his last bit of strength, he hefted Eden into the truck bed beside the girl in the tarp and surveyed his handiwork.

"Two for the price of one," he laughed, his voice a ragged croak.

As he backed out of the driveway, the wind howled around the old truck, rattling the windows and battering the roof. Ace could barely see out of the front windshield, but he steered the truck's wheels toward the old farm. The fury of the storm both worried him and reassured him.

*No one will be stupid enough to go out in this mess looking for anyone. By the time the hurricane passes, Eden Winthrop will no longer be a problem, and the girl will be safe under the ground in stall eight.*

An almost sad smile played around his mouth as he navigated the wet streets and fallen branches.

*The mission is almost over.*

Once he'd buried the remaining evidence, it would be time to find another mission. Maybe something further from home next time.

*Maybe some international travel is in order.*

Ace had liked Germany when he'd been stationed there. The thought of heading back to Europe as a civilian appealed to him. It was about time to enjoy new experiences; getting away from Florida, with its hurricanes, hot weather, and nosy people, sounded like a good idea.

As the truck rattled closer to the farm, Ace began to whistle.

# CHAPTER FORTY

Nessa stood in the doorway and gazed in horror at the nightmarish scene. The thick spray of blood on the wall seemed to fade in and out as fatigue washed over her. She rubbed at her eyes and tried to focus on the evidence, tried to formulate a theory as to what had happened in the once-cozy room. But her lack of sleep was becoming a real problem, and even the shock of the grisly scene couldn't seem to make her eyes stay open.

"I've gotta get some water."

The ragged words vibrated into the quiet air of the house, making Jankowski turn to Nessa with an impatient frown. His frown deepened when he saw her ashen complexion and glassy eyes.

"Don't move. I'll grab you a cup of water from the kitchen."

He fled down the hall, away from the gore, and Nessa glared after him in protest. She'd wanted to get away from the sights and smells that were making both her head and stomach spin.

"Fine, Jankowski," Nessa muttered, moving a few inches into the room. "Whatever you say."

She stopped just inside the doorway, knowing she would risk contaminating the scene if she went any further without protective clothing. The crime scene unit still hadn't arrived, and she wasn't sure how long it might take them to get through streets that were flooded, closed, or blocked by debris. She couldn't do anything to destroy trace evidence that might reveal the tragic events that had gone on in the house.

"Drink this."

Jankowski held out a glass of water.

Nessa gripped the glass with an unsteady hand and took a long drink, glad for any excuse to close her eyes. But even with her eyes tightly shut, she could still see the distorted face of the dead woman in the wheelchair.

"I tried to call Iris, but her voicemail just picks up right away. I'm guessing she's lost service."

Jankowski's comment stirred Nessa's brain back to life.

"Yes, she went out to help her parents. They live near the coast. She wanted to be with them when they evacuated."

"She sounds like a good daughter," Jankowski said, "but what we need right now is a dedicated medical examiner."

Nessa thought of the pictures in Iris's office, remembering the shy smile of her father, and the proud face of her mother.

"There's nothing she can do for the people here," Nessa said, trying not to look at the bits of brain sticking to the side of the desk. "Her time is better spent helping her family."

She felt Jankowski studying her.

*He's probably wondering why I'm not at home helping my family.*

The same question had already crossed Nessa's mind a million times, but there she was, hovering at the edge of a horrendous crime scene, waiting for crime scene techs that may never show up.

"Maybe I should try calling Archie Faraday," Jankowski suggested. "I think he lives nearby. Maybe he could help us out until Iris gets back."

"No!" Nessa snapped. "I don't trust that man, and neither does Iris. She won't thank us for involving him."

Melinda Woodhall

A flush of embarrassment and anger turned her cheeks pink as she looked away, not wanting to meet Jankowski's surprised stare. She took out her cell phone and tapped on the camera icon.

"Might as well start documenting the scene. If Alma and her crew can't get here, we'll have to do the best we can on our own."

"They'll be here soon, I'm sure, but suit yourself."

Jankowski walked to the foot of the stairs and gazed up into the darkness above.

"I'll go scout around upstairs. Make sure we haven't missed any other bodies."

"Yeah, and make sure no one's hiding up there."

But as Jankowski started thudding up the stairs, Nessa was confident he wouldn't find anyone else in the house. The scene clearly indicated a murder-suicide had occurred, and the perp was laying in front of her with his brains decorating the furniture. He wasn't going to give anyone any more trouble.

Nessa aimed her cell phone camera at different spots in the room, careful to get as many angles as she could without stepping further into the blood spatter. After getting several wide-angle shots of the full room, she took close-ups of the bodies, the spatter, and the weapon, before taking pictures of the other objects in the room.

She snapped a shot of the framed photos on the bookshelf. They showed the couple in much happier times: Terri Bellows in her wheelchair beaming at the camera, her husband cutting a birthday cake and wearing a pointy party hat, the loving couple raising champagne glasses in a celebratory toast.

*How did they go from that to this? Or was that all just an act?*

A large portrait on the wall displayed a young man in a military uniform. Nessa zoomed in and took a close-up. The uniform indicated that Dr. Adrian Bellows had been in the US Air Force.

Jankowski thudded back down the stairs.

"No blood, no bodies, no boogeyman," Jankowski called out, his voice artificially cheerful. "Nothing up there of any interest. At least not that I can see, but perhaps Alma and her crew can find something."

Nessa nodded and aimed her camera toward the desk. Jankowski stood close behind her, looking over her shoulder.

"You notice that he used his left hand to shoot himself?"

She jumped at his voice so close to her ear and spun around.

"Christ, Jankowski, give me some room."

She pushed past him and stomped down the hall, entering the kitchen in a huff. The air was heavy and silent. The only sound she could hear came from the tempest raging outside. Rain pelted against the windows and the wind howled around the rafters.

*It makes sense that he used his left hand. So, what's bugging me?*

Snippets of her recent conversation with Iris played through Nessa's mind. The medical examiner had determined that Helena Steele and Penelope Yates were killed by a left-handed perp.

Nessa glanced down at the suicide note on the table.

*He's admitted to killing both women. So, it all fits together, right?*

But something was nagging at Nessa. She felt as if she'd forgotten something or was missing a crucial piece of the puzzle.

*If only I wasn't so darn tired. I can't seem to think straight.*

She inhaled deeply and shook her head, willing her brain to perk up and help her evaluate the scene.

She aimed her cell phone camera at the note on the table, then began taking snaps of the rest of the room.

A calendar hung on the kitchen wall. Big looping words had been written in the box for the upcoming Saturday.

*Ace coming for lasagna.*

Nessa took a close-up photo of the calendar. She wondered what Terri Bellows had been thinking when she'd written the note about the lasagna. Could she ever have imagined her life ending so brutally before Saturday ever came? And what about Ace?

*No lasagna for you this week, Ace. Whoever you are.*

Unable to stop a huge yawn, Nessa closed her eyes and stretched, tempted to sit down at the kitchen table and rest her head.

*What harm could a few minutes of shut-eye do?*

Before she could answer her own question, her eyes returned to the suicide note, and the mention of Hope House. The girl Dr. Bellows had mentioned in the note had to be Kara Stanislaus.

*I've got to tell Eden. She'll want to know right away.*

Pity and regret surged through Nessa as she thought of the call she had to make. After so much loss and tragedy, Eden was once again going to be the recipient of bad news. The most devastating kind of news. Someone she cared about had been senselessly killed.

She pictured Eden's worried face at the police station only days before, warning them about Dr. Bellows. If only they'd listened then, a young woman might have been saved. They might have even been in time to save Penelope Yates and Terri Bellows.

A sick feeling settled into the pit of Nessa's stomach as she reached into her pocket and took out her phone. Had their reluctance to break protocol cost three innocent women their lives?

Nessa grimaced at the message telling her she'd missed six calls and had a dozen new text messages. She'd have to call Eden first. The least she could do was let the poor woman know what had happened to the missing girl she'd been looking for.

The phone rang four times then rolled to voicemail. Although Nessa was tempted to leave a message, she knew it wouldn't be fair. Her tired eyes scanned her missed calls. Eden's name was on the list, and she'd left a voicemail. Nessa tapped on the message and listened to Eden's anxious voice.

*"Nessa, this is Eden. I'm sure you're busy with the storm and...well, everything, but I think I may know where Dr. Bellows took Kara Stanislaus. I have an address...it's 3278 Ironside Way."*

The words sent a shiver down Nessa's spine.

*Could Dr. Bellows have taken Kara to the address on Eden's voicemail? Was her body buried there, waiting to be found?*

Nessa raced into the hall, calling out to Jankowski.

"You wait for the crime scene techs. I think I might know where Bellows has buried Kara Stanislaus."

\* \* \*

Nessa cursed the flashing lights ahead.

Another blocked road and another detour. She swerved around a barricade and pulled up behind a tiny car inching along the highway at ten miles an hour. Activating the bar of emergency lights on the Charger's dashboard, she sped around the little car, spraying up waves of water as she passed by.

The detour had taken her back by the police station, and she made a last-minute decision to pull in and see if she could corral a uniformed officer to go with her to the location on Ironside Way. The memory of arriving alone at the Old Canal Motel hovered in her mind, and she was starting to regret her hasty decision to go out alone.

Nessa ran into the police station lobby, shrugging off her dripping raincoat and looking around in dismay. The station seemed deserted. It was clear that everyone other than essential personnel had gone home long ago. The remaining staff were probably manning the emergency response center they had set up at city hall.

The lights flickered above Nessa's head. She wondered if the generator would kick in once the electricity went out.

*Hopefully, I won't be here long enough to find out.*

She hurried past the front desk and into the back, ready to confront Chief Kramer and demand he call up one of the on-duty officers to go with her to find Kara's body. Kramer had made the call not to question Bellows when Eden had first made her accusation. Now he needed to help her clean up the fallout from that decision.

The lights in the executive wing were still on, and some of the doors were open, but they all appeared to be empty.

*Most likely they're holding a press conference somewhere. Chief Kramer's probably posing with Mayor Hadley and Archie Faraday.*

Of course, Kramer would be relegated to the back row as usual. He wasn't as handsome as Mayor Hadley, or as distinguished as Dr. Faraday. Kramer was more of a man's man. The rough, coarse type of man that always seemed to enter a room like a bull in a china shop.

Nessa rolled her eyes at the image of the older men who'd pretty much run the town for years. They were the most visible members of the *good old boys' club* that made the rules and wielded the power in Willow Bay. It was a club that would never allow her or any other woman in, even if she had been interested in joining.

*Which I'm not. I don't give a fig about those old farts.*

Nessa stood in the doorway to Kramer's office and confirmed what she'd suspected. He was nowhere to be seen. She had started to turn on her heel and leave when she noticed the framed photo on the wall that she'd seen plenty of times before. But this time she couldn't look away.

A group of uniformed men stood at attention, their serious faces stoic under military caps. A young Kramer stood in the back line. Nessa instantly recognized his wide jaw and close-set eyes. Next to Kramer was a smaller man with unremarkable features. She'd seen the same man, in the same uniform, at the Bellows' crime scene.

Nessa walked into the office and stood in front of the photo. She bent forward and squinted at the tiny listing of names across the bottom of the group shot. Nessa's blood ran cold as she read the names. Airman "Ace" Kramer stood next to Airman "Doc" Bellows.

The red scrawling words on the calendar were starting to make sense now.

*Ace coming for lasagna.*

Nessa sank into the desk chair in front of Kramer's computer. She would look up the address on Ironside, see who lived there. She looked around for the mouse and saw that it sat on a US Air Force mousepad, positioned on the left side of the keyboard.

Nessa swallowed hard, trying to remember the last time she had been in Kramer's office. She vaguely remembered him using his left hand. But was she just imagining it?

*No. I'm a detective for goodness sake. I notice these things.*

A stab of fear shot through Nessa as her brain started to make connections. She took out her phone and opened up the photo app. She scrolled to the picture of Adrian Bellows cutting the cake, his eyes smiling under the party hat. He was cutting the cake with his right hand.

Hands trembling, she moved the cursor to the login screen and clicked on the *Guest Login* option. Within minutes she was searching Willow Bay's public database of property deeds. She typed in the 3278 Ironside Way address and waited for the screen to load.

The owner of the house was listed as Douglas Kramer. Nessa remained frozen, her mind refusing to accept what the evidence was telling her. She stared at the page, willing the information to change. Instead, she noticed an active *Additional Properties* link at the bottom of the page. Her hand moved the mouse as if it were compelled by an external force.

The screen loaded, displaying an unfamiliar address: a rural property outside of town. The property was zoned as agricultural-residential, and it had been transferred to Douglas Kramer in 1998.

Nessa was up and running toward the hall before she knew where she was going.

*I have to get to Eden before Eden gets to Kramer.*

Her phone vibrated in her pocket, and she stared down at the display with suspicious eyes.

It was Jankowski. Her finger hovered over the phone, but she hesitated. She thought back to the secrets Jankowski had kept from her about Reinhardt.

*Jankowski grew up in Willow Bay. He's been on the force for years. He may not be an old boy, but he's definitely one of the boys. Could he know what Kramer's been doing? Could he be part of it somehow?*

Nessa waited for the call to go to voicemail, and then raised the phone and tapped on Barker's number.

*If there's one man in town I trust, besides Jerry, it's Pete Barker.*

# CHAPTER FORTY-ONE

L eo tried calling Eden again; still no answer. He'd dialed her number as soon as Jankowski had kicked them out of the Bellows' crime scene but had gotten her voicemail. He hated to think she was going to hear the news about Kara Stanislaus from someone else. As much as he dreaded telling her that her suspicions about Dr. Bellows had been correct and that the therapist had already killed the missing woman, he couldn't bear to think of Eden having to deal with the heartbreaking news on her own.

"You guys want some coffee or tea or something?"

Barker stood in the doorway to the dining room that acted as his office. The index cards still lay scattered around the table, organized in messy piles that made little sense to Leo.

"Tea? After what I just saw? You gotta be kidding me, man. How about something a little stronger?"

Frankie paced the room, his erratic, jerky movements setting Leo's nerves on edge.

"I've got some beer," Barker offered, sounding annoyed.

"No, we all need to keep our heads straight," Leo snapped, his irritation rising. "No falling apart, and no getting drunk. There's still a hurricane out there; we might be needed to help around town."

Leo ran a hand through his disheveled hair and rubbed the stubble that was sprouting on his chin.

He studied a photo on the wall. Barker with a tall, thin girl wearing a high-school graduation cap and gown. She had long dark hair and inscrutable blue eyes.

The girl must be Barker's daughter. The one Nessa had told him about. The girl in the photo summoned thoughts of Kara Stanislaus, and Leo turned to look at Barker with a pained expression.

"And I still need to find Eden and break the bad news."

Barker held Leo's eyes and nodded, knowing only too well how difficult it could be to break the worst kind of news to people who had been hoping for the best.

Barker's phone buzzed on the table and Leo glanced down at it, surprised that the cell service was still active. Some of the cell towers must be up and running despite the hurricane's best efforts.

"It's Nessa."

He watched Barker cross the room and pick up the phone, curious as to why the detective would be calling in the midst of working a bloody murder-suicide scene.

"What's up, Nessa?"

Barker froze as he listened to Nessa's words.

"Hold on, Nessa. Leo and Frankie are still with me. I'm gonna put you on speaker so they can hear this, too."

Barker tapped his phone and Nessa's frantic voice filled the room, the background sounds of wind and rain letting them know she must be driving through the storm.

"I need your help, Barker. This is going to sound crazy, but you have to just trust me. We don't have time to get into all the details."

"I trust you, Nessa," Barker said, his voice all business. "What do you need?"

"I need you to go to Chief Kramer's house. The address is 3278 Ironside way."

"Okay, I'm getting my keys now," Barker said, pulling on his still-wet rain jacket and dropping his keys and wallet into a pocket. "But tell me why I'm going there."

"Chief Kramer and Adrian Bellows are old friends. I know it sounds insane, but I have information that leads me to believe Kramer killed Bellows and his wife."

All three of the men in the room gaped at the phone in Barker's hand, unable to process the words coming out of the speaker.

"Barker, you still there?"

"I'm here, Nessa. I'm just surprised."

"Is Leo still there?"

"I'm here, Nessa," Leo said, forcing himself to step forward and speak in the direction of the phone.

"Now, don't go ballistic, Leo. I need to tell you something, but you have to promise to keep your cool."

Leo's heart started to pound at the tremor in Nessa's voice. Whatever she had to say was bad. He closed his eyes and inhaled deeply.

"Tell me, Nessa. What's going on?"

"I think Kramer was the person who killed Penelope Yates and...your mother. I think he and Bellows may have worked together somehow, but I think Kramer was the one who actually wielded the knife."

Leo shook his head in confusion.

"How...why..."

"As I said, we don't have time for the details now. Please trust me. You and Eden saved my life, and now I'm trying to save...save Eden...if possible."

Fear coursed through Leo like molten lead.

"Where's Eden? Is she okay?"

"She went to check out an address. A place she thinks Bellows might have taken Kara. She doesn't know Kara is dead. She doesn't know the house belongs to Chief Kramer. She might be walking into a trap."

Barker put a hand on Leo's arm and squeezed.

"We're on our way. Nessa. But where are you?"

Leo rushed to the door. He looked back at Barker with impatient eyes, desperate to get going, but forcing himself to stay calm.

"I'm heading out to another place that Kramer owns. It's outside of town, and I have a feeling Kramer might try to run there. If he's already got Eden..."

The anguish in Nessa's voice terrified Leo, betraying her fear that Eden was in serious danger.

The possibility that Eden might already be dead sent a slash of pain through Leo.

But he couldn't let himself think of that now. He had to stay strong. If he could get to Eden before Kramer hurt her, he would move heaven and earth to keep her safe.

*If I get my hands on that bastard I'll kill him.*

Leo forced the murderous thoughts aside and raced down the hall and out the door.

A strong gust of wind knocked him back against the door as he stepped outside, and he had to lean against the relentless wind to get to his BMW.

Frankie jumped in the backseat and Barker flopped into the passenger seat just as Leo smashed his foot on the gas and sped out into the storm.

\* \* \*

The BMW roared through the slick streets, swerving and skidding without slowing down for fallen trees or standing water.

"Watch out, man!" Frankie complained from the back. "I'm getting thrown around like a damn rag doll back here."

Leo ignored everything but the road, knowing one wrong move could throw them in a ditch or against a tree and stop their rescue mission before it had gotten started.

"Up there to the right, then it's the second driveway on the left."

Barker pointed into the wall of rain in front of the windshield and Leo slowed down just in time to turn into a long, winding driveway that led up to a two-story house.

The windows had been boarded up against the storm and white sandbags had been piled up in front of the door.

The driveway was empty but led to a detached two-car garage. The garage door was securely closed.

"Let's see if anybody's home," Barker muttered, opening the car door and hurrying over to the garage.

He twisted the doorknob of the side door that seemed to lead up the stairs to the room over the garage. It was locked.

Leo ran around to the side of the garage and saw that the window had been boarded up with a thin piece of plywood. Frankie ran up next to him, his head bare, his hair slicked down over his head like a drowned rat.

"You get that side, Leo," he shouted. "I got this one."

They pulled at the wood, managing to rip one side from the wall. As the board fell away from the window Leo saw a flash of white inside the garage.

He wiped the windowpane with his hand and looked inside. Eden's white Ford Expedition was parked in the garage next to Kramer's shiny Cadillac.

As he stared in, Barker's face appeared in the window.

"Come on, I jimmied the lock."

Leo ran around to the door, Frankie fast on his heels. They entered the dark garage, hesitating to let their eyes become accustomed to the dim lighting.

Barker stood at the foot of the stairs.

He motioned to Leo to follow him, and the three men climbed up, pausing outside the closed door. Leo stared at the deadbolt on the door with growing rage.

"We need something to break this door down."

Frankie pounded back down the stairs. After a few seconds, he was back holding a small crowbar.

"Move back," Frankie commanded, swinging the crowbar around like a samurai sword.

He inserted the crowbar between the doorjamb and the lock and pulled back with all his strength. To Leo's amazement the doorjamb cracked.

Again, Frankie inserted the crowbar, this time a little further up on the door, and pulled back.

Apparently satisfied by another loud crack, Frankie dropped the crowbar on the floor and raised one, big foot, delivering a solid kick to the middle of the door. With a loud crash, the door banged open, revealing the room beyond.

Leo stumbled forward, his heart sinking as he took in the empty room. He turned to Barker, deflated.

"She's not here. Eden's not here."

But Barker was staring past him, looking at the old, wooden wall where eight photos had been taped.

He walked slowly as if in a daze, stopping in front of the pictures and gazing at the faces of the young women that had been kept in the room.

Leo looked from the photos to the bed frame and bare mattress. His eyes fell on the ankle cuff and chain shackled to the wall.

Anger and outrage exploded in his chest, making it hard for him to breathe. His eyes took in the pictures of the eight girls.

The last girl, the eighth victim, matched the description of Kara Stanislaus. She must have been in this room since she disappeared from the hospital.

"What kind of sick bastard did this?" Frankie sputtered, standing in the middle of the room looking queasy.

But Barker was still staring at the photos, his finger resting on the girl marked as number five. Over Barker's shoulder, Leo saw that the girl was tall and thin, with long dark hair and blue eyes. His heart stopped.

*Could that girl be Barker's daughter? Could she have been kept in this room? Is that why she never came home?*

"Barker? Are you all right?"

Leo stepped forward just as Barker's knees buckled. He steadied the big man who gasped for breath and clutched at his chest.

"Sit down, Barker. Just sit on the floor and catch your breath."

Barker lowered himself to the gritty wood floor and leaned his head against the wall, still struggling to breathe.

"Are you okay? You think this is another heart attack?" Leo asked, his eyes drawn back to the girl with the bright blue eyes.

"No, it's not my heart. Well, I guess in a way it is..."

Leo braced himself, knowing he needed to ask the question he didn't want to ask.

"Is that Taylor in the picture? Is that your daughter?"

Barker shook his head and cleared his throat.

"No, but...she's a dead ringer for my daughter. At first, I thought it was Taylor. In the dark, I thought it was...my girl."

Leo let out a relieved puff of air, as Frankie squatted next to Barker. He didn't say anything, but he put a thin hand on Barker's broad back and patted him awkwardly.

265

"When all this is over, I'm going to find her," Barker finally said, his voice a cracked whisper. "I'm going to find her and I'm going to bring her home."

Leo nodded and looked down at Barker, his own voice revealing the stress and worry that tore at him.

"I know you will, Barker. And I'll help you. Once I find Eden..."

"I'll help too, man," Frankie said, standing and looking toward the door. "If we survive this fucking hurricane."

Barker stared up at Leo, the color starting to return to his pale face and a spark of an idea in his eye.

"I think I might know where Kramer has taken Eden."

He struggled back to his feet and straightened his jacket.

"Nessa said Kramer owns property outside the city. I remember an old dairy farm that Kramer's old man owned years ago. The department held a few events out there when I first started."

Leo thought he knew the place Barker was talking about.

"Okay, let's go."

He hurried down the stairs and back out into the rain.

The BMW stood in a puddle of water and mud as Leo splashed across the driveway. As he opened the door to get in, he heard a sharp sound under the wind. He paused and looked around.

"Did you hear that?"

He turned to Frankie and Barker who were climbing into the car.

"Nah, I didn't hear any–"

Frankie paused and listened.

"Yeah, I heard that."

He darted around the side of the garage with Leo calling after him.

"We don't have time, Frankie!"

But seconds later Frankie emerged from the side yard, a worried furrow between his brow as he carried a sodden golden retriever.

"It's Duke!" Leo shouted, taking the dog from Frankie's arms. "Open the back door."

Barker swung open the door and Leo laid Duke on the backseat. Leo saw a patch of red fur and a wound on Duke's hind leg.

"He's been shot," Barker said, his voice outraged.

A cold certainty grew in Leo's mind and filled his veins with icy fear. The madman that had killed his mother, kept eight women locked in his garage, and shot an innocent dog, now had Eden. If she wasn't already dead, she soon would be.

Leo steered the car toward the farm, his eyes watching the darkening sky as he silently prayed they would make it out to the isolated farm in time.

# CHAPTER FORTY-TWO

Jankowski watched as Alma Garcia and Wesley Knox worked the bloody room. The senior crime scene technician and the junior forensic technician had arrived without fanfare just after Nessa's Dodge Charger had sped away. They'd gotten straight to work, stoic eyes expressionless behind protective hoods, and Jankowski assumed they must still be numb to the gruesome sights and smells of the scene after working the Penelope Yates homicide only days before.

Alma moved around the room with her camera, capturing photographic evidence and recording a detailed video of the entire crime scene. Occasionally she would stop and collect a physical specimen or jot a note on her scene log.

Wesley calmly examined the bodies, seemingly unperturbed by his sudden elevation to acting medical examiner. The young technician was taking the daunting assignment seriously, shooting his own photos of the bodies in situ, recording the vital statistics of the bodies, and preparing them to be transported back to the medical examiner's office.

Jankowski's phone vibrated on his hip. He dug into his pocket, hoping Gabby wasn't calling to continue her nagging.

He was confident their sturdy, concrete block house would hold up against the storm, but he wasn't planning to share that opinion with his ex-wife, and he wasn't about to desert an active crime scene as Nessa had done. The number looked familiar, but the caller's name didn't pop up on his display.

*Maybe one of the uniformed officers reporting in?*

"This is Detective Jankowski."

"This is Barker. I need a favor."

Jankowski raised his eyebrows and shook his head.

"I'm doing fine, thanks, Barker. Nice to hear from you."

Barker's voice came back hard.

"I'm not screwing around, Jankowski. I have confirmation of an active abduction in progress and a detective heading toward a perp with a gun without backup. You want to continue to bullshit, or you want to help?"

Jankowski looked at the phone, surprised by the panic he detected under Barker's words.

"All right, tell me what's happened."

"Eden Winthrop is missing. She's been abducted and her dog has been shot. Nessa's on her way to the scene, but she may not be aware the perp has a gun and is ready to use it. I can't reach her on her cell. I'm hoping you can reach her on the radio."

"Shit." Jankowski's stomach churned at the thought of both Nessa and Eden in danger. "Do you know who the perp is? Do you know where Eden's being held?"

Barker went quiet, and Jankowski could hear a deep male voice speaking in the background.

"Who's with you, Barker? What's going on?"

"Just listen for a minute," Barker said, his voice raw. "This is going to be hard for you to hear, but the perp who has Eden is someone on the force. Someone we both know very well."

The words echoed through Jankowski's head.

*Someone else on the force is dirty? Someone who has Eden?*

"Who is it?" Jankowski demanded.

Jankowski listened to Barker inhale deeply and exhale, as if he'd run a mile. A man's voice in the background urged Barker to hurry.

"It's Kramer. Chief Kramer has Eden."

Jankowski opened his mouth to laugh, then closed it again. Barker wasn't joking. He really thought Kramer was dirty.

"You're nuts, Barker," Jankowski snorted, but his mind was starting to spin. "Why would Kramer want to abduct Eden?"

"She found out what he'd done."

Anger was starting to color Barker's words.

"She found out he and Bellows were buddies. They were both involved with the killings of Natalie Lorenzo and Helena Steele, as well as Penelope Yates. And that's not all."

A sick feeling settled into Jankowski's stomach.

"What the hell are you saying, Barker?"

"I'm saying Kramer built a makeshift prison over his garage and he's been holding women in there. I saw the place with my own eyes. I saw pictures of eight different women he'd kept locked up. I think they might all be dead."

Jankowski shook his head, refusing to believe the lies Barker was spewing at him. For some reason, Barker had it in for Kramer.

He must be trying to set Kramer up.

"I don't believe you, Barker. How about I call Kramer right now and ask him what the hell is going on?"

"Kramer won't answer your call. He's busy trying to cover up his crimes. He'll do anything to cover up what he's done. He killed Helena Steele, Natalie Lorenzo, and Penelope Yates to cover his tracks, as well as Adrian and Terri Bellows. He won't hesitate to kill Eden and Nessa, too."

Jankowski stared over at the bloody bodies still displayed in all their gory detail across the hall.

"How can you say that Kramer killed Bellows? It was a suicide. We have the weapon. I read the note."

"Nessa told me Adrian Bellows didn't kill himself. She said she had proof. That proof is there at the scene. Look for it, Jankowski. I trust Nessa, and I think she's in danger."

Jankowski walked to the doorway and stared down at the gun clutched in the dead man's hand. Slowly his eyes moved to the pictures on the bookshelf, and he realized what had been bothering him since he'd gotten there.

"Bellows has the gun in his left hand," Jankowski murmured into the phone.

"What was that?" Barker asked, his voice fuzzy as the cell reception started to fade in and out.

"Nothing," Jankowski said, his jaw clenching. "It doesn't matter. Where's Nessa heading? What's the address?"

"It's the old dairy farm east of town. The one that old man Kramer used to run."

Jankowski knew the place. He'd driven by the crumbling fence a million times on the way out to the coast, and he'd watched the sign fading away over the years.

"She'll never make it out there in this weather," Jankowski said, but his words sounded unsure, even to his own ears.

He knew Nessa pretty well, even though they'd only been partners a few months. If anyone could find a way through a hurricane to help someone, it would be Nessa.

"I'll try to reach her on the radio. I'll keep in touch."

But the cell service had already dropped.

Jankowski knew he may not be able to reach Barker again; it was up to him to find a way to warn Nessa.

If what Barker said was true, she was heading into a situation even more dangerous than the category four storm swirling around them. Once again Jankowski dialed Tucker Vanzinger's number.

"I need your help, man. And I think I know how you can clean up that mess you left behind."

# CHAPTER FORTY-THREE

Eden opened her eyes; a soft clump of dirt fell to the ground in front of her. She tried to move her head, but it felt unbearably heavy, so she closed her eyes again, willing herself to go back to sleep. A grunt and another thud prompted her to try again. She wrenched her head to the side and forced her eyes open. A big man stood over her, a shovel in his hand. Another shovelful of dirt landed beside her.

A small camping lantern hung on a hook behind the man, lighting up the dim room, revealing his rough, weathered face.

*Chief Kramer? What is he doing? Why is he here...wherever here is?*

Eden's head ached as she tried to remember where she was and how she'd gotten there. Memories of the hurricane and her frantic drive to find Kara seeped back into her mind. The events of the day began to filter through her mental fog.

*I was looking for Kara. Dr. Bellows had an address in his satnav.*

A gust of wind slammed the wooden door open, and Eden flinched, alerting Kramer that she was awake. He threw down the shovel and squatted next to her, studying her with curious eyes.

"You waking up already?"

His words were matter-of-fact, and Eden was embarrassed that her lips wouldn't form a coherent response.

*Had she suffered some sort of stroke? Did Kramer find her passed out on the ground and drag her in from the storm?*

"I never tried Chloroform before. Wasn't sure how much to use."

Kramer's words confused Eden; she frowned up at him, unsure what he was saying.

*Chloroform? Isn't that what killers use in movies to knock people out?*

She closed her eyes, trying to concentrate, but her brain wouldn't cooperate. Her thoughts and memories still seemed hazy.

"But I had to do something to stop your meddling."

Kramer's voice sounded far away.

"You've caused me a lot of trouble, you know. I had to bring the girl here before I'd had a chance to enjoy her properly. And you made me have to kill Doc. That's the worst of it."

A shiver ran down Eden's spine as she absorbed his words.

*Is he saying he's killed someone? And that it was her fault?*

She kept her eyes closed, hoping he would think she had fallen asleep again.

*No, not asleep. I wasn't asleep, I was drugged. Like Kara.*

The thought of the missing woman flashed through Eden's mind like a lightning bolt, filling her with fear and dread.

*Where is Kara? Has Kramer done something with her?*

Eden forced herself to open her eyes again and look up at Kramer's craggy face. She recoiled at the hate in his close-set eyes.

"Ka...Kara."

The croak of her voice hovered in the muggy air. Kramer's eyes flashed in fury as he realized what she'd said.

"You stupid, bitch. You're still worried about that drug-addicted nobody? Well, there she is if you're so desperate to see her."

Kramer stepped back and pointed the shovel toward a wooden wall a few feet away. Eden forced her eyes to shift toward the wall. Kara Stanislaus lay there motionless, her dark hair spilling out around her, melting into the shadows of the little building.

Eden strained to move her hand. She wanted to reach out to Kara, wanted to see if she was still alive. But her hand wouldn't cooperate. It felt thick and unimaginably heavy. The realization that she couldn't move ignited a fierce panic. Eden's chest tightened and her throat constricted.

"Help…"

She tried to scream out, but her weak plea was swallowed by the roar of the storm outside the thin wooden walls.

"Nobody can help you now, Ms. Winthrop. You've gone and stuck your nose in my business for the last time."

His big work boot appeared next to her face, and her eyes rested on a rusty red splotch that marred the surface. She raised her eyes up to see Kramer frowning down at her, his hands as big as hams on his broad hips.

"You just couldn't let it rest, could you? Couldn't let me just finish up my mission and move on."

Eden tried to block out his angry words, tried to calm her breathing. If she panicked now, it could prove fatal. She had to concentrate on getting away.

*Just wiggle the toes on one foot. Start small.*

If she could wiggle her toes, then she might be able to move her foot. And if she could regain control of her feet and her legs, she might have a chance to get away.

"My old man warned me about women like you."

Kramer cocked his head, as if considering his own words, then burst out laughing. The odd, raspy sound sent shivers down Eden's spine.

"Of course, I never much listened to that mean old bastard. He let my mother make a fool of him and then spent the rest of his life taking it out on me."

Eden felt her toes responding; she switched her focus to her foot.

*Just focus on one foot at a time. You can do this, Eden.*

"It was the one favor my old man did for me. He made me tough. Made me realize I didn't need anyone or anything."

Kramer turned and picked up the shovel again.

"But enough about that old fuck. He's dead and buried, and I'm still here and, well, I've got some more burying to do."

A clump of dirt fell close to Eden's staring eyes.

"What...what are....you going to do with...Kara?"

Her voice was weak, but she managed to squeeze out the question. Kramer paused and looked back at Kara's motionless form.

"I'm gonna bury her like the others." Kramer sounded amused. "Why do think I'm digging this hole, just for the fun of it?"

"The others?"

Kramer's face lit up, and he again put the shovel down and crouched beside Eden, looking into her wide, green eyes.

"Yes, the other girls I brought here."

He motioned over to Kara.

"She's number eight in my...collection, I guess you could say. This old stable has eight stalls; once I'm done tonight, that'll be it."

A terrible understanding grew in Eden's mind. She was looking at a serial killer. An evil man who enjoyed collecting the lives of young women. A man who planned to kill Kara, then kill her, and then go on killing.

"Why?"

The question tore from her throat like a curse, causing Kramer to frown and glare down at her in sudden anger.

"Why what? Why did I kill the girls buried in here?"

He ran a meaty hand through his thick thatch of hair and then clenched both hands into fists. Eden shrank back into the ground, sure he was going to strike out at her. Instead, he stood, grabbed the shovel, and began digging again.

"I don't have time to waste jawing with you. I've got to get this done and get back to town before people start asking questions and come looking for me."

Eden moved her legs, a tingling sensation telling her that blood was starting to circulate again. She was regaining control. If only she could find a way to distract him long enough to try to stand.

"You must have...a reason," she said, trying to think of something to get him talking. She had to stall for time. "A man doesn't kill...for no...reason."

"Who said I didn't have a reason?"

Kramer was winded now, the effort of hefting the big shovelfuls of dirt bringing beads of sweat to his forehead.

"I started killing to protect a friend, actually. To protect the only real friend I ever had. But then, well, I have to admit I started to like it. And it made it easier to take what I wanted and not have any problems afterward."

He was panting now, and the hole was getting deeper.

"I learned to bury the evidence. That's what kept me out of trouble all this time. Until *you* showed up."

Eden moved her leg, and shifted her weight slightly, tensing her back and her arms. If she jumped up, would she be able to stand? Would she be able to run?

*But what about Kara? Even if I can run out of here, what will happen to Kara? Can I just leave her here to die?*

Kramer was now knee-deep in the big hole, and his sweaty face leered over at Eden.

"I'm gonna make sure you can't cause me any more trouble. After tonight you'll never cause anyone any trouble ever again."

His raspy laugh echoed through the stable, reverberating in Eden's ears and making her hair stand on end.

*He'll never let me out of here alive. I'll never see Hope and Devon again.*

The thought of her niece and nephew brought tears to Eden's eyes. She imagined their distress when she didn't come home. Would they ever know what had happened to her? Would they ever be able to find peace again after losing the only family they had left?

*But no, they still have Reggie. She'll take care of them. If I'm gone, they'll still have Reggie and Duke.*

The thought of the golden retriever stirred a memory. Duke had been with her at Kramer's house. Was he okay? Had the dog gotten away, or had Kramer done something to him?

If only she had waited for Nessa to call back, or asked Leo to go with her. Leo Steele's face hovered in her mind, and she wondered if Leo would look for her. If he never found her, and never found out what had happened to her, would she become his new quest? Would he spend his life blaming himself for not being able to save her?

Anger began to build inside her, pushing away the sadness and fear. She glared over at Kramer, knowing she had to try to stop him. The horrible man was going to kill her, and he would destroy her family along with her. If she didn't do something soon, he would take her life and hurt everyone who loved her.

A cold resolve flooded through Eden; she closed her eyes and forced herself to go limp. A plan was starting to form, but she needed to put Kramer at ease. She needed him to believe she posed no threat.

*But I am a threat, old man. I've killed before and I won't hesitate to kill again to save myself and protect my family.*

# CHAPTER FORTY-FOUR

A stab of pain shot through Kramer's back, forcing him to drop the shovel and wait for the pain to run its course. He couldn't quit now, not before the hole was deep enough, and not when he had two women laid out on the ground next to him. If anyone saw the light in the stable and happened by to check on him, he would be done for. He'd spend the rest of his life behind bars or end up strapped to a metal table having lethal drugs pumped into his veins.

*Just gotta get these two in the ground and get back to town.*

But the hurricane wasn't cooperating. The stable walls trembled under the sustained pressure of the wind, and the old wooden door rattled on its rusty hinges. Endless rain hammered down on the thin tin roof, and Kramer's head started hurting along with his back.

*At least the Winthrop bitch has stopped whining.*

He regarded the blonde woman's slack face, nudged at her leg with his dirty boot. The chloroform had done a good job. Now that Doc was gone, along with his easy supply of drugs, maybe Kramer would have to start using chloroform more often.

A gurgling sound by the door made Kramer turn his head. A muddy stream of water was flowing under the door, quickly pooling on the dirt floor. He ran to Kara and rolled her limp body to the side. He pulled the tarp from under her and dragged it across the floor, stuffing it into the gap under the door. Fear kindled inside him as he waited to see if the tarp would hold.

*What if the whole place floods? What will come out of the ground?*

The girls in the stable had been buried in the dry, hardpacked ground. They would remain safe and sound as long as the conditions in the stable stayed the same. He wasn't sure what might happen if the ground got wet or the surrounding area flooded.

He saw with relief that the tarp had stopped the water. He was safe for now, and he wouldn't let anything jeopardize the mission. Girl eight was going in the ground, and Eden Winthrop was going with her. Nothing could stop him; it was just like that old song.

Kramer picked up the shovel and began to sing under his breath, trying to remember all the words to the song he and Doc used to sing back in the good old days in Germany.

"Off we go into the wild blue yonder, climbing high, into the sun. Here they come zooming to meet our thunder..."

Kramer raised his voice as he began to warm to the words and the tune, eager to drown out the incessant rain and wind outside.

"Down we dive, spouting our flame from under, off with one heckuva roar! We live in fame, or go down in flame, nothing'll stop the..."

With a sudden, loud crack, the old door banged off its hinges and flew into the room, smashing into Kramer and sending him staggering back against the wall. He pushed the cracked wood away and held a fist up to the dark sky beyond the doorway.

"You don't want me singing that song?"

Kramer yelled out to an unseen face from the past, his long-buried resentment at being discharged from the service finally bubbling to the surface after all these years. The self-righteous men that had kicked him out of the force had turned their backs on him after he'd sacrificed years to serve his country. They'd taken the word of a whore over his. They'd failed him just like everyone he'd ever known.

He stared out into the storm with reproachful eyes, watching the heaving palmettos beyond as they waved and bowed and shuddered. The tarp flapped and skipped along the floor, before plastering itself to one of the walls. The stable creaked and groaned around him, and he shook himself into action. He had no more time to waste; the hole would have to be deep enough.

Water burbled and streamed into the room, turning the dirt floor to mud and forming puddles under Kramer's boots. He grasped Kara's ankles, feeling heat in her skin that let him know she was still alive, still a risk. He dragged her toward the open grave he'd prepared. Once she lay at the edge, he circled around and pushed her gently forward, applying just enough pressure to begin her slow slide down into the pit.

Collecting the tarp from the corner of the room, he held it out, preparing to drape it over her body, then remembered that he had something for her. He reached into his back pocket and pulled out the gold chain and cross that Doc had given him. He'd said the girl had been wearing it when he'd taken her.

*Best to bury all the evidence. It'll be safer that way.*

Kramer tossed the necklace into the hole; it landed on the girl's hand, prompting a gasp. Her hand twitched, then moved. She was waking up. He heard a noise behind him and spun around just as Eden Winthrop grabbed the shovel and swung it at him.

"Wake up, Kara! Wake up and run!"

Eden's scream sent a surge of adrenaline through Kramer. He lunged forward, grasping for the handle of the shovel, but then slipped in the mud and fell to one knee.

"Give me the shovel!" he commanded, his face distorted with rage. "Don't make me do this the hard way."

He released the shovel and stepped back, pulling out the gun in his belt holster. He didn't want to have to use it again. The Ruger wasn't his official service weapon, but Kramer knew the gun, as well as any bullets he fired, could likely be traced back to him. He didn't want to leave any evidence, but he'd do what needed to be done.

*Eden Winthrop is not getting out of here alive.*

Eden froze at the sight of the little gun gleaming in his hand.

Kramer raised the pistol, aiming between her wide, green eyes. His finger itched to pull the trigger. Once she was gone he would be safe again, and he'd feel no remorse, only relief. After all, by killing her, he was protecting himself.

*Wouldn't anyone do the same?*

Most people would deny it, but if he was honest, he couldn't blame himself for his actions. Was it his fault that Helena Steele had threatened to reveal Doc's link to Natalie Lorenzo? The information she had would have raised a number of unpleasant questions in the community for both Kramer and Doc.

And he'd warned Penelope Yates not to get involved when she'd come to him claiming Natalie must have been killed by the man who had fathered Natalie's son. He'd even arranged for her to go into the psych ward in an effort to discredit her so that he wouldn't have to kill her. But had she listened? No, after twelve years of silence she'd decided to talk to a private investigator. So, what choice had he had? He had to protect himself and his friend.

Of course, the situation with Doc and Terri was harder to accept, but it couldn't have been helped. If Doc had been arrested and questioned, he might have cracked under pressure. He was weak, after all. And Terri had been an unknown. It would be too risky to leave her out there, uncertain how much she really knew about Doc's activities.

He looked around at the stable walls and the numbers that marked each girl's grave. Had he killed them all to protect himself?

*Yes, in a way I guess I did. If I'd let them go free, they would have come back to haunt me, like the girl in Germany, and like Natalie Lorenzo.*

"Step back against the wall," he called out, waving the gun. Eden stepped back, still clutching the shovel.

"Throw me the shovel."

Eden hesitated and Kramer aimed the Ruger down at Kara, who was stirring in the pit below.

"Give it to me, now, or I'll shoot her."

Eden tossed the shovel forward, tears streaming down her face as she looked into the muddy grave.

"You make one wrong move and I'll put a bullet in your head."

Kramer stuck the gun back in the holster and picked up the shovel. He began scooping huge mounds of dirt back into the hole, covering Kara and causing Eden to cry out.

"No, please don't-"

Her frantic plea stopped abruptly, and she stood still, listening to the haunting howl of the wind in the night. A soft thumping sound beat above the wind. A *chop, chop, chop* that made Kramer's hair stand on end.

*What the hell is that?*

He turned to the door and stared out into the darkness beyond. As soon as his back was to her, Eden jumped, grabbing at the shovel with both hands. Kramer spun around, wrestling for control of the muddy handle, sensing even as he did that the real danger was behind him.

A huge gust of warm air blasted into the stable, as the *chop, chop, chop* grew louder. Kramer looked up to see the tin roof blow up and away as if torn from the stable by the hand of God, cartwheeling end over end into the night.

Kramer stared through the door, stunned by the flashing lights and whirring blades of the helicopter which was now visible in the old pasture. Rain and wind swirled down into the roofless stable, coating him with a sticky layer of grit and grime.

A bulky man wearing military gear and a rain jacket emerged from the helicopter. He crouched down to avoid the rotors and ran toward the quaking walls of the stable, his bulky combat boots splashing through the soggy pasture. As he neared the door he raised a hand in greeting.

"Hiya, Chief. It's me, Tucker. Tucker Vanzinger."

Kramer blinked rainwater out of his eyes, not sure if the weathered soldier in front of him could really be the cocky young detective he'd banished years ago.

"What are you doing here?" Kramer asked stupidly, his mind still reeling, his mouth operating in slow motion.

"I'm here to do what I should have done a long time ago," Vanzinger said, stepping closer and looking through the door. "You got anybody in there that needs help?"

Instinctively Kramer grabbed for his gun, pulling it out and pointing it at Vanzinger before he realized what he was doing.

"You shouldn't have come here, Tucker. Reinhardt and I warned you never to come back here. You should have listened."

Vanzinger regarded the Ruger with narrowed eyes and held up his hands in a placating gesture.

"Let's talk about this, Kramer. No one has to get hurt."

Kramer snorted derisively and waved the gun at Vanzinger.

"I should've killed you twelve years ago. But better late than ..."

A swift movement behind Kramer prompted him to glance around, but he was too late. The edge of the shovel smashed into his head with a resounding thud. Eden Winthrop's unforgiving green eyes were the last thing Kramer saw before his world went dark.

# CHAPTER FORTY-FIVE

Jankowski crouched behind the wooden wall waiting for a signal from Vanzinger. He pointed the barrel of his Remington toward the open doorway of the dimly lit stable and inhaled deeply, trying to steady his nerves. The shotgun felt strange in his hands; he wasn't used to handling anything bigger than his Glock outside the station's shooting range.

When they'd landed in the helicopter Vanzinger had instructed his co-pilot, a nervous-looking guardsman with the callsign Twitch, to stay in the chopper and get ready to take off at a moment's notice. Vanzinger had also insisted that he would approach the shed on his own and try to engage Kramer in conversation. The only thing he'd asked was to use Jankowski's service weapon, which left Jankowski with just the Remington to provide cover and back-up.

Before Jankowski could peer around the doorframe to get eyes on Vanzinger, the wall behind him was illuminated by the headlights of a car hurtling toward him on the rutted dirt road leading up to the farm. Not knowing if the driver of the car was a friend or foe, Jankowski knew he had to make a move before it was too late. He stuck the barrel of the shotgun into the room, then leaned forward to assess the situation.

"It's all good, Jank!"

Vanzinger's words reached Jankowski just as the speeding car screeched to a halt fifty yards away. It was a black Dodge Charger, the make and model favored by the WBPD.

"We've got company," Jankowski yelled back, sidestepping into the room, the Remington poised to swing either in or out of the stable as the situation required.

He saw at a glance that Chief Kramer lay in a heap on the muddy floor and that Eden Winthrop knelt beside him, a shovel gripped in her hands. He turned his face to the Dodger, holding his breath as he waited for the door to open.

*Could there be another dirty cop coming to backup Kramer?*

Jankowski raised the barrel of the gun hesitantly, unsure he would be able to pull the trigger. He couldn't imagine killing a fellow officer. It was the ultimate violation of the principles he'd lived by for most of his adult life. When he'd joined the force, he'd taken an oath to protect and serve the community, and he'd understood then that he was also making an implicit promise to protect his brothers in blue at all costs. It would be a hard promise to break.

He exhaled in relief as Nessa stepped out of the car and pushed back the hood of the yellow slicker to reveal her red curls.

*Make that my brothers and sisters in blue.*

Nessa stared at Jankowski, her eyes lingering on the shotgun cradled in his arms, her hand resting on the Glock in her holster.

"It's all clear, Nessa!"

His voice fought against the roar of the storm, then disappeared into the next gust of wind. When Nessa didn't move, he raised his arm and waved, motioning for her to approach.

Nessa still didn't move, even though her hair was now plastered in wet strands against her head. Jankowski squinted into the night, seeing in the light spilling from the Dodger that her mascara was running in black streaks down her cheeks.

*What's wrong with her? Is that the rain, or is she crying?*

His heart clenched at the fear he saw on his partner's face. She was terrified. In a sudden rush of understanding, he knew why.

The last time Nessa had approached a fellow detective on a dark and rainy night, she'd been shot. Although she'd been saved by her vest, she'd sustained serious head injuries and had been in the hospital for days. Her family was still trying to recover from the trauma of almost losing her. And now, here she was, brave enough to be standing in the rain once again, risking her life to save someone else.

Admiration surged through Jankowski. He bent and laid his weapon on the ground, then lifted his hands to show Nessa he understood her apprehension, and that he was unarmed.

Nessa nodded and began making her way over the uneven terrain, sloshing through puddles and crunching over broken branches and debris. As she drew closer Jankowski saw that she had unholstered her firearm and held it by her side.

"What's with the helicopter. Jankowski? Who's with you?"

She eyed the four walls of the stable, then looked across the field at the mangled remains of the roof. Before Jankowski could answer, Tucker Vanzinger stepped into the doorway.

"You must be Nessa."

Nessa raised her Glock and leveled it at Vanzinger's chest, then glared over at Jankowski.

"Who the hell is he?"

"He's Tucker Vanzinger, the guy that flew that copter out here to save you and Eden Winthrop."

Lifting both hands to show they were empty, Vanzinger stepped back into the room and motioned for Nessa to enter.

"Come see for yourself."

The rain slowed to a drizzle as Nessa followed Jankowski and Vanzinger into the stable, and the howling of the wind diminished enough for Jankowski to hear her intake of breath at the sight of Eden huddled in one of the stalls next to Kramer's crumpled body. She was scraping at the ground, struggling to maneuver the heavy shovel.

"Oh my god, Eden. Are you okay?"

Nessa hurried to Eden's side, shoving her gun back into the holster before taking the shovel from Eden's trembling hands. She put an arm around Eden's shoulders and looked down into the hole in the floor, a look of horrified understanding dawning in her eyes.

"Kara!" Eden forced the words out in a hoarse whisper. "We need to save Kara!"

Pushing Nessa's arm to the side, Eden began to claw at the dirt with her hands in desperation. Jankowski realized with a jolt of horror what Eden was trying to tell them. Kara Stanislaus was under the ground, but she might still be alive.

The shovel's slick handle slipped in Jankowski's grip as he began scooping mud and water from the hole, being careful not to harm the girl that lay beneath. He lowered himself into the hole and continued to lift mounds of dirt out of the makeshift grave until a patch of alabaster skin appeared.

Throwing the shovel up and over the edge of the hole, Jankowski bent to scrape the remaining dirt from Kara's motionless body with his bare hands. His heart thudded in his chest as he felt in vain for a pulse in her thin wrist.

"No pulse," he muttered, as he slid one big arm under her shoulders and the other one under her knees.

Vanzinger bent to take the lifeless girl from Jankowski so that he could pull himself out of the pit.

"Are we too late?"

Nessa's voice was thick with dread as she helped Vanzinger lay Kara on a piece of tarp next to Eden.

"I'll breathe," Vanzinger said, ignoring Nessa's question. "Jank, you do the compressions."

Vanzinger knelt next to Kara and tilted her head back, checking her mouth for obstructions before pinching her nose and blowing into her mouth. Her thin chest lifted with the breath, and Jankowski felt a twinge of hope as he knelt next to his friend and positioned his hands over Kara's chest. He laced his fingers together and began fast, firm compressions as he'd been trained to do, but had never been called on to perform in a real rescue before.

Adrenaline rushed through Jankowski, strengthening his arms and quickening his pulse. He had to remind himself to keep the compressions firm, but not push down too hard. If Kara made it through this alive, he didn't want to be the cause of bruised or broken ribs.

Just as Jankowski's hope was turning to despair, Kara coughed and wheezed. She turned her head to the side and retched out a mouthful of muddy water, her hands clutching weakly at something on her chest. A glimmer of gold shone from beneath the mud caked on her dress.

"Her necklace," Eden said, her voice trembling with emotion. "She has the necklace her father gave her."

Nessa stood and slid off her yellow slicker, draping it over Kara's thin body as the rain continued to trickle down.

"Let's get them to the chopper, Jank," Vanzinger said, stretching his back. "I have equipment on board, and we can have them at the hospital in no time."

"What about Kramer?" Jankowski asked, looking over at the big police chief sprawled in the dirt. "He got a bad blow on the head, but he's still breathing. Should we take him, too?"

A high-pitched voice sounded behind them.

"I'm not letting that maniac anywhere near Kara again."

Eden stood on shaking legs, staring over at Kara's battered body on the stretcher. Her eyes grew bright and hard when they shifted to Kramer. Nessa nodded and took Eden's arm, helping her out the door.

"I agree. I can secure Kramer and drive him back in my car. The storm is letting up, so I should be able to get him back to town without any problem."

"Okay, let me get Eden and Kara on the chopper and then I'll help you secure Kramer in your car."

Jankowski put an arm around Eden and helped her walk to the chopper. Twitch waited for them with anxious eyes. The jittery pilot reached down and hoisted Eden up into the cabin.

"We need a stretcher, man," Jankowski called to him. "I've got another female in there that can't walk. She'll need transport to the nearest hospital."

More headlights bounced toward the farm as Twitch lowered the stretcher to Jankowski and Vanzinger. The men watched a black BMW approach as they hustled back to get Kara. By the time they'd made it to the stable, Leo Steele and Pete Barker had jumped out of the car and were charging toward them.

Jankowski took a double take as Frankie Dawson exited from the rear of the car carrying a big golden retriever. Jankowski recognized the dog as Eden Winthrop's emotional support animal, Duke.

"These guys friends of yours, Jank?" Vanzinger asked as they lifted Kara onto the stretcher and began pushing her toward the chopper.

"I know 'em, but I wouldn't say they're friends."

A tattered palmetto frond got stuck in the stretcher's wheel, and Jankowski bent down to extract it. When he stood up, Leo Steele was standing next to him.

"Is Eden in there? Is she okay?"

The raw pain in Leo's eyes stopped Jankowski from coming back with his usual sarcastic retort.

"She's okay, and she's already on the chopper. But Kara needs immediate medical attention so no time to chat."

He pushed past Leo and helped Vanzinger and Twitch load the stretcher into the rear of the helicopter. He turned back to see Leo right behind him. Barker and Frankie hovered a few feet away, their faces grim.

"I need to see her," Leo pleaded. "I have to know she's all right."

Jankowski looked up at Vanzinger, then back at Leo. He shook his head and sighed.

"You go with them on the chopper, Steele. I'll stay here and help Nessa get Kramer back to town. Barker can help us and then drive your car back."

"What about me and Duke?" Frankie asked, his eyes jumping between Jankowski and Leo. "You aren't gonna leave us out here with a serial killer are you?"

Jankowski rolled his eyes and shouted up at Vanzinger.

"Tucker, how many passengers can you take with you?"

Vanzinger leaned out and looked at Frankie and Duke. He raised his eyebrows and shrugged.

"The two of them don't weigh more than a hundred pounds soaking wet," he said, his voice impatient. "They can come, but we need to hurry."

Frankie passed the dog to Jankowski and climbed into the copter. Jankowski felt the dog shivering in his arms, and a hot rush of disgust for Kramer rolled through him.

*Why would he shoot an innocent dog? He really is a heartless bastard.*

Leo had climbed aboard and turned to take Duke.

"Thanks, Jankowski," Leo said, swallowing hard. "I owe you."

Jankowski could see Eden crying with relief as Leo presented her with the dog, whose tail had started to wag despite his injuries.

"Get that dog a blanket!" Jankowski yelled up to Vanzinger.

He turned away from the sight of Leo and Eden huddled together over Duke. They were the picture of a loving family reunited, and as happy as he was for them, the sight made him feel more alone than he'd ever felt before.

"Okay everyone, get back!"

Twitch and Vanzinger closed the doors and soon the helicopter was hovering and swinging out into the gusty night. The flashing lights soon faded into the dark, and Jankowski turned back to Barker.

"Where's Nessa?" he asked.

Barker looked at him in surprise.

"What do you mean? She wasn't on the chopper?"

Jankowski's heart jumped into his throat. He looked at the ground next to the stable wall where he'd laid the Remington. The shotgun was gone.

"She's in there with Kramer, and he may be armed!"

Jankowski started to run toward the stable, but Barker held out a hand to restrain him.

"You can't go charging in there if he's got a gun. You won't be any help to Nessa if you get shot."

Jankowski felt for his holster. His Glock was with Vanzinger, flying away in the dark.

"Are you carrying, Barker?"

Barker's eyes widened as he saw Jankowski's empty holster.

"You've gotta be kidding me."

Jankowski slowly shook his head.

Before Barker could respond, they heard Nessa's distressed voice coming from the stable, followed by Kramer's deeper tones.

"I'm going in," Jankowski whispered to Barker, frustration at his helplessness turning to rage. "I'll kill him with my bare hands if I have to."

Barker grabbed for his arm, but Jankowski shook him off and stormed toward the stable, determined to save Nessa even if it meant risking his own life. After all, she had kids and a husband, while he had nothing to lose.

The lantern on the stable wall flickered, throwing eerie shadows over the stalls. Jankowski crouched and then jumped into the room, determined to put up a fight for the shotgun. Kramer was injured and weak, and Jankowski was confident if he took the older man by surprise, he would be able to overpower him.

Nessa gaped at Jankowski as he skidded to a stop next to Kramer. She held her Glock in her right hand and Jankowski's Remington in her left. Both guns were trained on Kramer. The police chief was bound and cuffed, his face red with indignation as he watched Jankowski take in the scene.

"Jankowski, you better talk some sense into your partner before you both do something you'll regret."

A flush of anger stirred in Jankowski's guts at Kramer's cold words. The old man actually thought they were stupid enough to be intimidated by his threats.

"No, Kramer," Barker said, walking in behind Jankowski. "You're the one that's gonna be doing the regretting. We know everything, and Leo has already informed the feds. They'll be waiting for you back in town I'm sure. Or at least they will be there once the storm passes through."

Nessa looked up into the cloudy sky.

"The rain's stopped," she said, almost to herself. "And the wind's dying down. I think we've been spared the worst of it."

"No, Nessa, the worst of it is right there in front of you."

Jankowski glared down at Kramer, resisting the urge to kick the big man that had caused so much heartache.

"Is this where you buried them?" Barker asked, walking to stand over Kramer. "Is this where you put the other girls? Is that what the numbers mean?"

Jankowski looked at the stalls, noting the numbers on the wall above each one. He turned to Barker and frowned, trying to understand what the retired detective was saying.

Barker picked up a shovel and moved to stand in stall seven.

"If I dig here, what will I find, Kramer? *Who* will I find?"

Kramer glowered up at Barker, his eyes shining with hate.

"You always were weak, Barker. You never had the stomach for the job. It's no wonder you had to quit."

Nessa raised the Glock and aimed it between Kramer's eyes.

"Don't make me mad, *Chief*. Barker's the best detective Willow Bay ever had. Better than ten of you and your buddy Reinhardt."

"It's too bad Reinhardt didn't finish you off, Nessa. I warned him you would cause trouble," Kramer hissed. "Women always do."

Jankowski picked up the shovel and waved it over Kramer's head.

"Enough talk, old man. Are you going to admit what you've done, or should I start digging?"

Kramer smiled up at Jankowski, but his eyes were bleak.

"I'm not saying anything else without my lawyer."

Jankowski sighed, then joined Barker in stall seven. As he began to dig, Nessa's cell phone buzzed in her pocket.

"Cell towers must be back up," she said pulling out her phone.

Her voice quivered as she spoke. Jankowski smiled as he listened to Nessa's side of the conversation.

"Hi, Jerry. Yes, I'm okay. The boys? Yes. I love you, too, honey, more than anything in the world. Okay. I'll be home soon. Bye."

Jankowski looked at Nessa and smiled at the new stream of tears on her cheeks, glad that Jerry and the boys would be waiting for her. But as he shoveled up another mound of dirt, uncovering a patch of tarp and a tangle of long red hair, he feared it would be a while before Nessa would have the chance to go home.

# CHAPTER FORTY-SIX

The softball thwacked against Cooper's bat and skittered down the line toward first base. The player at first dove for the ball but misjudged its speed, turning to watch as a tiny outfielder trotted over to pick it up and fling it toward home. By the time the ball was back in the pitcher's hand, Cooper was proudly standing on second base.

"Yeah, Cooper! Good job, buddy!"

Nessa shrieked and jumped next to Jerry, unable to contain her excitement at her youngest son's first double. It felt so good to laugh. And it was the first time in over two weeks that she'd been able to forget the horror and carnage Kramer had left behind.

"I'm going to take the boys to get pizza with the team," Jerry said, pulling her against him for a hug. "You go and see how Barker's doing. I know you must have a lot to talk about."

"You sure? I can go with y'all if you want."

Jerry shook his head, a flush of color rising in his cheeks.

"No, we'll be fine," he said, taking her hand. "And I'm sorry."

Nessa raised her eyebrows.

"Sorry for what?"

"For not giving you the space you need, and, well...for not trusting you the way I should. I know I acted like an idiot, thinking you and Jankowski..."

"No, you weren't being an idiot, Jerry. You were being human. But I want you to know I would never do anything to hurt you or the boys. I would never betray you. Not with Jankowski or anyone else."

Jerry swallowed hard and nodded, looking out over the crowd.

"I better go find the boys. We'll see you at home later."

Nessa watched him walk away, waiting until his tall figure disappeared into the crowd before she walked back to her car.

\* \* \*

A big, dusty pick-up truck sat next to Barker's little Prius when Nessa arrived. She parked her Charger along the curb and walked over Barker's well-manicured lawn to the front door.

"It's open," Barker yelled out after she'd knocked.

Loud male voices led her to Barker's dining room, which doubled as his office. The table had been recently polished and cleaned, and Barker sat with Jankowski on one side of him and Tucker Vanzinger on the other.

"You want some tea?" Barker asked, and Nessa saw that he had what looked like a cup of herbal tea in front of him, while the other men were holding bottles of Bud Light.

"Come on, Nessa. Have a beer with us," Jankowski teased, rolling his eyes at Barker's teacup.

"I'm fine, thanks. I've got my water with me."

Nessa held up her refillable bottle of water. She'd been pretty good about keeping it with her lately. She'd decided to focus on her health and her family. Those were the most important things, and she planned to hold on to them for dear life while she still had them.

"Tucker was about to tell us why he just up and quit the force all those years ago, weren't you, man?"

Jankowski grinned over at Vanzinger, who looked less than pleased to be the center of attention. Nessa saw that he was a redhead, like her, although his coppery hair was already streaked with a few strands of white. She ran a hand through her red curls.

*With my job, I don't imagine it'll take long for my hair to turn white.*

She watched Vanzinger's eyes darken as he began talking about his first year as a detective partnered with Detective Kirk Reinhardt.

"At first I was in awe of Reinhardt. It seemed like he knew everyone in town and seemed to have all the answers. Anytime we'd get assigned to a case he'd decide what had happened and who to blame within the first few hours."

Vanzinger took a swig from his bottle and scratched at his ear.

"Anyway, it didn't take too long for me to see that all those people that knew him, were actually a little afraid of him. He liked to intimidate people, I think. He intimidated me, for sure."

The room was quiet as Vanzinger thought about what to say next. He looked down at his hands and sighed.

"I'd already figured out he wasn't a good guy by the time we were assigned to the Helena Steele homicide. I'd seen enough by then to realize he was involved in something, although I didn't know details."

Vanzinger abruptly stood and stalked over to the window.

"Evidence would disappear when Reinhardt suddenly decided a perp was innocent, or new evidence might be handed in anonymously when he wanted someone to go down. I wasn't sure if he was getting paid to fix cases, or if he just got off on having the power to screw with people's lives."

"I vote that he got paid," Barker volunteered, "and that the power trip was just a bonus."

Nessa nodded but didn't interrupt. She could tell the story was difficult for Vanzinger to tell, and that he was stalling, delaying the part about what had happened to make him leave town.

"The Helena Steele homicide was my first murder scene, and it was a bad one. I'd never even seen a dead body, except in the morgue." Vanzinger looked queasy at the memory. "So, seeing the way Helena Steele had been sliced open..."

Sweat was beginning to bead on Vanzinger's forehead. He cleared his throat and took another long sip from his bottle.

"Anyway, I wanted to do right by the victim, and her husband seemed so torn up. I couldn't believe he'd done it. It just didn't seem to fit. And when the knife didn't have his prints on it and the time of death was estimated to be hours before he'd gotten to the house...well, I spoke up. I told Reinhardt I didn't buy the husband as the perp."

"Let me guess," Barker said, "Reinhardt shut you down, so you went to Kramer. Am I right?"

"Yeah, I told Reinhardt I was convinced Ken Steele wasn't our perp. He told me to keep my opinion to myself. For the first time, I felt threatened by him. I mean, I knew he was crooked, but I was still too naive to think he would go after another detective. So, I went to Kramer. Spilled my guts."

"What did Kramer say?" Jankowski asked, earning a glare from Nessa.

"He told me that reporting a fellow officer was against the code. He said he didn't need troublemakers like me on the force, and that he wanted my shield and my weapon. Just like that. I was stunned. Of course, I said I wouldn't do it, and Kramer laughed."

Vanzinger looked over at Nessa with bitter eyes.

"He said if I didn't leave town he'd make sure I ended up in jail or worse, He said he had evidence against me that would put me away for years. When I asked what it was, he just said, he didn't know but he'd think of something. By the time I left his office, I didn't want to be on the force anymore, anyway."

He sat down again and leaned back in his chair.

"I kept my mouth shut, but I also kept tabs on the trial. When Ken Steele went down I felt sick. I wanted to come forward...I thought about it..."

"But you didn't," Barker said, his eyes hard.

"No, I didn't."

Vanzinger raised his chin but wouldn't meet Barker's eyes.

"I thought nobody would believe me. Then when Ken Steele committed suicide in prison, I knew it was too late."

"If you'd come forward back then, maybe we could have stopped what happened after that." Nessa's voice was soft, but Vanzinger flinched as if she'd slapped him. "Maybe all those women wouldn't have had to die."

"Don't you think I know that?" Vanzinger's eyes blazed as he looked at the detectives around the table. "It kills me to know that by keeping quiet I've caused so many other people to get hurt."

Jankowski reached out to put his hand on Vanzinger's shoulder.

"Lots of cops have made the mistake of following *the code*, whatever that is. And you couldn't know the extent of Reinhardt and Kramer's crimes. At least you came forward once you did. You made it right in the end."

Vanzinger shook his head and sighed.

"My cowardice has cost people their lives, and I've got to find some way to live with that."

Nessa sipped at the water in her big bottle, trying to drown the resentment and anger she felt at hearing Vanzinger's story. It was hard to accept that he'd done nothing to stop an innocent man from going to jail. But if she was honest with herself, she knew she couldn't blame Vanzinger for what Reinhardt and Kramer had gone on to do. The men would have surely followed through on their threats if he had tried to expose them.

"You okay, Nessa?"

Barker was staring at her with his concerned, puppy dog eyes, and Nessa felt a rush of affection for the older man. He'd been through a lot as well, and yet he always worried about her. Always tried to make sure she was okay.

"It's been rough. I've been having trouble sleeping."

Nessa felt awkward admitting it in front of Vanzinger, but he was part of everything that had happened, and in a way, she felt he had a right to be sitting there listening.

"The crime scene out at the stable..."

She had to stop to gulp down more water.

"It's always there, you know? I can still see the remains...no matter how hard I try to block it out."

She closed her eyes against the images of the pitiful bones and hair entangled with decaying fabric. The remains of seven girls had been pull from the earth, and Iris and her team were still in the process of identifying them so their families could be notified.

"I know what you mean, Nessa," Barker said. "I've been waking up in cold sweats, thinking about that room over the garage. I still can't believe anyone could do that, much less a man I've known for over twenty years."

"He's not a man, he's a monster," Nessa muttered, clenching her fists on the table. "And I'll never forgive him for what he did to those girls."

As the men around the table nodded and finished their drinks, Nessa felt fear rise and mingle with her anger. Somehow she knew she would never be the same, and that the girls in the stable would continue to haunt her dreams for many years to come.

# CHAPTER FORTY–SEVEN

arker had insisted on driving his Prius up to Raiford so that Nessa could relax on the three-hour drive north. They'd impulsively decided to go to the Florida State Prison to meet with Vinny Lorenzo in person. Nessa wanted to ask him to identify Adrian Bellows as the man he'd seen leaving the Old Canal Motel on the night his mother had been killed. Barker wanted to tell Vinny that they'd identified his father through DNA testing. Barker even had a printout of the DNA test results with him.

"You sure you want to go through with this?" Nessa asked, studying him with her pale blue eyes. "You know how upset you got last time you saw him."

"That was twelve years ago, and this is different," Barker said, keeping his eyes on the road ahead. "This time I have something I need to tell him, and maybe I'll be able to get some closure at the same time."

Nessa turned her head to look out at the green fields whizzing by, keeping her voice casual.

"So, any more news on Taylor?"

Barker had shared his fright at seeing the picture of the girl who had looked so much like Taylor in the room over Reinhardt's garage. He'd also expressed his determination to track down his daughter and bring her home.

"No, I haven't had any luck yet. I thought Google could help you find anything, but so far...nothing."

"Seriously? You're trying to find your daughter using Google?"

Nessa raised an eyebrow as she turned to stare at Barker. He kept his face expressionless for another beat, then smiled.

"Well, I can't say I didn't try it, but I also have a few friends at the DMV and the credit bureau who've let me dig into their databases. Unfortunately, that got me about as far as Google. Nothing yet."

Barker's smile faded as he wondered how Taylor was managing to stay off the radar of the credit bureaus and the Department of Motor Vehicles. Could she really navigate the world without a credit card or driver's license? The worry that had been stewing in his stomach started again, and the burning pain soon followed. He'd have to get that checked out.

*Maybe I'm finally getting that ulcer I kept telling Taylor she was going to give me.*

His smile returned as he remembered the rare occasions he'd been home in time to have dinner with Taylor and Caroline. They'd all enjoyed swapping sarcastic remarks and lighthearted insults. He would nag Taylor about coming home late and keeping her room a mess. She'd complain that he smoked like a chimney and ate all the cookie dough Hagen-Dazs ice cream before anyone else in the house got the chance. Under all the teasing and complaining though, she'd been a daddy's girl. Or at least, he had thought she was.

"What are you smiling about?" Nessa asked, her eyes eager for happy news in the wake of so much sorrow.

"Just thinking about Taylor as a little girl," Barker admitted, his smile turning into a laugh. "She was always such a smartass."

"She must take after you then."

"She does in some ways, but she's so much smarter."

The ache in his stomach spread to his chest, and his laugh threatened to turn into tears.

"I've got to find her, Nessa. Whether she wants to see me or not. I've got to make sure she's okay. The world is a dangerous place, and I can't believe I've been a big enough fool to let her face it on her own for so long. No matter what it takes, I have to find her."

Nessa reached out and put her hand on Barker's shoulder.

"You'll find her, Barker. I know you will. You're the best damn detective I know. And the most stubborn damn detective, too."

Barker shook his head and sniffed, knowing he needed to change the conversation. Nessa had enough to deal with without him adding his worries on top of everything else.

He looked over at Nessa and cocked his head.

"How's Jerry doing? You two okay now?"

"Yeah, I think we are."

She shook her head and sighed.

"You won't believe what he was thinking."

"Let me guess. He was thinking you and Jankowski were doing the nasty. Am I right?"

Nessa sputtered in surprise, then started laughing.

"The nasty? Is that what you call it?"

Barker blushed a bright red, then started laughing, too.

"You know what I mean. He thought you were having an affair with your new partner, right?"

Nessa stopped laughing and nodded.

"Yes, that's what he was thinking."

Barker looked out the window and pretended to be interested in the sign for the next rest area.

"So, were you?'

Nessa froze, then turned in her seat to glower at Barker.

"Was I what?" she asked, her voice cold.

"Were you sleeping with Jankowski? And before you play the injured party routine, remember I've been in your shoes. I know how much it takes out of you to do your job."

Nessa gaped at him.

"So, what exactly are you saying?"

"I'm saying, if you turned to your partner for comfort, I'd understand. I wouldn't judge you."

Nessa snorted and looked out the window again.

"Did that trick ever work with suspects? The old *I understand why you did it and you can tell me* trick?"

Barker shrugged.

"I'm just saying…"

"Really? Me and Jankowski? You must think I'm desperate. Of course, I'm not screwing around with Jankowski. I wouldn't do that. No matter how bad things got."

She lowered her voice, the outrage draining away as fast as it had come, and looked down at her wedding ring.

"I just gotta do a better job of showing Jerry that he and the kids mean everything to me. I can't lose them."

Barker remained quiet as they drove on, but he had to admit he was relieved that Nessa hadn't started fooling around on Jerry. Barker was a romantic at heart, and he liked to think some couples could stay together no matter what life threw at them. That's how he'd thought of himself and Caroline. An unbreakable couple. But somehow life had thrown the one punch they couldn't duck. And now here he was, alone and still lost in his grief.

*Maybe I should go to counseling after all.*

He had a sudden image of Reggie Horn's bowed head at the cemetery. He'd asked Eden about her and she'd told him that Reggie was a therapist who'd lost her husband a few years back. Who could better understand his suffering than someone who had gone through it as well? He could ask her to counsel him.

*Maybe Reggie can help me get past the grief.*

He decided to store the thought away for later consideration.

\* \* \*

The Florida State Prison in Raiford had opened for business in the sixties, quickly earning a reputation as one of the toughest prisons in the country. Barker recalled that over two hundred prisoners had been executed over the years. He'd seen the resulting grave markers on the grounds around the prison, and as they drove up to the entrance he imagined the ghosts of the executed might still be trapped behind the silver razor-wire fence. He shivered despite the heat as he parked the car.

Once inside the big concrete building they went through the same security procedures as the other visitors, even though Nessa tried to flash her shield. The guard just looked at her with a deadpan expression and told her to please put her shield and all her other belongings in the tray.

Eventually, they'd made it through the maze of security, steel bars, and locked doors, and were released into a crowded room with long tables. Vinny Lorenzo sat at a table in the corner of the room, wearing a prison jumpsuit. He didn't look up as they approached.

Barker remembered Vinny as a twelve-year-old kid who found out his mother had been killed and that he was officially an orphan. The image of Vinny's dead eyes had stayed with Barker through the years, and he braced himself to look into those eyes again. He wondered if this time he would be able to see a resemblance between Vinny and the man he now knew was Vinny's father.

"Hi Vinny, they treating you okay in here?"

Vinny looked up, his expression guarded. He just stared at Barker, who realized the kid had inherited his mother's eyes. Natalie Lorenzo had left her son something after all.

"Hi Vinny, I'm Detective Nessa Ainsley."

A spark of something flared behind Vinny's eyes. He recognized Nessa's name. She'd been a victim of the man he'd worked for in the months leading up to his arrest, and she'd sat in on a few of the interrogations he'd gone through after he'd been captured fleeing from the Old Canal Motel.

"We found out who killed your mother," Barker said, not sure if this would be considered good news or bad news to the man in front of him. "And we found your father."

The spark in Vinny's eyes grew brighter, but he still didn't speak. He just waited and watched Nessa pull out the photo line-up she'd prepared. She showed him a sheet of photos. The men all looked pretty much the same. Adrian Bellows was the second to last man on the second row.

"You recognize any of these men? Did you see any of them when you were at the Old Canal Motel the night your mother was murdered?"

Vinny stared at the photos, his face expressionless. After a long beat, he lifted his hand and rested a finger on Adrian Bellows' photo.

"He looks older in this picture," Vinny said, his voice flat, "but it's definitely him. You say you guys caught him?"

Barker paused, then shook his head.

"No, someone killed him a few weeks back. He's dead."

Vinny looked down at the photo, then back up at Barker.

"Good. I'm glad he's dead."

Barker nodded, and Nessa picked up the photo lineup.

"So, you found out who my father is?"

Barker pulled out the DNA results.

"Yes, we did. And we confirmed it with a DNA test."

Barker laid a sheet of paper on the table in front of Vinny.

"Your father's name is listed in this report."

Vinny read the name on the sheet and frowned. He glanced up at Nessa and Barker, the mask of indifference gone.

"Douglas Kramer?" Emotion colored his words for the first time. "Willow Bay's chief of police is my father?"

Barker nodded, forcing himself to maintain eye contact. Vinny Lorenzo might be a killer now, but Barker tried to remember the boy he'd been before the world had ruined him. That little boy lived somewhere inside the killer, and Barker figured he deserved a little sympathy.

"Chief Kramer's been arrested and charged with multiple homicides. He knew your mother's killer, and we believe they molested her when she was just a teenager."

"So, I'm the kid of a killer?"

Barker thought about the question, not sure what to say. He looked into the eyes that had stayed with him over the last twelve years and wished things had been different.

*You can't change the past, but you can change the way you look at it.*

"You're the kid of a woman who loved you. Your mom was trying to get you back. Trying to make your father accept his responsibilities. That was why she was killed. She died trying to do right by you. That's what you need to remember."

Vinny frowned and picked up the DNA results. Slowly he crumpled the paper in his fist, then turned and motioned to the guard that he was ready to go. Barker watched him walk away, but when Vinny stepped through the door he looked back; he held Barker's gaze until the door had closed between them.

# CHAPTER FORTY-EIGHT

Kara stretched out on the twin bed, lifting her leg so that she could see the angry red circle of lacerated skin. The doctors had assured her that the physical scars around her ankle would fade over time, but she knew the mental and emotional scars would be harder to heal.

Although she'd been unconscious during the last traumatic day of her captivity, she still had nightmares about the room over the garage and had already suffered several terrifying flashbacks of waking up in the muddy grave. But worse than the nightmares and flashbacks was the guilt she felt about the other girls. She knew she shouldn't feel sorry for herself when she was the only one that had survived.

*Remember you are the lucky one, Kara. The other girls in that stable were not so lucky. Just be grateful you're still alive.*

Seven other girls had gone into the ground before her, and she wouldn't forget them or disrespect their memory by giving in to self-pity. She'd made a vow to herself that in the future the number eight would be her lucky number. A number that would stand as a symbol of her good fortune, her chance to live a good life. She promised herself that whenever she saw the number eight it would remind her to be grateful that she was still alive.

Sitting up on the bed, Kara looked around the room, glad to be safely back at Hope House, and eager to complete her treatment and get home. She'd called Anna the minute she was able and had begged her not to bring Niko down to see her until she had a chance to heal. She didn't want to worry Anna, and she didn't want to scare Niko. But she had been missing her family, and it was becoming harder to stay away.

A soft knock on the door brought Kara to her feet. Reggie Horn stood outside, a wide smile lighting up her face.

"How are you this morning, Kara?"

The director of the recovery center was normally cheerful, but Kara thought Reggie looked unusually happy. She wondered about the woman in front of her, realizing she didn't know much about the person she'd spent so much time with over the last two weeks.

"I'm good. Just missing my sister and nephew. Don't get me wrong, I mean, I love it here, and I'm so grateful to you and Ms. Winthrop for giving me a second chance, but I'm eager to go home."

Reggie's smile grew even wider.

"I don't blame you, dear. And it just so happens that Eden is on her way here, and she's got a surprise for you. Come see."

Kara followed Reggie down the hall and into the sunny meeting room. For an instant, she was back in session with Dr. Bellows, and her heart skipped a beat. Then her mind cleared, and she saw that the room was empty, although it looked like it had been decorated for some sort of party. Tears pricked at her eyes as she read the sign above the door: *Good Luck, Kara! We'll Miss You!*

"Does this mean..."

Kara turned to ask Reggie if the sign meant she was ready to go home, and her words stuck in her throat. Anna and Niko stood by the door. Niko held a balloon in his chubby fist, and Anna was smiling through her tears. For a long minute, Kara just stared at them, taking in the familiar faces that meant everything to her. Finally, she gasped out a happy shriek and ran forward to pull them into a bear hug.

"Why didn't you tell me you were coming? I've missed you both so much. Look how big you've gotten, Niko! Have you been good for your mommy? Let me hold you, sweetie."

The words flooded out, filling the room with joy. Soon the staff and residents arrived carrying a cake and a few wrapped presents. Kara turned to see Eden and Duke watching her with happy eyes. She ran to them, pulling Anna and Niko behind her.

"Ms. Winthrop, this is Anna, my sister. And this little guy is Niko, my nephew."

Eden grinned and ruffled Niko's soft curls.

"We've already had the pleasure of meeting," Eden said, her voice playful. "And Duke and Niko are already good friends."

"Ms. Winthrop came and picked us up this morning," Anna explained, turning grateful eyes to Eden. "She brought us here."

Eden nodded and took Kara's hands.

"And once we're done with our party, I'm going to take you all home to Orlando. It's time you're back with your family."

Kara's heart soared, then apprehension took over.

"But are you sure I'm ready? Will I be okay?"

Reggie spoke up behind Kara.

"You'll be better than okay, dear. And there's a friend of mine in Orlando, a wonderful counselor at a recovery center there, who is happy to work with you as an outpatient. I've already scheduled your first session with her for later this week."

Relief and gratitude washed through Kara as she looked around the group of women. They all seemed so happy for her, and it would be hard to leave their support behind. Hope House had become a refuge for her after her abduction. A safe haven in a dangerous world.

"I'll miss this place," she said, feeling tears on her cheeks. "And I'll miss all of you."

"You and your family are welcome to come to visit any time."

Eden smiled down at little Niko and Duke playing on the floor at their feet.

"And Duke would be up for a playdate I'm sure."

Kara watched Eden's eyes as they gazed down at Niko, and then over at Anna. Something in the kind woman's face seemed wistful, and Kara realized that Eden might be missing her own sister.

Eden would never have a joyful reunion with her sister. While Eden had been able to bring Kara and Anna back together, she would never be able to bring back Mercy. The thought made Kara sad, and she impulsively leaned in and hugged Eden, wanting to give back some of the comfort she'd received.

Eden responded by hugging her back, and Niko looked up and giggled at the women. Kara bent and pulled him into their circle and let herself just enjoy the moment.

# CHAPTER FORTY-NINE

L eo was on the phone with a client when Frankie stepped into his office. He motioned for Frankie to take a seat, but the lanky man began to pace the room with a nervous urgency, snapping his fingers and stretching his neck. Leo raised an eyebrow, wondering what had happened to get Frankie so worked up.

"Okay, what's wrong?" he asked, as soon as he'd ended the call.

"Whadda' you mean? Nothing's wrong."

Frankie dropped into a chair, then instantly jumped back up and crossed to the window. He stared out at the street, before turning to face Leo.

"You said you needed to see me, so, what's up?"

Leo regarded Frankie suspiciously.

"Why are you so nervous and jumpy? There's something different about you. What is it?"

Frankie snapped his fingers a few more times then sat down again. He crossed and uncrossed his legs.

"I've given up smoking, man. It ain't easy. I'm bugging out."

It took a minute for the unexpected words to sink in. Finally, Leo grinned and sat down across from Frankie.

"I'm proud of you, Frankie. I really am."

"Yeah, whatever, man. After seeing what smoking did to your pal, Barker, I figured I'd better quit before I wind up like him."

Leo laughed, glad to see that the partnership between the two men had ended with something positive.

"Well, I'm glad to hear it, whatever the reason. And I wanted to talk to you to say thank you."

Frankie looked confused.

"You tryin' to be funny? What did I do now?"

"No, I mean it, Frankie. You can be a pain in the ass, but you're a good guy, and I wanted to thank you for helping me find my mother's killer."

Frankie sat back in his chair; he lifted his head higher.

"I didn't do so much, Leo."

But Leo saw a happy shine in Frankie's eyes.

"These last few months have shown me who my real friends are, and who I can trust."

Leo leaned over and put a hand on Frankie's skinny arm.

"And I'm proud to call you a friend."

A flush of color spread over Frankie's face.

"Shit, don't go all mushy on me, man."

Frankie reached a jittery hand into his pocket; when he pulled it back out it was still empty. He'd forgotten he'd stopped smoking. The forlorn look on Frankie's face almost made Leo feel bad for him, but he thought he had something that would cheer him up.

"Wait here. I've got something for you."

Leo went out to Pat Monahan's desk. Her outbox had a stack of envelopes waiting to be stamped and mailed.

Leo rifled through the stack and found the envelope he was looking for. He walked back to the room and offered the envelope to Frankie.

"For your services on the case."

Frankie raised his eyebrows and took the envelope.

"Yeah, I've been meaning to ask you about getting reimbursed for those drinks I bought Penelope-"

His words faded away as his eyes scanned the check. He blinked and squinted at it, then looked up at Leo with wide eyes.

"I think you maybe added in one too many zeros, man."

Frankie put the check back into the envelope and held it toward Leo, the torn envelope shaking a little in the air between them.

"No, that's the correct amount."

Leo turned away without taking the envelope and crossed to his desk. He looked down, absently straightening a pile of papers, trying to come up with the right words.

"You risked your freedom for me, and you helped me find the bastard that killed my mother," Leo finally said. "That's worth a lot. I know money can't buy the things that count, but hopefully, I can use it to show you my gratitude."

For once Frankie seemed to be at a loss for words. He stared at Leo, cocking his head and frowning. Then he shrugged.

"Okay. Whatever you say, boss man."

Leo walked Frankie to the door, wishing him luck with his effort to quit smoking. He hoped it would last, but knew it was a long shot.

*Frankie has surprised me before. Let's hope he can do it again.*

Back at his desk, Leo picked up the pile of papers and reviewed his work. He'd finished filing the motion to have his father's guilty verdict thrown out.

With luck, his father's name would soon be officially cleared. And, more importantly, his mother's killer had finally been captured and was now facing justice.

Leo wondered how Kramer would try to get out of the charges. The evidence against him seemed insurmountable, but the wily old police chief had gotten away with so much over the years, Leo wasn't sure what he might try to pull now that he seemed to be cornered.

Although Kramer's own words may prove to be the final nail in his coffin. His confession to Eden in the shed that night would be hard to explain. He'd laid out all his dirty deeds and his reasoning behind them, and Eden had shared the information with the feds that had descended on the town.

And of course, there was the physical evidence. Leo felt a hollow ache in his stomach when he thought of his mother's sterling silver bracelet the police had found in Kramer's house.

Eventually, it would be returned to him, and he wondered what he would do with it. Would it bring him comfort in the years to come or just painful memories?

The search of Kramer's house had also turned up a collection of gruesome photos of the women he'd killed. His mother's picture had been in a pile along with pictures of the other women. Her dead body had been photographed and kept as a keepsake.

The thought of it made Leo feel sick, but he was glad the photo could be used as evidence to convict Kramer. Through her image, his mother would be one of the star witnesses against the killer.

Leo turned to stare out the window, his mind full of the evidence he'd sorted through in the last few weeks as he'd prepared the case for dropping the charges against his father.

He was convinced that once the feds had compiled all the evidence against Kramer, and added up the death toll from his crimes, he would be prosecuted, found guilty, and sent to death row.

It may take another twelve years to see final justice done, but Leo was now sure the day would come. He just wished the thought provided more comfort than it did.

*So, now that I've gotten what I wanted, why don't I feel happy?*

Perhaps too much had happened for him to ever be truly happy. Maybe it was too late. Just because Kramer had been caught, didn't mean he'd get his parents back. And it didn't give his parents back the lives they'd lost. They had been cheated out of their life together, and there was no way to go back and change that now.

Leo pulled open a drawer and took out a framed photo of his parents. He'd kept it on his desk for years, but had eventually stored it away, not wanting to see the constant reminder of how he had failed them. But now that he'd done what he could for them, maybe he should put it back on display.

He stared at the picture, taken only months before his mother had died. He admired her long, dark hair and fine cheekbones. She'd been a lovely woman. A woman still in the prime of life. And she'd gazed with such love at his father, who looked so happy, and so young. Leo realized with a jolt that when his father had died, he hadn't been much older than Leo was now.

Leo studied his father's dark hair and smiling eyes, aching for the man in the photo. Could that happy man have ever imagined the heartache and tragedy that lay before him?

*Can any of us really know what the future holds?*

Leo certainly had never pictured the road that he would end up traveling after his parents' death. The thought of everything he had given up in his quest to avenge his parents troubled him.

Had he missed out on having a family and future because of Kramer? Could he ever trust in someone enough to build a life together? His thoughts turned to Eden, and he wondered what she was doing, and if she was okay. After their joyful reunion on the helicopter, he'd tried to give her space to recuperate with her family. And he'd needed time to do what needed to be done to clear his father's name.

But lately, when he reached out Eden seemed distant and preoccupied. Perhaps she too was too damaged to trust in anyone again. Maybe it was too late for both of them.

As if his brooding had conjured her to his door, Eden stuck her head into his office and smiled.

"Duke and I thought we would stop by and surprise you!"

The golden retriever looked over at Leo with sleepy eyes and then sat at Eden's feet with a yawn.

Melinda Woodhall

"You'll have to excuse Duke," she said, laughing. "We just had a long drive back from Orlando. And he's a little tired."

"I don't know if I'm more excited to see you or this big guy," Leo teased, rising to give Eden a kiss, and then stooping to scratch the soft fur on Duke's back. "I've been so worried about him. It's great to see him up and about. And it's great to see you, too."

Eden stretched her hands above her head and sighed.

"We've just said goodbye to Kara. She's safely back in Orlando, ready to start a new life at her sister's house. I think she's going to be all right."

Leo nodded and considered her wistful expression.

"And what about you? Will you be all right?"

Eden lifted a hand to his cheek and shook her head.

"I'm tired of talking about me and how I'm doing," she said, her voice growing playful. "I came by to see how *you* are. You've been through a lot and I know it's been hard on you. So, I wanted to try again."

"Try again? What exactly are we going to try?"

Leo's mind began to paint a very interesting picture, but Eden laughed and shook her head.

"Don't get too excited. I'm suggesting we try to have a night in at my place. Maybe get some take-out and wine."

Leo's heart jumped at her words.

"That sounds like the best idea I've ever heard."

Eden beamed at him, then blushed.

"Of course, I may be able to get Barb to have the kids stay over at her place for the night if I ask nicely."

Pulse racing, Leo picked up his keys and followed Eden outside to his car, thinking maybe he'd misjudged the situation after all. He pulled onto the highway and headed toward her house just as the first stars began to appear in the autumn sky.

# CHAPTER FIFTY

Heavy footsteps on the stairs alerted Eden and Leo that Barb was on her way down, and they drew apart quickly, cheeks flushed and eyes bright. The older woman smirked as she bustled into the living room and took note of their guilty faces.

She called back up the stairs in an amused voice, "Come on, Hope and Devon. It's time for us to go."

Lucky darted in from the kitchen and jumped onto the sofa between Eden and Leo. The little Yorkie nestled into the pillow and peered up at Leo, ready for some attention.

"Lucky, you get over here right now," Barb called, unable to stop herself from laughing at the look of dismay on Leo's face. "You're coming with us."

Eden stood and hugged Hope and Devon as they trailed out the door after Barb. She would drop them off at the movies and then pick them up and take them back to her place once the movie was over.

"You two stick together and be careful," Eden called after them. "No leaving the theater or talking to strangers."

Hope rolled her eyes and Devon stuck his thumb up and grinned as they pulled away in Barb's big Buick. Eden watched the car disappear around the corner, her chest tightening with love and gratitude. She looked up at the stars and closed her eyes.

*They are wonderful kids, Mercy. I wish you could be here to see them.*

As the stars twinkled overhead, Eden felt that Mercy was there somehow; she was a part of them all now. And as long as they were together, Mercy would be with them.

Leo stepped up behind her and looked up at the stars, his cologne and warm skin making her dizzy with desire. She sank back against him and he wrapped his arms around her.

*It's so good to feel something other than fear.*

As she turned to face Leo, his cell phone vibrated in his pocket.

"Don't worry about that," Leo murmured, pulling her inside and closing the door behind her.

"No, you'd better get that. Someone might need you."

*Although I doubt they need you as much as I do.*

Eden forced herself to walk back into the living room and sit on the sofa. She waited for Leo to take out his phone.

"It's Barker."

He smiled apologetically and tapped to answer the phone.

"Hey Barker, how'd the trip go?"

Eden looked at him with curious eyes, already wondering where Barker had gone, and why it involved Leo. Perhaps her recent investigative work was turning her into a busybody after all.

"How did Vinny take the news?"

Eden recoiled at the mention of Vinny Lorenzo, instinctively looking toward the stairs even though Hope was gone. She tried never to mention Vinny's name when Hope was around. She worried that her niece's happiness would be dimmed by memories of the man who had abducted her and tried to kill her only months before.

"Okay, thanks for the update."

After Leo ended the call, Eden couldn't help asking questions.

"Did Barker really go see Vinny? What news did he have?"

Leo nodded and ran a tense hand through his hair. His mood had darkened at the mention of the man who had caused so much trouble.

"Nessa and Barker both went up to Raiford. Nessa wanted Vinny to ID Bellows, and Barker wanted to give Vinny the results of the DNA test they did to find out the identity of his father."

"So, what happened?"

Eden was reluctant to talk about Vinny Lorenzo on their night alone, but she had to know.

"Vinny was able to ID Bellows," Leo said, his eyes hard. "Said he saw him at the Old Canal Motel the night his mother was killed."

"And how did he react to Bellows being his father?"

Leo looked at Eden with raised eyebrows.

"So, you didn't hear about the DNA results?"

Eden shook her head, confused.

"No, what did the results say?" Eden asked, but before Leo could answer she added, "And If Bellows isn't Vinny's father, then why would he have killed Natalie?"

"Chief Kramer is Vinny's father."

Eden gasped, trying to digest the information.

"So, Kramer and Natalie?"

A deep furrow appeared on Leo's forehead as he explained what the investigation had uncovered so far.

"From what we can piece together Bellows and Kramer were in the military together in Germany. Kramer ran into some trouble and was dishonorably discharged. Something about drugging a local woman and attacking her. But Bellows wasn't implicated. After Bellows left the service he came looking for Kramer. We think they've been partners in crime ever since."

Disgust bubbled up inside her.

"Partners? You mean, they worked together to abduct women?"

Leo nodded grimly.

"That's what it looks like. When Natalie accused Bellows of being her son's father, both he and Kramer were at risk. Perhaps even they didn't know for sure who Vinny's father was. They just knew they had to stop Natalie from talking."

Eden tried to comprehend the extent of the men's depravity.

"And Kara? And the other girls in the stable?"

"We think Bellows selected girls who were unlikely to be missed. Young women with a drug addiction or some other problem. Mainly women who had run away from a bad home life or were in some other trouble that made them unlikely to go to the police."

"And he just passed them on to Kramer? Why would he do that?"

Eden stared into Leo's eyes, but she could see that he didn't know why. Perhaps no normal person could ever understand the mind of deranged killers like Bellows and Kramer. Perhaps it was better that they couldn't.

"I can't explain it," Leo admitted, holding her hands in his. "Perhaps in some sick way, they were trying to protect each other. Maybe they used that as an excuse to justify murder."

Leo's words felt like a punch in the gut. Eden recoiled and pulled away. She had tried to pretend she could have an honest relationship with Leo, but now she knew she never could. Not unless she told him the truth about what had happened the day Mercy died.

That day she had killed a man. A man that had at one time been Leo's client. She'd blocked the memories of what had really happened for years, but eventually, she'd remembered everything. And while she had assured herself that she'd done it only to protect Hope and Devon, deep down she knew that wasn't the only reason.

She had wanted to take revenge on Preston for killing her sister. She had wanted to kill the man that had taken away the person she'd loved most in the world. So, yes, she had killed Preston to protect Hope and Devon, but she had also killed him out of anger and fear and rage.

*How can I have a real relationship with a man who doesn't know what I've done? And what would he say if I told him the real reason why I did it?*

Leo stiffened, sensing immediately that something had changed. "Eden? What's wrong?"

Eden stood and paced across the room, keeping her back to Leo. She knew she had to make a decision. Either tell him the truth, the whole ugly truth, or let him go for good. There couldn't be a middle ground. Either she trusted him, or she didn't.

Leo stood and walked toward her, but he didn't touch her. He seemed to sense that she was upset and that she needed space between them. He hovered in the middle of the room, a worried frown on his face.

Eden turned to him, her eyes bright with unshed tears.

"I...I killed someone."

Her voice cracked on the words, and she dropped her head into her hands. When she looked back up, she saw that the blood had drained from Leo's face. He stared at her with unwavering eyes.

"Okay, now tell me what happened."

His voice was low and patient. He was ready to listen.

"I shot Preston." She choked on the words, hating herself for crying, but unable to stop the tears that flowed. "I killed my sister's husband."

Leo stepped forward, his face stricken, but his arms reached out to gather her against him.

"Oh my god, Eden. Why?"

She pushed against his chest and looked up into his face, needing to see his expression. Needing to know what he was thinking.

"Why?" she asked, her voice broken. "Preston had already killed Mercy. He was going to kill the children. He told me so. He told me to leave, but I wouldn't. I grabbed the gun, and I shot him. I did it because...because I wanted him to die. I wanted him dead. And I wanted Mercy's children to be safe."

Eden held Leo's eyes, refusing to look away.

"I'm glad I did it. And if I had it to do over again, I'd do it again."

Leo squeezed his eyes shut and inhaled. When he opened his eyes again they were clear and sure.

"You're not a killer, Eden. You're not like Bellows or Kramer or Preston, who all killed innocent people, and ruined innocent lives. You save lives. You help people."

His voice faltered, then grew strong again.

"You've helped me...more than you'll ever know. Because of you, the man that killed my mother is behind bars. You risked your life to do that. Killers don't help people. Killers don't save people. You do. You're one of the bravest people I know."

Eden let out a cry of relief, not realizing until that moment how much she had needed Leo to understand, and how badly she wanted to be with him without any lies or secrets between them.

"I'm sorry, Leo, for not trusting you sooner."

Eden took his hand and led him back to the sofa.

"I was scared. It took me a long time to admit what I'd done even to myself, and the only other person who knows is Hope. She was there. She saw everything."

"God, the poor kid." Leo shook his head. "You've all been through so much."

Eden smiled sadly and took his big, warm hand in hers.

"I guess that's why you fit right in here. We've all been through so much and so have you. Who else would understand?"

Leo squeezed her hand and looked at her with hopeful eyes.

"So, you think I fit in with your family?"

Eden grinned and nodded.

"Yeah, I think you do. But maybe you could start spending lots of time over here with us, just to make sure."

"That sounds like the best idea..."

But Eden had already pulled him in for a kiss.

When she looked up Duke was sitting next to her, staring at them with dejected eyes.

"Either he's jealous, or he needs to go out," Leo teased.

"I think it may be a little of both," Eden agreed, standing and walking toward the kitchen. "You coming, too?"

Leo jumped up and followed Eden out the backdoor. As they walked behind Duke through the quiet neighborhood, Eden knew she would be foolish to think the danger and hard times were behind her.

As long as she tried to help women in need, she would be putting herself in the way of men who wanted to harm them. She had made a vow to honor her sister's memory by saving other women, and she would never allow herself to break that promise.

But as she walked next to Leo, his strong hand in hers, she realized maybe she didn't have to fight the bad guys all on her own. Eden suddenly felt lighter as she followed Duke down the street and into the starry night beyond.

## Continue the Mercy Harbor Series Now...

Want to find out what happens next with Eden, Leo, and the rest of the gang in Willow Bay? Then continue reading the Mercy Harbor Thriller Series now with:

*Catch the Girl: A Mercy Harbor Thriller, Book Three*
by Melinda Woodhall.

Melinda Woodhall

And don't forget to sign up for the Melinda Woodhall Newsletter to receive bonus scenes and insider details at www.melindawoodhall.com/newsletter

# ACKNOWLEDGEMENTS

WRITING A BOOK IS USUALLY A LABOR OF LOVE that requires a writer to spend quite a bit of time tucked away from the people she loves. I'm grateful to have an understanding family that gave me both the time and love I needed to write this book.

I feel unbelievably lucky to have the constant support, encouragement, and love of my husband, Giles, and my wonderful children, Michael, Joey, Linda, Owen, and Juliet.

My sisters, Melissa and Melanie, my brother-in-law, Leopoldo, and my in-laws, David and Tessa, make my life infinitely better through their ongoing encouragement.

I couldn't dream up or write a better family in any book.

As I was writing this book I kept remembering how much my father enjoyed reading near the end of his life. Every time I saw him, he would have a book in his hand or mention a book he was reading. I realize now that his appreciation for a good story and the pleasure books brought him during difficult times, inspire me to write.

And always, I know the origin of everything I am, and everything I write starts with my mother. She taught me to love books, and for that, I'll always be grateful.

# ABOUT THE AUTHOR

**Melinda Woodhall** is the author of the page-turning *Mercy Harbor Thriller* series. After leaving a career in corporate software sales to focus on writing, Melinda now spends her time writing romantic thrillers and police procedurals. She also writes women's contemporary fiction as M.M. Arvin.

When she's not writing, Melinda can be found reading, gardening, chauffeuring her children around town, and updating her vegetarian lifestyle website. Melinda is a native Floridian and the proud mother of five children. She lives with her family in Orlando.

Visit Melinda's website at www.melindawoodhall.com.

**Other Books by Melinda Woodhall**
*The River Girls*
*Girl Eight*
*Catch the Girl*
*Girls Who Lie*
*Her Last Summer*
*Her Final Fall*
*Her Winter of Darkness*
*Her Silent Spring*
*Her Day to Die*

Printed in the USA
CPSIA information can be obtained
at www.ICGtesting.com
LVHW040235021023
759869LV00008B/229